SCARLET WOMAN

Shivers coursed through Melinda as Blake locked her to him. For a brief, poignant moment he stared down at her. Open. Pliable. Susceptible to her. His tremors shook her, and her nerves tingled with exhilaration when she heard his hoarse groan of capitulation. Then his mouth was on her and his tongue stabbed at her lips until she opened and, at last, had him inside of her. His big hand gripped her buttocks and she undulated wildly against him as his velvet tongue promised her ecstasy, plunging in and out of her and testing every crevice of her mouth. Strong and commanding like the man himself. Hungry for all of him, she spread her legs and he rose hard and strong against her. She slumped into him and might have fallen if he hadn't lifted her, carried her to the sofa, and sat down with her in his lap. For a long while, he sat there, rocking her and stroking her, soothing her with a tenderness she'd never known.

Other books by Gwynne Forster

SEALED WITH A KISS
AGAINST ALL ODDS
ECSTASY
OBSESSION
BEYOND DESIRE
FOOLS RUSH IN
SWEPT AWAY
SECRET DESIRE

Published by BET/Arabesque Books

SCARLET WOMAN

Gwynne Forster

BET Publications, LLC
www.bet.com
www.arabesquebooks.com

ARABESQUE BOOKS are published by

BET Publications, LLC
c/o BET BOOKS
One BET Plaza
1900 W Place NE
Washington, D.C. 20018-1211

All Kensington Titles, Imprints, and Distributed Lines are available at special quantity discounts for bulk purchases for sales promotions, premiums, fund-raising, and educational or institutional use. Special book excerpts or customized printings can also be created to fit specific needs. For details, write or phone the office of the Kensington special sales manager: Kensington Publishing Corp., 850 Third Avenue, New York, NY 10022, attn: Special Sales Department, Phone: 1-800-221-2647.

First Printing: July 2001
10   9   8   7   6   5   4   3   2   1

Printed in the United States of America

ACKNOWLEDGMENTS

To Brother Simba, co-owner of Karibu Books, Hyattsville, MD, and an exemplary man of strong moral fiber. In my research for this book, Brother Simba shared with me his experiences as a volunteer teacher and counselor to African-American youths during their incarceration at the District of Columbia's Lorton Prison and after their return to society. Brother Simba inaugurated a study group at Lorton (The African Development Organization), and he remains a mentor to those young men who accept his counsel. My thanks also to my husband who supports and encourages me in everything that I undertake.

Prologue

Melinda looked out of the only window in her tiny one-room apartment and saw nothing. Not the children jumping rope and playing hopscotch, nor the single mothers who sat on the stone bench beneath a big white oak tree escaping the late-August, Maryland sun. Over and over, her mind replayed Prescott Rodgers's proposal. Marry and live with him in his home and brighten his life by doing for him what he couldn't do for himself. He wanted her to read to him the classic literature of the English language. Although he was a brilliant man, dyslexia had deprived him of the pleasures of reading and writing. He had contacted the high school at which she taught English, offering to pay a student to read to him. None found the idea attractive, and she eventually volunteered to do it one or two hours weekly at no charge. But his tales of his world travels, especially his wanderings through Italy, so intrigued her that the few weekly hours soon became a daily ritual, a treat to which she looked forward each day.

A self-made man, inventor of a film-developing process, a fluid for contact lenses, and a type of eyeglass lens, all of which yielded hefty royalties, Prescott Rodgers had amassed a fortune. He lived a reclusive life, fearing scorn because he could not learn to read.

"We're both lonely," Prescott had argued, "and we have much to give each other. I know the chemicals I've worked with all these years are shortening my life, and I'd like to spend what's left of it in your company. Marrying me would still the tongues of those curious about your daily visits."

"Well, I . . . I don't know—"

"Will you accept a marriage of convenience? That's selfish of me, I know, because you're young, and I'm sixty-eight years old."

As a married woman, she would escape much of her father's intolerance and authoritarianism, and she would have a companion. Musing over her own life of loneliness—for which her father's self-righteousness and his indictments of all who disagreed with him were largely responsible—she reasoned that at last she would have a niche. She would belong with someone. Melinda added up the advantages, shoved the doubts and disadvantages out of her mind, and agreed.

She married Prescott Rodgers in a private ceremony in the office of Blake Edmund Hunter, Prescott's lawyer, with only Hunter and her parents as witnesses.

Prescott gave her a monthly allowance of $1,100 for her most personal needs, provided her with a housekeeper, and bore all other expenses. She read to him each morning, entertained for him, sparing though it was, and enjoyed the remaining four and a half years of his life as his wife.

Chapter One

Melinda Rodgers sat in Blake Edmund Hunter's law office on that damp, mid-May morning, dumbfounded, as he read aloud her late husband's will. She was to set up a foundation for remedial reading and the acquiring of literacy that would meet the needs of both children and adults and have it fully operating within a year of his death. She must also marry within the year.

If she failed to fulfill either requirement, the house in which she lived and everything else—except for one million dollars to rehabilitate homeless people—would go to a charity of Blake's choice.

"It doesn't surprise me that he'd want that foundation," Melinda said to those present—Blake, her parents, and her best friend—"but as much as he valued individual freedom, I can't believe he'd attempt to force me to get married."

"You just have to carry out his wishes," her father, the Reverend Booker Jones, said. "You wouldn't be foolish enough to throw away all this money. The church needs some repairs."

"Now, dear," Lurlane Jones said, in a voice soft and musical. "Our Melinda is in mourning; we mustn't push her."

Melinda watched Blake Hunter lean back in his desk chair and survey the group, his sharp, cool gaze telling them that he judged them all and found them wanting. She tried not to look at him, lest she betray her feelings.

"I really wouldn't have thought it of Prescott," she said, "but I guess you never truly know a person."

She glanced toward Blake, and her heart turned over at the softness of his unguarded look. She told herself not to react, that she had to be mistaken. He had shown her respect but never liked her, and she doubted he had or ever would have any feelings for her, though Lord knows he lived in her heart and had since the minute she met him.

With his cool, impersonal gaze back in place, he immediately confirmed her thoughts. "Don't think you can play at this, Mrs. Rodgers, and you're not allowed to hire anyone to do it for you. You have to do it yourself and to my satisfaction."

His sharp words and unsympathetic attitude surprised her, for he had always appeared gracious and considerate toward her during her husband's lifetime. "As my husband's close friend, I expected that you might give me some advice, if not help, but I see I'm on my own. I'll be in tomorrow morning to talk this over with you."

His left eyebrow shot up, and he nodded in what appeared to be grudging appreciation. "I'll be here at nine."

"Let's go, Rachel." Melinda said to the friend she'd asked to be with her when the will was read. But she noticed that the woman got up with reluctance, almost as if she didn't want to leave.

"You do what that will says," Booker Jones roared in the

descending elevator. "We can't afford to lose one brown cent of that money. We need it to do the Lord's work."

"Melinda will do what's right. So stop fussing," Lurlane said.

Melinda didn't respond. Her father taught his parishioners that money was the root of all evil, but he never said no to it.

"Is he like that all the time?" Rachel asked Melinda as they walked down one of the main streets of Ellicott City, Maryland. "My father hardly ever raises his voice."

"Your father isn't a preacher," Melinda reminded her. "If other pastors are like my father, they're always right. He talks over everybody and across everybody, because when he opens his mouth the world is supposed to shut up and take heed."

"Girl, you go 'way from here," Rachel said. "He's a good man. Last Sunday, he preached till he was plain hoarse and couldn't say another word."

"Yes, I know he's good, and I bet he started whispering into the mike. Nothing shuts up my father."

"He's a righteous man."

"You're telling me? He's the only one on earth. I wish he'd understand that he can't mold people as he would clay figures just because he believes they'd be better off."

"Now, Melinda. You don't mean that."

She did mean it. Her father believed in what he taught, but he was driven by a secular monster, the one that made you want praise and acceptance. Tired of the subject and uninterested in Rachel's views of Booker Jones, Melinda stopped talking. Who knew a man better than his family?

"Rachel, why do you think Prescott put that clause in his will forcing me to remarry? I just can't figure it out."

"Me neither, girl, and Blake Hunter is going to see that you do it or lose everything, including your house."

Melissa shrugged. "I'm not worried about that, because I never intend to remarry."

Rachel stopped walking. "Was Mr. Rodgers mean to you? I'd have thought an older man would be sweet as sugar to a woman less than half his age."

Melinda smiled inwardly, aware that the comment reflected the local gossip about her and Prescott. "My husband treated me as if I were the most precious being on this earth. He . . . he was wonderful to me. Those four years were the happiest of my life."

"Well, I'll be! I guess there's no telling about people. Maybe I'd better start looking for an older man. I'm thirty-two. With a fifty- or sixty-year-old man, that ought to stand for something." Rachel didn't say anything for half a block, and then she spoke with seeming reluctance. "How old do you think Blake Hunter is? And how come he's not married?"

"Why would I know?"

"He was your husband's close friend, wasn't he?"

"They never discussed the man's private affairs when I was around. I know practically nothing about him."

"I'll bet you know he's a number ten."

"A what?"

"A knockout. A good-looking virile man who makes you think things you couldn't tell your mother."

So she'd been right. Rachel hadn't wanted to leave Blake's office. The woman was after Blake. She told herself to forget about it. Nothing would ever happen between Blake Hunter and herself.

Melinda walked into the redbrick colonial she'd shared with Prescott and froze when she realized she'd been expecting to hear his usual, "That you, dear?" *Get a hold of yourself,* she said aloud, squared her shoulders, and headed for her bedroom, determined to meet the rest of her life head-on. The sound of Ruby vacuuming the hall carpet reminded her that the upkeep of the house was now her responsibility.

"We have to talk, Ruby," she told the housekeeper. "I don't

understand it, but Mr. Rodgers didn't provide for you in his will, and I can't keep you on here. I'm afraid we'll have to separate.''

"He paid my wages for the entire year after his death, Miz Melinda. And last year, he drawed up a real good pension plan for me. Only thing is, I has to work here for the next twelve months. He done good by me.''

Melinda swallowed several times and told herself it didn't matter that Prescott had left his housekeeper better fixed than his wife.

"Is Blake Hunter in charge of your pension and wages?''

"Yes, ma'am. My pension starts thirteen months from now, and Mr. Blake will send me my salary every Friday, just like he always done.'' She coughed a few times and patted the hair in the back of her head. "If I was twenty years younger, that man wouldn't be single. No siree. That is one sweet-looking man. A face the color of shelled walnuts.'' She rolled her eyes toward the sky and wet her lips. "Them dreamy eyes and that bottom lip . . . *Lord.*'' She patted her hair. "Honey, that is *some* man.''

Imagine that. "He's a hard man,'' Melinda said, thinking of how lacking in compassion for her he'd seemed when he read the terms of her late husband's will. Harsh terms, and so unlike Prescott. "But if anybody could break through that wall he's got around himself, Ruby, I expect you could.''

Ruby put the can of furniture polish on the table and shook out the chamois cloth she used for polishing. "Miz Melinda, that man just can't help being hard. He done nothing but work from daylight to dark six days a week from the time he could walk till he finished high school. His daddy cracked that whip.''

She stared at Ruby. Surely the woman was mistaken. "He told you *that?*''

"No, ma'am. He sure didn't, but I heard him telling Mr.

Rodgers that and a whole lot more. That man been through somethin'."

Melinda's eyes widened, but she quickly replaced that with a bland facial expression. No point in letting Ruby know that anything about Blake interested her. She'd had two shocks in two minutes, and she had a hunch she'd get more of them. She leaned against the wall and waited for Ruby's next shot. Her impression of Blake had been of a privileged youth from an upper middle-class family. How had he become so polished? Ruby's high-pitched voice interrupted Melinda's musings.

"Working a boy like Mr. Blake's daddy done made him work would amount to child abuse these days," Ruby said, warming up to the subject. "He said his folks was poor as Job's turkey."

"Well, he certainly overcame it," Melinda replied and walked rapidly up the wide stairs, richly carpeted in Royal Bokhara. However, realizing that she'd practically run from the talk about Blake because she didn't want to think of him, she slowed her steps. As executor of Prescott's estate, the man would be a fixture in her life for the next twelve months, and she'd better learn to handle the consequences.

Blake Edmund Hunter looked from one woman to the other as Melinda stood to leave his office and Rachel Perkins remained in her chair gazing at him. Another one of nature's stupid tricks! Rachel wanted him so badly she was practically salivating, and Melinda Rodgers didn't know he was alive. His gaze followed Melinda's svelte physique, straight, almost arrogant carriage and sweetly rounded buttocks as she strolled out of his office. He wanted her and had from the minute he first saw her, but he was Prescott's friend, so he hadn't let himself give in to it when Prescott was alive. He was damned if he'd succumb to it now.

If anything turned his stomach, it was a gold-digging woman, an unfaithful wife, or a treacherous friend. She hadn't given him reason to believe that she would be unfaithful to Prescott, and he was grateful for that, because she'd been temptation without trying and he wouldn't have considered disloyalty to Prescott.

Yet, as much as he desired her, he had reservations about her. For instance, that virginal innocence she wrapped around herself didn't fool him. She was less than half Prescott's age, and nobody could make him believe a young, gorgeous woman like her had married an old, solitary recluse for love. She'd married Prescott Rodgers for his money, and Blake would see that she carried out the terms of that will, *or else*. That clause Prescott had inserted requiring Melinda to marry within a year or lose her inheritance . . . He squeezed his eyes shut, and told himself the lump in his throat had nothing to do with that.

He answered the phone, grateful that its ringing had derailed his thoughts. Dangerous thoughts.

"Yes, Lacy. Look, I'm sorry but I have to deal with this will."

"But you can leave it long enough to have lunch with me."

He glanced at his watch and banged his left fist on his desk. Softly. Reaffirming his intention to stay away from her. "I'm having lunch at my desk today, and for goodness' sake, Lacy, please don't pout. It's so childish." He could imagine her lower lip protruding in what she considered a sexy come-on.

"You're busy every time I call."

Leaning back in the chair and closing his eyes, he told himself not to show annoyance. "Lacy, I told you I'm not ready for a relationship, and I haven't said or done anything that would make you think otherwise. I'm sorry."

In his mind's eye, he could see her lighting a cigarette and taking a long drag, a habit he hated. "Maybe this weekend?"

She had the tenacity of Muhammad Ali smelling victory, but he refused to be roped in.

"I'm longing to see you," she whispered

He wished she wouldn't beg. Three dates didn't amount to a commitment. "Yeah, right! I'll . . . uh. Look, Lacy, I wish you well. I'll see you around."

He hung up, but he doubted that ended it. Any other woman would know that he'd just broken ties with her, such as they were, but not Lacy Morgan. He'd never seen a human being with thicker skin.

He walked over to the window and looked down at the flowering trees, but they didn't engage his thoughts. What would happen to Melinda if she couldn't do as Prescott's will required? His long, tapered fingers rubbed his jaw, and he shook his head as if to clear it. The Rodgers account was but one in his portfolio, and several others required his attention. He pushed the intercom button.

"Irene, could you come in and take a letter to Folson?"

"Yes, sir."

Now here was a woman he admired: always professional, and she expected him to be the same. So he wasn't prepared for her comment.

"Blake, I don't see how Melinda is going to set up that foundation. People here don't think highly of her since she married Mr. Rodgers. And to make things worse, she never once went anyplace with him from the time they married till he died. Some say they weren't really married, that she just lived with the old man."

His jaw twitched, and he knew he grimaced, for her blood reddened her light skin and she lowered her eyelids. *So much for her unfailing professionalism.* He looked over a few notes and dictated the letter.

"Anything else, sir?"

With his elbows propped on the desk, he made a pyramid

of his ten fingers and looked her in the eye. "Yes. There is. I was Prescott Rodgers's witness when he married Melinda Jones in this office in the presence of her parents. That's all."

He didn't care for character assassins any more than he liked gold diggers, and he hated feeling protective toward Melinda, but he did. Feeling a flush of guilt, he tapped his Mont Blanc pen on his desk. If she couldn't establish that foundation, he wasn't sure he'd be able to live with himself. He'd insisted that Prescott include that provision in the will and had worded it himself. If she ever found out . . .

Melinda dressed carefully that morning, choosing a white linen suit—she wasn't going to mourn in black; Prescott had made her promise she wouldn't—a blue and white striped linen blouse and navy accessories. She wanted to look great, but she didn't want Blake to think he'd ever entered her mind.

"Come in, Melinda, and have a seat," Irene said, when she opened the door. "He'll be with you in a second."

Looking around the reception room, she marveled at its decorations, carpets, paintings, and live green plants—elegance without ostentation.

"Good morning, Melinda. Nothing pleases me like promptness."

She stood, accepted his extended hand and wished she hadn't, as her heart lurched, and fiery ripples spiraled up her arms. His gaze seemed more piercing than ever, or had he noticed what that physical contact with him had done to her?

"Hello, Blake. I've thought this over and figured that I can either try to comply with this strange bequest or walk away from the entire thing." At his quick frown, she added, "Neither one of those provisions is easy to comply with, but I've made up my mind to do all I can to get that foundation up and operating. Reading is what brought Prescott and me together, and I know how dear this project would be to him.''

His frown deepened. ''What do you mean by that?''

So Prescott hadn't confided that problem! She lifted her left shoulder in a dismissive shrug. ''Long story. Let's get started on this.'' Something flickered in his gaze, but she discounted it as being impossible. Blake Hunter had no feelings for her.

She made notes as he talked, suggesting names of people she should contact, and providing her with tips about their personalities and attitudes. Once, when she glanced up at him and saw the softness in his fawnlike, brown eyes, she had to stifle a gasp and quickly turned her attention to the tablet in her lap.

''Your father wants to be on the board,'' he said. ''I can't advise you about that, but I'm sure you'll want board members who can get along with each other.''

Laughter flowed out of her at the thought of her father cooperating with any group of eleven people anywhere in the world. She looked at Blake. ''Do you know anybody in this town who can swear to having had a gratifying conversation with my father?'' She'd often thought the problem with her father was his longing for acceptance, but she would never allow herself to say that.

What was certainly mischief gleamed in his eyes. ''I didn't know you knew that. What he's like, I mean.''

''Blake, I lived in the house with him until I went away to college.''

His big body settled itself in his desk chair, relaxed, and he twirled a pencil, the only playful thing she'd ever seen him do. ''I'll bet you thanked God for college.''

She leaned toward him, enjoying this unfamiliar side of him. ''Did I ever! I put on some lipstick before the train left the station.''

A smile played around his lips, mesmerizing her. ''What

about your soul? Weren't you afraid you'd burn in hell for that worldly deed?''

"Tell you the truth, it didn't cross my mind. Do you think a bird worries about the cage after it flies out? Not for a second. I thought, *'Free at last!'* ''

Suddenly, his demeanor changed, and she supposed he'd only temporarily forgotten himself, that it was back to business.

"I'll ask Irene to type out this list of prospective board members along with their street and e-mail addresses and their phone numbers. This will take time, so the sooner you get on it, the better.''

"Yes, *sir!*''

His eyebrows went up sharply, but she didn't care if he recognized her insolence. He couldn't change faces with her like a chameleon and expect her to accept it.

"You're not as easygoing as you appear to be, are you?''

She put the tablet in her pocketbook and stood, preparing to leave. "I didn't know anybody thought me easygoing. That is a surprise.''

"Real little tiger, eh?'' he said, walking with her to the door.

She whirled around and he towered over her, inches from her body. *Get a grip on it, girl.* "Tiger, lion, or leopard. Cross me, and I claw. But unless you step out of line, you'll never get so much as a hint of my feline side.''

She wanted to back away from him, but the door trapped her. She didn't like the feeling that pervaded her body, a strange hunger that she suspected had nothing to do with food. He didn't move, and she didn't want him to know what his nearness did to her. Then his pupils seemed to dilate, and his nostrils flared. *Oh, Lord, please let me get away from here without making a fool of myself.*

Summoning all the strength she could muster, she whispered, ''Would you please open the door?''

He reached around her in what felt like a half caress, though she knew it wasn't, and turned the knob. She stepped backward and nearly lost her footing, but he grabbed her and pulled her toward him.

"What   ?"

She glanced over her shoulder as Judd Folson walked in for his eleven o'clock appointment. And from the man's knowing expression, she didn't doubt that he assumed he'd caught her in Blake Hunter's arms a week after she buried her husband.

She raised herself to her full height—nearly six feet if you took into account her three-inch heels—and looked him straight in the eye. "Good morning, Mr. Folson. Lovely day, isn't it?"

The man nodded in reply, gaping as he did so, and she realized that Blake's arm remained around her waist. She stepped away, stood against the doorjamb, and made herself smile.

"Thanks for your help, Mr. Hunter. I hope Irene can get that list to me in a day or two and I can get started." Nervous words, and she knew it.

But he didn't answer, only stared at her with those piercing eyes and nodded his head, before turning to Judd Folson.

"Have a seat, Judd," Blake said to his visitor, though his thoughts remained with the woman who'd just left. "I just looked over your suit."

"Man, if you could work with that nice little tidbit hanging on to you, I take off my hat to you."

In the process of sitting down, Blake stopped seconds before touching the chair. "What tidbit are you talking about?" Folson was a good client, but that didn't mean he could make a rude statement about another one of his clients. About to slap his right fist into the palm of his left hand, he caught himself and sat down.

Folson shifted uneasily in his chair, and Blake didn't have

to be told that the man noticed his testiness. "Well, I thought you and she were . . . not that I blame you. She's just about the best-looking . . . uh . . . woman around here, and after four or five years as Mrs. Rodgers, she must be—"

Blake interrupted him, because he knew that if he heard him say it, he'd pick him up out of that chair and . . . He told himself to calm down.

"Mr. Folson," he began, though he normally addressed the man by his first name. "I was opening the door for Mrs. Rodgers who stood with her back to it, and when you almost knocked her down, I grabbed her to prevent an accident. I assume you would have done the same."

"Well, sure. I . . . I just thought. Never mind. What do you have for me?"

Blake opened the file and outlined for Folson his options in respect to property he wanted to sell. "You'll get top price for it now, but it's impossible to predict its future value. Depends on property changes in the neighborhood and whether we get aggressive growth in another part of town. My advice is to sell now, take your three hundred percent profit, and consider yourself lucky."

"All right, let it go. I need to get rid of some holdings anyway."

"I'll keep you informed."

He wanted the man to get out of there. He bowled and played soccer and basketball at the same club as Folson and sometimes with him, though he wouldn't call him a friend, but right that minute, he wanted the man out of his sight. He stood, signaling the end of the appointment.

Folson shook hands and went on his way, but Blake walked back and forth in his office until he forced himself to sit down. He let out a sharp whistle as the truth exploded in his brain. Melinda Rodgers's behavior as she walked toward that door was solid evidence that she reciprocated what he felt, and she'd lie if she disowned it. Now, how the devil was he supposed to handle that?

He answered the intercom buzzer. "Yes, Irene."

"Melinda Rodgers on two."

"Hello, Melinda. What can I do for you?"

"Hello, Blake. I have some questions that occurred to me since I left your office. First, is that clause stipulating that I have to marry within a year legal?"

What was she getting at? "It's legal. Why do you ask? You thinking about contesting it?"

"Contest it? Why should I do that? He was entitled to specify his wish. I just don't understand it."

Angry now at himself for his softness toward her and for having reprimanded Folson in her defense, he spoke sharply to her. "It shouldn't be difficult for a woman like you to find a husband. If it's known that you're looking for one, you can have your pick. So, that certainly won't be an obstacle to your inheriting Prescott's estate. Your problem is setting up that foundation."

Her lengthy silence was as much a reprimand as any words could have been. Finally, she said, "And the foundation. Are you sure someone else can't set that up and I approve it?"

"Trust me, you'll do as the will states. That, or nothing. If you want that inheritance, get busy."

He thought she'd put the telephone receiver down and left it, until he heard her say, "Is there a provision in that will that allows me to replace you as its executor?" Her tone, sharp and cold, was meant to remind him that he was her husband's employee, a fact that he never forgot.

He looked down at his tapered and polished fingernails. Perfect. You could even say he had elegant hands. But at that moment, he wanted to send one of them crashing through the wall. Replace him, indeed!

"For whatever reason you'd like to have my head, Melinda, don't even think it. You and I will work together until this is settled."

"I don't suppose you're offering to help me fulfill that second clause in the will."

She let it hang, loaded with meaning and the possibility of misinterpretation. Thank God for the distance between them; if he'd been near her, he didn't know whether he'd have paddled her or . . . or kissed her until she begged him to take her. He told her good-bye at the first opportunity and hung up, shocked at himself. Prescott was dead, but even so, he didn't covet his friend's wife. Melinda had pushed his buttons, but the next time, he'd push hers. And she could count on it.

If she wasn't mistaken, something had happened between Blake and herself while they stood at his office door. For a few seconds, her whole body had anticipated invasion by the wild, primitive being within hand's reach, and she'd been ready to open herself to him. Men who stood six feet four inches tall and had a strong, masculine personality weren't all that uncommon. But add those warm fawnlike eyes that electrified you when he smiled and . . . She grabbed her chest. Oh, Lord. . . . If she could only avoid him.

Melinda dreaded going to church that next Sunday. Custom allowed her to stay away the first Sunday after becoming a widow, but not longer. After the service, she went to her father's office on the first floor of the church, not so much to visit with him as to avoid the condolences of her father's parishioners who huddled in groups at the entrance to the church and on its grounds. She knew what they thought of her, that they believed only wicked women wore high heels, perfume, and makeup and that she had married Prescott for money. For all their righteousness, only one of them had come to sit with her during her husband's final illness.

"You seem tired, Papa," she said. "Maybe you need a vacation."

"Can't afford it. You get busy and set up that foundation, otherwise you'll lose that money."

He wasn't going to inveigle her into putting him on that board; once the word was out, no one else would sit on it.

"I'll get started on it, but I wish everybody would remember that Prescott hasn't been gone three weeks. I need time to adjust."

"Didn't mean to rush you, but you have to make hay while the sun's shining, and people will be more likely to help you now while your grief is fresh."

Melinda hadn't associated her father with greed. Maybe he really did need money for the church. Best not to comment on that. "Yes, sir. I'd better be going. See you soon."

She patted his shoulder and jerked back her hand, remembering that he didn't like being touched. She'd like to know what would happen if he unlocked his emotions, but she wouldn't want to be there. The thought brought Blake Hunter to mind. Now, there was a man who probably controlled the blinking of his eyelids.

After parking her four-year-old Mercury Sable in front of her parents' house, she went in to see her mother. "Why weren't you in church this morning, Mama? You aren't sick, are you?"

"No, honey. Your father had a miniconvention yesterday, and after cooking and serving that gang, I was too tired to get out of bed this morning."

"Papa ought to get you some help. You're practically a slave to those preachers and the members of that church."

Lurlane Jones rolled her eyes and looked toward the ceiling. "Bring me Aladdin and his magic lamp; I'll get some help a lot quicker that way. Your father does what he can."

Her mother had the looks and bearing of a woman of sixty, though she'd just turned fifty, and her father looked as if he hadn't lived a day longer than forty-five years though he'd recently passed his sixtieth birthday.

"It's sapping your life, Mama. The hardest work Papa ever does is preach his sermons, and since my brothers and I are no longer here to help you, you're slaving here all day and half of some nights. You won't catch me doing that for any man. Never!"

Lurlane tightened the belt of her robe and began brushing her long hair in a soothing, rhythmic fashion, as if expressing pleasure with her life and all around her. "We're of different generations, Melinda. When you find a man you love the way I love your father, you'll understand."

Melinda's head came up sharply. "Are you suggesting that I didn't love Prescott?" It hadn't occurred to her to wonder what her parents thought of that marriage, and they hadn't let on.

"You loved him as a friend, a pleasant companion, and only that. You're still an unbroken colt, as your grandfather would say, but that'll change before long."

"My life, the part I held to myself, wasn't secret after all," she said to herself, walking rapidly out of the dining room to escape the sound of the ticking clock—a source of irritation for as far back as she could remember—knowing that her mother would follow. She wrapped her arms around Lurlane, kissed her, and left.

Driving home with her mind on her options, she was glad she'd invested in blue chip stocks most of her teacher's salary and every penny of the allowance that Prescott gave her each month. The payoff was having enough money to support herself while she studied for a Ph.D., and enjoying the choice of remaining among the gossipmongers of Ellicott City or leaving the town. But she could not dishonor Prescott's wishes that she set up that foundation, so school would have to wait one more year.

As she entered the house, she heard Ruby say, "She's not back yet, Mr. Blake. Maybe she stopped by Reverend Jones's house. She does that some Sundays."

Melinda rushed to the phone that rested on a marble-top table in the hallway. "Hello," but he'd already hung up. She looked down at the receiver she held, while disappointment weighed on her like a load of bricks.

Every molecule in her body shouted, "Call him back," but he would want to discuss business, while she . . . She went into her room, threw her hat and pocketbook on her bed, and looked around. Blake Hunter had aggravated her nerves and irritated her libido for almost five years, and it hadn't gotten the better of her. She wasn't going to let him mess up her mind now.

She ignored the telephone's insistent ringing. "Yes, sir, she just walked in. Yoohoo! Miz Melinda, it's Mr. Blake."

"Hello, Blake." Did that cool, modulated voice belong to her?

"Hi." A pause ensued, and she wondered why, as her heart-beat accelerated.

"What is it, Blake?"

"I hope you didn't decide to put Reverend Jones on the foundation's board of trustees."

She stared down at the phone. "I thought we had an understanding about that."

"Yeah. Well, I wanted to be sure."

"Not . . . to worry." The words came out slowly as she realized he'd changed his mind about something, and that her father's membership on the board was not the reason he'd called. She sat on the edge of the bed, perplexed.

"Why are you calling me, Blake?"

"Didn't I just tell you—"

"No you didn't," she said, interrupting him. "But if that's

the way you want it, fine with me.'' Angry at herself for seeming to beg the question, she added in a voice that carried a forced breeziness, ''Y'all have a nice day.''

''You bet,'' he said and hung up.

Pressing him hadn't gained her a thing; she might even have lost a few points with him.

Chapter Two

The biggest error he'd ever made. What the devil had come over him? He'd feasted his eyes on her, eaten at her table, wanted her for nearly five years and kept it to himself. Not once had he done anything as stupid as making that phone call. He'd swear that, until yesterday, she hadn't had an inkling as to how he felt about her. The thing to do was get his mind on something and somebody else. To make himself useful. He put on a pair of jeans, a T-shirt, stuck a baseball cap on his head, got into his Mercury Cougar, and headed for Metropolitan Transition Center in Baltimore, a state facility for short-term prison inmates.

As he entered the institution, he met a priest he'd often seen there. "Got three new ones today," the priest said. "Tough kids. I expect you can do more for them right now than I can."

Blake didn't like the sound of that. "Where are they?"

"Up on 9XX3. Jack will send them down."

"Thanks. As soon as one leaves here, two or three replace him."

The priest shook his head. "And they're so young."

Blake sat on the uncomfortable sofa, drabness facing him from every angle, and waited for the young men. Why would a person risk going back there once he regained his freedom? Yet the prison held dozens of repeat offenders. Finally, the boys arrived, none of them over eighteen.

"I'm Blake. A lot of the guys here take my course in criminal law. Would you like to join?"

"School? Juku, man," the oldest one said. "Man, that's like an overdose of Nytol."

Blake shrugged and pulled his cap further down on his forehead. "I make it cool, man. One of the brothers learned enough law to get his case reopened. I wouldn't think he's any smarter than you."

"I gotta keep my lines open, man. Otherwise, while I'm in here, my territory'll go up for grabs."

The youngest of the three looked at Blake, attentive, but unwilling to cross the leader.

"How long are you in for?" Blake asked the older, talkative one whom he'd sized up as the leader.

"Eighteen months. Why you take up your time coming out here?"

"We brothers have to hang together," Blake said. "The street's mean; it can suck every one of us in like quicksand."

"Man, I ain't fooled by your jeans and sneakers," the older one said. "You don't know nothing 'bout the street, man. It's a pisser out there."

Blake had been waiting for that. It always came down to *are you really one of us?* He rested his left ankle on his right knee, stuck his hands in the front pockets of his jeans, and leaned back.

"I hustled the streets of Atlanta till I owned them. You name it, I did it—running errands on my bike, shining shoes, selling shoestrings, peddling books, peanuts, even the Holy Bible. I delivered packages, did whatever I could to make a living and keep myself in school." He had their attention now, and he'd keep it. "Every cop knew me, and I knew every junkie on the street, but I wasn't their customer."

"Did you rat on them?"

Blake raised an eyebrow and pasted a look of incredulity on his face. "I'm sitting here talking to you. Right?"

"Cool, man. My name's Lobo." The older one held out his hand, palm upward. "Put it right there, man. You're mega."

He supposed that was a compliment, so he thanked Lobo.

The others introduced themselves as Phil, who hadn't said anything previously, and Johnny, who was the youngest of the three. Two potential gang members if he'd ever seen any.

"I'll be here next Saturday at three o'clock when I teach criminal law. Hope to see you brothers in the class." He picked up the bag he'd rested on the floor. "Meanwhile, I brought along a few things you might like to share—some chocolates, writing pads and pens, deodorant, soap, aftershave, things like that. See you Saturday." Rule number one, never overstay your visit.

Lobo extended his hand, and Phil and Johnny did the same. "Chill out, brother," Lobo said. "You da man."

Blake let himself grin. Getting their confidence was the first step. Later, he'd try what the correction institution didn't bother to do—work at correcting them.

When he got outside, it surprised him to see the priest sitting against the hood of his Cougar. "How'd you make out?" the priest asked him.

"I made a dent, but not a very deep one. They've been there less than a week and already they're a little gang."

"Not very encouraging," the priest said. "How'd you get into this?"

Blake walked around to the driver's side of his car. "I'm going to Ellicott City. If you're headed that way, I'll give you a lift."

"I'm going to Baltimore."

"A couple of years back," Blake said, as he headed into Baltimore proper, "I had a client, a young Moslem man, who told me he'd managed to turn some of the brothers around, giving up one day each week to teach in the Lawton Prison Program. He impressed me, and I decided to do something similar."

"I wish I knew how he did it."

"He had his successes as well as some failures, you know." He slowed down to avoid colliding with one of Maryland's road hogs. "By the time we get to these criminals, most are too far gone for help, but I decided to try with the young ones." He paused for a minute. "I'm not being disrespectful, Father, but it might help if you learned the language of the street and took off that collar. They don't want to be corrected, so you have to be subtle."

"Thanks. You don't play golf by any chance, do you?" the priest asked him.

"You bet. I'm no Tiger Woods, but I occasionally shoot around par."

"Then maybe we could go out together some Saturdays after your class. My name is Mario Biotti."

"Blake Hunter. It'll be a pleasure."

He dropped the priest off in Baltimore, and headed home. He loved junk food but didn't allow himself to have it often. Today, however, he pulled into Kentucky Fried Chicken and ordered a bucket of southern-fried buffalo wings, french fries, buttermilk biscuits, and coleslaw. Walking out with his treasure, he patted his washboard belly, assuring himself that he could occasionally indulge in junk food and keep the trim physique in which he took pride. As he opened the door of his car, he heard his name.

"Mr. Hunter. Well, this is a pleasant surprise."

Rachel Perkins. Just what he needed. "Hello, Miss Perkins," he said, remembered his baseball cap, and went through the motion of tipping his hat. "Great day we're having," he added, getting into his car as quickly as he could and igniting the engine.

Her obvious disappointment told him he'd escaped an invitation that he wouldn't have wanted to accept, and a grin crawled over his face as he waved at her and drove out of the parking lot. He'd always enjoyed outfoxing people, and Rachel Perkins was outdone.

At home, he put the food on the kitchen counter, washed his hands, and was preparing to eat when the telephone rang.

"Hi, Callie. What's up? I was going to call you as soon as I ate."

"Nothing much. Mama said Papa's still poorly, but I haven't been down there since we last talked. He keeps driving himself just as he always did, even though we send him money and he doesn't have to do it."

"He's a hard man, and that extends to himself. Thank God I got out of there when I did."

"Tell me about it. I have to thank you for insisting I get my General Education Diploma and for sending me to college. No telling what I'd be doing now if you hadn't."

"Water under the bridge, Callie. You only needed a chance. Why don't you come up here for part of your vacation? You haven't seen my house yet."

"Maybe I'll do that. Don't forget to call Mama."

"I won't. Hang in there."

He hung up and walked back into the kitchen with heavy steps. He dreaded going to Six Mile, Alabama, but no matter what his father's shortcomings, his mother needed his support, and he'd have to get down there soon. He sat against the kitchen counter, propped his left foot on the bottom rung of a step stool, and bit into a piece of chicken. Somehow, it failed to satisfy him as it usually did on those rare occasions when he ate it. He put the food in the refrigerator and went out on his patio. What the devil was wrong with him? He was hungry, but had neither a desire nor a taste for food, and that didn't make sense: he loved to eat. Maybe he needed a check-up.

The phone rang again, and he raced to answer it. "Hello. *Hello?*"

The caller had the wrong number. He slammed his left foot against a leather puff that he'd bought in Morocco and considered himself fortunate to have chosen that rather than the wall as a means of relieving his frustration. *Damn her, anyway.*

Melinda looked over the list of people Blake suggested for membership on the board of the Prescott Rodgers Foundation, as she'd decided to call it, and ran a line through the name of Andrew Carnegie Jackson. The man's parents named him Joseph, but he changed it, claiming that Joseph reminded him of the song "Old Black Joe." A man with money, he'd said, ought to have a name to go with it. Hardly a social event took place in Ellicott City that someone didn't make a joke of it.

She stared at the name Will Lamont, and grabbed the phone with such recklessness that she jerked it off the table and the receiver fell on the floor.

"What are you trying to do to me?" she asked, her voice sharp and cutting, when Blake answered the phone. "Will Lamont is head trustee at my father's church. I can't put him on this board unless I appoint my father too."

"Then scratch off his name."

"That's exactly what I did. How could you—"

"If he's off the list, what's the problem? I gave you a bunch of names. Do what you please with them."

Her fingernails dug into the flesh of her palm. "Thanks so much. You're supposed to be helping me, but it's clear you're waiting for me to blow the whole thing." She held the phone in her left hand and pounded softly and rhythmically on the desk with her right fist.

"So you think I'm an ogre? Fine. I like that; it means I don't have anything to live up to."

She wanted to . . . What *did* she want? She'd better rope in her thoughts. "Prescott talked about you as if you could change the direction of the wind. I wish you'd show *me* some of your virtues. So far, you're batting pretty low."

"Well, I'll be doggoned. You want to see some of my virtues. Why didn't you say so? I'll be happy to oblige you."

She looked down at the print of her little fingernail in her right fist and shook her body, symbolically shedding the goose pimples that his words brought to her arms. Suggestive words that imbedded in her brain images of his beautiful fingers stroking her flesh.

Angered that he seduced her so easily, she said, her voice crusted with ice, "What are you talking about?"

"Me? Same thing you're talking about. Why?" The words came out almost on a laugh. Mocking. Yes, and accusing. "Did I say something wrong?"

She escaped to the safety of talk about the foundation and the list before her. "Who drew up this list, you or Irene?"

"I gave her the names. She did the rest. She's extremely efficient."

She didn't give two hoots about Irene's efficiency, and she was sure he knew it. "Did you put these booby traps in here intentionally, or did you have temporary lapses of political savvy?"

"I don't have such lapses. If you see a name on that list,

it's because I intended for it to be there. I don't mix foolishness with business."

"I see." She couldn't help needling him, even though she knew that was a substitute for something far more intimate. "One of your virtues. Right?"

She heard the wind swoosh out of him and prepared herself for biting words, but the expectation didn't materialize.

"Think over this conversation, Melinda, and let me know what you make of it. Any disinterested person would think you're after more than you're receiving. Think about what you want before you get in too deep."

She had to let that stab go by, because he'd changed from teasing to baiting, and she refused to bite. "Since I'm not a disinterested party, I won't be able to judge. Right?" She began walking back and forth from her desk to her bed. "The will says you're to help me; if you don't, I'll do it without you."

"You might as well cooperate with *me*; it will be done to my satisfaction or there'll be no foundation and no inheritance."

She swore under her breath. "A person with a flea brain could see through what you're doing. I refuse to fail, because that would make you happy."

She imagined that one of his mesmerizing grins had taken possession of his face when he said, "You don't want me to be happy?"

"Does the sun rise in the north?" she asked him. "This isn't getting me anywhere. See you." She hung up and immediately wished she hadn't. Jostling with him had been fun, and while they were at it, she'd had a warm, cozy sensation, far from the forsaken feeling she had now.

An hour later, his belly full of calories, Blake lay flat on his back on his living room floor listening to Ledbetter sing the blues. He wasn't contented, but he felt a lot better than he did before she called to chew him out. If only he had a firm handle on whatever was going on between them.

He voiced his frustration with a satisfying expletive. She could raise hell and threaten all she pleased, but she'd fulfill the terms of that will or she'd be just another widow. She married Prescott for money, and if she wanted to get it, she'd have to earn it. She could heat him to boiling point; it wouldn't make an iota of difference.

Melinda decided to tackle Judd Folson first and get that over with. Too bad that he'd misunderstood the scene with Blake and her when he'd walked into Blake's office.

"Good morning, Mr. Folson. This is Melinda Rodgers. I'm calling to—"

"Oh, you needn't worry, Melinda. Blake explained that he had to catch you when he opened the door. I didn't—"

The nerve of him. She told herself not to react. "Mr. Folson, my late husband's will requires that I establish a foundation to support remedial reading here in Ellicott City, and I'm inquiring as to your willingness to serve on the board. I'm canvassing twelve of the town's leading citizens. It's a charity foundation, so there's no honorarium for this." She heard a sound like someone clearing his throat and waited for the verdict.

"The leading citizens, eh? Well, now, that's right decent of you. You can put my name down."

Martha Greene agreed to serve, but not before she let Melinda know what she thought of the Reverend Booker Jones. "That man thinks everybody's headed straight for hell, everybody but him, that is. It's a wonder you turned out as well as you did."

Melinda closed her eyes tight. Ten more to go, and she could shake Ellicott City dust from her feet, except for Christmas and Mother's Day. *Turned out as well as you did! Grin and bear it, girl,* she admonished herself. *It'll soon be in the past.*

"Then you'll serve, Mrs. Greene? Thank you so much. My husband would be pleased."

"You think I'm doing it for him?" the woman shot back. "I'm signing on because of all the people around here who can barely read a street sign. Prescott Rodgers stayed as far away from the citizens of this town as he could get. Anybody would have thought he was scared we'd absorb some of his money."

Just a sweet, loving human being. "Whatever your reason, Mrs. Greene, I do appreciate your help."

She hung up. "Whew." That was as much as she could take for one evening. She went over the lesson plans for her classes in American literature and contemporary fiction writing, got ready for bed, and put on a Billie Holiday CD. Jazz, Mozart, and Brian McKnight ballads could lull her into contentment every time. She sat on the floor with her back against her bed and closed her eyes to let the sound of Billie singing "Why Not Take all Of Me?" wash over her. Within seconds, Blake Hunter filled her thoughts, and then she could feel his fingers gently loving her neck, face, arms, her belly, thighs, all of her. She gripped the coverlet on her bed as he hovered above her, and when he wiped tears from her eyes, she felt the dampness on her face and knew that she cried.

Melinda got to school the next morning, but she'd tossed in bed all night begging for the sleep that never came, and every muscle in her body ached. When questioned about her obvious fatigue, she explained to Rachel that working on the foundation had worn her out.

"I thought maybe you'd been out with that fine brother who's handling Prescott's will."

"You saw him the last time I did."

Rachel lowered her gaze, and Melinda couldn't help noticing

the look of embarrassment on the woman's face. "Are you suggesting that I'm seeing Blake socially?" she asked Rachel.

"Well . . . uh . . . no, but you know how people talk."

Melinda didn't press Rachel, but the woman's words failed to placate her. She'd noticed her fascination with Blake, and Melinda didn't blame her. Who would? Blake Hunter wasn't just handsome; his tough, masculine personality and riveting presence jumped out at you, and you had to pay attention to him. Any female between the ages of eight and eighty with warm blood running through her veins would give the man a second look.

"What are they saying about me and Blake Hunter? What *can* they say?"

Rachel patted Melinda's shoulder and looked as if she wanted to deny her statement. "Girl, our folks love to gossip. You know that."

She stared down at Rachel, who stood little more than five feet five inches in her three-inch heels. "It isn't just 'our folks' who gossip; all small-town people gossip; they don't have much else to do." Seeing the relief on Rachel's face, she knew the woman had been saved from embarrassment. Or maybe from lying.

Later that afternoon, the school's superintendent called Melinda to his office. "Mrs. Rodgers, I understand your late husband's will contains provisions that aren't favorable to you. I was—"

"Who told you that? As far as I'm concerned, there's nothing bad in that will."

"But I heard you'd been disinherited, and I thought you might ask Mr. Blake to settle some money on the school."

She propped her hands on her hips and glared at him. It wasn't easy to ring her bell, but he'd just managed to do it. "Is that all, Dr. Hicks?" Without waiting for his answer, she spun around and left.

On an impulse, she stopped by Blake's office on the way home. If he couldn't do something to arrest the awful gossip, she'd chuck the whole thing.

"Melinda. What a surprise," he said and stood when she entered his office. "What can I do for you?"

She explained the reasons for being there. "It started yesterday with Judd Folson. Even Rachel's repeating these stupidities. I'm fed up."

The tips of his fingers warmed her elbow. "Come on in." He didn't go to his desk as she would have expected, but led her to the leather sofa that rested beneath a collection of paintings by African-American artists and sat there beside her.

"Tell me about it." His voice conveyed an unfamiliar softness, a tenderness, maybe even an intimacy. At least she thought so.

"It's . . . I know a lot of people don't like my father, and I understand that. I even accept it, because he's a big dose for me sometimes, but what did Prescott ever do to anybody?"

"Ordinary people envy the rich, Melinda. He didn't have to do anything to anybody."

Her eyes widened, and her pocketbook slipped from her lap to the floor. She caught herself, but not quickly enough to hide her shock. He picked up her pocketbook and put it on the sofa beside her.

"Why are you surprised? The poor have hated the rich since the beginning of time."

She couldn't help staring at him. "Rich? What do you mean, *'rich'*? I know Prescott was well off, but rich?"

Now, she had obviously surprised *him.* "Prescott Rodgers was worth millions, and his estate will earn royalties probably for as long as people wear glasses and use cameras."

She slumped against the back of the sofa and slowly closed her mouth. "I never dreamed . . . Prescott never talked about his finances, and I didn't question him about them. I knew we were well off. We had what we needed, but if he hadn't given me anything more than the first real peace I'd had in my life, I would have been contented."

He stared at her for so long that she decided she'd lost his sympathy, that she'd better leave. But he restrained her with a hand on her shoulder, a hand whose warmth she felt to the marrow of her being.

"Don't go. Please. This takes some getting used to."

"Why? What did you think? That I—"

He cut her off. "Don't say it. Right now, I don't know what to think. Prescott talked freely to me about his affairs, or at least I think he did, so it didn't occur to me that he didn't share them with his wife."

She didn't like the chill that settled in her chest. "There was no reason why he should have." She stood and walked to the door, giving him no choice but to follow her.

"If you want to take over the matter of that foundation, it's all right with me," Blake said.

"You know I can't do that. I've sworn to do as he wished, and I can't sidestep my integrity and live with myself."

His voice behind her, so close to her ear, sent shock waves throughout her body, and she had to will herself not to turn around.

"I . . . I'll help you with it. Maybe . . ." His breath seemed to shorten, and his words became rasping sounds. "We'll . . . like I said, I'll help you."

And then it hit her. His opinion of her didn't differ from what the rest of Ellicott City thought about her. "You don't believe me, do you? You think I knew and that I can't wait to get my hands on Prescott's money, don't you? Isn't that right?"

The sudden coolness of her body told her he'd stepped away from her back. She saw his hand on the doorknob and remembered that moment two weeks earlier when it had rested on her waist. Protective. Possessive. He turned the knob, and when she risked a glance at him, she bit back the gasp that nearly sprang from her throat. Desire, fierce and primitive, shone in his eyes.

"What do you want me to say?"

The words seemed to rush out of him. Perhaps he'd found some kind of reprieve, had grabbed the opportunity to reply logically, but without saying anything meaningful. She didn't answer. But she hurt. Oh, the pain of it, shooting through her like a spray of bullets tearing up her insides. The ache of unappeased desire, and the anguish of knowing he thought so little of her. With her hand covering his, she pulled open the door and rushed down the corridor to the elevator. He didn't think well of her, but he wanted her. She didn't know if she could stand it.

He watched her rush away from him, her hips swaying almost as if in defiance above the most perfect pair of props a man ever looked at. Seconds earlier, he'd come close to doing what he'd sworn never to do. As she reached the elevator, he closed his door and leaned against it. It wouldn't do for her to look back and find him watching her. She needed his help; without it, the good people of Ellicott City would laugh at her, and he couldn't bear to see her ridiculed.

A man confided things to his lawyer, but to keep his wife in the dark about his wealth . . . He ran his hand over the hair at the back of his head. He didn't believe she was lying, but something didn't jell. A woman who'd been married for almost five years ought to know how to finesse a man's revved-up libido. Any man's. But she didn't make small talk, didn't joke, didn't say anything that would have cooled him off. That level of naivete in a twenty-nine-year-old widow was incomprehensible. He should keep his distance, but he didn't see an alternative to sitting with her while she contacted the people on her list.

She'd had time to drive home, so he called her. "Melinda, this is Blake. Suppose you stop by after school, and we'll go through your list till we get twelve people to agree to serve. The sooner we do this, the better."

Her long silence annoyed him until he let himself remember that she was probably as shaken by their near-encounter as he. "All right," she said at last in a voice that suggested disinterest. "I want to finish it as soon as possible."

He believed that, but not her feigned disinterest. "Till tomorrow then."

She hung up, obviously discombobulated, and he was certainly at the root of her discomfort. While he tried to think of a way to smooth their relationship without indicting himself, the phone rang.

"Reverend Jones on one," Irene said.

"Hunter. What may I do for you, sir?"

"I just talked with that daughter of mine. She doesn't seem to understand my position in Ellicott City. If anybody should be on that board, it's me. You're her advisor, so I'm depending on you to set her straight."

Here we go! He sat down and, to make certain he stayed calm, he picked up a red-ink pen and began doodling. "Reverend Jones, my job is to advise my client, not to dictate to her, but I've warned her that it's best not to give either a political or a religious flavor to the board. Further, I've suggested that she exclude from consideration members of her family and of Prescott's family." He hadn't, but the words might convince Jones not to ride hard on Melinda.

"That's bunkum. Rodgers didn't have any family. At least not that anybody around here ever heard about, and they can't come in now and start demanding the man's money when it belongs to Melinda."

"You needn't worry about that, sir. Have a good day."

He hung up and considered the pleasure he'd get out of

pitching something—*anything*—across the room. Booker Jones planned to aggravate him to distraction, and he'd probably do it from the hallowed perch of his pulpit.

His anticipation of Booker's tirade proved prophetic. Melinda forced herself to go to the Third Evangelical House of Prayer—her father's small church—the following Sunday morning and hadn't been seated for ten minutes when she realized that her personal affairs would be the text of her father's sermon.

"Children, obey your parents. That's a commandment. But does my own daughter obey it? I say to you, parents, don't be discouraged, as I am not discouraged. They will perish, every last one of them. But our reward will come, and oh, how beautiful it will be. Let them know that money is the root of all evil. Let them know that they will burn in hell. And brothers and sisters, it won't be a little blister, and there won't be any salve to put on it . . ."

Tuning him out, all she heard was the drone of his voice. Getting up and leaving wasn't an option, so she sat there and let herself think of pleasant things. Her life with Prescott and the peace and contentment she'd known with him. But as she reminisced, it came to her forcefully that Prescott had treated her as if she were a child, taking care of her material needs, giving her an allowance, never broaching the subject of sex— not that she'd have welcomed it. She'd gone from one father to another one, and neither had prepared her for her encounters with Blake Hunter. A tough man with a soft core, she surmised, and a masculine persona that fired her up and awakened the womanliness in her. She hadn't known the meaning of the word *lust* until she first looked into his eyes and he stared at her until her nipples tightened and her blood raced as if she were in a marathon.

She wanted to close her eyes and think about him, but didn't dare for fear her father would think she slept during his sermon. At last the choir sang the closing hymn, and she rushed out of the church.

"Didn't Reverend Jones really preach today? Bless the Lord," one of the sisters said to her.

No way was that woman going to make her concur with her father's accusations. "My father speaks his mind," she told the startled woman and brushed past her.

With her heart lodged in her throat, she knocked on Blake's office door the next afternoon at three-thirty. He opened the door, smiled, and her pulse kicked into overdrive.

"Hi."

Not *hello,* but *hi.* She looked up at him and tried to smile back, but she suspected she hadn't succeeded. What had caused this about-face?

"Hello. Uh . . . hi."

If he noticed her lack of composure, he didn't let on. "I wish you'd brought some fries or something. I didn't get any lunch. Been preparing for a trial tomorrow morning."

"I could go get some," she said, wondering at his turn of mind.

His fingers touched her elbow, and he walked with her to his desk. "No need for that. I'll order something by phone. What would you like? I'm having french fries and ginger ale."

"You haven't eaten since breakfast, and you're ordering french fries?"

A sheepish expression flashed across his face. "Come to think of it, all I had for breakfast was a glass of V-8 juice."

She shook her head in wonder. "How can you look the way you do if you don't eat properly?"

His eyebrows went up, and she knew she'd said the wrong thing.

"How do I . . . Never mind. Most days I eat bran flakes and a banana. That better?"

"Decidedly," she said and put forth a lot of effort to prevent his seeing how relieved she was that he hadn't finished that sentence. When he'd eaten the french fries, he opened both bottles of ginger ale, wrapped a napkin around one, and handed it to her.

"Ready?"

She nodded. "Ready as I'll ever be."

A grin converted his whole face into a thing of beauty. She'd better concentrate on that board of directors, or anything other than him that would occupy her mind. The man was safer in a less jovial mood.

"Let's try Alice Pride first," Blake suggested. "She craves social status, so she ought to be a shoe-in."

And indeed she was. "I'm just too glad to do some good for my town," Alice said. "Just let me know when you're calling the first meeting. I'll be there."

And so it went for the first two calls. Then Melinda dialed Luther Williams and told him the purpose of her call.

"What?" she asked, and her face must have mirrored her horror at Luther Williams's indictment of her, because Blake snatched the phone.

"This is Blake Hunter. We're working on setting up this foundation according to Rodgers's will. What's the problem, Luther?"

"Well . . . I . . . You know what everybody says. I mean, you don't expect me to join in with a kept woman to—"

"What the hell are you talking about, man? This foundation was Prescott Rodgers's bequest. And what do you mean by trashing a woman's reputation on the basis of gossip? That's slander."

Melinda put the list on the desk, picked up her pocketbook that she'd placed on the floor, and started for the door.

"Oh, no, you don't," he called after her and slammed the receiver into its cradle. "Is that all it takes to make you tuck your tail in and run? Is it?"

She whirled around and slammed into him. "You don't know what it's . . . like," she whispered, as the fire began to blaze in his eyes. The belt on his trousers touched her belly. So close. Lord, he was there, and she could have him. She closed her eyes to hide the temptation before her.

"You're not a coward, are you? You won't let them beat you down. I won't let you run. Do you hear me? Stand up to them. Show the bastards you don't care what they say."

"Bu . . . bu . . . but I . . . I *do* care. I do."

Shivers coursed through her as he locked her to him. Startled, she looked into his fierce eyes, then dropped her gaze to his mouth and parted her lips. For a brief, poignant moment, he stared down at her. Open. Pliable. Susceptible to her. His tremors shook her, and her nerves tingled with exhilaration when she heard his hoarse groan of capitulation. Then his mouth was on her, and his tongue stabbed at her lips until she opened and, at last, had him inside of her. His big hand gripped her buttocks and she undulated wildly against him as his velvet tongue promised her ecstasy, plunging in and out of her and testing every crevice of her mouth. Strong and commanding like the man himself. He held her head while he plied her mouth with sweet loving, stroked her back, her shoulders, and her buttocks until she sucked his tongue deep into her mouth and feasted. When his hand went to her breast, she pressed it to her while his fingers twirled her turgid nipple. Hungry for all of him, she spread her legs and he rose hard and strong against her. She slumped into him and might have fallen if he hadn't lifted her, carried her to the sofa, and sat down with her in his lap.

For a long while, he sat there, rocking her and stroking her, soothing her with a tenderness she'd never known.

"It wasn't any use, was it?" he said at last.

She knew what he meant and didn't pretend otherwise. "Looks that way. But it shouldn't have happened. I have enough problems as it is."

"I won't argue with you about that. We have to work together on this foundation, and don't forget, there's one more clause."

"How could I forget *that?*" she asked, getting to her feet. "I think I'd better go now."

"Do you want me to . . . Can I drive you home? I mean . . . do you need me for . . . something?" He gasped it, as if releasing the words pained him all the way to his gut.

She shook her head. "I drove, but thanks."

He walked with her to the door and stood looking down at her. Nobody had to tell her what he was thinking or what he wanted. Suddenly, his right shoulder lifted in a quick shrug, and she knew he'd won over temptation. At least one of them had sense. If he'd kissed her again, she wouldn't have left the way she entered. That much strength she doubted she had. But what about tomorrow and the next day and the next?

He winked at her and grinned. "Don't worry, Melinda. There isn't much I set myself to do that I can't manage. See you tomorrow."

By the time she reached her car, her breath came in short gasps, but that didn't explain her inability to steady her fingers enough to get the key in the ignition and start the vehicle. After a few minutes, she gave up. Why had everything become so difficult? She wanted to lay her head on the steering wheel and wake up in Italy, Switzerland, Kenya, or anywhere but Ellicott City.

The people had the same character as the town: museum pieces, all show and little substance. If she got involved with Blake, the busybodies would assume they'd been right all along, and if she stayed in Ellicott City, she didn't see how she could avoid it. He might have the mental toughness of a samurai warrior, but she'd been in his arms, and she knew how badly he wanted her. The next time . . . For five years, she'd hungered for him, locked him in the privacy of her heart and the recesses of her mind, never revealing to anyone what she felt and how it pained her. And now, he'd transformed her into a hot and passionate woman, a willing lover. She didn't believe in lying to herself, so she didn't promise herself she'd resist him.

Blake stood at the window in his office and looked down on Old Columbia Pike where he could see the top of Melinda's green Mercury Sable. Why didn't she drive off? He didn't want to become involved with her, but he'd had her in his arms, felt her tremors, smelled her heat and tasted her sweetness, and he wouldn't bet five cents that he wouldn't touch her again. When a woman wanted him as badly as she did . . . He swallowed hard. His hands had roamed her body and she'd relished it, had opened herself to him, as uninhibited as a tigress in heat. And he was starved for her.

"Blake, I've been buzzing you," Irene said, and he turned to see her standing in the doorway between their offices.

"Oh, thanks. What is it?"

"Lacy Morgan's on line one."

He swore. "Tell her I emigrated to Alaska."

"What? I beg your pardon."

What a great idea. "You heard me. Tell her exactly that."

"Bu . . . but . . . How do I phrase it? I can't just lie."

"Tell her I told you I moved to Alaska." He snapped his finger. "Oh, yes, and I didn't leave a forwarding address, a phone number, fax number, or an e-mail address."

She stared at him as if he'd lost his mind. "That is an order, Irene."

"Yes, sir . . . I mean, Blake."

His laughter followed her rapidly retreating figure, a cleansing release that he'd needed and needed badly. With luck, Lacy Morgan would consider herself insulted. Now, if he could just straighten out the rest of his life that easily. Not a chance. He grabbed his briefcase, got in his car, and drove to the Patapsco River where the swiftly moving water never failed to soothe him. He looked at the late-day sun, slowly dying, its rays filtering through the leaves of the oak and beech trees that towered in the distance. A light, fresh breeze frolicked against his body, cooling and refreshing it. Pretty soon it would be night and, as on every other night, he'd be all by himself. He took his cell phone out of his briefcase, pulled air through his front teeth, shrugged, and put the phone away. He didn't want to hear any voice but hers.

Chapter Three

"Who is it?" Melinda called downstairs to Ruby when she heard the doorbell.

"Uh, it's ... Mr. ... What did you say your name was?"

"Humphrey. Jonas Humphrey."

"Jonas Humphrey, ma'am."

Now, who could that be? She knew Prescott's few associates, or thought she did. During the last two years, Blake had been their only visitor. But after that bombshell Blake had dropped about her late husband's finances, she couldn't be sure about anything concerning Prescott. She kicked off her bedroom shoes, stuck her feet in a pair of loafers, and went downstairs.

"I don't think we've met, Mr. Humphrey. What can I do for you?"

"Well, miss"—he looked around, shifting his gaze from

place to place as if appraising the room's appointments—
"could we sit down, perhaps? I'd like a soda or anything cold,
if you don't mind."

She knew a shifty look when she saw it, and she wasn't
going to be taken in by this interloper. "Would you please tell
me why you're here?" she asked the man. Around forty or
forty-five years old, she supposed, he projected self-confidence,
though she wouldn't have credited him with a right to it.

She leaned against the piano and trailed the fingers of her
left hand rapidly over the bass keys in a show of impatience.
"Well?"

He cleared his throat and looked approvingly at the Steinway
Grand. "I don't suppose you know it, but my beloved Heddy
passed on about six months ago, and I find the burden just too
heavy to bear. When your dear father was preaching night
before last, it came to me clear as your hand before you that
he was leading me straight to you. I own a little shop down at
the end of Main Street." He took a card from his pocket,
handed it to her, and she read *Humphrey's Firewood*. "It's not
much, but everybody around here needs wood."

Where was this leading? "What does all that have to do
with me?" she asked him, though she'd begun to guess the
answer.

"Reverend Jones said a woman shouldn't be alone, that she
needs a man's protection. I'm sure he taught you that from
childhood. Well, since we're both alone, and . . . well, I thought
we might get together. I see you like music. I do, too." He sat
down and crossed his knee, though she remained standing. "I
got all the records Sister Rosetta Thorpe and Hank Williams
ever made. I had one by Lightnin' Hopkins, but my dear beloved
smashed it one day when she got mad with me. God rest her
soul."

She'd had enough. More than enough, in fact. "Mr. . . . er

. . . Humphrey, did you say your name was? I am not interested in getting married. Now, I'd appreciate it if you'd excuse me.'' She called Ruby. "Would you please let this gentleman out? And, Ruby, don't let anybody else in here unless you know them.''

The door closed, and Ruby called up to her. "All right, ma'am. He said he knowed Mr. Rodgers. I'm telling you some of these mens is the biggest liars.''

Had her father put that man up to proposing to her? She sat down and telephoned him.

"Jonas Humphrey?'' he asked her, a tone of incredulity in his voice. "You mean that thief down on Main Street? Why, he'd steal a cane from a blind man. Of course I didn't send him over there. You watch out, girl, because they'll be hearing about that will. Not that it would hurt you to get married. A woman shouldn't be alone—''

She'd heard that a hundred times already. "Sorry, Papa, but I have to go. Talk to you again soon.''

"All right, but you come to prayer meeting tomorrow night.''

She dressed and rushed to meet Rachel at Side Streets Restaurant. The historic old mill pleased her more than the wonderful seafood served there. Its quaintness gave her a sense of solidness, of permanence. They had barely seated themselves when Ray Sinclair entered with his latest girlfriend. In her single days, she'd been enamored of Ray, but he had ignored her, often seeming to make a point of it. The day he stepped in front of her and got into the taxi she'd called, her affection for him dissipated like chaff in a windstorm. But on this occasion, he seated his date, left her at the table, and walked over to speak with Melinda.

"Terribly sorry to hear of your great loss, Melinda. If I can do anything to help, just snap your fingers.''

She leaned back in the booth and spoke with dispassion. "I don't need anything, Ray. My husband provided well for me and, if he hadn't, I provide well for myself. Nice seeing you."

Rachel's eyes seemed to have doubled in size. "Why'd you dust him off like that? He's the most eligible man around here. If that doesn't beat all—"

Melinda threw up her hands. "When I had a crush on him before I got married, he flaunted it, showed me as often as he could that he thought himself too good for me. Now he wants to know what he can do for me. I guess he's been listening to all the gossip, or maybe he's heard about the will. That poor girl he's got with him is welcome to him."

She'd hardly walked into her house when her phone rang. Ruby had left for the day, so she waited for the voice on her answering machine.

"I was wondering if you might like go with me down to Lake Kittamaqundi for the Fourth of July celebration. It's nice and casual. Give us a chance to get reacquainted."

Why was she supposed to recognize his voice? She did, but he didn't need to know that. "Who is this?" she asked.

"This is Ray," he said, obviously crestfallen.

"Now let me see, hmmm. I'll have to let you know."

"We'll have a good time. I'll order a picnic basket, some wine, and . . . Listen, we'll do it up big."

"Are we still talking about watching kids shoot marbles and dogs play catch down by that lake?"

"Uh . . . well, there's the fireworks, you know. Anyhow, I'll call in a day or so to see what you decided. I'm glad you're going. It'll be great."

It wouldn't hurt him to hope; he might recall the many times he'd let her hope and pray, and all to no avail. Of all the men in Ellicott City, Ray Sinclair was least likely to get a second glance from her.

If she were certain of the reason for his sudden interest, she might be amused, but she remembered Luther Williams's insulting suggestion, the awful accusation that had brought her into Blake's arms, and she no longer felt like playing games with Ray. Who knew what he'd heard or what he wanted? Tomorrow, she'd work on that foundation, much as she hated doing so. But the sooner she finished it and got out of Ellicott City, the happier she'd be.

He knew it was a dead giveaway, opening the door before she'd hardly had time to ring the bell, but the entire day had been one long wait for three-thirty.

"Hi." He meant it to sound casual, and he hoped it did, but he didn't feel one bit nonchalant about her. "Ready to tackle that list?" he asked, mostly to remind her, if not himself, that they were together for business and not social purposes.

"That's why I'm here. Whether I'm ready for it is something else." She was looking directly into his eyes as if searching for something important. It wasn't a stare, more like an appraisal. Or a question, as if she didn't really know him and wanted answers about him.

And she was getting to him, too, so he made light of it. "I don't have crumbs around my mouth, do I?"

The back of her right hand moved slowly over his left cheek in a gentle, yet astounding caress. "Your mouth is perfect. Let's tackle the mayor first."

"What do you mean by that?"

She threw her briefcase on the sofa and walked away from him in the direction of his desk. "I mean the mayor will probably be difficult, so let's call him and get it over with."

He caught up with her and stopped her with a hand on her

right shoulder. "Baloney. You know I wasn't talking about the mayor. You walk in here, make a suggestive remark, caress me, and then stroll off as if all you've done is toss a piece of paper into the wastebasket." He pushed back his rising irritation. "Honey, you play with me, and you will get burned as sure as night follows day."

She stepped away from him. "Oh, for goodness' sake. I was just being pleasant."

He imagined that his face expressed his incredulity; he refused to believe she didn't know a come-on from a pleasant pat. "Pleasant? Yeah. Sure. And I'm standing in the middle of the Roman Forum."

"Oh, don't make such a hullabaloo over a simple, friendly gesture. If you wanted to hear some real corn, you should have been in on the conversations I had with two would-be suitors today."

His head snapped up. "Who? You mean—"

"One guy proposed marriage, and the other one's an egotist who thinks all he has to do is phone me. Biggest laugh I ever got."

She could see the perspiration on his forehead, and he knew it, but he couldn't do a thing about it. He couldn't even reach for his handkerchief, because she'd glued her gaze on him. He laid his head to one side and decided to go for broke.

"Not bad for one day. At this rate, you can't miss. If we can finish this list, you'll be free to get on with that other business."

Now what had he done? She'd wilted like a crushed rose. He looked downward and kicked the carpet with the toe of his left shoe, ashamed that his words—spoken to hide his own feelings—had bruised hers. The urge to take her in his arms and soothe her almost overwhelmed him, but he knew the consequences if he gave in to it. He'd tempered his opinion of her, but too much remained unexplained, and not all of it was pretty. The wisest thing he could do would be to keep a good solid distance between them. With her standing there open and vulnerable, a defenseless beauty, he laughed to himself. If he was serious about staying away from her, he'd better pray for sainthood.

She straightened her shoulders and sat down, and his admiration for her soared.

"Good afternoon, Mayor Washington," Melinda said, and continued with her reason for calling. "I hope I can count on you to serve."

She held the phone away from her as if to protect her eardrums, and he took it. He'd rather not get on the wrong side of His Honor, the mayor, but he said, "Frank, this is Blake Hunter. I'd be careful about that kind of talk if I were you." He winced as he thought of Melinda's ordeal with the people of Ellicott City. "Mrs. Rodgers is setting up a foundation as prescribed in her late husband's will. If you slander her as you were doing, she'll sue you, and as representative of her husband's estate, I'd have to take you on."

"You?" The mayor sounded as if he was stunned.

"You got it. I'd rather not do that, buddy, but you know me. I'll bite the bullet every time."

"Sorry, brother," the mayor went on, "but ... you know she's not fit for something so important as that foundation is to this community."

Blake tightened his fist, then he ground his teeth. *Count to ten, man,* he told himself, loosening his tie. "Have you forgotten that there won't be a foundation unless she sets it up?"

"In that case the money goes to the city. Right?"

"A million will go to the city for the benefit of the homeless alone and the rest to a charity event or organization of my choice. It will pay for you to cooperate."

"That's not the way I read it. If necessary, we'll go to court."

"Forget that, buddy. You'll only be wasting time and money."

Melinda grabbed the phone. "Excuse me, Blake, but I just want to tell the mayor that he will not serve on this board, not now or ever. That's right, sir." She hung up.

"You just made an enemy, but he deserved it. Let's get on with this."

Well after seven that evening, they could count twelve people who were willing to serve on the board. Melinda leaned back in the chair, locked her hands behind her head, and blew out a long breath.

"I'm pooped."

He didn't doubt it. "Me too. How about something to eat? Let's go around the corner to Tersiguel's. I feel like some decent food."

"Fine. Where's the ladies' room? I need to freshen up. I'll eat what Ruby cooked for me some other time."

"There's one just off Irene's office. I thought you were too pooped to bother with hair and lipstick and things like that."

"Mr. Hunter, I never get that tired."

They'd barely seated themselves when Martha Greene paused at their table. "Oh, how nice to see you, Mr. Hunter! Good evening, Melinda." From hot to freezing in less than a second.

Melinda searched Blake's face for the question she knew she'd find there. "What is it?" he asked her.

"As far as I know, I've never done anything to offend her, but she seems to enjoy being rude to me."

His eyes softened with what she recognized as sympathy, but she didn't want that, not from him or anyone else. He reached across the table, evidently to take her hand, but withdrew before she could enjoy the warmth of his touch.

"I believe I reminded you once that most people envy the rich, but when a woman is both rich and beautiful, women will dislike her and men will turn cartwheels for her. Even so, Martha Greene isn't known as a charitable person."

Flushed with the pleasure of knowing that he thought her beautiful, she lowered her gaze. "You don't know how happy I'll be when the will is settled and this business is history."

The expression in his eyes sliced through her, and she knew that somewhere in those words, she'd made a blunder. A serious one, at that.

"I imagine you want to get on with your life," he said, "especially after having spent almost five of your best years in semiretirement. But don't forget that when you finish this round, you've got to show me a marriage certificate."

She knew that she gaped at him; she couldn't help it. Her fingers clutched the table, knocking over the long-stem glass of white wine that soaked the tablecloth and wet her dress.

"You kissed me and held me as if I were the most precious person in the world, and now you can say that to me. You're just like all the others." As though oblivious to the wet tablecloth and the dampness in her lap, she gripped the table and leaned toward him.

"You at least know that Prescott was happy with me, that I made his life pleasant, and that I was loyal to him. You know I never looked at another man, because I didn't look at you."

"Look! There's no need to—"

"Yes, there is. You listen to me. It happened the minute you opened your office door for Prescott and me when we went there to be married. And the first time you came to our home I knew that what I felt for you twenty minutes before I took my marriage vows was definitely not superficial. From then on—at least once a week for almost five years—I had to deal with you. But you didn't know it, and don't tell me you did. You don't know what it cost me, and you'll never know. So don't sit there like a judge-penitent and pass sentence.''

She tossed a twenty-dollar bill on the table, grabbed her purse and briefcase. ''I'll eat whatever Ruby cooked. I'll . . . I'm sorry, Blake.''

Walking with head high, away from the source of her pain, her eyes beheld only a blur of human flesh and artifacts. She didn't see the gilded candles on the hanging chandelier, the huge bowl of red and yellow roses on a marble stand beneath it, or her reflection in the antique gold-framed mirrors that lined the walls. Only the gray bleakness of her life. But none of those who accused her would ever see one of her tears. The gossiping citizens of Ellicott City irritated her. But Blake's words bored a hole in her. She got into her car and sat there, too drained to drive. Should she fault herself for having let him hold her and show her what she'd missed? Maybe she shouldn't have allowed it. *But I'm human, and I've got feelings.* After a while, she started the car and moved away from the curb. ''You're dealing with your own guilt, Blake,'' she said aloud, and immediately felt better. ''You wanted your friend's wife; well, take it out on *yourself.*''

Blake washed his Maryland crab cakes down with half a bottle of chardonnay wine and considered drinking the whole bottle but thought better of it. He shouldn't have plowed into her, knowing he'd hurt her, but she had infuriated him with her tale about the men who wanted to marry her. He knew she'd attract every trifling money hunter and womanizer in Howard County and maybe farther away than that.

As much as he wanted her, he didn't intend to get in that line. Her apparent eagerness to gain control of Prescott's millions didn't sit well with him, especially since she hadn't once shown the grief you'd expect of a woman recently widowed. His left hand swept over his face. It wasn't a fair accusation, and he knew it. Not everybody grieved for public consumption. He didn't covet another person's wealth; he made a good living and had every comfort that he could want, but he'd earned it. He'd worked for every dime he had, and he couldn't sympathize with, much less respect, anybody who didn't work for what they got. He let out a long, heavy breath. How had it come to this? She was in him, down deep, clinging to the marrow of his being, wrapped around his nerve ends. Way down. Right where he lived.

"Oh, what the hell. If it hasn't killed me so far, it won't!" He paid the check and left her twenty-dollar bill on the table for the waiter.

He walked into his house, threw his briefcase on the carved walnut dining-room table, and looked at the elegance all around him. Thick oriental carpets covered his parquet floors; Italian leather sofa and chairs; silk draperies, fine walnut tables and wall units and fixtures, and fine paintings adorned his living room. All of it aeons away from the days when water soaked his bed every time it rained, and wind whistled through the cracks of the house in winter. The memory depressed him, and he wondered if the hardships of his youth had made him a tough, cynical man. He hoped not. Shaking it off, he telephoned his mother in Alabama, his thoughts filled with the one problem he'd never solved. His relationship with his father.

"How's Papa?" he asked her after they greeted each other.

"Just fair. I think he's tired, and I don't mean ordinary tired. I sense that he doesn't feel like going on."

"You serious?"

"I wish I wasn't, son."

"I don't like the sound of it," he told her. He'd gotten the same feeling when he spoke with his father the previous morning. "I'll be down there tomorrow."

After hanging up, he remembered his promise to visit Phil and Johnny. The warden had separated them from Lobo, who'd set up business as usual there in the jail. Blake called the warden and asked him to explain to the boys that he'd see them on Sunday.

"I'd hoped to hold my grandchildren," his father told him, "but none of the three of you bothered to get married yet." His thoughts appeared to ramble. "You had a tough life, but you made something of yourself, and I'm proud of you. I know I seemed hard, maybe too hard, but we had to live. Make sure you find a girl who'll stick with you through thick and thin. One like your mother."

The old man's feeble fingers patted Blake's hand. He'd never thought he'd shed tears for his father, but when he walked out of the room, they came. And they flowed.

He didn't want to use Melinda, but when he boarded the plane in Birmingham, his only thought was to have her near him. It might be unfair to her, but life wasn't fair. Right then, he knew he could handle most anything, if she was there for him. As soon as he walked into the terminal in Baltimore, he dialed her on his cell phone, and when she didn't answer, he felt as if the bottom had dropped out of him. Surely she didn't mean that much to him.

"It's because I know I'm losing my father," he rationalized. As a child, he'd almost hated the man who'd driven him so relentlessly. How often he'd wondered if he worked so hard to save young boys from a life of crime because he'd had neither a childhood nor the freedom that adolescence gives the young. What the heck! He put the car in drive and headed for the Metropolitan Transition Services Center.

For the first time, he thought his private visit with the young boys—this time, Johnny and Phil—was less than rewarding, because he didn't feel enthusiasm and couldn't force it.

"You got a load, man?" Phil asked him.

He shrugged; it wasn't good policy to share your personal life with the prisoners, who tended to focus on themselves.

"You not sick?" Johnny's question surprised him, because the boy hardly ever showed interest in anyone.

"I'm fine. But I think my father is dy . . . isn't going to make it."

"That ain't so good," Phil said and, to his astonishment, the boy put an arm around his shoulder. "It sucks, man. I know how you feel."

Another time, he would've asked Phil about his father, but right then, he was grateful that at last he had a bond with the boys, even if that progress grew out of his own grief. At the end of the hour, he knew their time together had been productive. Driving home, it came to him forcibly, a blast like a ship's signal in a fog: he'd reached them not because of any ingenuity on his part, but because he had needed their comfort. They understood that and accepted him because *they* had been able to give something to *him*. It was a lesson he hoped never to forget.

Shortly after he got home, he answered the phone and, to his disappointment, heard Lacy's voice.

"I called you half a dozen times," she said in that whining voice that made his flesh crawl. "At least six times."

"Right. You said that a second ago. I was at the prison with two boys I'm working with."

"Why would you waste time with those thugs? When they

get out, they're going right back to dealing drugs and shooting innocent people.'' As if she'd been wound up like a top, she held forth on the subject of bad, hopeless children.

''I think every kid deserves a chance to make something of himself, and I'm doing what I can to help.'' He looked at his watch. With more things to do than he cared to contemplate, wasting ten minutes listening to Lacy's prattle didn't please him. He closed his eyes, exasperated. ''These two boys are serving time for petty theft, and there's hope for both of them.''

He imagined that she rolled her eyes and looked toward the ceiling in a show of disinterest when she said, ''If you say so.''

''Lacy, this is one more way in which you and I are as far apart as two people can get. You don't care what happens to those kids; I do.''

''Oh, for goodness' sake! Are you taking me to Lake Kittamaqundi on July Fourth for the Urban League picnic?''

''I have no plans to go, Lacy. Count me out.''

''But everybody's going, and I don't want to miss the fun.''

She still hadn't gotten the message. He didn't want to hurt her, but he wasn't going to that picnic with her. ''I'm sorry, Lacy. If you want company at the picnic, you'll have to ask someone else. Okay?''

After a few seconds of silence, her breathy voice with its sexual overtones bruised his ears. ''I don't want to go with anyone else, but I can't drag you over there.'' A long pause. ''Can I?''

''No, you can't. See you around.'' For a woman of classic good looks, he couldn't figure out why she sold herself so short, insisting on a relationship with him, although he told her in many ways that it wasn't going to happen.

He thought of calling Melinda, apologizing to her and telling her he needed her, but he couldn't do that. In his whole life, he'd never let anybody see him down.

"Hold your head up and push your chin out even if you're dying," Woodrow Wilson Hunter had preached to his children, drilling it into Blake, the last of the three to leave home. There had to be a gentler method of nurturing a boy into manhood; at times, he still felt the pain. He ate a sandwich and stretched out in bed to struggle with himself and his feelings for Melinda until daylight rescued him.

The telephone rang as he walked toward the bathroom to get his morning shower, and thinking it was probably Lacy, his first inclination was to ignore it. But he heard his sister Callie's voice on the answering machine and rushed to lift the receiver.

After listening to her message, he asked, "When did it happen?"

"About half an hour ago. I'm on my way there now."

He hung up, slipped on his robe, and walked out on the balcony just off the dining room. An era of his life was over, and yet it hung ajar. Unfinished and devoid of the explanation he needed but would never get. He stared out at the silent morning, at trees heavy with leaves that didn't move. Air still and humid. Heavy, like his heart. Everything appeared the same, but it wasn't. He went inside and telephoned Melinda.

Melinda dragged herself out of the tangled sheets and sat on the side of her bed. If she packed up and left town, she wouldn't miss the place or the people. However, the losers would be those who lived in a world of illiteracy and who relied on information that they couldn't evaluate and thus rarely questioned. If only she could avoid Blake Hunter until that board was operating to his satisfaction, the gossipmongers would have to find another subject. Weary of it all, she decided not to bother with the board that day.

"Now who could that be at eight o'clock in the morning,"

she said aloud when the phone rang. "Not Ray Sinclair again, I hope."

"Melinda, this is Blake. I can't help you with that board meeting today. I have to cancel our appointment."

"But ... What's happening, Blake? You told me I should go ahead with it, and I figured I was on my own from now on. What's going on?"

Strange that he'd forgotten that; he took pride in having an almost infallible memory. "I'm sorry I plowed into you the way I did the other night when we were supposed to be having dinner. I shouldn't have said those things, and I don't know why I did because I didn't believe them." He supposed he'd surprised her, because she considered him a hard man.

"Something's wrong. I know it is. What's the matter, Blake?"

Her words and the compassion in her voice took him aback. He didn't want to unload on her, but if he started telling her about the hole that had just opened in him and that grew bigger by the second, if he told her what he felt ... "My ... my father died, and I have to go to Alabama for a few days."

"Your father? I'll be right over there."

"Melinda—"

"You ... Maybe you shouldn't be alone right now, and anyhow, I want to be there with you until you leave."

Those words caressed his ears like a sweet summer breeze. He couldn't discourage her, because he wanted, needed to see her.

"You might need me for something," she went on, as though oblivious to his silence. "I'm coming over."

He sucked in his breath. If she knew how he needed her ... He hardly trusted himself to be alone with her. "I'll be here." was all he managed to say.

He showered quickly and dressed, certain that if he opened

the door for her while still wearing only his robe, he'd destroy what there was of a relationship with her.

Twenty minutes later, he opened the front door, and the rays of her smile enveloped and warmed him like summer sunshine. Without a word, she reached up, and he knew again the delicate touch of her lips on his mouth, warm and sweet. But he didn't kiss her; if he did, he wouldn't stop until they consummated what they felt.

"No point in saying I'm sorry. You know that," she said. "I just . . . well, I needed to be here with you."

His heartbeat accelerated so rapidly that, for almost a full minute, he couldn't catch his breath. He shouldn't encourage what was happening between them, because he was neither sure of her nor of himself.

"I'm glad you came. It's so strange, knowing he's gone and we never resolved our differences. After I matured enough to understand him and why he drove himself and everyone around him crazy the way he did, we ignored the issues between us, pretended they didn't exist and got along with each other. I wish I'd confronted him."

Compassion for him shone in her eyes with such fierceness that he had to steel himself against the feeling that slowly snaked its way into his heart.

"Didn't he love you?"

His fingers pressed into his chest as if he could push back the pain. He wished she hadn't asked that. "I don't know. I wish I did. Yesterday. I was down there yesterday, and he told me he was proud of me. So, maybe. I don't know."

With a tenderness that shook him, her arms wrapped around him, held and caressed him, and he closed his eyes and let himself relax and absorb the loving she offered. She seemed to be telling him that he needed love and caring and that she wanted to give him that. Her fingers squeezed him to her, and then she released him and stepped back.

"What time is your flight?"

He studied her eyes, needing badly to understand what he saw there, and he didn't want to make a mistake. "That reminds me, I have to check the Baltimore-Birmingham flight schedule."

She patted him on the back. "I'll do that. You pack. See? I told you you might need me for something."

He had to get out away from her before he did something foolish. "I . . . uh . . . there's a phone out in the hallway." He grabbed a suitcase from the closet in the foyer and headed for his bedroom without looking at her.

"There's a Delta Airlines flight at eleven-forty. I'll drive you."

"I was going to drive and leave my car at the airport."

"And it probably wouldn't be there when you got back."

He shrugged. "This is true, but if you drive me, how'll I get home when I come back?"

She didn't look at him when she said, "You'll call me, tell me when you'll be back, and I'll meet you. Simple as that."

He didn't know her reasons, and he didn't want to ask, because he wasn't sure he had anything to give in return. "I can't let you do this, Melinda."

"Why? You want an affidavit stating that you're not obligated to me? Give me a pen and a piece of paper."

When he grabbed her shoulders, he surprised himself more than her. "It isn't that I don't trust you—"

"What about my integrity? Do you believe in that? Do you?" Her lips trembled, and her eyes held a suspicious sheen.

His fingers moved from her shoulders to her back and then gripped her waist. "Yes. Yes, damn it. Yes!"

Her lips parted to take him in, and desire slammed into him, hot and furious and overpowering. The sound of her groans of sexual need shook his very foundation, and against his powerful will, he rose against her hard and hurting while she feasted on his tongue. He had to . . . Caught up in the fire she built in him, he wrapped an arm around her shoulder and the other around her buttocks and lifted her to fit him. She straddled him, hooked her ankles at his back, and moved against him with a rhythm that sent hot needles of desire showering through his veins.

"Melinda. Melinda!"

"Huh?"

He set her away from him as one would a pan of boiling lye. Then, realizing that he might have hurt her, he folded her in his arms and hugged her. Her breath came fast and hard like that of a marathon runner at the end of a twenty-six-mile race, and he held her as he strove to regain his own equilibrium.

After a few minutes, he trusted himself to speak. "Something's happening here, and it . . . it doesn't want to be controlled." A half laugh tumbled out of him; he'd never been one to dodge responsibility, and when it came to fanning the fire between them, he was the guilty one.

"I'd like to know what's funny so I can laugh. It's gotta be an improvement over what I feel."

She'd begged the question, so he had no choice but to ask, "What do you feel?"

She looked at him with the expression of one staring at the unknown. "Need. Confusion. Loneliness. A lot of stuff that makes me feel bad."

He had almost relaxed when she said, "And I feel something for you that I shouldn't, because you don't want me to feel like this. But don't worry; you're as safe with me as a lion cub surrounded by a pride of lions."

He wasn't sure he wanted all that security, but it wouldn't hurt to have it while the coming eleven months revealed her future.

Her father raised her to want only what was good for her, and though years had passed since she'd believed his every word, she conceded at the moment that she'd be better off if she'd never wanted Blake Hunter. But on the other hand, she was glad she hadn't died without feeling what she experienced when he had her in his arms kissing and loving her.

Get your mind on another level, girl, she told herself as she let him ponder her last words. "We'd better get started," she said after minutes had passed and he hadn't responded to her assurance as to his safety. "No. Wait a minute, is there anything in the refrigerator that will spoil? Any plants? Pets?"

A frown clouded his face. Then he smiled, and she wondered if he'd done that intentionally to make her heart race and butterflies flit around in her stomach.

"I forgot about the refrigerator." He dumped the handful of fruits into the garbage disposal. "That's it. I'm the only thing here that breathes. Come on."

He picked up his suitcase, took her hand, and walked to the door. "You're a special person, Melinda. Very special." He looked beyond her and spoke as if to himself. "And very dear." She didn't speak. How could she when she didn't know what those three words meant? They walked to her car, and when he paused at the front passenger's door, she handed him the car keys.

"Since you're apparently not a male chauvinist, why don't you drive?"

He stepped around to the driver's side and accepted the keys. "You mean if I'd asked to drive, you would have objected?"

"You got it."

"You think that means I'm not a chauvinist?"

She got in and closed the door. "It's a pretty good indication. But if you are, you'll let me know; that's an ailment a man can't hide."

"Now wait a second. Who's being a chauvinist?"

"Not me, I was just stating a fact."

"That so? Do you know that much about men? I wouldn't have thought it."

"Whoa. I didn't realize a married woman—or a widow for that matter—was expected to account for such things."

He looked over his shoulder, moved onto Route 144, and set the car on cruise. "And I didn't ask you to, but you have to admit there's a certain freshness, an innocence about you that one doesn't associate with a woman who's had almost five years of marriage. But maybe this isn't the time to get into that."

How much did he know about her marriage to Prescott? "I'm not sure I follow."

His quick glance sent a chill through her. A man didn't discuss his marriage with his attorney, did he?

"You mean about the innocence? Could be it's just the way you are with me. Whatever. I like it."

She folded her hands in her lap, stared down at them, and made herself relax as he turned into the drive leading to BWI airport. "No comment?" he asked.

"Some other time. No point in getting into a deep discussion that we can't finish."

A grin danced off his lips. "In that case, I'll repeat those words the minute I get back here. Be prepared."

They walked into the terminal minutes before his flight was called. He put his ticket in the breast pocket of his jacket, took her hand, passed the security checkpoint, and reached the gate as boarding began.

Blake dropped his suitcase on the floor and clasped both of her shoulders. "I'm never going to forget this, Melinda. Never. You can't possibly know what your being with me these past couple of hours means to me. I'll call you."

She hardly felt his kiss; it passed so quickly. But she recognized in it a new urgency. Or maybe it sprang from a deeper need. She didn't know, and she was afraid to guess. She walked slowly back to her car thinking that she had no idea where in Alabama he was headed.

Chapter Four

Callie ran to him with arms open and tears glistening in her eyes as he stepped into the terminal. Wordlessly, they held each other, seeking comfort in shared sorrow. Although she was two years older, once they became adults he'd treated her as a younger sister. He'd always loved her, and as a small boy, had followed her constantly unless there was work for him to do. He picked up his suitcase, and they walked arm in arm to her car.

"Thanks for meeting me, Callie. How's Mama doing?"

"Pretty good. She said she expected it, though she hadn't thought it would be so soon."

"Neither did I, and I was with him yesterday. How'd you know I'd be on that plane?"

"It was the next one in from Baltimore, and I knew you'd make that one if you could."

He remembered Melinda's comment about his lack of male chauvinism just as he was about to ask Callie for the keys to her car, and he smothered a laugh. Instead, he asked her, "You want to drive, or you want me to drive?"

The startled expression on her face was evidence that he ought to mend his ways. "You're going to sit in the front seat beside me while I drive?"

The laugh poured out of him, until he stopped trying to stifle it and leaned against the car, enjoying it.

"What on earth are you laughing at?"

He told her, leaving out what he considered irrelevant. "Maybe she was telling me something. Do you think I don't have enough respect for women?"

Both of her eyebrows shot up. "You? No, I don't think that. You're a man who takes charge, and I expect you'd want to drive even if it was John's car."

He opened the driver's door and held it for her. "You drive. As for me driving John's car with him sitting there, you and I both know he'd have to be deathly ill. Did he get in yet?"

"He'll be in tonight."

Much as he disliked facing what he knew awaited him, it was nonetheless good to have the affection and support of his siblings, John and Callie. He knew they'd all be strong for their mother, but did they hurt as he did and did they feel cheated of a father's love? Maybe some day they'd talk about it.

Whatever he'd expected, it wasn't the smile with which his mother greeted them. "I'll be lonely when y'all leave," she told them, "but he wouldn't want us to sit around with long faces."

He hugged his mother and walked into the house, feeling the difference the second he stepped across the threshold. The windows were wide open, and the curtains flapped in the breeze that flowed through the rooms. He turned to look at his mother with what he knew was an inquiring expression.

Her smile radiated warmth and contentment. "The last thing he said to me was 'enjoy what's left, and let the sunshine in.' I'll love him as long as I breathe, but I aim to do that starting now."

The pain began to crowd his heart. Maybe it wasn't the time, but he couldn't hold it back. "You loved him so much, as hard a man as he . . . he was?"

With a vigorous shake of her head, she said, "He wasn't hard. I know he seemed that way to you children, but the day he married me, he promised I'd never want for anything. Sometimes he worked all day and most of the night to keep that promise. I hurt for you all when you were growing up, and I didn't like to see how you felt about him, but he taught you the values that would see you through life."

"Mama, when I was ten or eleven, I'd get so tired I couldn't even run."

"I know, son. And I remember how he held my hand and cried at your college graduation as you stood up there and gave that speech, top student in your class."

She turned to Callie. "When you got your degree, he said we'd go to your graduation even if his strawberries rotted on the bushes while we were gone, and you know the value of those berries and what they meant to him. He loved all of you." She sniffed and blew her nose, fighting back the tears, but her eyes remained dry.

"John surprised us with these air conditioners he designed for his company," she went on, "and your father walked all the way to Mr. Moody's house and asked him to come down and see what John did. He was so proud of you all."

Her arms wound around his shoulder, reminding him that he could count on her when everything else failed, and it had always been that way. "You were the one he worried most about," she said with a wistful smile, "because you are so strong-headed, and you were so angry with him. Let it go, son.''

Why did the price of forgiveness have to be so high? He looked at his mother with new insight about the way their family life had been when he was young and bitter, and now he had to know more. ''Did he ever tell you he loved you?''

Her lips parted in what was clearly astonishment. ''Yes. All the time. Not always with words, maybe, but in numerous other ways. Let it go, son. Let the sunshine in.''

Blake lifted his shoulder in a shrug. ''I guess I have to. The trouble is I wanted to love him.''

''You children made his last years beautiful. He had a lovely home, more than enough for us to live on even if we didn't work, and for the first time in his life, he had a little leisure time.''

''I'm glad we could do it.''

John arrived that evening and they finished the funeral arrangements while they reminisced about their childhood. Blake didn't like the drama and commotion that accompanied southern mourning, and he was glad to have a moment alone. He walked out to the front gate where the summer breeze carried the scent of roses and the clear moonlit night brought him memories of his childhood. And loneliness. He went inside for his cell phone, came back and telephoned Melinda. Maybe it didn't make sense, but he needed to hear her voice.

''I've just been thinking that I had no idea where you are,'' she said after they greeted each other.

''I'm in Six Mile, about twenty miles outside of Birmingham. It's small, barely a hamlet. Here's my cell phone number. Call me if you want to.''

''I will, and I'm glad you called me. How's your mother taking this?''

''Philosophically as usual. I guess it's worse for me than for Mama and my sister and brother, because my relationship with him was so much poorer than theirs, but I'm making it. Being with John and Callie, my older brother and sister, and talking things over with them puts a clearer perspective on my childhood. I'll be fine.''

"How'd you get there from Birmingham? Rent a car?"

He leaned against the gate and inhaled the perfume of the roses. Strange how the floral scene reminded him of Melinda. Bright. Cheerful and sweet. "I'd planned to rent one, but Callie met me." He told her of Callie's reaction when he asked her whether she wanted to drive her own car. "I'll have to be more careful. Callie says I'm just a guy who takes charge, but that can seem overbearing. What do you think?" He realized that he wanted her to think well of him, and that surprised him, because he didn't remember ever caring whether anyone liked him. He had to do some serious thinking about what Melinda Rodgers meant to him and what, if anything, he'd do about it.

Her voice, soft and mellifluous, caressed his ears and wrapped him in contentment. "I think you're tough, and I imagine you can be overbearing, but you haven't treated me to any of that, so I don't know."

"What were you doing when I called?"

"I . . . uh—"

"What?" He told himself to straighten out his mind, lest his imagination get out of control.

"Well, I was lying here looking up at the ceiling, and don't ask me where my mind was."

"Would I be presumptuous to think your mind might have been on me?"

"Roses are red and violets are blue."

He laughed because he couldn't help it and because so much of something inside of him strained to get out. "I wouldn't take anything for that. Go ahead and keep your secrets."

"Are you going to let me know when you're coming back so I can meet you?"

He closed his eyes and let contentment wash over him. In the seventeen years since he'd left his paternal home and the mother who'd nurtured him, he'd forgotten what it was to have someone care about his comfort and well-being. Irene made a stab at it, but he didn't cooperate because he didn't want an office wife.

"I said I would, and when I tell you I'll do something, I do it if it's humanly possible. Remember that. I'll see you in a couple of days."

"Can I do anything for you while you're away?"

"Thanks, but . . ." It occurred to him that she could, but he hesitated to involve her. He hadn't heard from Ethan in over two weeks, and if the boy got into trouble again, he'd be a three-time loser, which meant he'd be an old man before he got out of jail.

"If you don't mind, call this number, ask for Ethan, and find out how he is. Tell him where I am and that I want him to call me tomorrow night. Don't give him your name, telephone number, or address. Just say I told you to call him. If he's in trouble, call me back."

To her credit, he thought, she didn't question him about his relationship to Ethan, but promised to do as he asked.

He didn't want to leave her with a cold good-bye, but their relationship didn't warrant much more. So he merely said, "Talk to you again before I leave here," and she seemed to understand.

"I'll expect that," she said. "Take care of yourself."

He hung up and went inside. He didn't feel like dancing, but he walked with livelier steps.

Two days later, Blake stood at his father's final resting place, dealing with his emotions.

"If you had wound up in jail or as an addict," his mother

said, "maybe you'd have grounds to hate him. But look at you. He must have given you something that inspired you to reach so high and accomplish so much."

What could he say? She looked at it with the eyes of a woman who loved both her husband and her children; she wouldn't lay blame. He wished he were in the habit of praying, because he could use some unbiased guidance right then.

Gloria Hunter's fingers gripped his arm. "Let it go, son. If you don't forgive your father, you'll never be able to love anybody, not the woman you marry, not even your own children." His mother tightened her grip on him as she whispered, "Please let it die with him."

Strange that he should think of Melinda at a time when he was finding his way out of the morass of pain and bewilderment that dogged him and had been a part of his life for as long as he remembered. What did she feel for her father? It was suddenly important for him to know if she loved Booker Jones, a man who few people in Ellicott City, other than his family and parishioners, seemed able to tolerate.

His mother's words bruised his ears. "Son, you've got to let it go."

In his mind's eye, he saw again his father stand, tears streaking his cheeks, when Columbia University conferred the doctor of laws degree on his younger son. As pain seared his chest, he knelt and kissed the sealed metal casket. When he stood, his mother's arms enfolded him, and he didn't think he'd ever seen her smile so broadly or her eyes sparkle so brightly with happiness.

Melinda waited until late the next morning before she tried to locate Ethan. She supposed he might be a relative, since Blake didn't have any children. She amended that. He didn't have any that she knew of.

"Ethan ain't here," the voice of an older female said in answer to Melinda's question. When asked where she could find him, the woman advised, "Look down at Doone's poolroom over on Oela Avenue facing the railroad. If he ain't there, I couldn't say *where* he is."

She couldn't find a phone number for Doone's, but though she was wary as to what she might discover there, she got in her car and drove to the place.

"Whatta ya want, miss?" a big bouncer type of a man asked her.

"I'm looking for a boy named Ethan."

He pointed to one of the pool tables. "Right over there. Hey, Ethan, a lady's here to see ya."

Melinda watched the boy amble toward her. An attractive, neat kid whom she imagined was about sixteen years old, she wondered what he was doing in a poolroom so early in the day.

"Ethan, do you know Blake?"

Recognition blazed across his face, and since he showed interest and wasn't hostile, she decided to smile to indicate her friendliness.

As quick as mercury, his look of recognition dissolved into a frown. "Yeah. I know him. What's the matter with him?"

"He has a family emergency and had to go out of town. He wants you to call him tonight. And please do that, Ethan, because he's worried about you."

Ethan looked hard at Melinda and narrowed his eyes as though making up his mind about her. "You sure he's all right?"

She nodded. "I'm sure. Will you call his cell phone number?"

He stuffed his hands in his pockets and looked past her. "Uh ... yeah. I shoulda called him, so he'd know I wasn't in no trouble. But I got this job staking balls late nights to early morning, so . . . I shoulda called and told him. Tonight, you say?''

''Yes. Tonight.''

''Okay. See you.'' He started toward the table, then turned back to her. ''Oh, I forgot to thank you for coming by.''

She told him good-bye, but she couldn't get him off her mind. He didn't seem like a criminal, but she supposed that wasn't something obvious to the eye.

When she got back home, Ruby accosted her right at the door. ''Miz Melinda, how come all these mens calling you? I left the messages on your desk, but it don't look good to have all these mens calling here when you just been a widow. Six months from now when you needs one, that'd be a different matter. Oh yes,'' she called, as Melinda walked up the stairs, ''Miss Rachel said for you to call her. That woman sure is nosy. I told her I ain't seen Mr. Blake in this house since poor Mr. Rodgers passed. God rest his dear soul.''

She looked at the names of her callers: Leroy Wilson, Frank Jackson, Roosevelt Hayes, Macon Long. She didn't know any of them, but she knew what they wanted: a chance to help her spend her late husband's money. She tore up the messages and telephoned Rachel.

''Hey, girl. What's going on?'' Rachel asked.

''Good question, Rachel. Any time you want to know what's going on here, who's been here and what I'm doing, ask *me*. That'll save Ruby the trouble of telling me what you asked her.''

''Tight-lipped as you are? I wanted to know, so I asked. Really sorry, Melinda. I—''

''Now that we've got that settled, Blake hasn't been inside this house since Prescott passed. Should I tell him you asked?''

''Of course n . . . Well, if you want to.''

She didn't intend to play games with Rachel. They would either remain good friends or they wouldn't, but she was a grown, unattached woman and she didn't have to answer to a soul.

"Rachel, I'm meeting Blake at the airport in Baltimore tomorrow, and I can't swear he won't come into my house or that I won't go into his and stay awhile."

Silence hung between them. "Then you *have* got something going with him," Rachel said after some minutes, her voice arid and hollow. "I thought so." Suddenly, she appeared to brighten. "Well, if he makes your top twirl, honey, go for it."

She didn't believe her, but neither did she blame the woman for a gracious stab at face-saving. "Say, have you ever been to that Great Blacks In Wax Museum in Baltimore?" she asked, deliberately changing the subject.

"No. Want to go tomorrow?"

Melinda couldn't help laughing at Rachel's transparent effort to go with her to the airport to meet Blake. "Sorry, I can't go tomorrow. I'm meeting Blake. Remember?"

After making small talk for a few minutes, they hung up. But before she could pull off her shoes, the phone rang again.

"Melinda, honey, this is Ray. I'm just confirming our date for July Fourth."

She gripped the receiver and considered slamming it back into its cradle. The nerve of him trying to force her to let him display her at that fair for the benefit of local citizenry. "We don't have a date, Ray. I told you I'd think about it. I've done that, and I've decided not to go with you. Thanks for being in touch after all these years. Now, if you'll excuse me, I have a lot to do." She hung up. Five of them in one day, and Lord knows how many more such overtures she could expect. She didn't wait long for the next one.

Minutes later, a man identifying himself as Salvatore Luca claimed to have seen her on Main Street, inquired as to who she was and was anxious to meet her. At least he hadn't come right out and applied for the job of husband.

"There must be some mistake, Mr. Luca," she said in her sweetest voice. "I haven't walked along Main Street in I don't know when. Hope you find her."

She settled down to study the list of twelve people whom, with Blake's help, she'd chosen for the board, but she couldn't get interested in the task of selecting the board's officers. Why had Prescott saddled her with something for which she had no taste and worse, with the stipulation that she marry within the year or lose the inheritance, a modern-day coup de grâce?

Cold tendrils of fear shot through her. She got up from the richly inlaid walnut desk, walked to the window, and looked down at the goldfish pond in the back garden, but the colorful creatures didn't amuse her. Not even the gentle breeze that brushed her face when she stepped out on the porch off her bedroom gave her pleasure. Maybe nothing ever would again. She turned away from the blackbirds that perched on the porch swing waiting for the crumbs she usually enjoyed feeding to them and walked slowly back into the house. It couldn't be true; she wouldn't let it be true. Blake couldn't be like all the others, maneuvering for the money her husband had earned despite a handicap that would have bested most women and men. She didn't want to think that of him, but he was certainly making the road rough for any other man.

She picked up the tablet containing the names of the board members they'd selected, and her gaze fell on Salvatore Luca's name. She'd written it there, idly, as she spoke with him. She pitched the tablet away from her, lifted the receiver of the ringing phone, and slammed it back in its cradle without answering it. Fed up. With no school until September, she didn't have to stay in Ellicott City. Not once in her life had she had a vacation, and she was due one. When the phone rang again, she ignored it.

"Miz Melinda," Ruby called, "Mr. Blake's on the phone."
What timing! "Hi. What time shall I meet you?"

He seemed to hesitate. "You sure you want to?"

Taken aback by his perceptiveness, or maybe it was his sixth sense, she softened. "Of course I'm sure. What time?"

"Four-twenty. Delta."

"How are things with . . . with your family?"

"About what you'd expect, I suppose."

"You. What about you, Blake?"

"I don't know. Burying your father makes you look at yourself and your life with a critical eye. Let's say, I'm making it."

She didn't know how to take that, but she suspected that he was being brutal with himself, judging himself in the harshest terms, and she hurt for him.

"Don't judge yourself unfairly. You're one terrific guy. Come on home, Blake, and stop thrashing yourself. You don't deserve that."

"I wish it was that easy. See you tomorrow."

She'd pulled back, and nothing would convince him otherwise. That was her right, but he wished she'd done that before he began to need her. He didn't want to misjudge her, and he was fairly certain that he didn't, but at gut level he sensed a coolness definitely at odds with the warmth that leaped out from her to him the morning he left Baltimore for Six Mile. Hell, he'd handled worse, and this wouldn't break him. As he strode into the terminal, he wouldn't have been surprised if she'd changed her mind and decided not to meet him.

She rushed to him, but her arms weren't open wide to receive him. He walked now with heavy steps, as though moving against a strong force. The uncertainty of what awaited him and the pain of what he'd left in Six Mile crowded his thoughts and weighed him down. He hadn't realized what he felt for his father . . . and for her.

"Hi." She reached up to hug him, and he drew her close and soaked himself in her sweetness.

"Hi, yourself," he said, substituting those words for genuine communication. "Thanks for meeting me."

She smiled at him, and he saw warmth in her eyes, but not the intimacy that had burned in her gaze and sizzled in her arms when she'd held him that morning in his apartment.

"Don't thank me. I couldn't have stayed away."

Four days earlier, she'd said, "I need to be here with you." He digested the difference, hooded his gaze, and picked up his bag.

"Let's go," he said, and she reached for his free hand. He let her hold it.

"So what happened since we talked the other night?" he asked her as she headed out on Route 144. "Been doing some thinking?"

"You could say that. Five strange men and one not-so-strange called me yesterday, and none of them gives a hang about me." She swerved to avoid a van when it moved into the center lane. "Somebody told those guys about that stupid clause in Prescott's will, and they're all after money at my expense. It's never going to happen."

So that was it. "And you soured on all men, including me, just because some of the brothers see a good thing and go after it?"

Her quick glance was less than flattering. "One of them wasn't a brother. 'I saw you on Main Street and had to know who you were,' " she mimicked. "I haven't been on Main Street in a solid year. The guy's never seen me. A good lie, though."

"What do you mean?"

"He was prepared to spend time with me and get me to fall for him. Trust me, that beats guys like Jonas Humphrey, who just dropped by my house and said he was prepared to marry me. He should live so long."

Before he could respond to that, she changed the subject. "I've decided I need a vacation, and I'm going to take one. I need to get away from all this. Time enough to worry about that board when I get back. Of course, if you feel you'd like to set it up, be my guest."

So they were back to that. The passion that consumed him while the plane crept at a snail's pace from Birmingham to Baltimore had already begun to cool, but now it deserted him.

"If you don't want Prescott's estate, at least consider the people in this county whose lives will be enhanced if they develop good reading skills."

She drove up to his house and cut the engine. "I'm going to see it through if it takes me five years."

He knew his bottom lip dropped, and he stopped himself when he started grinding the teeth on the left side of his jaw. "You can be exasperating. In all the years I visited Prescott, I never saw in you any semblance of belligerence. Always the gentle, smiling hostess."

She turned to face him and lifted her shoulder in a shrug. "Things have changed. I'm on my own now."

While he stared down at her, he had the pleasure of seeing her eyes darken in recognition of him as a man. "Yeah. Well, don't go overboard, and it wouldn't be a bad idea to examine your tires when you get home." He couldn't help grinning when she raised her eyebrows and parted her lovely mouth, clearly perplexed.

"Why?"

"Considering how you took that curve when we came off the highway, your tires are probably split. I wouldn't make a habit of that, if I were you. " He opened the door and paused. Small talk. A sure sign that he wasn't saying what he felt any more than she was.

"I . . . uh . . . suppose you'll let me know your plans?"

"Sure I will." Her airy tone was forced or his name wasn't Blake Hunter.

So be it. He didn't say good-bye, because he didn't feel like it. Once inside his house, he dropped his suitcase on the floor and paced back and forth along the hallway connecting the foyer and dining room. He'd been on fire, and she'd cooled him off as thoroughly as if she'd sprayed him with ice water. She wouldn't have to do that a second time.

Melinda had prowled from room to room in that big house ever since finishing her supper. The darkened skies heralded an approaching storm but, uneasy, as she tended to be during storms, she walked around her bedroom looking at its mauve and lavender silks in the romantic setting that had never witnessed romance.

Without considering what she did, she sat on the edge of her bed, reached for the phone, and dialed Blake Hunter's number. Her heart palpitated at the sound of his deep, sonorous "hello," stunning her into recognition of what she'd done.

"What is it, Melinda?" His voice had the tone of a command as if he knew she'd started to hang up and forbade her to do it. She'd forgotten about caller ID.

Frantically, she searched her mind for a reason to have phoned him. "Uh . . . I wanted to know if Ethan called you."

"Yeah. Right."

"What does that mean?"

"He called. Thanks for finding him. I'd rather he wasn't working in a poolroom, but at least he has a job and he gets to it on time."

Since he didn't believe her, she'd lay the onus of the conversation on him. "Ethan interested me. Who is he?"

"Ethan is one of the young boys that I'm trying to help

straighten themselves out. He's fifteen, and he's already been in jail twice. He promised me he's going to school in September, and keep at it till he gets his high school diploma.''

"He showed genuine concern for you, asking me repeatedly if you were all right.''

"Not many people have shown an interest in him.''

"*Oh!*''

"What is it? What's the matter.'' The urgency in his voice said he cared and cared deeply. "I ... uh ... Isn't that thunder?''

"Sounds like it. Best not to use the telephone during electric storms. I'll—''

"Wait. I think somebody's at my front door. But at this time of night ... I don't know who it could be.''

"Check it. I'll wait.''

The thunder loomed closer and louder, but she forced herself to creep down the winding stairs and turn on the camera that hung just below the eaves at the front door and displayed the visitor on an indoor screen while taking his picture. She didn't know who that man was or why he'd come, uninvited, to her home. He rang the bell, this time following it with a heavy knock on the door. She checked the locks and alarm system and raced back upstairs.

"I've never seen him before,'' she told Blake after describing the man.

"You're sure the house is secure?''

"I think so. Prescott installed a very expensive system, though we never had to test it.''

"Relax. I'll call you later, but wait till you hear my voice on your answering machine before you pick up. All right?''

He hung up before she could answer, leaving her to wonder why he would concern himself when, only a few hours earlier, she'd deliberately thrown cold water on their budding relationship. The doorbell rang persistently, but she ignored it, knowing that the camera would document the caller's every move.

A clap of thunder, a flash of lightning, and tremors raced through her body. Another sharp crack of thunder and she covered her eyes with her hands, but between her fingers, she saw the flashing light. When the telephone rang, she raced to it but, remembering Blake's warning, waited until she heard his voice.

"I'm parked across from your house. A man dashed away from your front gate, but I didn't see his face. Anyhow, he's gone." Flashes of light almost blinded her, and thunder bellowed like a foghorn in her ear.

"We'd better hang up," he said. "It's dangerous to talk by phone during this storm."

"I'm coming down to let you in."

"Melinda! I don't think—"

She hung up and ran downstairs. Whether to have company during the frightening storm or because she longed for him, she didn't know and didn't want to question her motives. She peeped out of the window as he streaked through the rain, and opened the door as he reached it.

Nearly soaked, he stood before her, gazing down at her. She didn't look at the door as she slammed it shut with her left hand, because she couldn't take her eyes from him. He wouldn't let her. His aura possessed her as he stood there wet and wild, his legs wide apart and his hands balled into tight fists. Shaken, she moved to him and lay her head against his chest. He let her wait and then, as if driven to it against his will, crushed her to his wet body. She wanted his mouth on her, but he denied her, though he held her now as if he cherished her.

"Why did you want me to come in here? Why?"

"I . . . I didn't think—"

"Well, think about it right now. What do you want from me?"

"I wanted a reconciliation, some evidence that . . . that—"

"That I want you? Is that it? Evidently, you didn't need that when you met me at the airport today."

She shook her head. "I'm . . . I'm scared of lightning, and I—"

"Not good enough. If all you wanted was company, you could have opened the door for that man who was so anxious to get in."

"That's not fair, and it's unworthy of you."

"But it's all right for you to try dangling me as you would your little puppet, huh? Don't even think it. I could die wanting you, before I'd put up with that. I meet a woman as an equal. Period. Tell me why you asked me to come in here."

" 'Cause I . . . Oh, Blake. Hold me and . . . and—"

His mouth possessed her, hard and demanding, but when she parted her lips for his tongue, he stepped away.

"You and I have to decide where we're heading, and this isn't the time. I sensed when you met me at the airport this afternoon that you've developed strong misgivings about me. Brand-new ones. I don't know why, but it's the reason you backed off."

He rubbed the back of his neck and closed his eyes briefly before reclaiming her with a mesmerizing gaze. "I admit I'd rather not get involved with you, at least not now, and you can figure out some of the reasons. We're both ambivalent, so what do we do about it?"

"Who's the . . . the woman who interests you?" She hadn't planned to ask him. Not ever. But there it was.

His eyes widened at her boldness. "No woman has a claim on me."

She didn't want him to leave, and she didn't know a graceful way of keeping him there. "There's a dryer downstairs, if you want to dry your clothes."

She wanted to wash the grin off his face. He had an irreverence, a wickedness that excited her. "What's amusing?"

"You are. I'm your guest. Sure you don't want to dry them for me?"

Annoyed at his brazenness, she cocked her head to the side and let her lashes lift at snail's speed. "I don't mind looking at your washboard belly and those fabulous biceps or anything else you care to display. As far as I'm concerned, the male body beats the female's by miles."

Emboldened by her own words, she pinched his cheek as she strolled past him on the way to the door that led to the basement. "A man like you? God's perfect art? Go ahead and strip; I sure as heck won't turn my head."

His words stopped her. "I've done things I regretted, Melinda, and I probably will again. But I think you ought to know that whenever I step out of line, I know full well what I'm doing, and I'm prepared to take the consequences, regret or not. Keep that up, and in a minute I'll have you on this floor, buried as deep into you as I can get."

She imagined the lover he'd be and could hardly contain herself, but she bluffed. That was all she *could* do. "You'd need my cooperation for that."

The fire of desire blazed in his eyes. "And I'd have it. You know I would."

Knowing that her feelings for him were so transparent distressed her, but she held her own. "If you could read my mind," she said cryptically, a smile shimmering around her lips, "you wouldn't be standing over there. Maybe you want to dry off at home." She hoped that would bring him down a peg.

But it didn't. He half laughed. "I was planning to do that all along. You may be immune to male nudity, but when I strip in a woman's presence, baby, I mean business." His grin, devoid of warmth, told her he wasn't amused. "Be sure and keep a good watch," he said. "If that guy shows up again tonight, call me."

"Why?"

"I'll enjoy dealing with him. Sleep well."

"You too. And, Blake, thanks for coming over here."

He opened the door with great care, stepped outside and looked around; then he was gone.

She slept fitfully as Blake Hunter danced in and out of her dreams, mesmerizing her with the heat of desire in his hypnotic eyes, walking away from her with long strides. Never looking back. Then he held her hand as they strolled down Rome's Via Veneto while Prescott described the pleasures to be found in Rome, Florence, and Venice. She began thrashing in bed when Blake laid her beside the Trevi Fountain and rose above her as she prepared to receive him. His moans of pleasure awakened her.

Startled by the implications of her dream and by its vividness, she got up and sat on the side of her bed. How had such a strange and tantalizing experience lodged itself in her subconscious? Rome and Venice were Prescott's favorite cities. He told her so many intriguing tales about them that she felt as if she'd been there. Could her intuition be telling her that she ought to get away from Blake or, perhaps, from Ellicott City? That she needed to witness life from another corner of the world? She walked to the window and looked out at the full moon. Didn't she deserve to be more than a monument to a memory?

"Italy?" Her father roared when she told him of her plans. "You can't go over there. I hear tell those men walk behind women and pinch their backsides. I won't have my daughter—"

"Papa, I'm going to Italy. Prescott told me so many wonderful stories about it that I feel as if I've been there many times. He'd close his eyes and paint the most wonderful pictures of Rome and Florence for me. Other places, too, but especially those two cities. Don't worry about those guys; I'll wear a girdle and frustrate them like the devil.''

"You'll wear ... Girl, do you know who you're talking to?''

"Yes, sir.''

"And what about that board you have to set up and the husband you're supposed to be finding. Melinda, girl, you're going to fool around and lose millions. You get busy, and don't bring me no Italian son-in-law. You hear?''

He passed the phone to her mother. "Enjoy it while you can, honey,'' Lurlane advised, "and bring me some pretty postcards.'' Melinda said she would.

Shortly after noon, she stepped out of the front door to see whether the storm had damaged anything. Only the limbs of a young crab apple tree lay on the ground, for which she was grateful. The big footprint in the middle of the patch of begonias she'd set out the day before reminded her of the previous night's visitor, and she phoned Blake to ask if he'd like to see the man's picture.

While she waited, she mentioned the incident to Ruby.

"Don't no mens come here to see me. I values my neck too much to let that happen. My husband wouldn't hold for no stuff like that.''

"Well, what do you think he was after? It was late, and he didn't want to leave.''

"I guess they thinks widows is needy. Like my husband says, though, there's women and then there's *women*.''

Later, Ruby looked at the pictures. "I seen eyebrows like them before, but otherwise I ain't got no idea who he is. I tell you one thing, though; that man's nervous and shifty, which means you don't want him 'round you. I'd keep them pictures for the police; they might come in handy." She answered the doorbell. "It's Mr. Blake, Miz Melinda."

"I . . . uh . . . I'm going downtown in a few minutes to book a flight to Italy. I need a change," she told him after they'd talked for a while.

"Italy? Why on earth are you going *there?*"

"Prescott talked about that country and the people so much that I imagined being there. I need a change, and I . . . I've decided to experience the place for myself."

His intense stare was just short of intimidating, but her father had given her plenty of opportunities to fold up, and it had yet to happen. If he couldn't manage it, no one could.

"You can't hide from life, Melinda. If it's a change you need, I'd say go and have a great time. But if you're trying to escape the reality of your circumstances, nothing will have changed when you get back here. If you need me, you have all of my phone numbers. I'll be here for you."

Her face must have mirrored the question in her mind, for he added, his voice somber and minus its velvet beauty, "That's right. I'll be here for you. I'll always be here for you no matter what. I'd appreciate knowing when you plan to leave."

"I'll call you."

Two weeks later, having already imprinted Florence in her memory for all time, Melinda strolled down the Via Veneto, Rome's most famous street. Her mind bulged with memories of the vivid dream in which she walked that street hand in hand with Blake.

She felt a rubbing on her buttocks and whirled around. If one more man made a pass at her or tried to pinch her, she was going to collapse in giggles. Flirting had to be the national pastime. A country full of handsome men, but she saw and didn't see them; Blake had taken a seat in her head and refused to move. She sent him an e-mail: *If you were here, this would be the time of my life.*

When she got up the next morning, she found a computer reply on the floor just inside her room door. *If I thought you meant that, I'd be tempted to take a much-needed vacation.*

She replied: *You'd be tempted, but your self-control would take care of that. See you when I get back.*

But he didn't give her the last word: *If you ever learn how to handle my self-control, we won't be having exchanges such as this one. See you when you get back.*

Chapter Five

The next day, Melinda strolled through the Vatican Museum with Winnie McGhee, an American woman she had met on a tour the previous afternoon. Having agreeable company added another dimension to her stay in Rome, especially while sightseeing and that all-important Italian pastime, dining. Italians treated food with the respect due it and dined with gusto. But when it came to art, it was so much a part of their lives that they seemed to leave the museums to the tourists. Nothing she'd read prepared her for the beauty and richness of the Vatican Museum's art collection, and she said as much to Winnie.

"And nobody told me I'd probably walk at least ten miles while I was in here," Winnie said of the museum. "If they had, I would've worn my Reboks. Lord, but my feet are killing me," she moaned, for at least the third time.

"Maybe you'd better rest tonight. We can see the night life another evening."

"They don't hurt *that* bad. My cousin works at the U.S. Embassy, and he said if we meet him there at five o'clock this afternoon when he gets off, he'll take us for cocktails and then to dinner. Dress up. Michael is real fancy."

Melinda put on a short black dinner dress and brightened it with a rose quartz necklace and earrings. Black shoes and bag and a black cut-velvet stole completed her attire. To her amazement, Winnie had dressed entirely in apple green, a color Melinda detested. Michael waited for them in the embassy's reception room—an ordinary-looking chamber dominated by a huge American flag and an imposing marine—along with an Italian who worked at the embassy as an interpreter.

The Italian's eyebrows shot up in appreciation when he saw Melinda. *"Ehhhh! Bella!"* he whispered as he kissed her hand. If cousin Michael had intended the Italian for Winnie and himself for her, the Roman had quickly changed that scenario.

The quintessential Italian male. A number ten if she'd ever seen one, and like all Italian men of his ilk, he knew it. Evidently, Enrico didn't like apple green any more than she did, because he made no secret of his preference for her.

As the evening progressed, she decided that nothing could compare with the Italian passion for people watching or with their food, which the four of them enjoyed in an upscale restaurant that featured gourmet delights.

"I will show you the whole world," Enrico assured Melinda as they walked down the Via Veneto that night toward her hotel, which faced the Borghese Gardens and the famous Villa Borghese. He spread his hands in an expansive gesture. "The whole world."

Deciding to go with her wicked streak, she replied, "But I only have another week of vacation. We can't see the rest of the world in one week."

Obviously feigning shock, he clasped his hands to his broad chest. "Ah, signorina, I could live with you a lifetime in one day." They entered her hotel and he stopped walking, looked down at her, and frowned. "You would desert me when I have at long last found you? All my life, I have been searching for you."

She patted his arm. "Same here, so I guess we're both lucky I took this vacation. Thanks for a great evening." She took a step toward the elevator.

His dark eyes seemed to get blacker, then flash with fire before he half-lowered his long, curly black lashes. *"Cara mia, what kind of men do they have in the United States who don't teach a beautiful signorina how to tell a man good night?"*

She wouldn't laugh. She wouldn't let herself. But her lips parted in a full grin, which Enrico accepted as acknowledgement of his wisdom.

"I know one man back in the States who I'm going to ask that question, and he'd better have the answer."

He grasped both of her forearms. *"You are not married?"*

"Not anymore."

He crossed himself, looked toward heaven, and let out a long breath of relief. Then he seemed to panic. "But if you are divorced, the Blessed Mother will not countenance my . . . er . . . loving you."

She swallowed a laugh, though she sympathized with him because he'd just shot himself in the foot. "I was thinking that, too, Enrico, and I'm so glad you're such a wonderful, righteous man. I'll say good night." She squeezed his fingers, and made it into the elevator before he could recover from his enjoyment of the halo she'd draped over him.

She walked into her room, kicked off her shoes, and fell back across the bed, exhausted by the day's activities. From the corner of her eye she noticed the flashing red light on the telephone and considered not answering it. She'd had enough of Enrico's delicate, less-than-serious pursuit for one evening, though he was fun and she suspected his antics amused even him.

Melinda considered erasing the message without playing it, but it occurred to her that many women would love to have Enrico's attention. *I'm in Rome,* she remembered, reason enough to cut the Romans some slack.

"Hello."

"Signora," the front desk clerk said, "I am sorry to bother you, but please check your messages. The same gentleman has called you three times this evening. Buona notte."

"Good night."

Now who could that be? She lifted the receiver and punched the red button. "You must be having a great time." Blake Hunter's voice caressed her like layers of soft satin. "When you get in, call collect."

Hearing his voice stirred up conflicting feelings in her, reminding her of what she'd left behind and what she'd have to deal with the minute she set foot back in Ellicott City. Not to speak of her deep and unsatisfied longing for him. A glance at her watch told her that if it was midnight in Rome, it was six o'clock in the morning in Ellicott City. But he'd said call him, and though his voice didn't convey a sense of urgency . . .

She dialed his number. "Hello, Melinda."

"Is there anything wrong, Blake?"

"Not that I know of. Why?"

She rolled her eyes toward the ceiling. The man could be so exasperating. "You called me three times?"

"Yeah. I wanted to talk with you. Rome's a fast city; should you be out at midnight?"

"I wasn't hanging out on the street all by myself. Is that what you wanted to talk with me about?"

"I'm glad you found a friend to do things with. Sightseeing

can't be too much of a thrill all by yourself. Is this friend an American?''

Might as well have a little fun. "Well, yes and no."

"Yes and . . . Run that past me again."

"I said—"

"I know what you said."

She smothered a laugh. "She's an American, and he's . . . uh . . . He's Italian.''

''At least you don't have to worry about the language. Are they married?''

The laughter broke through, and she had to let it roll. "Not that I know of.''

''What's so amusing?'' His voice didn't indicate that he found anything to laugh at. He'd switched from hot to cold as quickly as that, and the teasing lost its appeal for her.

"I was having fun. I'm glad you called me, Blake."

''I'll try to believe that if you give me some more evidence.''

"There's plenty of that, but you don't want it. Remember?''

"Hell, Melinda, let's cut out this circus. I miss you."

"Uh . . . me too."

She heard the sudden thumping of her heart, and the marbles jockeying for position in her belly made her dizzy. Giddy with expectation, she clutched the receiver and waited.

"When are you coming home?"

"Next Sunday." He already knew that.

"I'll be waiting for you."

He wasn't getting away with that. She detested misunderstandings, and that sentence reminded her of a molted animal; it was and it wasn't.

"Do you mean you'll be waiting for me at the airport?"

''That and more.'' The slight unsteadiness of his voice, deep and suddenly hollow, set her heart to thudding so hard that it frightened her, for she could recognize the truth when she heard it. And what was *her* truth? She had six days in which to settle that with herself.

"I'll be there Sunday."

"All right. Good night, babe."

The next afternoon, Melinda joined with Winnie for an organized bus tour of Ancient Rome. "Stay as close to me as you can get," the guide told his group, as the thirty-some tourists assembled in front of the Catacombs at San Sabastiano just off Via Appia Antica, the Appian Way, near where, it is said, Christ appeared to Peter.

"I thought this was where the Christians hid out during the Inquisition," Winnie said upon learning that they were about to enter the underground Christian burial site.

"No way. When they got here," Melinda explained dryly, "they'd finished hiding. Trust me."

The group followed the guide into the black labyrinth of the past along path after path of rows upon rows of boxes, the final resting places of the long-ago departed. "I'm getting out of this dump," Winnie said. "Ain't been no air in this place in eighteen hundred years."

"Hurry up, Winnie. If we get left down here, we'll never get out."

"Both of my feet hurt. I'm walking fast as I can."

Melinda didn't want to panic, but dread and unease had settled over her. "I don't even hear the others, Winnie."

"I know, but I have to rest."

"Go right ahead, you'll be in good company. Some of these good people have been resting down here since the second century A.D. According to my guide book, this is the only cemetery in Rome that was available for Christian burials throughout the Middle Ages."

"Well, I hope they've been happy down here. I hate this place."

"In that case, walk faster or you may never get out."

"But I—"

"We're way behind. I can barely hear the guide, and I can't see a thing. I'm going to walk faster. If you park yourself down here to rest, girl, I'll see you in heaven."

"You can't leave me."

"Not if you keep up with me, I can't. But I'm not getting left down here, so come on."

She grabbed Winnie's hand and all but dragged her along the dark, dank path. Seeing a shaft of light, Melinda decided she was getting out there; she didn't care where the guide and his followers were.

"So there you are," the guide said as they emerged into the glaring sunlight. "I was afraid we would have to leave you."

Melinda remembered that standing akimbo with *both* fists on your hips was supposed to be unladylike, but that didn't cause her to desist. "Are you telling me you would have left us down there to rot?"

The man lifted his right shoulder in a lazy shrug. "I had a one-way ticket. To go back for you would cost me six hundred lira. With that, I can buy bread."

You could have bought a lot more than that with the tip I'm not giving you, Melinda said to herself. Noticing that the group listened to their conversation, Melinda turned to them, raised her arms as if in surrender, and said, as dramatically as she could, "Imagine! My life for a loaf of bread." The group rewarded her with a spirited ovation.

"What am I going to do?" Winnie asked no one in particular. "My feet feel terrible."

"Buy another pair of feet and quit griping," a woman of around eighty advised.

"Or find another way of calling attention to yourself," a Scandinavian blonde said in an air of disgust.

"Wasn't it great?" Winnie asked when they were back on the bus and headed for the Quirinal, the highest of Rome's seven hills, for a view of the city at sunset, renowned as an awesome sight.

Melinda stared at Winnie with what she supposed was a withering look. "Sure, and you're in Germany right now reclining against the Brandenburg Gate."

"Oh, pooh," Winnie said. "It was fun. Where'll we go tomorrow?"

Melinda leaned back in her seat, took a deep breath, and let a grin creep over her face. "Tomorrow, I am going to let you give your feet the rest they deserve."

For the next five days, Melinda drifted around Rome, partly in awe of the art, architecture, and remnants of Roman glory and partly dazed by Blake's subtle promise. She'd withstood so much adversity that she couldn't think of anything she feared, except lightning and coming to terms with Blake. A strong, sensual and possessive man, nobody had to tell her that if he made love to her, he'd own her heart and her whole being. And she was hungry for him, had been for five years, starved to come alive in his arms, to know at last what she'd missed.

The trouble was, he wasn't sure of her honor; at least, he hadn't been the last time she saw him, and eight or nine days alone with his thoughts wouldn't likely have changed that. What had changed, she figured, was the seesaw between his intellect and his libido, and his intellect wasn't winning this one.

Melinda's dilemma didn't approximate Blake's battle. "I know I'm not cheating Prescott, that if he were alive, I wouldn't contemplate any kind of intimacy with Melinda," he said aloud in the privacy of his bedroom. "Then why can't I just let go and enjoy what I want so badly that I can't sleep at night?"

"Your honor is all you have," his father had preached to

him and his brother. "Don't touch another man's wife." It was as much a part of him as his name.

He finished dressing in jeans, a Chicago Bulls T-shirt and sneakers, got his baseball cap, and headed for the Metropolitan Transitional Services Center in Baltimore. Thinking of the place, he shook his head. It was an institution for inmates with short-term sentences, and no ambiguous title would change that. He parked, went inside, and signed in at the warden's office.

"How's Lobo doing?" he asked the warden.

The man pursed his lips and moved his head from side to side. "Rotten. The kid's trouble waiting to happen. He knows it all. Would you believe he started organizing a gang right in this prison?"

"Yeah. I believe it, but that doesn't mean he's hopeless."

"He can serve the rest of his time over in Hagerstown. I got enough problems."

"He was a bad influence on Phil and Johnny, but I hate to see him go to Hagerstown."

"The boys'll be down in a minute. By the way, you seen Ethan?" The warden's cynical attitude toward youthful criminals was one of the reasons why so few at that institution made an effort to reform.

"I saw him a few days ago. He has a job, and he's trying to stay straight." The disbelieving stare the warden leveled at him didn't surprise him.

"You talking 'bout the same Ethan? Well, that's a miracle if I ever heard of one."

Blake raised his shoulder in a quick shrug. "No miracle whatsoever. He just needed a little help."

Blake took a seat. He'd learned not to stand when the boys came down to meet with him. Most were short, and his six-feet-four-inches height seemed to intimidate them. When he was sitting, they were equals. He didn't have a long wait for Phil and Johnny.

"Thanks for getting that school to take us," they said in unison. "The principal interviewed us and said we could stay together," Phil added. "He said we'd keep each other out of trouble."

"In two years, you'll finish high school," he told them. "You're getting another chance." He looked at Johnny. "Pretty soon, you'll beat me at chess; there isn't much more I can teach you. So I found a chess instructor for you when you get out. You could be a champion if you work at it."

"Oh, I am. I can beat every guy in here now. Who woulda thought a game like that could be so much fun?"

"What happened to Lobo?" Phil asked Blake.

"Seems he doesn't want to get his act together, so they're sending him to Hagerstown."

"Whew. That brother's full of it, man," Phil said. "He wanted to organize a distribution ring for when we get out, but I told him no way. I'm in here for snatching a woman's pocketbook; that heavy stuff could get me sent to Westover."

He'd never asked them why they were incarcerated, not wanting to put a wall between himself and the boys, but he had their confidence now, so he felt comfortable asking Johnny, "What about you?"

"I was shoplifting, but what I got wasn't worth this trip." His shoulders sagged. "Nothing woulda been. No matter how hungry you get, man, in here you gotta wait till somebody feeds you."

Blake watched, awed, as Johnny sliced the air above his head. "I had it up to here, man." What a difference from the day he met them!

Sweet music to his ears. Some of the boys he worked with changed their lives, but a lot of them went back to jail. He consoled himself with the thought that it was worth the effort if only one became a successful citizen, husband, and father.

"I can't stay long today," he said. "I have to meet someone at the airport." And he had to go back to Ellicott City and dress, because he wouldn't have dared visit those boys wearing a business suit, shirt, and tie. They threw him a high five, and he headed for home and then—Melinda.

"You look good," he said, taking her bags. She didn't offer him a kiss and he didn't expect her to. "Relaxed and refreshed. Yeah. You look . . . great."

Her smile was what he'd waited for. Warm and generous. "There aren't any flies on you," she said. "You look terrific, and you haven't even left town." She stopped and worried her bottom lip in that way she had just before one of her wicked utterances.

"Hmmm. You didn't leave town, did you, Blake?"

He felt good. Lord, he felt good. He was living and breathing again. The hell with it. He put his free arm around her and squeezed her to him as they walked through the terminal.

"I went to Baltimore."

"Silly. That's not what I meant and you know it."

He moved his arm from her waist and took her hand. "You know how it is, sweetheart; when the cat's away . . ." Enough of that.

The happiness he felt nearly overwhelmed him. He wasn't used to it. At the bottom of the escalator, he stopped and stared down at her. He didn't know what she saw in his face when she looked at him, for he had never felt so vulnerable. She sucked in her breath and wet her lips and he bent to her mouth. Her arms crept up his chest to his shoulders, and then he could feel her fingers at the back of his head just before she parted her lips and invited him in. The heat of desire, frustrated, long bottled up, plowed through his body, and he locked her to him and plunged his tongue into her sweet welcoming mouth. She sucked on it, pulling it deeper while her hands caressed his head and the side of his face, and the sound of her moans excited him until his libido warned him of what would come next. He wanted to let himself go, but it wasn't the time or the place.

It wasn't easy to release her, but what choice did he have? They were in the airport, even if the escalator shielded them. But he knew that if they'd had privacy, he wouldn't have stopped unless she asked him to.

He did his best to reduce the sexual tension, putting his arm loosely around her waist and continuing toward his car. "Is that Italian fellow expecting to see you again?"

He nearly stopped walking when a burst of giggles escaped her. That was one trait he would never have associated with Melinda Rodgers.

"What's cracking you up?" he asked, putting her bags in the trunk of his car. He opened the passenger door for her, hooked her seat belt, and got in. She laughed aloud.

"What's funny?"

"That Italian will not be looking for me because he's under the impression that I'm divorced. He's a practicing Catholic and isn't about to get mixed up with a divorced woman."

He quirked an eyebrow and told himself to keep his gaze on the highway, but he'd give anything for a good look at her right then. "Why did you tell him that?"

Her laughter rolled over him, the sweet music of a master musician. "He asked if I was married, and I said not anymore. I guess I don't look old enough to be a widow, or maybe the world thinks we Americans get divorced whenever we're bored. I don't know."

"You could have straightened him out."

"I congratulated him on being a religious gentle— What *is*

this? He wanted an affair. Are you saying I should have encouraged him? Pull over to the shoulder and let me out of here."

"Hey! Do you think I'm crazy? I just wanted to satisfy myself that you didn't want the guy."

"Didn't want him?" she fumed. "I was in his company one evening. Is that what you think of me?"

He couldn't help laughing though he knew she'd get madder. "If truth be known, it happened to me the first time I looked at you, and it's only gotten worse day by day for the five years since."

"Humph. You're a man. That's the way men do things."

He pulled up to her house, cut the motor, threw his head back, and roared with laughter. "And you sure are a female. Lord, I missed you, and I didn't even know why."

Her head snapped around so that she faced him. "If you know now, be sure not to keep it to yourself. I hate the darkness, real or imagined."

He looked at her and allowed himself a grin that dissolved into a laugh. "A great philosopher once said, 'Knowledge is truth; nothing can be known.' I'm with him."

She stared at him for long minutes before swinging her long legs around and getting out of the car. "You're crazy. You know that?"

"Maybe. I don't know. Something's happening."

She reached in her pocketbook for her door keys, put the key in the lock, stopped, and turned around to look at him, amazement splashed over her face. "You have laughed more since you walked into that airport terminal than in all the years I've known you. At least, around me." Her voice softened. "Do you . . . uh . . . have any idea why?"

Maybe because he was so glad to see her, but he certainly wasn't going to tell her that. Her question sobered him. "Beats me. I'm not in a habit of analyzing myself."

She turned around, opened the door, took a few steps inside, and stopped.

He sensed that something wasn't right. "What's the matter?"

"I smell a cigar. Nobody's smoked a cigar in this house for as long as I've lived here. And this is definitely the odor of a cigar."

He sniffed the air. She was right. "Maybe Ruby had company."

"Blake," she said, her voice strained, "I gave Ruby a vacation. She's in Virginia visiting her mother, and she left the day before I did and won't be back until day after tomorrow. Ruby's husband doesn't smoke. So what can this be?"

He unhooked his cell phone from his belt and dialed the police department.

Two officers searched the house, the gardens, and the pool, but didn't find anyone, nor did they find evidence of tampering. But they confirmed that the smell of cigar smoke also permeated the den upstairs.

"Don't stay here tonight," Blake said. "Until we can get a guard posted here, I want you to stay in a hotel."

"That's not a bad idea," one of the officers said, as they walked to the front door. "If the guy didn't find what he was after, he'll be back. If you need us, call. Meantime, we'll cruise by ever so often to check things out."

She thanked them and dropped into the nearest chair, the euphoria in which Italy had draped her no longer evident. "I don't want to go to a hotel. How could anyone get into this house without leaving some evidence of forced entry?"

He knelt before her on his haunches. "That person could have a key, could have had one for years. Consider changing the locks and the security system." He jumped up. Where was his head? "Wait a minute? Did you leave that security camera on?" He knew before she spoke, from the expression on her face, that she hadn't done it.

"What about the man who wanted to get in here that night just before you left for Italy. Did you get him on camera?"

She sprang from the chair, ran to the front door, and rewound the camera. *Not an inch of film, used or unused, remained.*

Panic streaked across her face. "It's empty. Oh, my Lord. That's what he came in here for."

He rushed to her and put his arms around her. Logic said that was only one of the things the man had wanted. The point was, what did he want that night and why did he go in the den and no other room?

"Did Prescott have any relatives that you knew of? He told me he was adopted, an only child, and that both of his adoptive parents were dead. Is that what he told you?"

Though she tried to hide it, he could see fear in her eyes, stark and real. "That's what he told me. He said he was lonely as a child and always wished he had siblings or cousins." She frowned, obviously searching her mind. "Maybe you should check his past business associates. Did anyone ever stay here with him? This . . . this beats me, Blake."

"Tell you what. Let's put a roll of film in that camera and set it. I'll have a guard stationed front and back tonight. You can stay with me . . . if you're willing to chance it, or—"

"What do you mean if I'm willing to chance it?"

It wasn't a moment for comedy, but the way she stood there, hands on her hips, ready to take a dare, he couldn't help grinning at her. "You can risk the tongues of the local gossipmongers, or . . ." He stopped laughing and let all that he felt for her shine in his eyes. "Or you can risk me."

After contemplating his words, she let him know what she thought of her own strength as well as his character. "Since Prescott died, I've realized that the good people of Ellicott City think I'm tarnished and they'll probably always think it."

Her lips worked furiously, almost trembling, and he could see how close she was to tears. But she pushed her shoulders back and raised her head, ready to deal with the problem *and* with him. "Truth is, *you're* not even certain that I'm not what these people think I am. But I can stay with you in your house without risking anything. I'm never going to let myself down, and I'd bet on your pride and that awesome self-control of yours anytime."

Maybe she was sure; he certainly wasn't. He might be uncertain about his attitude toward her but definitely not about want he wanted and needed. "I think it's best you have the house secured. I can take care of that tomorrow morning, if you'd like."

But she seemed preoccupied. "That man was about . . . I'd say around fifty-five or sixty, from the picture the camera took. I'm not too good at drawing, but I think I could sketch him near enough."

He stared at her. "You mean you looked at the pictures and rewound the film?"

"Yeah. I did."

She sketched the man as she remembered him and gave the drawing to Blake. "I think I'd better stay in a hotel tonight."

He handed her his cell phone, and with the operator's assistance, she called the Sheraton and reserved a room.

"I'll drive you. Call me in the morning when you're ready to come home."

On the drive back to Baltimore, he kept thinking about the sketch. He'd never seen the man, who probably wasn't a relative. The answer was right at the forefront of his mind, but he couldn't pull it out. He would, though.

Her words interrupted his thoughts. "Prescott never told me much about his business, and I didn't ask. I knew he'd closed his laboratory and that he couldn't work with chemicals any longer. But that's about all. Ruby answered the phone, so I didn't know who called him."

It didn't make sense to him that a wife wouldn't be interested in her husband's affairs. "Didn't you ever ask him about his friends and associates?"

"You're the only one of his associates that I met, and if he had any other friends, I didn't know about them. When we met, I suspected he'd been very lonely, and little things he said gave me the impression that many of the movers and shakers in Ellicott City resented him."

A glance told him that she'd drifted into the past. "He was such a great storyteller; through his reminiscences, I saw the world. As I told you, it was his tales of Italy that prompted me to go to Florence and Rome." She settled down in the leather-cushioned seat and sighed. "He was a good provider and a wonderful companion. I was contented."

He nearly hit the brakes. What a way for a woman to speak of her husband! Not a word of love or affection. A young, sensual woman who got scorching hot whenever he touched her. It didn't make a bit of sense, and he'd have to give it a lot of thought; if she hadn't married for love, then what for? He'd spent the past week grappling with his doubts about her motive for marrying Prescott and had decided to give her the benefit of the doubt. But she'd just popped that balloon. His gaze drifted to the speedometer, and he lessened the pressure on the accelerator. It wouldn't do to get a ticket for driving seventy miles an hour in a fifty-five zone, but the shock of her words had taken his mind off the need for careful driving. He was a lawyer, and investigating people was a part of his business. He didn't intend to continue in ignorance about a woman who, if she knew it, could bring him to his knees.

The next morning, Melinda stood in front of the Sheraton waiting for Blake and hating herself for not haven driven to Baltimore in her own car. She'd spent half the night trying to figure out the reasons for his on-again off-again passion. In the airport terminal, he'd kissed her as if he were afraid she'd evaporate, but a couple of hours later at the hotel registration desk, he'd forced a grin and said, "See you in the morning." *And what about your own indecisiveness*, a niggling voice demanded.

Before Blake could get out of the car and walk around to her side of it, she opened the passenger's door, threw her small hand luggage in the backseat, and got in. "Thanks for coming."

"My pleasure. I've had a guard posted around the house, and as soon as you get home, we can call a security agency."

"You don't think I should keep the one I have?"

"Whatever you think best," he said, surprising her by leaving the decision up to her. "Might be a good idea to change though, because there's no telling who the culprit is."

During the trip home, their conversation consisted of banalities, impersonal words to cover self-consciousness and fill the space vacated by intimacy. At the front gate, he introduced her to Tillman, the guard, and walked with her through the downstairs portion of the house where she met Hawkins, who'd posted himself on the back porch.

"You ought to be safe with these fellows here." He gave her the phone number of the security company. "This one has an excellent reputation; Tillman and Hawkins are their men." She made an appointment for later that day and thanked him.

When he looked at her as though scrutinizing every pore of her face, she could see the conflict in him and his unwillingness to let go whatever misgivings haunted him at the moment and prevented him from taking her in his arms. Self-control was a thing to admire, but as far as she was concerned, that much of it could shackle a man. If he ever let himself go, she wanted to be there.

Suddenly impatient with his uncertainty, she started for the front door. "I may call you this afternoon after I work out a slate of officers for the board. I'm anxious to get this over with."

This time, it would be she who did the brush-off. "Thanks for the lift." She opened the door and waited.

But he wouldn't be rushed or dismissed. "Call me as soon as the security man finishes. I want to check it out before he leaves."

At her raised eyebrow, he said, "As executor of this estate, I'm responsible for it until I can legally turn it over to you. See you this afternoon."

Displeased because he'd had the last word, she saluted him. "Yes, sir." But if it nettled him, he didn't let her know it.

She watched him drive off and wondered if she'd ever be a normal woman in a normal relationship with a normal man. When he'd laughed so happily after they met in the airport and been so sweet and loving, she'd begun to hope he'd won his battle with his conscience or whatever objections he had to their relationship. But he hadn't changed—or maybe he'd backtracked—and if she didn't get that board in order and get out of Ellicott City, she didn't know what she'd do. The phone rang, and when she heard her father's voice, she actually welcomed it. How could she be so forlorn that she welcomed the lecture she knew he'd give her?

"You're back. Weren't you going to call your parents?"

"Hi, Papa. I stayed in Baltimore last night, and I was so tired I crashed the minute I got in my hotel room. How's Mama?"

"Just fine, thank the good Lord. What's wrong with your big house you couldn't stay there? You were by yourself, I hope. I don't trust Hunter. The man sees a chance to get rich just like all these other good-for-nothing gigolos. You watch that fellow."

"He's legally responsible for this estate, Papa. That's all."

"I'd like to know why he's so dead set against having me on the board."

"Papa, if I put you on the board, I have to put a clergyman

of every other faith and denomination on it. This isn't supposed to be a board composed of religious advocates.''

"We're outstanding citizens, and that's all the will specified. If a man of God can't be trusted, who can?''

She rolled her eyes toward the ceiling and resisted pulling air between her teeth. "Twelve of you together would be a twelve-man wrestling match. Prescott would have hated it. The list is complete, and not a man of the cloth is on it, Papa.''

She could imagine that he frowned and rubbed his chin as he did when frustrated. "Well, at least you didn't embarrass me. But you come to prayer meeting tomorrow night. You got to feed your soul, child, you hear?''

"Yes, sir. Love you, Papa.''

"I know, girl. I know. Bye now.''

She phoned Rachel. It was a loose friendship, but she valued it nonetheless. At least Rachel didn't blame her for Booker Jones's arrogance.

"Hey, girl! You back? Tell me you brought one of those tall, dark, and handsome Neapolitans with you.''

"I didn't go south of Rome, and if I saw a Neapolitan, I didn't know it. What've you been up to?''

"You know me, girl. I do as little as possible when it's hot. I've been looking for a date for the fair, but not a single nibble so far. You wouldn't by chance be going with a certain sexy lawyer, would you?''

In the six years she'd known Rachel, the woman had yet to show an interest in a man who was interested in her. It was incomprehensible that Rachel, a feminine, chocolate-brown woman with large dreamy eyes, couldn't find a man to love and who would love her. Of course, she had flitted away five of her best years with Ron, and not because she loved him, but in order not to be alone. From where Melinda sat, having Ron would be worse than being alone.

She'd better discourage Rachel. "Why do you want to know

about Blake? You spent a couple of hours sitting across his desk from him when he read Prescott's will to us. If he was going to make a move, he'd have done it by now. Rachel, learn to like the men who like you; if you don't . . ." She let it hang.

"I know. But you can't blame me for . . . Oh, what the heck, I'll ask Ron to take me."

Ron. Melinda hurt for her friend. "Honey, it's time you did something about him. I've got to get to work on this board. See you later."

"I'm sure glad you're back home, even if you did come back by yourself. See you."

One by one, she rejected as chairperson of the board each of the individuals she and Blake had considered. Then she remembered that when Prescott died, Betty Leeds called to ask if she could help her and sent a basket of flowers to the memorial service. The only one who did so. As she reflected on that period, she realized for the first time that many people resented her husband's wealth and accomplishments. She'd thought they snubbed her because she'd married a man more than twice her age and assumed she did it for his money, but she was learning that they didn't like him, either. For whatever reason, their harsh judgment hurt.

The security company's man replaced the security system and knocked on the door of the den where she worked. "I've finished, ma'am. Nobody can get into this house without a key or sounding a loud alarm that rings here and in our office, in which case, the police will be here in ten minutes."

She remembered that Blake wanted to look over the system and called him.

"I'll be there in a few minutes."

Her call surprised him, because he'd expected her to ignore that request. He'd meant it, but he'd also needed an excuse to go back to her, to be near her. He rubbed the back of his neck and walked from one end of his den to the other, back and forth. It was moving so fast, too fast, and yet, he couldn't stop it. Didn't want to stop it. And why should he?

His gut instinct told him she was honest. She had to be; if she'd told him the truth, she'd wanted him for almost five years. He'd been in her home visiting with her husband, and he'd dined at her table more times than he could count, and not once had she let him know that he attracted her. Yet, now she admitted wanting him from the minute she laid eyes on him. And he believed her, because he only had to touch her and she became a torch in his arms. He needed her. That sweet, innocent smile could seep into him and tie him in knots.

But so much about her mystified him, and he was too smart to get entangled with . . . Hell, he *was* entangled. He . . . When he saw the sunset over Lake Kittamaqundi, he longed to share it with her. Something so ordinary as his brioche and morning coffee would fail to satisfy him when he longed to let her taste it. And he no longer found solitude when he sat alone at the edge of the lake with the breeze whipping around him.

He sat down and dropped his head in his hands. How long had he loved her? And he loved her. Oh, yes. No mistake about that. For what other reason would he think about her when he was arguing a case and writing his briefs? Why would he lie awake at night aching for her, and why didn't he ease that ache with another woman?

For a full fifteen minutes after he reached her house, he sat in his car, telling himself to cool down, that loving her didn't mean he had to lose his perspective.

Finally, he went inside, checked the doors, windows, and gates as well as the additional cameras installed at the front and back doors. "It's sound," he said to the man and gave him his business card. "Send the bill to me at this address."

"Right. I'm glad you're pleased."

* * *

"Wait a minute," she said to Blake as he started down the stairs. "There's supposed to be some kind of alarm in this walk-in closet. I should have told the security man about it. At least, I think Prescott said it's an alarm."

"Which closet?"

She pointed to a door in the hallway next to the den. "This one right here. It's full of stuff Prescott stored in there. I've opened the door and looked, but I've never been in it."

Slowly, tentatively, her hand turned the knob, and she opened the door and stepped inside. A box fell, and then another and another. *"Blake!* Help me with this thing!"

He was already there, pushing the box back on the shelf. "I've got it. Find the light switch."

It was then that he felt her hips cradled against him. Then she turned, and her breasts flattened against his chest, her breathing accelerated, and when he tried to twist away from her he knocked over a stack of heavy boxes. Fearing that they might have hit her, he grabbed her. And then her scent filled his nostrils, her breasts heaved against his chest, and he could feel her tremors. He had to get away from there. He had to . . .

"Melinda where is the li . . ." Good Lord. Her mouth was there, the hard tips of her breasts teased his pectorals, and she shifted her body against his. His blood thundered in his ears, and then . . . She clicked on the light, and he looked down at the wild, hungry woman in his arms. He supposed she saw the inevitable staring her in the face, because she bolted from that closet, and he followed her out of it to where she leaned against the wall, panting, her eyes closed.

They stood there as if in a trance until she opened her eyes, and his gaze followed hers as she looked across the hall at the open door of her bedroom.

"He . . . uh . . . You think that man did a good job?" she

asked him. "I mean . . . he . . . uh . . . wasn't here but three hours."

She rubbed her hands up and down her sides almost rhythmically, and he watched their movement fully aware of the significance. As if seeking privacy or a means of escape, she half-turned from him.

But he'd seen her tight nipples outlined beneath her jersey T-shirt, pointed and erect, and when she swallowed not once but several times, his blood began to race and his heart slammed against his chest, pounding like a pagan drummer. He should get out of there, but he knew he wouldn't.

"You want me to leave?"

Her shoulders jerked forward as if he'd frightened her, and she stopped stroking her thighs, folded her arms and rubbed them almost as if she punished them.

"I said, do you want me to leave? Do you?"

When she spun around to face him and gasped, he knew his emotions blazed on his face.

He jammed his hands into his pockets and stepped closer to her, knowing that if he put his hands on her he'd have a hard time removing them. She still hadn't answered him.

"I'll leave this minute if you want me to. Tell me what you want."

"I . . . I . . . Blake, for heaven's sake, what do you want from me?"

Her trembling body swayed toward him, but he kept his hands in his pockets. He'd fought it until he couldn't. He was tired and . . . he loved her . . . and . . . and needed her as he needed his beating heart.

He barely recognized the dry, hollow tones that came from the depth of his being. "I want you. That's what I want, and if you don't tell me to leave here, I'm going to have you. You want me. I can see it. I smell it. I've needed you for years. All you have to do is say the word *go*."

Over his shoulder, she looked at the mauve and lavender bedroom in which she'd slept alone for almost five years, and the pain and loneliness of it settled on her once more. All the nights of tossing in that bed while he'd loved her only in her heart and mind came back to her with punishing force. And she loved him and had for . . . for so long. When he stood before her like that, strong and manly but vulnerable, open and pained, she could neither deny him nor herself.

"You . . . first you want me and then you don't. I'm human, Blake, and . . . and I hurt . . . I—"

He interrupted her. "And I hurt. Either tell me to leave or come here and put your arms around me."

She looked at his outstretched arms and forgot about reason. Forgot that tomorrow he'd be sorry. Forgot about what the people thought of her and what he probably thought. *I'm twenty-nine years old, and he's the only man I've ever wanted, ever loved. I'll regret it, but I don't care. At least I'll know what it is to lie in his arms.* She made herself look into his eyes and the expression in them nearly unglued her.

"Melinda!"

He spread his legs, emphasizing his manliness, and his nostrils flared as his aura seeped into her. She swallowed the liquid that accumulated in her mouth, inhaled his scent, tasted him, and her blood roared in her ears as she stared at his outstretched arms.

Maybe she moved on air; she didn't know how she got to him, but his big hands were locked on her, holding her. She raised her face and knew the power of his unleashed passion as his mouth possessed her. She parted her lips and his tongue danced in her mouth, mating with every crevice of it, taunting and teasing. Laying claim. And possessing. His hands claimed her buttocks, then skimmed over her arms, her neck, and her back. Her heart began to hammer out an erratic rhythm as he twirled his tongue in her mouth. His lips. His smell. His hands. All of him. He possessed her.

Her breasts ached so badly. Why didn't he do something to them? She needed . . . Grabbing his hand, she rubbed her left nipple with his palm and moans pealed from her throat. When he attempted to raise her T-shirt, she jerked it over her head and threw it across the room. In seconds, her bra was on the floor, his hot mouth opened over her nipple, and spirals of unbearable tensions shot through her, straight to her heaving center until she let out a keening cry of helpless surrender.

"Take me to bed," she pleaded, as he suckled her. But he moved to the other breast and nourished himself until she cried out, "Blake, something's happening to me."

His head snapped up, and he stared down at her, but she pressed her face to his chest. His hands stroked her back with such tenderness that she almost cried.

"That's my room right over there," she whispered. He couldn't leave her. Not now.

He took her hand and stopped at her bedroom door. "Are you sure? If we go any further, I don't know if I'll be able to stop."

She did her best to smile. "I won't want you to stop."

He threw back the covers on her bed, stepped behind her, and caressed her breast. At the touch of his fingers on her naked flesh, hot darts of desire zoomed straight to her love portal. Shaking, she turned around to face him. He lifted her and laid her on her bed, and when she made as if to remove her pedal pushers, he stilled her hand. While he pulled them off slowly and methodically, her nerves rioted in her body. He stood there looking down at her, as she lay there nude but for little more than a G-string, and desire roared through her with awesome force.

She watched him disrobe, impatient for what was to come. When he knelt beside her bed and kissed her from her head to her feet, her hips swayed involuntarily, but he wouldn't be rushed. At last, she spread her legs and raised her arms to him in a gesture as old as woman.

"Honey, please. I'm going out of my mind."

But he kissed her thighs, moving to the inside of them slowly upward until he reached her woman's secret. Methodically, as if they had always been his to love, he opened her folds and kissed her until her hips moved upward to meet his rapacious lips.

"Blake," she moaned. "I can't stand it."

"All right, love." He climbed into the bed beside her, gathered her into his arms, and let her feel all of him, from his powerful shoulders to his full hard length, and she gasped in surprise. His kisses were showers of fire, and with his lips locked to her nipple suckling her, draining her of will, her womb contracted. Frantic for relief, she lifted her hips to receive him, but he wasn't ready. He pulled her nipple deeper into his mouth and let his fingers drift to her petals of love, where he teased, stroked, and tantalized until she screamed aloud. She felt a gush of liquid, and he rose above her, sheathed himself with a condom, and stared down into her eyes.

"Look at me, Melinda. I want you to know that it's me loving you. Think about me and nobody and nothing else."

"Yes. Oh, yes."

His lips brushed hers. Then he twirled his tongue around her nipple and suckled her while his fingers stroked the most intimate part of her until she writhed beneath him. Frustrated, she reached down and took him in her hand.

"That's right, love. Yes, oh, yes. It's what I want you to do. Take me in, sweetheart."

She brought him to her, lifted her hips for his entry, and a scream tore from her lips as he drove home.

He stared down at her. "What in the name of . . . What happened? You couldn't be—"

She nodded as he kissed the tears that streamed from her eyes. "Ours was a marriage of convenience. I was lonely, and he needed a companion."

"Well, I'll be."

"Blake, don't. Please don't leave me like this."

He gathered her to him and buried his head in the curve of her neck. "I'm ashamed. I've done you such an injustice."

"It's all right. I . . . I just want you to love me. It's all I ever wanted from the minute I saw you."

"And it's all I wanted. You're precious to me. Do you understand? How do you feel?"

"I feel like I need something to happen."

He levered himself on his forearms and kissed her eyes, her cheeks, her nose, and the curve of her neck. She turned her head in the hope of feeling his lips on her mouth, but they caressed her chin. At last, he gave her the thrust of his tongue, deep, commanding. Laying a claim. He smiled down at her, a tenderness in his eyes that she hadn't seen before. And then his lips closed over her aching nipple, and he pulled, tugged, and suckled until she contracted around him. He reached down and stroked the nub of her passion until her hips undulated, heat seared the bottom of her feet, and jolts of electricity whistled through her veins as a strange pumping and squeezing began in her center.

"Blake, please. I think I'm going to die right now."

He began to move, slowly and carefully, as if testing, but she didn't want that; she wanted to explode. "Honey, please."

"Are you okay?"

"Yes. Yes."

He thrust slowly, then faster and faster until, finally, he let her have his power. With one hand beneath her buttocks, he stroked, then teased, moving in circles.

"Tell me what you feel. Do you think I'm hitting the right

spot. It should get more urgent with each stroke. Tell me what's happening, baby."

"I don't know. I think if I don't burst wide open, I'm going to die. It's terrible and it's ... Oh, honey, it feels so ... Oh, Lord!"

He increased the pace, kept his hand between them and stroked her until the squeezing, pinching, and pumping shook her from head to feet and her whole being erupted into a vortex of ecstasy, and she released a keening cry.

"Oh, Blake. Blake. What are you doing to me?"

"I'm loving you." Then he drove masterfully, and when the rhythmic movement around him ceased, he gripped her to him and, with a powerful shudder, collapsed in her arms.

They lay locked together as one, his body within hers. Speechless. Undone by the force of what they'd just experienced. She prayed that he wouldn't tell her he was sorry.

After a few minutes he separated them, but continued to lie above her. "Are you all right? Tell me how you feel."

"I'm ... I guess I'm kinda in shock. If I'd known that I'd be this way with you, I wonder if I would have been a virtuous wife. I feel ... liberated. A whole woman. I feel fabulous."

He stared down into her face. "You're not sorry?"

She shook her head. "No. How could I be? What about you? If you are, I don't want to know it."

"I'd have to be an idiot to regret an experience like this. No, I am not sorry." He seemed to search her, looking for she couldn't imagine what.

"What is it?"

"I never dreamed you were ... uh ... untouched. Why didn't you tell me? I would never have been so careless. I would have taken pains not to—"

"You couldn't avoid hurting me. At least it was over in a second."

He grinned in that way that she loved. "We're going to readjust this whole scenario."

"What do you mean by that?"

"When I look at you, think of you, I don't want to associate you with Prescott, because you were never his, and now . . . now, you'll never be any man's but mine."

Not associate her with Prescott Rodgers? Her eyes widened. He was kidding himself.

Chapter Six

When he would have separated their bodies, she locked her legs around his hips and held him to her. Though shaken by the enormity of what he'd just experienced, a sadness pervaded him at the thought of what had *not* happened. He looked at the woman who smiled up at him, sweet and trusting, as if he were her whole world. She'd given him everything, and he had felt her love and trust, but he hadn't been able to let himself go, to give himself up to her, open and exposed. He'd never been able to do it, not once with any woman, because that meant baring his soul, exposing his insides. But this time, he'd been so sure . . . because he loved her. For the first time in his life, he loved. And still . . . He closed his eyes and tightened his grip on her, fighting off the loneliness he suddenly felt. She would accept and cherish whatever he gave her, however he gave it, at least for now, because she loved him. But the time would come when she would need all of him. He kissed her eyes and her sweet lips and thanked God that he'd brought her to a powerful climax. He'd done his best to give her everything, and he had. *All but myself.* He knew now that until he resolved his conflicts about her, he couldn't give more.

"You're so pensive, Blake."

He tried to make light of it. "This is a time for reflection. First time I've . . . uh . . . initiated a woman, and believe me, sweetheart, it takes a mental adjustment."

"Is that bad?"

So she was anxious. "Would you call being alive with every atom of your being shouting to the heavens a bad thing? How could you think that?" he asked, striving to put her at ease.

"I'm not an expert on the minds of men. Just about everything they do surprises me."

He made himself grin, though he wasn't in a grinning mood. "Whoa. That's a man's line. Are you telling me—"

She interrupted. "Do you think I expected ever to be in this bed with you? Not even after you kissed me until I got the shivers. You said it wouldn't happen, and I believed you."

He could almost see his gloom evaporate. He laughed. Laughter was one of the gifts she'd given him. And how precious it was!

"I believed me, too," he said when he could stop laughing. "I'll have to learn to be more reliable."

Her fingers moved slowly over his face, as if seeing him with her senses rather than with her eyes. "Not about this, I hope. But I don't suppose I have to knock myself out thinking about it. Once the genie is out of the bottle . . ."

Lord, he loved her. If only . . . Until he could master himself, he'd make sure she didn't want or need any other man. He sucked her nipple into his mouth, put one arm around her shoulder, a hand beneath her hips, and began to move.

* * *

Hours later, he walked with her down the stairs holding her fingers so tightly that they hurt, but she didn't remove his hand because she knew he was fighting with himself. He had the proof that Prescott had not consummated their marriage, but did he believe the reason she gave him? The truth? And if he did, would he punish himself with the notion that he'd taken his friend's wife? When he'd been loving her, she'd never felt so cherished, and when she'd exploded beneath his driving passion, she knew she'd never stop loving him. He'd made her feel like a queen, the only one alive, but right now something separated them and she suspected it was his conscience.

At the door, she said, "You know Ruby's off today. I could cook you something quickly."

He shook his head. "I'll get a sandwich when I get home." Then he gazed at her with a look that said he wanted something, but she couldn't imagine what because she didn't feel his sexual tension. Perhaps he was trying not to show it, she mused, for he'd moved back from her.

"You said you weren't sorry."

He shook his head as the fawnlike eyes she loved let their brilliance bore into her, seeming to penetrate her soul. "I am not sorry, Melinda, and I never will be. We'll talk tomorrow." His kiss on her lips fired her for a second, and then he was gone.

Several mornings later, reading her mail, Melinda stacked seven letters in a pile and considered throwing them out. Reading them would be a waste of time; every letter would reveal a man who wanted to ride Prescott Rodgers's gravy train.

The handwriting on one letter persuaded her to open it. Goose bumps popped out on her arms when she read, *One of these days, lady. One of these days.* There was no signature, only a post office box number that she suspected would prove phoney. Maybe she should show it to Blake. However, after a minute, she discarded the idea, she'd fight her own battles.

"Miz Melinda," Ruby called. "A gentleman says he wants desperately to speak to you. I shore do wish I'da been a widow before I got married. It must be somethin' having a pack of mens chasing you. Course I'da still married Piper. You wanna talk to this man?"

No, she didn't want to talk with him. "Take his number, Ruby, and I'll call him. I'm busy right now."

"Yes, ma'am."

Later, looking at the name Ruby had written down, she threw her hands up in disgust. She'd never heard of the man. If she put an ad in the paper saying she'd made her choice, that wouldn't stop it. She'd have to ask Blake to figure a way out of it.

She answered Ruby's knock on her bedroom door. "What is it, Ruby?"

"My Piper said the mens where he works is all talking about you having to get married before a year's up. They said if you choose one of them, that one would agree to help the others support they families. Not including my Piper, mind you. Is that why all these mens is calling here? If you sick of it, I can just tell 'em you already found the man."

"I'd rather you didn't do that. I'm not going to marry a fortune hunter. Period. Maybe I'll keep all these letters and write a book."

Ruby's laughter always seemed to start in the pit of her belly and reverberate from the ceiling. And this time, she gave it full rein.

"What you gon' call it? 'Ducking Work'? Or maybe 'Unearned Income'? I declare these mens is somethin'."

"Or maybe I'll call it 'Wagging The Dog.' "

"And that's just what they's trying to do."

Melinda completed the slate of officers for the board of the Prescott Rodgers Foundation, called them, ascertained their willingness to hold office, and mailed the list to Blake.

"You could have given them to me over the phone," he told her. "You're not avoiding me, are you?"

After years of having to pussyfoot around the truth, from then on she intended to tell it like it was. "You know how it is with me, Blake. Nothing has changed. But I can see that you need a little space, so it's your move."

"Look, I—"

"I don't want to hear any reasons; just let me know when you get it straightened out."

"I . . . I want to see you." His voice reached her as a hoarse whisper. "You . . . you're everywhere. This house is full of you."

"What do you think of the officers I chose?"

"Damn it, Melinda, didn't you hear what I just said?"

Don't do this to me, Blake. Don't make me hurt any worse than I do already. "I heard you, but I'm not listening. I can't."

She'd never heard him sigh, and hearing it now shocked her. "I know what you're saying and why, and I . . . well, I don't blame you. But can't we at least see each other sometime?"

She thought for a moment. They certainly could. "I've just decided I'd like to go to the Urban League's July Fourth dinner dance. Want to take me?"

"I thought the league was sponsoring a picnic down at Kitta-maqundi Lake. I threw the invitation in the wastebasket."

"And you obviously didn't read it. If you got an invitation, you're also invited to the dinner dance. The picnic isn't invitational; it's open to the public."

"I'd love to go with you. What's the dress code?"

"Black tie. I'll be wearing a long white chiffon."

"I wouldn't miss it. The local gossipers will have a ball, but don't let that rankle you."

"If I'm with you, they can nose-dive into the lake for all I care. Look, I don't think I need those guards anymore. The house is secure. Having them here is a waste of good money."

Now what had she said? His long drawn-out silence annoyed her. "Blake, you don't have to be so obvious. If you disagree, please say so. After all, you're the one who's running this place."

"Then I say the guards remain until they're no longer needed."

"Yes, sir! I have to prepare the brochure explaining the board's purpose and how it will function. See you."

She hung up without waiting for his response, and she wished she hadn't. She hurt so badly. Nothing would make her believe he didn't care for her and care deeply, but she knew that until he worked out whatever was bothering him, he'd pulled the reins on himself and on a relationship with her.

Her mind wouldn't stay on the brochure. She could go out and buy shoes, but she hadn't worn the last pairs she bought when she got into a blue funk. Maybe if she called her mother. She began to dial but hung up before she finished. The phone rang, and she raced to it.

"Hello."

"You sound as if you've been running or exercising. Sit down; we have to talk."

Something began eating at her insides. "What is it, Blake?"

"Sweetheart, I can't explain my behavior, because I don't fully understand it. I know this much: you're precious to me. My body, my emotions, and my heart know what they want, but my head isn't with them, and I've operated on mental power alone ever since I was sixteen."

"Blake, you don't have to explain yourself."

He went on as if she hadn't interrupted him. "Nothing else

would account for my wanting you and caring for you all those years and being able to keep it to myself. You were right, I never planned to consummate what I feel for you, but I . . . I needed you so badly. Don't think I used you; I wanted to give you everything a man could give a woman.''

"And you did, almost.''

"Almost?''

"You haven't given me yourself yet.''

He didn't deny it. "We need to spend time together, see where we're headed, and I don't mean time working on Prescott's board.''

"We're going to that dinner dance. That's a start.''

"I'll be at your place around five-thirty that afternoon. It'll take us about half an hour to get to Baltimore.''

"I'll see you then.''

But he didn't hang up. "Kiss me?''

"Oh, Blake. It's not good enough. Bye.''

He'd come around. She didn't doubt it for a minute, and she didn't intend to make it easy for him. She phoned Agnes's Designer Originals.

"Agnes, this is Melinda Rodgers. Do you still have that white chiffon MacFadden gown in size twelve?

"I knew you'd come back for it. It's here.''

Melinda thanked her and hung up. "I feel like a teenager,'' she said aloud. "When I walk in there with Blake Hunter . . . I can hear the buzz right now. In that tux, he'll have women gushing all over him.''

She let the phone ring four times before answering it. "Hello.'' She half expected, hoped to hear Blake's voice, but only silence greeted her ears. Then, breathing, heavy and rhythmic, followed by a man's harsh laugh. She slammed down the receiver. Shaken beyond words. With guards at the doors, he couldn't reach her, so he'd terrorize her by phone. "Not on your neck. You needn't even think it," she said aloud. In the future, she wouldn't lift the receiver unless she knew the caller.

"Thanks, Ruby," Blake said.

He stood at the bottom of the broad staircase and watched Melinda, loveliness personified as she glided down the stairs. She didn't look down at the steps, but gazed into his eyes like someone charmed. And he hoped she was. Her white chiffon gown billowed as she seemed to float toward him. When she reached the bottom, she held out her hand and smiled, but he could only stare at her. Bewitched.

"Hi."

He told himself to get with it, reached for her hand and held it. "You are so beautiful, so lovely."

Her smile widened, and her lashes lowered over her dreamy eyes, light brown pools of enticement that could make a man do things he'd regret. He wanted to take her back up those stairs and love her senseless.

"You look wonderful," she said. "I expect I'm going to have to fight off the females tonight."

"What about me?" he asked as they started for the door. "You don't think the guys out there tonight are going to let me have you to myself, do you?"

She laid her head to one side and looked at him from beneath those long lashes. "If you don't want me to dance with anybody else, just say you don't, and it'll be your arms only."

Fortunately, they'd cleared the front steps or he might have tripped. "Slow down, Melinda. If I ever heard a loaded remark, that was it."

She slipped her arm through his as they walked half a block to his car. "Loaded or not, a simple yes or no will do it."

He helped her fold her skirt across her knees, hooked the seat belt, and closed the door. As he walked around the car, she reached across the driver's seat and unlocked the door for him. He could get used to the company of a woman like her.

Easing the car away from the curb he remembered her comment. "You want me to respond to that remark? Come on, Melinda. If I don't say no, my name is Mudd. Right?"

He glanced toward her as a smile frolicked around her lips. "Something like that. By the way, how many women invited you to take them to this affair?"

"Two. You and Rachel what's-her-name. I've already disappointed a few by declining such invitations, and they don't ask me anymore. Put your hand over here where I can touch it without causing a wreck."

Her hand warm and soft beneath his, the delicate scent of her perfume, and that aura of peace that she never failed to project made him feel like a special man.

"You're a treasure," he said though he hadn't meant to voice his thoughts.

"Thank you. You're not bad yourself."

He hoped she meant that as a compliment. He stopped for the red light and looked across at the Wayside Inn. "Jonas was in my office today, and he said the Wayside Inn recently refurbished its Banneker Room."

"Really? I thought they did that a couple of years ago. It's amazing the pride this town has in Benjamin Banneker."

"Why not? After the Ellicott brothers, he's the town's most famous son. An astronomer, surveyor, and clock maker, the first black scientist this country produced."

"And has he got a family tree! His grandmother was a white slave holder who bought two African men from a slave ship. The same year, 1692, she freed all her slaves and married the slave from that ship. His name was Bannaka. One of her four daughters, Mary Bannaka, married a freed slave, and he took her surname, which they changed to Banneker. She gave birth to Benjamin Banneker, who inherited all of her property."

Blake took the exit off Route 95 and headed for Calvert Street. "The man traveled in fast company, too," Blake continued. "He carried on a steady correspondence with Thomas Jefferson on the injustices of slavery. You can find numerous monuments to Banneker in this part of the country."

"I know, and I'll bet half of the African-American high-school seniors have never heard of him."

"Yeah. And a pity, too. Here we are. Stay put, and I'll go around there and make sure you don't ruin that dress."

She took his arm as they entered the great hall. He'd escorted numerous beautiful women to such affairs, but this one had the eye of every man they passed. From the mirrored wall he could observe her carriage, elegant and graceful. And she paid no attention to her admirers. What a woman!

They'd been given seats at table seven, and it pleased him to see that he'd have Duncan Banks, the noted journalist, for company. Banks stood as they arrived. "Man, I've had my fingers crossed in the hopes we'd have good company. It's great to see you."

He shook hands with Duncan and made the introductions. "Duncan Banks is a friend of long standing, Melinda. This is his wife, Justine Taylor Banks. Duncan and I met in undergraduate days when Morehouse, which was my school, debated Howard, Dunc's school."

"Who won?" Melinda asked.

"They're still debating that question," Justine said. "I'm a psychologist, who's staying home with our two-year-old daughter. In the meantime, I write a syndicated column."

"I teach high-school English and English literature," Melinda said. "Seems to me we're in related fields."

Duncan leaned forward. "Right. Bring her over to see us, Blake."

"Yes, and soon," Justine said. "We could spend a weekend down at our place on the Chesapeake Bay. What about it?"

He looked at Melinda and prayed she'd show enthusiasm for the idea. These people were his closest friends, and he wanted them to love her.

"I'd love that." She turned to him, her eyes bright with excitement. "Can we?"

He nodded, too full of emotion to trust words. He turned and caught Duncan's hard stare and knew that his friend had summed up the situation and reached the right conclusion, that Blake Hunter had finally fallen in love. And there would be questions and more questions. He'd take them as they came.

Duncan's hot gaze roamed over his wife, resplendent in red silk. "Dance with me?" Her smile was that of a woman in love, and she held out her hand to her husband as he approached her.

"How long have they been married?" Melinda asked

"About three years, but being around them is like being on a couple's honeymoon. Deepens your faith in love and marriage."

Her stare spoke volumes. If he didn't know better, he'd say she'd looked right through him. "And your faith in the institution of marriage is shaky?"

"I wouldn't say that exactly but, as a lawyer, I get a constant parade of husbands and wives who behave as if they've never liked, to say nothing of having loved, each other. It makes one wonder."

She leaned back and folded her hands in her lap, exuding an aura of serenity. "What about those who stay together?"

He lifted his left shoulder in a shrug. "I've wondered about that. Whether they're happy or . . ." Leaning toward her, he whispered, "What about you and Prescott? If he had lived, would you ever have asked him for a divorce?"

"You mean if, having made my bed hard, I would have remained in it?"

He reached for her hand and stroked it. "I didn't mean to

be rude. Heck, I don't know why I bothered to ask, because being the woman you are, you would have stayed to the end."

"Yes, I would have," she said, her eyes glistening suspiciously. She blinked rapidly. "Prescott was honorable, and he deserved my fidelity." Her fingers trembled within his hand.

Now he'd done it. He stood and held out his arms to her. "Come here, baby. Come here and let me hold you."

"B . . . Blake, there're several hundred people in here."

"Then dance with me. Anything just as long as I can get you into my arms."

She stood, and he hugged her to him quickly before taking her hand and walking with her to the dance floor.

"I thought you weren't coming tonight."

Melinda moved her head from Blake's shoulder and stared at Ray Sinclair. "Ray, I assume you know Blake Hunter. I did say I wasn't coming, but I changed my mind."

"Mind if I cut in, old man?" Ray asked Blake.

She nearly laughed aloud when Blake looked around as if to see where the voice was coming from. "You talking to me, buddy?" He looked at her, his eyes twinkling in that mischievous way he had. "Baby, you want to dance with this fellow?"

"Me? Why . . . no. I promised you all my dances tonight."

"Sorry, pal. The lady says no."

Ray Sinclair had a temper, it seemed, and didn't take putdowns easily. "I see you cut yourself in, Hunter. You're making sure you're the guy who gets control of old Prescott's fortune. You may be fooling Melinda, but I'm on to you."

Blake missed a step, recovered, and swung her out as if he'd planned it. Then he stopped the dance. "I will give you a chance to eat those words, Sinclair, or answer to the charge of character assassination. Now get as far away from me as you can.''

She was certain he hadn't planned on making a statement that would set the tongues of Ellicott City's gossipers into perpetual motion, but what was done was done. He looked at Ray Sinclair, who seemed unaware that he'd just been threatened with a civil suit. ''I mean what I said. You'll regret that remark. Now, go find whoever you came with.''

Evidently deciding to cut his losses, Ray greeted a man who passed nearby and walked off with him, immersed in what had to be a phony conversation.

''I didn't mean to embarrass you,'' Blake said to Melinda, ''but he got off easily. I didn't grow up besting guys with clever words; in my set, we swung our fists. Sinclair was fortunate: It's been years since I settled issues that way; and besides, he showed off in a place and at a time when he knew I wouldn't split his lip.''

''I'm not embarrassed. I just wish it would end.''

''Yeah. I guess you do. Let's finish this one later,'' he said, referring to the dance and the fact that Ray's ill-timed interruption had sullied the sweetness of being in each other's arms.

''I assume from his remark that he would like to help you comply with the terms of Prescott's will.''

She resisted sucking her teeth, but stopped walking, turned and looked at Blake. ''Ray hasn't said that, but after years of treating me as if I were an incurable disease, he's probably heard about Prescott's will, and now he's driving me crazy with his concern for my welfare. Can you think of something I can do to call off these men? They're acting as if I have to pay in order to get married. I don't give a hoot if I—''

His expression, fierce and forbidding, halted her words. Surely the evening was ruined, but he splayed his hand on her back and followed her to their table. As he seated her, he whispered, ''For tonight, let's not deal with problems. I want to enjoy being with you. All right?" His lips brushed her cheek so quickly that she might only have imagined it. She glanced up and saw Duncan's knowing gaze fixed on her.

Duncan's smile was one of indulgence, such as one might bestow on a child. "Unless you're better at it than the rest of us, don't try winning an argument with Blake. It's usually a waste of time."

She imagined that surprise showed on her face, because she thought she'd won some points with him. But maybe she hadn't, and issues she'd thought they'd settled would have to be fought out again.

"Come on, Dunc," Blake said. "I'm not that tough. You'll scare her off."

Duncan let a half smile play around his mouth, and she knew he'd just made up his mind about her. "I doubt that. I think you've met your match, and it's about time."

She looked at Justine. "They're talking over my head."

"It's a habit of theirs," Justine replied, "but not to worry. They're as dependable as homing pigeons, and they don't surprise you . . . once you get them figured out, that is."

Melinda looked at Blake, who sat at her left, and what she saw made her heart beat faster, but he quickly hooded his eyes, masking the passion she thought she'd seen. Yet, in that second, he touched her soul and she reached for him, involuntarily. He grasped the hand she held out to him and moved his lips. She didn't know what he said, only that, for him as for her, it was a moment of intense intimacy.

From the orchestra, the sexy growl of a tenor saxophone wailed out the blues, and Blake squeezed her fingers. "We didn't finish that dance."

Seconds later, he had her on the dance floor with one arm around her waist and the other around her shoulder. The saxophonist began to play a song about the wonder and beauty of a woman's loss of innocence in the arms of the man she loved, and she put her head against his shoulder while the music and Blake Hunter transported her out of herself.

She tingled with exhilaration, her heart light, as they moved to the beat and the mood of the music, his body shifting provocatively with every step. She told herself she wouldn't give in to him, but he held her close, possessively as if he had the right, and she let him drown her in the seething passion of the moment. Though she fought for control of her senses, his aura claimed her and wouldn't release her. His fingers rubbed circles in the middle of her back, causing waves of excitement to wash over her. She stumbled and missed a step.

"Blake, what's come over you? Are you trying to . . . What are these people going to think about us dancing this way?"

He brushed his lips across her forehead, looked down at her, and grinned. "The men will want to murder me, and the women would like to tear you to shreds. Let them think whatever they like."

"Easy for you to say; I'm the one they'll be talking about."

He stood still and swayed them to the pulsating beat. "Not if Ray Sinclair decides to ignore what I told him. People will talk, Melinda."

"When my father says that, he always adds, 'but make sure they aren't talking about you.' "

The saxophone stopped its wailing and Blake walked them over to the bar at the far end of the ballroom. "He certainly called attention to you last Sunday, or so I'm told."

"Again? I wish he'd stop using me for his examples of a disobedient daughter. Whenever his text begins with the Ten Commandments, I know who he did his research on."

"What would you like?" he asked her when they reached the bar.

"If you're going to dance the way you did on that last number, I'd better stick to ginger ale."

"Didn't you like it?"

"Yes, but—"

His eyes held no mirth, only the look of a man who intended to make himself clear. "If you enjoyed it, that's all I care about. You were with me in every step; in fact, you encouraged me."

"*Me?* I encouraged you? You did your doggoned best to reduce me to putty out there in front of all these people."

"No, I didn't. I just danced, and you liked it. You swung yourself into me and let me feel every line of your body." He winked, daring her to deny it.

Her bottom lip dropped and she gaped at him, but that didn't faze the man. "Yeah, you liked it," he went on. "Baby, you fit me like a glove, standing or lying down."

"*Blake!* It's not nice to remind me of things like that."

The bartender put the glasses of ginger ale in front of them, and Blake handed one to her.

"What's not nice? I'm proud of the way you responded to me. Any man would be. So don't get bent out of shape because I bragged about it. I'm only talking to you."

She relented, because her wild surrender in his arms wasn't something a man would forget. She certainly wouldn't. "But I'll bet people can look at me and tell what kind of things you're saying to me."

"Okay." He started to laugh, this new Blake, and she primed herself for a wicked remark. "You're lousy in bed." He pinched her cheek. "That make you feel better?"

"Wait till we leave here."

He laughed and his eyes sparkled as if happiness suffused him. "If you're planning to make me eat those words, we can leave right now."

She sipped her ginger ale, enveloped in his joy. "Oh, you! Your bark is worse than your bite." She'd almost told him that she could be so happy with him, but she knew that such words would have darkened his mood.

His irises seemed to change from light brown to black.

"Don't depend on that. Most times, I don't have a problem with keeping my counsel, but you do strange things to me." He touched her elbow and walked with her back to their table.

The waiters served the dinner, and she toyed with the roast beef, peas, and potato croquettes, but had little interest in the food. Blake wanted space, a chance to deal with his feelings about a relationship with her. As a moral man, he set high standards for himself and, she suspected, for her as well. She knew she loved him and would be happiest if he were her life's mate, but she held out little hope for that. Wanting and needing her, even loving her, wouldn't make him ignore his conscience altogether. He'd capitulated to his libido and made love with her, but she'd bet that when he was alone with his thoughts, he thrashed himself for having done it.

"I hope we can expect you at our place one weekend soon. Our little town of Curtis Bay sits in a tiny inlet at the very edge of the Chesapeake Bay," Justine said, getting Melinda's attention. "The water's great right now, and the place is idyllic." She glanced at her husband. "Perfect setting for lovers. I hope you'll come."

Melinda couldn't help looking at Blake for his reaction. "I'm all for it," he said. "How about it, Melinda?"

Was he admitting to his friends that they were lovers? The man needed a good talking to. Then he grinned sheepishly, as if he'd read her thoughts, and she didn't care that his friends knew they'd been intimate. "Say when," she said, directing the words to him. "I'd love to go."

"We'll let you know," he said to Duncan. "Maybe a couple of weeks from now."

Later, Blake stood in the foyer of her house, holding her right hand and smiling down at her as if she were priceless. "I'm enjoying our time together this evening, and I want us to spend more time in each other's company, this kind of time."

"You mean—"

"I mean being friends, getting to know each other, giving us a chance to find out whether we want to continue what we started. We know we want each other but ... well, for me, that's not quite enough."

She scrutinized his face, his whole demeanor, and saw only the honesty that was so much a part of him. "Thanks for the company. I wouldn't have thought you'd be such an erotic dancer. But come to think of it—"

"Whoa. I thought you didn't want to talk about that, but if you do . . ."

She held up both hands, palms out. "All right, all right. I take it back. Give a kiss and go home."

His hands grasped her shoulders, and his mouth brushed her lips, but when she parted them, he didn't give her his tongue, but squeezed her gently and withdrew. "Honey, you know where that leads. I'll call you tomorrow."

She watched as he paused on the steps and spoke with the guard, then strode across the street, got into his car, and drove off. Blake Hunter enthralled her, but from then on, she planned to try and keep that to herself.

Blake reread the agenda for the board's first meeting and prepared for fireworks. In a few minutes, the group would assemble in his office. He answered the door and was relieved that Martha Greene was the first to come. If Melinda had arrived first, their being together in his office would have been more fuel for the wagging tongues. Melinda and the others walked in shortly thereafter, and after reading the relevant portion of Prescott's will, Blake asked Melinda to open the meeting.

She thanked them for coming and for their willingness to direct the foundation. "I have appointed the following officers," she told them, and though Blake didn't hear grumbling, disapproval mirrored itself on most of their faces.

She named the officers and added, "Blake Hunter, accountant and chief executive officer. The officers will serve for a term of two years, except that, as executor of my husband's estate, Mr. Hunter shall serve permanently as accountant and CEO."

"It's customary for the board to elect its own officers, isn't it?" Martha Greene asked, clearly offended by having not been given a post.

Blake shook his head. "As executor of the will, it was my decision to make. This was simpler."

He thought the meeting surprisingly free of conflict, but for him, the wonder of it all was the smooth way in which, as president, Betty Leeds handled it. She smiled at a potential troublemaker and then proceeded to ignore him. He was going to enjoy working with the Prescott Rodgers Foundation's board of directors.

The meeting adjourned and, as he was telling Betty Leeds good-bye, half of his sentence remained unuttered, and his mouth dropped open. Melinda Rodgers was walking out of his office in what appeared to be animated conversation with Alice Pride. And, apart from "hello," she hadn't said one word to him since she'd walked in the door.

The next morning, she called almost as soon as he walked in the office. He hoped she called to explain ignoring him the previous morning, but if she knew she'd done that, she didn't consider it worthy of mention.

"Blake, I know it won't be easy, but you have to find a way to call off these guys who want to marry me for Prescott's money."

"Now wait a minute. You're asking me to announce that you've chosen the guy, or that you're engaged? Is that it?"

"Blake Hunter, you are not dense, so stop pretending that you are. I want these men to leave me alone, and since you're in charge of . . . of all this, do something to get rid of them. Just don't tell them I've already chosen someone."

"Why not? What're you saying? You're getting married or aren't you?"

Her tone carried an icy veneer. "I will not have anybody think I'd marry a man for the sake of an inheritance."

"But if you don't get married within the next seven months, you *will* lose it, and I'll be unable to help you."

He could almost feel the arctic air blasting him through the wires. "You're some piece of work. Good-bye!" She hung up.

He understood people; that was part of his job. But he'd never understood what made women tick, starting with his mother. Why couldn't Melinda just come right out and tell him what she wanted him to do? He took the mobile phone off its cradle and dialed her number.

"What's this all about, Melinda? Yesterday morning, you walked in here, stayed for two hours, and all you said to me was hello and thanks. You didn't even bother to say good-bye. If anybody's a piece of work, seems to me it's you."

"Yesterday morning, I was keeping temptation away from you, since that's what you seem to want."

"Don't hand me that. What could happen in the presence of Martha Greene and the rest of that bunch, huh?"

"You want space; I'm giving you space."

She was hell-bent on driving him up the wall. He walked over to the window and looked down on Columbia Pike at the white oak trees swaying in the breeze. Why couldn't she . . . ?

"Melinda, stop pretending. I'm facing the conflicts I have about a committed relationship with you, and you know that. It's not settled in your mind, either, so—"

"You can't speak for me, Blake. I know what I want and don't want. Now will you please call off these wolves? How'd you like it if a string of women asked you to marry them so they could hop on a gravy train? If you don't put a stop to it, I'm leaving town. I'm fed up."

He took a deep long breath before letting the air out of his lungs. "I'll do my best, but right now, I can't imagine what that will be if I can't say you've made a choice."

"You'll think of something. This whole will was an act of ... of ... I'll be in touch. Good-bye."

The heaviness around his heart surprised him. "Be careful, Melinda. If one of us is in pain, the other is subject to feel it. Not many people have experienced feelings as powerful as those we share. So don't trash this. I certainly will not. Bye."

"It all depends on you, love. I know where I stand. Bye."

His sharp whistle split the air as he walked back to his desk and placed the phone in its cradle. He wished he could say the same.

Chapter Seven

The Reverend Booker Jones sipped the last of his morning coffee, the one cupful that he allowed himself each day, since more than one would be a sinful indulgence, and patted his wife's hand.

"They've ignored me and all I stand for in this community, Lurlane. My own child didn't want me on her board of trustees."

Lurlane squeezed his hand, though she knew that nothing short of an appointment to the board of the Prescott Rogers Foundation would console him. "Dear, you know if she put you on that board, she'd have to put a preacher of every faith and denomination on it. Then what would she have? A duplication of our annual conference of religious leaders."

He swallowed a forkful of grits and scrambled eggs and waved the fork at her. "What's wrong with that?"

She smothered a smile. "As much as you complain that in fourteen years, the conference has never passed a unanimous resolution, how can you ask?"

His stare disconcerted her, and his lips quivered, not in anger, she knew, but from the pain of rejection. "The Lord will bring down my enemies. Every last one of them will perish for what they've done to me." He got up from the table and went to the phone. "I don't even have a grandchild. The boys are so busy making money that they don't send here, and look at Melinda. Twenty-nine, almost thirty years old and not a child to show for it. The Lord told us to be fruitful and multiply."

"Back then, there weren't more than a couple of million people on earth, Booker. Now, there're more than six billion. Seems to me like there's been too much multiplying."

"You'll have to pray about that," he told her, dialing Melinda's number.

"Booker, the poor child has enough problems. That will specifies twelve board members, and she's already chosen them. There can't be more."

He hung up. "She could've put our Paul on that board. Her own brother, and a professor, too."

Though she hurt for her husband, she believed Melinda had done the right thing. "Board members have to be residents of Ellicott City. Remember?"

With pursed lips and a deeply furrowed brow, he paced the floor. She wished he wouldn't upset himself so much over things he couldn't control. He went back to the phone, and she knew he'd chosen another target.

"You cooked up this whole thing, Hunter," he said, "because you intend to keep Melinda for yourself and walk off with all that money. Not as long as I breathe. You hear me?"

He stared at the receiver, and he didn't have to tell her that

Blake Hunter had hung up on him. When he reached for the phone again, she stopped him with a gentle tap on his shoulder.

"Don't call her when you're angry. She has enough to worry about."

With Ruby at the market, Melinda answered the phone. "Hello."

"My name is Arthur Hicks. Is this Melinda Rodgers?"

Exasperated, she rolled her eyes toward the ceiling and blew out a harsh breath. She'd fix him. "Yes. What can I do for you?"

"Well, somebody told me you was lookin' for a husband and you'd settle some . . . er . . . funds on him soon as he married you. I'm strong, healthy, and good lookin', and I ain't got no er . . . re . . . sex diseases. How long would I have to stay married to you?"

Melinda held the receiver at arm's length and stared at it. Then her anger dissolved into uncontrollable laughter.

"What's the matter. What you laughing at?"

"Sorry," she said, when she could control the laughter. "I was laughing at a guy named Blake. That deal is off."

She hung up, got in her car, and headed for Columbia Pike. Maybe when she signed Prescott's property over to him, Blake would get the message. And when women started chasing him for it, he'd understand how it hurt to be the object of a money hunt.

"How nice to see you, Melinda," Irene said when she opened the door. "Come right in." Had Irene's smile been malicious, or did she imagine it?

"He's in there," Blake's secretary said. "Go on in."

After hesitating for a second, Melinda opened the door

to Blake's inner office and stopped in her tracks at the sight of Rachel leaning across Blake's desk, her face inches from his.

She blinked. "What's going on here?"

Rachel jerked around toward the door, startled. But she quickly summoned her aplomb, straightened up, and patted her hair as if to suggest that it had been disarranged.

Then she smiled. "Hi, Melinda."

I'm not falling into that trap, Melinda said to herself. *She needs a reality check if she thinks she's made me jealous.*

"Hi, Rachel." She forced a friendliness that she didn't feel. "Make any headway since you've been here?" She had the pleasure of seeing bright red creep over Rachel's fair skin.

"I don't know what you're talking about," Rachel said.

"Yes, she does," Blake cut in, not bothering to hide his amusement. "But everything's exactly as you left it."

That was music to her ears, not that she'd thought differently. "I need to speak with Blake, privately," she said to Rachel. "If you wait out there with Irene, we could have lunch together. Want to?" She sounded bitchy, but she couldn't resist getting some of her own. She'd deal with Rachel later, too.

Blake stood. "Would you excuse us, Rachel?"

At least he didn't give a reason. She stepped aside as Rachel approached on her way out and smiled broadly, though Rachel looked at her with what could only be described as guilt.

"Irene, would you please show Ms. Perkins out? And next time, be sure I've given her an appointment." He flipped off the intercom and looked at Melinda.

"Which do you believe? What you saw or what I said?"

She tried to make herself smile, but it didn't work. Instead, her bottom lip dropped and stayed there as his seriousness registered. She mentally snapped her fingers; he wanted absolution. He stepped around the desk, took hold of her shoulders, and stared into her face.

"I need the answer to that question."

A fast quip sat on the end of her tongue, but she couldn't utter it. Blake Hunter was dealing with a deep uncertainty and the pain that went with it.

"I know Rachel's aggressive, and I know she's interested in you."

"Meaning what?"

"I believe you. Why wouldn't I?"

He continued to gaze into her eyes, triggering a swell of passion, and though she fought it with every ounce of willpower she could muster, she swayed toward him. He needed no further inducement to lock her in his arms.

"Blake, think. Think. You're pulling me under, but you're not ready for it."

His lips brushed her eyelids, nose, and cheeks, and she struggled beneath the power of his onslaught. "Honey, listen to me. Please. Oh, Blake. Don't make me care more than I do when you're so uncertain about us."

The unsteadiness of her voice emphasized her distress. "Don't. Don't let me love you."

But her words were lost to the storm that raged within him and that burned in his fiery gaze. "I need you."

Then his mouth settled on hers, thrilling her and shocking every nerve in her body. She parted her lips and groaned in pleasure as he filled her with his velvet tongue, searching, probing and claiming what he knew belonged to him alone. When he gripped her buttocks and pressed her to him, she tried to raise her body to fit his. She had to . . . to feel him, to know that he needed her the way she needed him. But immediately, he backed away from her.

"I've never used that sofa over there for anything other than sitting," he said with a wry smile, "but, woman, you make me feel things and do things that surprise the hell out of me. I want to take you over there and love you, and I want it so badly it hurts. But I can't make myself do that, and you wouldn't allow it."

She didn't look at him. He had her on fire, and by the time she would have realized where she was, the act would have been completed.

He tipped up her chin. "There could never be anything between me and Rachel Perkins or between me and any other woman, so long as you're in my life."

She stared at the carpet. "That reminds me why I came here. I want to sign off that will. The board is operational now, and I'm not going through with the rest of it." She sliced the air above her head. "I've had it up to here with that will. Do what you have to do. I don't know what got into Prescott." She walked away, turned, and walked back to him. "Imagine his insisting that I find a husband and get married. Was he mentally okay when he wrote that?"

"He was, and furthermore, you know he was. That clause is the one he insisted on most. He was as lucid as you are right now, so you can't contest it."

"I can't . . ." She stared at him for a long minute. "Be seeing you." She had to get out of there before she said something she needn't bother taking back.

Blake watched as she nearly ran from his office. She hadn't been angry about Rachel, and he supposed he ought to be thankful for that, but something had to be done to ease the friction between them. Making love had left them needing another kind of resolution, a meeting of minds. With that, they could be soul mates. But that wouldn't happen if he couldn't get to the bottom of her cavalier attitude toward that enormous fortune.

Either Prescott had given Melinda money from a source he didn't know about—and that was certainly possible—or she wanted to prove to the people of Ellicott City that she didn't marry a sixty-eight-year-old man for his money. But to throw away millions? Shaking his head in bemusement, he dialed Wayne Roundtree in Baltimore. That's what she wanted, so he had to do it.

"What can I do for you, buddy?" Wayne asked him.

Blake explained about the will and Melinda's request.

"You sure that wouldn't attract more men?"

"That's possible and it's a problem, man. She's fed up, and I don't blame her, but she won't let me announce that she's made a choice."

"And she's right," Wayne said. "Whoever she married, even years from now, would be considered that choice."

Blake's heart constricted, and he had to struggle to get his breath. "I . . . uh . . . hadn't thought of that, but I've gotta do *something*." He thought for a few seconds. "All right. Run a short story and end it with a statement saying she decided to forfeit the will rather than marry a man she doesn't love. Just tell the truth."

He'd forgotten the possible damage that one of Wayne's whistles could do to an eardrum. Wayne reminded him. "Who'll believe that? If *you* didn't tell me it's true, I wouldn't even print it," Wayne said. "Man, that boggles the mind."

"Yeah. Mine too."

"Okay, check the front page, lower right-hand corner, day after tomorrow."

"Thanks, man. I owe you one."

She'd probably be ready to eat fire when she saw that story on the front page of *The Maryland Journal,* but that was what she'd said she wanted. He didn't question his sense of relief or the smile that lingered on his face for the next few hours.

"What is this I'm seeing, girl?" Booker Jones asked his daughter, holding a copy of the *Maryland Journal* inches from her eyes. Apparently having decided that the phone wasn't adequate for what he had to say, he'd driven to Melinda's house and banged on the door with such force that Tillman, the guard, had restrained him.

"It's true," Melinda told him, "but I didn't write the story printed in that paper."

"Then who did? No. Don't tell me he's busy plotting to take over and get control of all your money." With his hands clasped at his back, he paced the length of the living room. "Lawyers. I never did trust 'em. Bunch of crooks."

She wouldn't have put the story on the front page, but at least it was where you couldn't miss it. And it must be working, because she hadn't had a call all day.

"Papa, you're misjudging Blake. He did what I told him to do."

He glared at her, his eyes fierce and threatening. "If you fool around and lose that money, I'll . . . I'll disown you."

How could he get so angry about money, which he claimed to be the greatest source of evil? His Adam's apple bobbed furiously above his white clerical collar, as he looked at her.

"At least think of your mother. I do what I can for her, but you don't know how happy I'd be if she could have a little time to herself, to enjoy her life, be her old self." He looked into the distance, as though caught up in a dream. "She deserves the best, more than I'll ever be able to give her, considering my small congregation." He wasn't posturing now, but battling tears.

"Papa, I . . . I don't know what to say."

Suddenly, without another word, he turned abruptly and rushed out of the house.

She called her mother. "Mama, please see if you can calm Papa. He's so upset that I'm afraid for him."

Lurlane didn't seem concerned. "Well, don't be. He's pretty strong. Besides, he tells the church folk that money's the root of all evil, and I tell him he ought to practice what he preaches. Is there anything between you and Blake Hunter?"

"*What?*" she gasped. "Who said so?"

"Honey, you two have been the talk of this town ever since that Urban League shindig. Is it true?"

Was it? Melinda asked herself. "We're trying to work out our feelings for each other. We . . ."

She could imagine her mother rolling her eyes when she said, "I don't speak Greek, Melinda. What is he to you?" Lurlane Jones never let up till she had what she wanted.

She didn't lie to her mother. "I . . . uh . . . I love him, Mama."

"And what about him?"

She told the truth as she knew it. "I think he loves me, but he isn't sure about a relationship between us."

"Then I'm glad that story's in the paper today. You ought to marry Blake Hunter. I'd like to know what he's got against a relationship with you. There wasn't anything going on between the two of you while your husband lived, was there?"

She gave Lurlane a synopsis of what had happened since they'd first seen each other, omitting the time they made love.

"Well, child, that's a hot potato. You be careful. Men don't buy what you give 'em for free, and Blake Hunter's no different, I don't care how good a man he is."

She didn't want to talk about Blake, not with her mother or anyone. They'd come to terms or they wouldn't. Whatever happened, there'd never be another man in her life. "Mama, have you forgotten that I'm a recent widow?"

Evidently unimpressed, Lurlane replied, "You lost your best friend, and I sympathize with you. But you listen to me. If you lost Blake Hunter, you wouldn't be acting so brave; you'd be dying inside, and everybody would know it."

"You're being melodramatic, don't you think?"

Lurlane pooh-poohed the remark. "Why do you think Prescott put those strange clauses in his will? He wanted you to get married, and that business about the foundation meant working knee to knee with Blake Hunter. I'm not so sure he didn't have Blake in mind for you. Prescott loved you, though I'd bet my neck he never once kissed you, except for that peck on the cheek at the wedding ceremony, not to speak of—"

"Mama, don't you think you're overstepping?"

"Sure I am, but I've made you think, and that's all I wanted."

She told her mother good-bye and went to the den to go through the morning mail. One envelope with long, back-slanted handwriting got her attention because it didn't have a return address. She opened it. Yet another threatening letter, one that bore a handwriting different from the first one. She stared at words that were meant to unnerve her and dialed Blake's number.

"What does it say?"

She read, "You can put a dozen guards around your house, but I intend to get what's mine." It was unsigned. She described the handwriting.

"It's either forged or someone is trying to camouflage his handwriting," he said. "I'll be over to look at it."

"When?" She could have kicked herself for letting him know she was anxious to see him.

"Now, if you're not busy. I'll finish this brief in a couple of minutes. Did you see the *Maryland Journal* today?"

She should have called to thank him, and she would have if seeing the story on the front page hadn't vexed her. "Yes. Thanks. I hope it works."

* * *

She opened the door for Blake, looked at him, and told herself to turn off her emotions. She'd brought the letter down with her so he'd know he wasn't making a social call. At least, she hoped that was the message he'd get.

He looked at her, gave a slight half laugh, and said, "Mind if I come in?"

"Oh, yes. Yes, of course." She creased the side seam of her skirt with her right hand, shifted her weight from one foot to the other, and rubbed her left arm.

"Is it too much to ask if I could have a seat?"

Irritated at his self-assurance and his deliberate effort to let her know that he detected her nervousness, she got back her normal cool persona and strolled into the living room, giving him the impression that he could follow or stay where he was. He walked in and sat down. She knew he'd won their tug of wills when he asked if she'd like him to leave.

"You haven't looked at the letter," she said and didn't try to keep the testiness out of her voice.

He shrugged in that casual, I-don't-care way that he had; then a friendly heart-stopping smile eclipsed his face. "I didn't know. You seemed kind of, well . . . uncomfortable." He opened the letter and read the short note, then studied the envelope for what seemed to her an inordinate amount of time.

"Well?"

"I'm not a handwriting expert, but I'm convinced it's a man who's trying to fake his own handwriting. I can have this evaluated, if you'd like."

She crossed her knee and swung her right foot, a habit she'd begun as a teenager when she had to listen to one of her father's long and rambling lectures. Now swinging that foot helped steady her nerves.

She nodded. "And maybe fingerprints too?"

He shrugged again. "Well, if you want me to, but I don't think that will tell us much. This person apparently knew Prescott, so he might not be a criminal, in which case his fingerprints wouldn't be on record."

She stopped swinging her foot and leaned forward. "You know, this is the third threat I've received in the past few weeks."

"And you didn't tell me?" he roared.

"I figured that with the guards here and the other new security measures, the place is impenetrable."

"This isn't Fort Knox, and when you leave the house, you're at the man's mercy."

"If he knows something of his is in this house, why doesn't he stop the stealthy business and ask me for it?"

"Good question. It's my guess that Prescott didn't think the man was entitled to whatever it is he thinks he has a claim on, so he plans to steal it. I'll tell the guards to be extra cautious. Well, if that's all, I'll be going."

He stood and she had no choice but to follow him to the door. By pretending he had no interest in her as a woman, he was getting some of his own back, and she had only herself to blame. She had wanted to see him, but she'd been ashamed to let him know how much and, instead of greeting him warmly, had been overly cool.

It rankled her that he could look at her dispassionately, as if he had no personal interest in her, the way he was looking at her right then.

"Now that your story is on the front page of the region's biggest newspaper, what are your plans for complying with the conditions of the will?"

"I don't have any," she said, laying back her shoulders and letting her defiance show in her bearing.

He leaned against the wall beside her front door and seared her with a stare that nearly disoriented her. "If I let you walk

away from all this . . ." He flung his arms out as if to encompass
her home and all that would be hers. "Prescott was my client,
but we were also close friends, and he trusted me to see that
his wishes were carried out to the letter."

"If the two of you were so close, you must know why he
tried to force me to get married. If he didn't trust me with his
fortune, why should I care what happens to it?"

"You don't believe what you're saying. Look, Prescott was
a self-made man. He got where he was by working hard night
and day. No one helped him or even comforted him when he
needed it. You were the first person to share his life, and even
that was superficial. So don't think unkindly of him."

She glared at him. "Can you see me forcing myself to be
intimate with a man I don't care for in order to inherit what is
rightfully mine? From what you know about me, can you envis-
age that?"

"Where in that will does it say it has to be a man you don't
care for? It specifies that you marry within a year of the funeral.
In a year's time, a person could fall head over heels in love."

If she wasn't already in love with a man who didn't consider
himself a candidate, her treacherous heart seemed to shout. "In
the nearly five years of our marriage, Prescott showed me only
gentleness and considerateness. I never dreamed he had this
mean streak."

"He wasn't mean. I tried to talk him out of that clause, but
he insisted on it. 'I know what I'm doing,' I remember him
saying, 'and it'll all turn out just the way I want it to. You'll
see.' Those were his exact words."

She waved her hand in dismissal, because she no longer
cared about the inheritance, though she meant to see the foundation grow and flourish. "So he knew I wouldn't hold still for
it, didn't he? Well, it's no skin off my back. I wasn't born into
wealth, and Prescott didn't live the life of a rich man. I won't

miss it." She slapped her hands together as if to wipe them clean of the entire affair. "It's history."

"By the way," he said, and put his hand on the doorknob, "Martha Greene complained that she should be paid for sitting on the board. I told her what the will specifies, and said we'd be sorry if she decided to resign."

"But she can't. I'd have to start interviewing again." Her hand went to her mouth, and she supposed her eyes widened to twice their normal size when it occurred to her that Martha Greene might have accepted membership in order to undermine the foundation. She said as much to Blake.

"Maybe. I'm not so sure. She likes prestige, and this board will have that. But if you want to talk to her, to try and persuade her, go ahead."

She couldn't believe her ears. "You mean you didn't do that?"

"Definitely not. She's already got an inflated opinion of herself. I just let her know she'll miss something."

"Like what?"

He told her about the reception he planned for the board. "It's on me."

"But ... but why?" Her father's words drummed in her ears. With effort, she pushed them aside. "That's expensive."

"My pleasure. You changed your mind about spending a weekend at Curtis Bay with Duncan and Justine?"

"No, but since you hadn't mentioned it, I figured you'd changed *your* mind."

He took his hand off the doorknob and stepped closer to her. "Before I commit myself to anything—I mean anything—I make certain that I want to do it. It may take me a while to get to that point—in fact, it usually does—but once committed, I'm not likely to change." His gaze flickered with a fire that she knew well, but only briefly. "Do you understand what I'm saying?"

She nodded. Nothing had ever been clearer; his words were a reflection, no, a translation, of his behavior with her. Her heart beat faster, and it softened, as she had known it would. She reached up, kissed him quickly on the cheek, turned, and rushed up the stairs. If he touched her, she would explode.

"You may speed up those stairs, but when you get to the top, you'll wish you were down here with me." His words brought her to a halt, and she stood on the stairs with her back to him. "It doesn't matter how much space you put between us, where you go or how long you stay there, you'll come back here to me, because I'm in your blood just as you're in mine."

She whirled around. "Of all the . . . the—"

He didn't wait for her to find the words. "You're going to have to deal with this, just as I am. It isn't what we feel for each other that's in question; we're both clear on that. Our problem is doubt. Your doubt and my doubt."

"Speak for yourself."

"That I am. You're uncertain of me and my objectives."

"How can you say that?"

He raised his right hand as if to ward off more words. "For what other reason would your behavior toward me be so inconsistent?"

"And yours isn't?"

"We react to each other. I do or say something that makes you question me. The same happens with me. I thought I had worked it out while you were in Italy, but this . . . this uncertainty surfaced again." He walked to the bottom of the stairs and gazed up at her. "Are you willing for us to try and get to know each other? Really know and understand each other?"

She took a couple of steps down toward him and stopped. "You can make the sun shine, the moon rise, and stars burst in my head, and you can make me so damned mad I can't see. I'm not so dense that I have to take a course in order to understand you. Be yourself. Lay all your cards on the table, and I won't have a problem reading you.''

He put his foot on the bottom step. ''Don't you come up here,'' she whispered. ''Don't . . .''

He took the steps three at a time, picked her up, and carried her to the top. ''You tell me I can make the sun shine and expect me to turn around and walk out of that door? That's proof you don't understand me. Put your arms around me.''

''Blake . . . th . . . this is crazy.''

''I know it, baby. I know it. Kiss me.''

She looked up into his hungry eyes and parted her lips, but he only gazed down in her face until she wanted to scream her need to be in his arms. And then his mouth possessed her, his big hands gripped her shoulder and her hips, and at last she had the gratifying hot thrust of his tongue. She clung to him as he savored every crevice of her mouth. She wanted, needed more. Frantic for all of him, her hand went to his belt buckle. Immediately, he broke the kiss and cradled her gently in his arms.

''It isn't enough for me either, but I promised myself I'd give us a chance, and I mean to do that. Will you help me?''

Still drunk on him, she closed her eyes, took in a deep breath, and expelled it slowly. ''If you tell me how, I will.''

''That's what I mean by getting to know each other.''

She wanted to tell him she knew he wasn't sure of her honor and integrity, but if she did, he wouldn't lie about it, and that would be the end. So she'd wait.

''I'll have to play it by ear,'' she said and meant it. This man refused to compromise where his needs were concerned, and who could blame him?

''All right. I'll get an expert to look at this letter, and then I want to have a word with Ruby.''

''You don't think she—''

''No, but she might be able to tell us something about the

people who knew Prescott and visited him before you and he were married. She's worked here for more than twenty years."
He hugged her. "I'll be in touch."

She listened until she heard the lock click on the front door; then she went into her room to try and sort out her feelings. But the phone rang almost at once, disturbing her thoughts.

"I see Hunter's wound you around his little finger." Ray Sinclair's voice came to her without the obsequious sweetness she'd once heard in it. "Too bad. I'll bet you didn't know you're playing second fiddle to Lacy Morgan."

"I'm what? You must have read the *Maryland Journal* this morning. You gave it your best shot, Ray, you and a bunch of other money hunters, but be a sport and let it lie. If you don't, I may publish the names of the men who tried to get on that gravy train."

"I'll sue you."

"Really? Your messages are still on my answering machine. Good-bye, Ray."

She hung up and grabbed her stomach as pains shot through it. Lacy Morgan had the looks and body of a sex siren and the aristocratic bearing of a sovereign. *Only an idiot would think a man with Blake's looks and achievements would be unattached,* she said to herself. But he'd taken her to the gala and the way he'd danced with her and held her on that dance floor had been nothing less than a public statement. She had to console herself with that knowledge.

Half an hour later, her phone rang again, and she had an impulse to ignore it. After several rings, she answered.

"This is Tillman out front, Ms. Rodgers. A man's been driving past here in a rented Chevy. I got a look at him through me field glasses, and I'll try to photograph him with the zoom lens on me camcorder. Just wanted to let you know."

"Thanks, Mr. Tillman. I hope he drives past again."

"Oh, he will. He's been past here a dozen times already. Be in touch."

Just one more thing to deal with. She'd married and lived with Prescott Rodgers and known almost nothing about him apart from what he'd shown her of his personality. Maybe she'd been naive in marrying him.

She looked at the program she'd outlined for the board's next meeting. A television and radio campaign to enroll functionally illiterate adults in literacy classes and the disbursement of funds for after-school remedial reading programs. Maybe if she proposed that the board appoint Martha Greene chairperson of the media campaign . . . She went to the phone and paused. Better see what Blake thought of that. Martha could be a pain.

"Martha's trying blackmail," Blake said. "She wants an office on the board. Nothing will convince me that that status-conscious woman will resign from the board of the Prescott Rodgers Foundation. Forget about it and see whether she comes to the next meeting."

She told him about Tillman's phone call.

"Yes. He phoned me, and I expect we'll have something to go on. With these fingerprints, the handwriting, and some pictures, we ought to be able to figure out who this guy is and what he wants. Where's Ruby?"

"She's off on Thursday afternoon. She'll be in tomorrow."

"I hope she can identify the man. Of course, we may be dealing with two different men. Duncan wants us to come out this weekend. How about it?"

"Well, I . . . I guess I need to get away from this town's stifling heat."

His lengthy silence served as a reprimand. "Any other reason why you'd consider going there with me?"

She couldn't help laughing. "Certainly not because of your . . . uh . . . magnetism or that commanding aura of yours. You have a great pair of hands, but I wouldn't think they'd have any bearing on my decision to spend a weekend with you. I love the water. Yes. That could be it.''

She heard him clear his throat. "You have a way of getting fresh with me when I'm nowhere near you. But, lady, I will remember your words. A great pair of hands, indeed!''

"I always did take my punishment well. Just ask my folks.''

"Punishment? Is that the way it strikes you?''

Laughter bubbled up in her, and she let it out and with it the terrible tension that had dogged her since he'd left her house earlier that day. "Honey, what's in a name? Whatever you call it . . . Being with you is . . . magical. Hang up. I have a lot of work to do.''

"Same here. I'll be by for you shortly after noon on Friday. Kiss me?''

She made the sound of a kiss, hung up, and congratulated herself for not having asked him about Lacy Morgan.

Blake read again the analysis of the handwriting on the letter Melinda gave him. The writer was not a schizophrenic, but a man trying to hide his identity. The fingerprints weren't on record. So, as he'd suspected, the man wasn't a convicted criminal, but if he tried getting into that house again—with or without a key—he'd go to jail. No doubt, he'd had at one time a business relationship with Prescott, who must have kept papers in his home that he hadn't shared with his attorney. He'd have to speak with Melinda about that.

He packed his bathing, surfing, and fishing equipment in the trunk of his car, went back inside, and called Ethan.

"How's the new job?'' he asked the boy. He'd gotten him away from that poolroom as quickly as he could.

"It's great. My boss says he'll buy my books and pay my transportation to and from night school if I'll do what you do.''

"What's that?''

"He wants me to talk to kids about what happens when you get into trouble and go to jail and how to stay straight. I told him I'd do it."

Some made it and some, like Lobo, wouldn't. Ethan had the drive to become a respectable citizen. "I'm proud of you, Ethan," Blake said. "If you need me, you know my cell phone number."

"Thanks. Hang in there."

"You bet, and you do the same."

He'd better call his mother and tell her where he was in case she needed him. Finding her in good health and high spirits heightened his anticipation of the weekend and what it might bring for Melinda and himself. He meant to keep an open mind about her and let the chips fall where they may.

At a quarter of twelve he parked his car in front of her door. "I have something for you, sir," Tillman said to Blake as he walked up the steps to Melinda's front door. "Pictures I took with me camcorder. You can look at 'em in there on the TV. I don't think he knows I took 'em because he's driven by here twice today."

"Thanks. If he continues, I'll suggest to Mrs. Rodgers that she indict him for harassment."

"That's what it looks like to me, sir," Tillman said.

When Blake rang the doorbell, his breathing quickened in anticipation of the sight of her. She opened the door, smiled up at him, and everything around him seemed to glow, but he needed more. All night, he'd wrestled with her words, "an inheritance that's rightfully mine," and doubts about her reasons for marrying his friend had once more filled his head almost to bursting until it ached.

"Aren't you coming in?" she asked.

How fresh and beautiful she was in that yellow sundress! "Hi. Where's Ruby? I want to show you two something. Could you turn on the VCR so I can hook up this camcorder?" They sat down to watch, and when the green Chevy came into view, Blake froze the frame.

"Recognize this man, Ruby?"

Her answer was a good while coming, so he glanced at her and saw that she was concentrating intensely. Finally, she said, "Can't say as I do, Mr. Blake, though he do remind me of the picture Miz Melinda showed me. Still, they's a little somethin' familiar 'bout that face. It's just that the parts don't go together."

Now that was something to think about. "What about you, Melinda? Recognize him?"

She also took her time answering. "He's the man who came to this door before I went to Italy and who I caught on the surveillance camera. I'm sure of it."

He flicked off the camcorder. "Yes. From that sketch you drew, I thought as much."

"Not long after I come here to work for Mr. Rodgers, he had a friend what used to visit pretty often, usually on the weekend," Ruby said. "He stayed in the guest room and come and went pretty much as he pleased. I thought they was working together on somethin'. But that man had salt-and-pepper hair, almost white, and wore black horn-rimmed glasses. What keeps reminding me of him is this man's eyebrows."

"Do you remember that man's name?" Melinda and Blake asked simultaneously.

"Sure 'nuff. I seed him and fed him often enough. Reginald Goodwin or maybe Goodson. No. It was Goodwin."

Ruby slapped her thighs and got up from the chair. "I ain't said they is the same, and I ain't said they ain't. But you don't 'spect to see two different men with bushy eyebrows arched up like that, lest they's father and son. Wouldn't even happen with two brothers what wasn't twins."

Blake looked long and hard at her. Ruby was a smart woman.

He'd have that angle investigated. "You've been a great help," he told her.

Reaching for Melinda's hand, he asked her, "Ready to go?"

She nodded, absentmindedly, he thought. But what woman wouldn't be disturbed learning that her husband hadn't shared with her things that were important to him?

Chapter Eight

Blake drove along Route 40 thinking of the tapes that Melinda had selected for the drive to Curtis Bay. Blues, jazz, and Mozart. He glanced quickly in her direction.

"You didn't happen to bring any Joe Williams CDs, did you?"

" 'Every Day I Have The Blues,' " she said and promptly put it on.

That song always gave him a lift, even though it was blues, and as he always did when he heard it, he sang along with Joe, straight through the hair-raising ending.

"I would never have dreamed it," Melinda said. "My Lord, you can sing, and the blues at that. What else do you want to hear?"

If it hadn't been so hot, he'd have rolled down all the windows and let the breeze blow over him and around him. He felt good. "Play anything you want to. Say, you didn't bring 'Early One Morning,' did you?"

"I don't get in my car without it. Buddy Guy's the man. You bet I brought it."

He put the car on cruise control and let the moment have its way with him. "I want to go through your music. You wouldn't own a recording of 'Carmina Burana,' would you?"

She slid further down in the bucket seat, folded her arms, and closed her eyes. The picture of contentment. "I have worn out two LPs, and I just bought a CD recording a couple of weeks ago. Don't tell me you like that too."

He could hardly believe it. "Honey, I shave by that music."

He reached over and stroked the back of her hand. "Maybe this thing between us isn't so implausible as it seems."

Then she said something that shook him to the core of his being. "Is that why you don't believe in it? Because you think it's inconceivable?"

He switched off the cruise control and slowed down. "Is that what you think?"

She nodded. "You want to believe, but you're not there yet. You take a giant step forward, but something happens, I don't know what, and then you take a step and a half back. Did you realize that?"

"There's some truth in that, I suppose, but what's in my heart never wavers." From the corner of his eye, he glimpsed the broad grin playing around her mouth.

"Maybe one day you'll tell me exactly what's in your heart. Keeping a lid on what's in mine is becoming a problem."

He wished they were holding hands and walking right then. It was a strange way to strengthen their understanding of and feelings for each other, sitting in a moving vehicle and hardly touching.

"We're almost there," he said, "and I don't even remember

when I turned into Route 695. Let's exit at the foot of the Francis Scott Key Bridge and walk along the bay. Right now, I feel confined." Her head snapped around and she stared at him.

"That's right. It's the one thing I can't tolerate: being where I don't want to be. And right this minute, I want to feel the fresh breeze."

"You mean you want to feel free."

"I want *us* to be out there, just the two of us, alone with nature. Sometimes I walk along the Patapsco River, usually around sunset, letting the cool air refresh me. It's invigorating."

He brought the car to a halt and got out. She met him as he walked around to open her door. With her hand in his, he walked down to the edge of the Chesapeake Bay to stroll the path that he'd walked alone so many times. How different it seemed now as they walked hand in hand.

Not far from shore, one fish and then another jumped out of the water as if they were playing leapfrog, and she tightened her fingers on his. "Did you see that? Those two fish?"

"Yeah. Sometimes, late in the day, they put on a show. I've promised myself I'm going to find out why they do it. When I see that, I put my fishing gear away; at least on the Patapsco River, if they're jumping, they don't bite. Out on the bay, they seldom jump."

"You love the water, don't you?" she said. "So do I. It's liberating. Makes me feel free. Uninhibited."

Water gave him that same sense of oneness with nature. He felt as if he floated in a sea of contentment. Everything seemed so right, so perfect as they strolled beneath the shade trees. He stopped walking and faced her.

"Sometimes, like this minute, I feel in my gut that you're the woman for me. And for all time. Whether we're teasing, arguing, mad at each other, or making love, I'm fully alive when I'm with you. And then, that certainty will slip away from me. Can you understand that?"

She nodded, but he didn't see how she could understand what puzzled him about himself.

Her gaze was soft and her face had that tenderness, that sweetness of expression that made him want to lay his head against her breast and feel her arms around him.

"I suspect something in your past, your childhood perhaps, causes you to need a guarantee before you'll take a chance on us, and on other things, too, I imagine. But, Blake, there's no guarantee when it comes to a relationship with another person, not even if that person is your parent. You know that."

He walked with her to a bench that rested beneath a huge willow tree whose branches hung low in picturesque splendor. "Let's sit here out of the sun for a minute. Are you too warm?"

"No. The breeze is wonderful."

He slung his right arm around her shoulder and held her hand with his left one. "You may have touched on something important. I wouldn't swear to it one way or another, because I don't spend time trying to figure why I do or don't do a thing. But if I was scared to take a chance, I wouldn't have a bachelor's degree, not to speak of a doctorate."

"Until a few months ago when Ruby told me about your childhood, I had assumed from the way you carried yourself that you came from a wealthy family. You were the most polished man I'd ever had close contact with."

"I learned from my teachers, my classmates, from men to whom I delivered packages in their posh offices. My father didn't have time for the niceties; he worked twelve or fourteen hours every day except Sunday, and when we kids weren't in school, we had to work along with him. Life was rough. Hard. When I look back, it seems unreal."

As if she divined his needs, her arms went around him and the love she gave seeped into him, a healing potion. "But you stepped over every obstacle. You should be proud. I'm proud of you."

He thought of Lacy, of her whining and superficiality. Melinda was real. He could lose himself in her, but it wasn't the time or place for that, so he focused on her words. "I don't think I'm exceptional, only that I wanted it so badly I would have worked at any job, made any sacrifice to escape that harsh life."

She drew back and looked him in the eye. "Since we're learning each other, help me understand this: you're so hard on people. Why?"

"I can't tolerate people who're not prepared to earn what they get, who want the rewards without working for them, who cry about how bad their lot is without doing anything to improve it. If you call that hard, I'm hard."

She seemed pensive, as though musing over his words and their meaning. "Not many people are as strong as you are. For all my father's blustering, he's never seemed strong to me, not even when I was a child."

He stood, suddenly aware that the strength he projected was a part of his attraction for her. He said as much.

She grinned. "You kidding? When I first looked at you, I wasn't seeing strength. Come on, let's walk a little."

"I'm not going to ask what you did see, because you won't tell me."

"Hmmm. I just said 'Oh, Lord, please don't do this to me. I'm a married woman.'"

Laughter rumbled within him and he let it out with joy. "That's exactly what I said, except that I reminded the Lord that *you* were a married woman."

He looked up at the willow branches that drooped almost to the ground and urged her closer. She gazed up at him with lips parted, and he flicked his tongue across them, waited to savor the torture of anticipation, and then plunged into her. When she pulled him deeper, tremors plowed through him from his head to the soles of his feet. He jerked back and stared at her, and all that he felt for her leaped from his lips of its own accord.

"My God, you move me to the pit of my gut."

"If we could only open ourselves up to whatever comes, just think how special it would be."

He nodded, and started with her to the car, his head splitting with anxiety. Even if they cleared every other hurdle, she'd never forgive him if she knew it was he who'd insisted that she couldn't inherit Prescott's estate unless she set up that foundation. He'd known Prescott's preoccupation with illiteracy and how it circumscribed people's lives, but he hadn't been overly concerned about that problem when he wrote that clause in the will. He'd done it because he hadn't believed that a twenty-five-year-old woman would marry a man Prescott's age for any reason other than money, to loll around in luxury as long as the man lived and to be rich when he died.

He didn't return to the highway, but drove along the side road near the water. "We ought to do this more often," he said. "There's something irresistible about wide open spaces. One day, I'm going to have a house on a hill with God's green earth, trees, and water as far as I can see. A place where my kids can romp undisturbed and unafraid, where I can see daybreak in the morning and moonrise in the evening."

His gaze took in the stately willow trees, shrubs, and black-eyed Susans that lined the roadway. Beauty as far as he could see. One couldn't help but feel the power and beauty of nature.

She must have felt it too, for she asked, "Are you telling me you want to go back to your roots?"

"Heavens, no! But I don't want my children skipping rope on concrete. What about you?"

"I've only lived in Ellicott City and College Park, Maryland, where I attended the university. But I can imagine the delight of feeling the morning dew cool under your toes. Does Duncan have grass around his lodge?"

"He sure does, but don't expect a rustic old lodge; his place is a lodge in name only. You'll see in a few minutes. We're less than a mile from Curtis Bay Hamlet. It's a tiny place at the edge of the Chesapeake Bay, right on the water."

He drove up to the two-story, redbrick house and parked. "Here we are."

She got out and gazed around. "You're telling me, this isn't a lodge! It's your quintessential upscale dwelling."

He took their things out of the trunk and started toward the house. "Where's everybody?" she asked.

"Probably at the beach. Or maybe they didn't get here yet." He opened the door with his key. "How many bedrooms do you and I need, one or two?"

"Since that's not a serious question—"

He interrupted. "Just checking. But you're right next door to me, so keep those coals bedded down." He couldn't help laughing when she exhaled sharply and stuck her fists on her hips. "Okay, okay. Just teasing. You're right there." He pointed to the open bedroom door at the top of the stairs. "See you later."

As far as she knew, she'd never walked in her sleep, but she didn't remember ever having slept that close to temptation, either. She unpacked, hung up her clothes, opened the window, and looked out at the Chesapeake Bay. The curtains flapped in the breeze and she stripped, flung her arms wide, and let the cool salty air caress her naked body. She heard his steps, dashed to the closet, and put on a robe, but he didn't pause at her door. She stretched out on the bed, testing it for comfort, and a knock on her door awakened her nearly two hours later.

"Are you all right?" Justine called to her. "I've begun to worry."

She got up and opened the door. "I guess this is what happens when you're not used to fresh air. I'm fine. Thanks for having me."

"We're delighted. Come on down and meet our daughter."

She scrubbed and buffed her face, put on a pair of white shorts, a yellow blouse, and white espadrilles, let her hair down, and skipped down the stairs. Voices led her to the patio on the shaded side of the house, where Blake stood and walked toward her as she stepped onto the patio.

"I almost whistled," he said, "but I figured I'd better be on my good behavior." He stepped to within inches of her, took her hand, and smiled down into her face. "You're so lovely and so . . . so perfect in that getup."

She knew that what she felt right then blazed on her face, but she didn't care. Not with this black Adonis towering over her within kissing distance, telling her she looked great. His fawnlike eyes darkened to obsidian, and his Adam's apple moved rapidly while he looked at her. Mesmerizing. His masculine aura swirling around her like sea foam in a storm. If she didn't corral her thoughts, what he read on her face wouldn't be conducive to polite, company patter.

Her effort to do so didn't succeed. All she could think of as he stared down into her face was the way she'd felt when he lay embedded deep within her, rocking her to the stratosphere.

Teasing and taunting until he forced her to give herself up to him. Driving her out of herself until she died a little.

She watched his breathing quicken, his stance widen, and his pupils dilate, and didn't doubt that he'd read her thoughts. Then, as if to suggest that he'd bewitched her deliberately, he winked, and she knew he'd brought himself under control.

Determined not to let him get the better of her, she reminded him of his earlier admonition to her. "Keep the coals bedded down? Is that what you said? Take some of your own advice."

He laughed, and oh, how she loved to see him open up and let the joy flow out.

"I never saw you laugh so freely and so much until I got back from Italy. Now you laugh a lot, and I love to see it."

He took her hand. "Come around here and meet Tonya. I'm her godfather, and I want you to know that I can do no wrong."

She stopped. "Who's her godmother?"

Both of his eyebrows shot up. Then a grin spread over his face. "Leah, Wayne Roundtree's wife. Why?"

She winked at him. "Just checking."

As soon as he picked up the child, her little arms encircled his neck, and she kissed his cheek repeatedly. "Unca Bake," she said as he walked with her over to where Melinda stood. It was a picture that she could not have imagined.

"Hello, Tonya." She reached for the child, but Tonya wouldn't leave Blake.

"This is Melinda," he told Tonya. "I want you to like her."

Tonya scrutinized her, decided she wasn't interested, and focused her attention on Blake. "She'll come around."

"Maybe," Justine said. "She loves men. I suspect that's due to her passion for Duncan. She idolizes him."

Duncan rounded the side of the house and hopped up on the patio. "Glad you could join us, Melinda. I see you've met my daughter."

"She's a darling, the image of Justine," Melinda said.

He glanced at his wife and grinned at what she surmised was a private joke. "She is that, all right, though I was the last person to see it. I thought we'd cook out tonight. Tomorrow morning, we can go fishing." He looked at Blake. "Unless you'd like to take Melinda for a cruise."

"I'd love that, provided she wants to get up early."

"You name the time. I'd love a boat ride." she said.

"Okay. Leave here at five-thirty?"

When she hesitated, Justine said, "I'll lend you my alarm clock. The bay is heaven that time of morning when you're out there almost all alone. You can make coffee after you get on board."

Melinda reclined in a lounge chair and watched Blake play with Tonya, listened as he exchanged ready quips with Duncan and Justine. Lighthearted, witty, and playful. A different man. She looked up and saw Justine watching her and wasn't surprised when the woman took a seat beside her on the lounge chair.

"Something tells me you're wondering who this Blake is. Right?"

"Pretty close. How did you guess?"

"For weeks, I've watched him unwind. He seems to laugh just because it feels good to do it. Oh, he reverts occasionally, but that doesn't last long."

"He's softened. I don't know what happened, but I love seeing him like this."

"Duncan believes this is the real man, that he buried this side of himself while he made his way up."

"But I've known him for five years, and—"

"Maybe he's changed because he doesn't have to fight so hard with himself."

"What do you mean?"

"My guess is that you're at the center of this. You're a free woman now, and he needn't feel guilty because he wants you."

A gasp escaped her. "He told you about that?"

"He shared his feelings with Duncan, because they're close friends, and he needed one, believe me. I first noticed this new playfulness and even frivolity in him when you were in Europe. He must have come to terms with himself. You're good for him. Very good for him."

"Blake, can you get the potatoes to roasting and throw the salad together? This'll be ready in about fifteen minutes or so," she heard Duncan say.

"Excuse me," Justine said. "I'd better take Tonya. If Blake puts her down, she'll scream. I think she feels she owns him. Be back in a minute."

If playfulness in Blake surprised her, seeing that chef's apron over his white Bermuda shorts challenged her credulousness. She blinked her eyes a few times, getting used to the picture, enjoying the sight of him picking over meslun lettuce leaf by tiny leaf.

"We turn in early," Justine told her after dinner, "because we get up with the sun, but make yourself comfortable. I'll put the alarm clock on your night table." She reached for Duncan's hand. "Come on, husband, I have a few things to say to you."

And the right to say them, Melinda thought. She watched Duncan kiss his wife on the side of her mouth, take her hand, and then, as if he'd already forgotten his guest, glance over his shoulder at them and murmur, "Night."

She didn't want Blake to read her thoughts, to know what seeing that woman leave them to enjoy married bliss with her husband made her feel, didn't want him to know she envied Justine Banks. So she closed her eyes, but he seemed to draw her gaze the way a flame draws a moth, and she opened them and looked at him. There was no mistaking the blazing fire in his now obsidian orbs or what this signified. Suddenly frightened at the power he held over her, though he probably didn't imagine it, she found the strength to look away from him and get up from the chair.

"S . . . since I have to get up before five o'clock, I think I'd better turn in. See you tomorrow morning."

"Yeah. I have to put some ashes on what's left of that fire, so you go on in. I'll . . . uh . . . be out here on the patio when you come down in the morning."

He turned away, and she knew he didn't think he could risk a good night kiss. She certainly couldn't. She paused on her way upstairs. Hadn't Blake seen Duncan pour half a bucket of ashes on those coals? Maybe he was doing that to take his mind off what he really wanted.

First one thing and then another conspired to interfere with her getting a good night's sleep. The infernal clock ticked mercilessly beside her ear, counting off the seconds of the rest of her life. She hated ticking clocks because she didn't like being reminded constantly of her mortality. Exasperated, she put the clock under the bed where she couldn't hear it. In a few minutes, she dozed off to sleep, where Blake awaited her with his taunting and teasing, offering himself to her and then withholding what he knew she so longed for. Furious with him, she bolted upright and was getting out of bed to give him the reprimand he deserved when she awakened, realized she'd been dreaming, and fell back in bed. Defeated. Finally, she slept.

Melinda managed to get safely down the stairs with barely open eyes and make her way to the patio where Blake leaned against the railing, alert and smiling, looking as though he'd already swum a few laps. With her eyes closed, she shook her head slowly and carefully. As heavy as her head felt, in her clouded state, she could easily damage it.

"Hi," she said, "don't tell me you're a morning person."

"Hi, yourself. Guilty as charged. And you're not."

She swayed toward the wall. "No, sir-ree. I've been congratulating myself ever since I realized I'd gotten my eyes open."

"I see your sense of humor is working before sunup. Have you noticed that we're identically dressed?"

"Really? What am I wearing? As far as I'm concerned it's still night. I did well to recognize you."

His left hand went to his chest in a gesture of feigned humility. "Woman, I'm crushed. We're wearing white slacks and sneakers and light blue, collared T-shirts."

"Thank God I'm decent."

He took her hand and started to his car. "The boat's only a few blocks away, but considering your . . . er . . . condition, I wouldn't dare suggest you walk that far."

She could feel the breeze as he sped along the little road beside the shore. "At this rate, I'll wake up," she said.

"It's a bit chilly, but Duncan keeps sweaters on the cruiser. You'll be comfortable." He grinned. "Yep, if I have to keep you warm with my body."

"At five-thirty in the morning, give me blankets."

He drove up to the dock, got out, walked around, and opened her door. "You *are* sleepy, if you didn't rush out of this car before I could get around here."

He stood inches from her, letting her feel the electrifying magnetism of his hot gaze. "I'd enjoy the pleasure of awakening you about this time one morning and seeing how you respond when it's me and not the clock that arouses you."

She shrugged, aware that he jostled her, but lacking the energy to defend herself as she normally would. "Even *I* know the answer to that," she said.

"And . . ."

"And I'd wake up. I might sleep past daybreak, but definitely not past sunrise."

Obviously he remembered that she'd said he could make the sun shine, as his laughter seemed to swell joyously until he doubled up with mirth, thrilling her with the joy he communicated to her. She could listen to him laugh forever. His eyes sparkled and his white teeth gleamed, and she thought what a pleasure it would be if she could stay with him always.

He sobered up, let his fingers rest gently at her elbow, and said, "Now you're waking up.

"Here we are," he said, walking up the gangplank to the sleek, thirty-foot cruiser. He turned and waited for her. "This is the *Tonya Girl.* Let me give you a hand."

But she stood still, her eyes wide as she stared at it. "This is Duncan's boat? I thought it was something small like a fishing boat with maybe an outboard motor. Good grief, you could spend the night in this thing."

"Want to?"

"I . . . I don't know. I've never been on a boat before, much less slept on one. You know how to operate this thing?"

"You betcha. Duncan and I learned to navigate this baby when he put the down payment on it. Justine is learning too. Come on. I'll make some coffee, and then we'll get going."

He brewed a pot of coffee and toasted some bagels, which they consumed as they stood on deck. Minutes later they headed for the open bay. She stood beside him admiring his deft handling of the helm. What else did he do that she didn't know about?

"Blake, tell me about yourself. Out here in Curtis Bay, you're a different man. So free, relaxed. I'd even say loose. Are you happy here? Is that it?"

She hadn't meant to make him frown, but he did. "Loose? I don't know. Happy? I could be. Maybe this lifestyle suits me. I hate being confined, and out here . . . well, I wish I could explain it. Happy will have to do, I guess."

"My Lord, look at that." Colors began to streak across the sky. Blue, red, gray, and orange, mingling, dancing, and suddenly competing for space and position. They gazed in awe as the orange and red streaks battled for prominence until bright red streaked across the horizon and the sun broke through the clouds.

His hand gripped her elbow, and she looked up and saw the fierce look on his face. "You told me I made the sun shine. Do you remember that?"

Of course she did, but she only looked at him and said nothing.

"Did you say it, or didn't you?"

"I said it."

When he grabbed her shoulders, she knew he meant business. He'd let her go the night before, and he'd do it now if she wanted it that way. He stepped back and stared down at her, his hands balled into fists, his stance wide, and his nostrils flaring. She looked at his pectorals, prominent beneath his blue T-shirt, and saw his Adam's apple move rapidly. His breathing quickened, and she could smell the sizzling man in him, feel his hands possessing her body, and taste him. Yes, she could taste him. Her gaze met his and hot pinions of desire shot arrow-straight to the center of her passion. She wanted to . . . to . . . Frustration gripped her and she closed her eyes.

"Come here, Melinda. I need you, baby."

Her eyelids flew open and her lips parted, but she couldn't move and couldn't speak. If he'd only . . . "Can't you just . . ."

"Let me know if you want me. Tell me. I still ache from last night. Do you want to make love with me?"

"Yes. Yes." With her arms open, she sped to him, and he wrapped her close to his body.

"I'm crazy for you. Do you hear me? I'm on fire for you."

Why didn't he move, kiss her, do something? "Isn't there a bed downstairs?" she asked him.

She glimpsed the wild savage expression on his face just before he lifted her and ran downstairs with her. "What about the boat?'' she asked as he opened the door to the captain's quarters.

"I dropped anchor. Kiss me. Honey, open your mouth and kiss me.''

She reached for his belt and pulled his shirt from it, ran her fingers beneath it, up his chest to his sensitive pectorals, and felt the shivers that raced through him. He held her head and plunged his tongue into her mouth, simulating the act of love until she began to undulate against him, demanding more. She knew he wouldn't be delicate this time, that he'd been strung out with desire for her so long that he'd just take what she gave. When she stepped away from him and pulled off her T-shirt, he reached for her, pulled her nipple into his mouth, and suckled her until her escalating moans echoed in the distance.

She fell across the bed and raised her arms to him, and within seconds, he was there with her wrapped in her arms. He tugged her slacks and panties over her hips and threw them aside, then quickly disrobed. She slid down beneath him and kissed his belly, flat, hot, and all male.

"No, baby. I can't handle that.'' He pulled her up, locked her hands above her head, and took his pleasure in her breast, sucking, nipping, kissing, and pinching until she thought she'd go mad. He kept her hands immobilized above her head, and with his lips fastened to her nipple, she felt his fingers trail slowly down to her feminine center. Her entire nervous system shimmered, out of control, and she squirmed, twisted, and flailed in frustration until his talented fingers reached their goal. She raised her body to hasten contact with his hand and feel that unbelievable fullness begin to gather inside of her and drive her crazy. She gave no thought to her dancing hips as he strummed her as a lyrist plays a lyre.

"Blake. Oh, Blake. I can't take more. You've got to—''

"You're not ready yet, baby.''

"I am. I am.''

His fingers danced faster in pursuit of their goal, tantalizing, teasing, and stripping her of her will. When his lips covered her own, she eagerly opened to his searching tongue and moaned in pleasure as he possessed every centimeter of her mouth.

Then he tugged at her nipple, released it, and gazed down into her face. "You like that, don't you?"

"Yes. Yes. I love everything you do to me."

He sucked the other one until she let out a keening cry and the liquid of love flowed over his fingers.

"Blake. Honey, please get in me. *Get in me!*"

"All right, sweetheart." He slipped on a condom and rose above her with his gaze fastened on her eyes. "Take me. Take me in."

She clutched him with her fingers, and in her haste to receive him, raised her body for the sweet thrill of his thrust. He found his place within her, sank home, and at last, he lay deep within her where he belonged.

Her heart took off when he smiled down at her and said, "Relax now."

"I will. I will."

With one hand beneath her buttocks, he shifted his hips and began to thrust. "Relax, honey, and don't hold back. Let it go, baby. Give yourself to me."

She quit struggling for release, locked her ankles across his hips and her arms around his waist, and moved with him. Right away heat seared the bottom of her feet and she thought she would surely die when the swell of climax threatened and then eluded her. He increased the pace and the pinching and squeezing began, but he drove faster and faster until she cried aloud.

"Blake. Oh, Blake, love me. Love me." He thrust power-fully, demanding her submission, until she erupted into ecstasy.

"I do. I do," he said and, draining himself of his essence, he collapsed in her arms.

She looked at his head on her breast and swore that no other man would touch her. He was hers and she wasn't going to let him go.

"How are you feeling right now?" he asked her.

"Queen of the world. I don't think I've been happier. What about you?"

"Unbelievable, sweetheart. Unbelievable."

"I want to sleep, but if we don't go back, they may think we stole the boat," she said.

"Not hardly."

"Then what *will* they think?"

The grin that played around his mouth was answer enough, but he made it crystal clear. "They'll think we're doing whatever it is lovers do." He slipped his hands beneath her hips and squeezed her closer to his body. "Mind if I get some juice? I'm kind of hungry. I'll be right back."

She put her hands over her head and stretched long and lazily. Gazing toward where he'd lain seconds earlier, she imagined the pleasure of awakening beside him every day for the rest of her life. With his pillow clutched to her breast, she smelled his scent, then buried her face in the sheet and inhaled the must of their lovemaking. She couldn't get enough of him.

"I brought you some orange juice."

She pulled herself up and leaned on her right elbow. "Thanks. We didn't eat breakfast. A bagel is nothing. I'm starved."

"I can cook some bacon and scramble two or three eggs. Okay?"

Was he serious? She supposed her disbelief was mirrored on her face, because he set the juice glass on the little table and stared at her.

"What is it? You want to go back?"

Beg him? Having learned that there were more effective ways, she lay back on the bed, patted the space beside her, and then stretched her body suggestively. She didn't purr, but if he didn't get the message soon, she would.

"You want me to—"

She threw aside the sheet in an unmistakable invitation for him to join her. "I thought you said you're a morning person," she needled, when he slipped between the sheets and joined her.

"Yeah, but after what you did to me a few minutes back, I'm not my normal self."

She leaned over him, and when her nipples grazed the hair on his chest, her pulse skittered and the echo of her escalating heartbeat hammered in her ears. She brushed his lips with a soft kiss, then his eyes and his neck. She wanted to explore him, every inch of him. The sparkles of anticipation in his wonderful eyes was all the encouragement she needed, and she let her palms graze his pectorals, barely touching them. His breathing accelerated, and she twirled her tongue around first one nipple and then the other until his body jerked upward. Her fingers trailed down his body, and she assured herself of his readiness, then wrapped her arms around his waist and kissed his belly, cherishing every inch of him until he began to squirm out of her embrace. But she gripped his thighs and loved him.

"Baby, watch that," he yelled, reached down and pulled her from him. "Whew. That was close," he whispered as if to himself.

He reached down for the packet that lay beside the bunk and she shielded him, then he pulled her on top of him and positioned her legs so that she straddled him, open to his penetration. He tested her for readiness, found what he needed there, and drove home. It was fast, furious, and powerful. Then he flipped them over, smiled down at her, and loved her until she screamed aloud her satisfaction and he collapsed, shattered, in her arms.

He levered himself on his forearms. "I'm too heavy for you."

But she clasped him to her, fighting off the unease she already felt that he might slip away. "You're not too *anything* for me; you're what I need."

She could feel his love then, as he gazed into her eyes, open and vulnerable. Flaccid within her. "You're precious to me," he said, his voice a cracked, hoarse whisper. "But so many hurdles. So much ..." He attempted to withdraw from her, but she held him.

"It's so good, holding you this way."

But he separated them nonetheless, leaving her bereft of the protection she'd felt while he lay within her. "One thing I know, Melinda, this isn't going away any time soon, probably never. I have to come to terms with it. You may already have done that; I don't know."

He still had questions, did he? Well, so did she. "What's Lacy Morgan to you?"

He sat up. "Is that a serious question, or are you changing the subject?"

"Serious question."

"I dated her a few times because I was interested, but that quickly petered out. After that, she invited me several places and I went with her. Twice. Then I called a halt to it. She's tenacious, and doesn't want to let go. I have never been intimate with her and don't plan to be. That answer your question?"

She let out the breath she'd been holding. "Sure does."

"Now, what about us? If you're not going to get married by next March, that means giving up your inheritance. If that's what you're thinking of doing, I'd like to know why."

"Let me out of this bed," she said, throwing the sheet off her nude body.

He restrained her with an arm around her shoulder. "That's not an idle question. I want to know why and I think I'm entitled to an answer." His voice softened, pacifying her with its warmth and masculine tenderness. "Baby, don't put bricks in our path. It's hazardous enough as it is. Talk to me."

"I already told you I can't marry another man I don't love, not even if he's a friend, sweet and kind to me. I don't want money that badly."

"Is that your only reason?" His eyes mirrored intense anxiety, and she could see that he held his breath. But could she open her soul to him when he hadn't told her he loved her? She let her hand caress his cheek.

"Do you think I could lie this way with any man but you?"

He sucked in his breath. "Could you?"

"I can't even imagine it."

He wrapped his arms around her and pressed gentle kisses to her lips, eyes, cheeks, and forehead, cherishing her with such tenderness that she couldn't hold back the tears. She knew she'd love him forever.

Shortly after noon, they sat on deck eating the breakfast of scrambled eggs, bacon, and toasted bagels that he'd cooked. "I feel like I could eat a horse," he said, getting up from the table. "Let's see if there's any fruit in the refrigerator. Woman, you gave me a workout."

She swallowed her coffee and yawned with as much dignity as she could muster. "We don't want to mention what you did to me. Say, do you know, we never did see the sun come all the way up?"

"But did it rise?"

"Honey, you made a miracle. Who would believe the sun could rise half a dozen times in the same morning?"

Joy suffused him, and he supposed she could see it in his eyes, the smile on his face, and in the movements of his body. "Yeah. How 'bout that?"

He loped downstairs to the galley for whatever additional

food he could find. How could you love a woman with every atom of your being right down to the recesses of your soul if you weren't sure you trusted her integrity? Maybe he was the problem, not she.

The refrigerator yielded frozen ice cream sandwiches and fresh peaches, and he found a bunch of ripe bananas on the counter. He collected his treasures along with some paper napkins and dashed back upstairs. She wasn't going anywhere, but he still couldn't wait to get back to her.

"It's one-thirty," she said when they'd finished eating and cleaned the galley. "They'll think we drowned."

"Quit worrying about what they think. They want us to enjoy ourselves. You think I'd rather fish with Duncan than be here with you?"

"Hope not," she said and pulled the straw hat down until it almost covered her eyes.

"Where's the linen closet? I want to change the bed in the captain's quarters."

He tipped up the brim of her hat, and ran his index finger down the bridge of her nose. He had to touch her someplace and, if they were ever going to turn that boat around and head back, her nose was the safest place. A cloud covered the sun, and he looked up. He didn't like what he saw, so he dashed downstairs to alert Melinda that they had to lift anchor and go. She stood beside the bunk bed holding their soiled sheets close to her body, her eyes closed and an expression of rapture on her face that zonked him. He felt the rush of blood to his loins, but he had to control it, because that sky held threatening clouds.

"Honey, we have to hurry." Her eyes flew open and she gaped in surprise, but he took care not to let her know he'd shared that moment with her. He made the bed while she found the laundry bag and put the sheets in it.

When they got on deck, he saw that the sky had darkened

and the clouds hung lower, and goose pimples popped out on his arms. He'd never been on that bay in a storm, not even with Duncan at the helm. He pulled anchor and headed for shore, but in less than five minutes, he heard the roar of thunder.

Chapter Nine

At the first clap of thunder, he knew he had trouble on his hands, probably the fight of his life, one that would test his nerve and fortitude—not to speak of his skill—until he anchored that boat in Curtis Bay harbor.

If I get there, he said to himself. A glance toward where Melinda sat minutes earlier made him do a double take. Where on earth was she? The deck chair in which she had been sitting was empty and he hadn't seen her go down the steps. Forced to concentrate on navigating the boat, he couldn't leave the helm and look for her. His heart slowed down to a stop when lightning streaked across the horizon, a blazing light as far as he could see, and the loudest, most threatening noise he'd ever heard roared right over his head.

He looked around. Not another boat in sight, and that left him alone on that vast bay. a sitting duck for lightning strikes.

He did the only thing he could do, opened the throttle as far as it would go in a daring attempt to race ahead of the storm. Where the devil was Melinda?

He reached into the cabinet below the helm, got the foghorn, and called, "Melinda, are you all right? Come here where I can see you."

Lightning danced across the horizon in a spectacular display of nature's graphics, and thunder roared and crashed over and around him, booming its awesome power. His flesh seemed to crawl as the sky loomed black and dangerous, and he'd never seen the waters of the bay so dark and ominous. Suddenly, the wind rose and the dark water seethed in a newly menacing turbulence, so that the *Tonya Girl* began to roll. He grabbed the foghorn and called Melinda again.

"Baby, I can't leave the helm. Come where I can see you and know you're all right. Do you hear me?"

At last he heard a voice, but the high, whipping wind carried the sound away from him, so he turned toward it, and when he did, he saw her white pants silhouetted in the afternoon darkness.

"Melinda!"

"Blake. Honey, will we . . . will we make it?"

He couldn't guarantee it, not with the weather and water conditions deteriorating by the second.

"I'm giving it my best shot. You all right?"

"I'm . . . uh . . . I'm fine. Just trying to get used to the way the boat's rocking."

Lightning bounced off the water all around the *Tonya Girl*. *Any minute now, we'll get a strike,* he said to himself.

He noticed that she'd wrapped her arms around her middle, evidently trying to stave off the tremors, and he didn't blame her for being scared; he wasn't exactly jumping for joy himself. Thunder rumbled in the distance, and he knew that within seconds it would blast over his head and all around them. As he expected, another blinding light flashed around them, and then the thunder crashed so violently that it almost deafened him. He pulled Melinda to him with one hand while gripping the helm with his other one. She burrowed into him.

"We'll make it, baby. We've got to." She covered her ears with her hands, and he hurt for her. "Go on back down before it starts raining."

She looked up at him. "If you can stand up here in this, so can I, and I'm not leaving you. I went down to the ladies' room, not to get away from the storm."

"I thought you were afraid of these storms."

"I am. It's childish, but I'm petrified of lightning."

"Then go back—"

"I'm not leaving you here alone. You may need me."

He didn't argue because he wanted her where he could see her and know that she was safe. "If I can just get us there before it rains, though it's so close I can smell it."

"Me too. How can it be so dark this time of day? It's so eerie that it's almost . . . you know . . . exciting. Wonder what causes this?"

"Beats me. I couldn't stand my ninth-grade geography teacher, so I didn't listen to anything she said, which may account for my ignorance about the elements."

"Why didn't you like her?"

"She was mean to me. She didn't respect me because I was poor, couldn't dress like the other kids, and didn't have time for school plays and other extracurricular activities. One of the first things I did when I got my law degree was look her up and send her an announcement. I got a bang out of that."

Drops of rain sprinkled their bodies. "Would you look under there and get those yellow slickers, please? I almost forgot about them." She did as he asked, and they'd barely put them on when a deluge pelted them.

He saw a searchlight in the distance about where he figured

the marina would be. Surely Duncan wouldn't stand on the dock in that dangerous electric storm. He eased up on the throttle, reducing speed. *I hope that light isn't a mirage,* he said to himself. But as he neared it, he didn't see any other lights and guessed that there'd been a power outage. But his only concern was getting Melinda into Duncan's house unharmed. Lightning blazed around them, and the thunder blasted his ears, but he thought only of the safe harbor within his reach. The darkness slowly receded as rain pelted them. They'd endured twenty-five minutes of pure terror.

"Baby, we're almost there. We've made it." He eased into Duncan's assigned berth, cut the motor, clasped Melinda to him, and held her. Torrents of rain drenched the slickers they wore, but there by the boat's helm, they held on to each other, mute.

"Good Lord, you gave us a scare."

She turned at the sound of Duncan's voice. "This is the worst storm I've ever seen on this bay," Duncan said. "You all right?"

She wasn't all right; for the first time since those clouds had suddenly become black, she gave in to her fear. Tremors shook her body, and she knew Blake could feel them even through those heavy raincoats.

"We're all right," she heard Blake say. "But I'll remember that scene for the rest of my life."

"But you made it back here like a seasoned sailor," Duncan said. "As the Bard noted, 'All's well that ends well.' You two go on to the house. I'll secure the *Tonya Girl.*"

She followed Blake's gaze upward. "Would you believe that?" he asked. "Now that we're safe, it's beginning to look like two-thirty in the afternoon." He shifted his gaze to her face. "If you're okay, I'd like to help Duncan with this. It'll only take a couple of minutes."

His arms still held her, and as she looked into his face, at the caring and deep concern it expressed, she knew she would be dealing with a different man, one who knew exactly what he wanted, but would have to scale high hurdles in order to force himself to achieve it. But that didn't bother her because, now, she knew him. If he'd mastered that boat in his death-defying battle with the storm, he would master Blake Edmund Hunter.

They didn't speak to each other while he drove the few blocks to Duncan's house. Talk would have been anticlimactic. They had deftly communicated their feelings in those moments when their emotions had been raw and their hearts bare.

"You were wonderful," she said later when they stood on the back porch pulling off their raincoats.

She couldn't figure out why he was reluctant to accept her compliment, but he was. When he looked at her, his smile barely touched his lips. "You're the one. You told me you were afraid of lightning, yet you stood there in the midst of those petrifying flashes because you thought I might need you." He tipped up her chin with the index finger of his left hand. "In that storm, a lot of men would have been shaking, terrified. You're an awesome woman."

She didn't want to be awesome. She wanted to be the woman he loved. "You're dynamite on the water," she said, seeking levity. "I'd like to settle with you in a houseboat, or any kind of boat. Something tells me you dance your best dance on the waves."

"Not quite," he said, and a shadow covered the gleam that had brightened his eyes. Surely there wasn't room for sadness after what they'd just come through. "Not quite," he said again.

The back door swung open, and Justine rushed to them. "I thought I heard you down here. We've been out of our minds with worry." She looked at Blake. "Did you have any problems?"

He rubbed the back of his neck, pursed his lips, and seemed to muse over his answer. "Problems? You bet. It wasn't just the weather, though that was awesome. I had to battle the churning in my stomach and, yeah, my faith. If you've ever been tested, you know what I mean."

She nodded. "If you know my story, you know I've been there. The important thing is that you're safe."

" And that you will never again forget that cardinal rule." Blake spun around at the sound of Duncan's voice.

"Rule?" Melinda asked.

"Never take a boat out on this bay or any other body of water without checking the weather forecast. This is August, man. We can get a storm every afternoon. I should have warned you, but . . . ahem . . . I expected you back by eight o'clock this morning."

"Now, honey, you're meddling. We wanted them to enjoy themselves."

Duncan looked at his wife and winked. "And they didn't disappoint us either, baby."

Justine's smile broadened into a full, lusty laugh. "Sorry, Melinda, Duncan didn't mean to embarrass you. We can have lunch whenever you're ready."

Melinda looked at Justine. Deadpan. "Embarrass me about what?"

When Blake nearly doubled up in laughter, she lifted her chin, laid back her shoulders, and strutted past Justine into the house. "You're as nutty as a pecan grove, all three of you," she flung over her shoulder to the chorus of laughter that followed her.

Blake sat on the edge of his bed thinking of their ordeal in the storm. Through it all, he'd been outside of himself, dealing with it as if only Melinda were threatened and he had no duty to himself, only to her. But for a second after he reached the marina, the bottom had nearly fallen out of him when he reflected on the extent of the danger. *I've got to get back to Ellicott City and clean up the mess back there,* he said to himself. *I want my life in order.*

After changing into a short-sleeved yellow sport shirt and white Dockers, he shoved his feet in a pair of sandals and loped down the stairs.

"We're eating in the kitchen," Justine said. "The sun's out, and it's too hot and muggy to eat on the patio."

Blake sat beside Tonya's high chair, and immediately she held out her arms to him.

"Uncle Blake has to eat, Tonya," Duncan said, but the child ignored him and reached for Blake.

Eating with Tonya in his lap would tax his ingenuity as well as his dexterity, but he loved to hold her. "She'll cooperate, won't you, Tonya? Going to be good?' he asked her.

She nodded and reached for him again. "I'm good. Unca Bake, pease kiss," she said.

He unbuckled her and took her into his arms, and she bounced and bubbled with laughter. Then she kissed his cheeks. He looked at her. "You give me something special," he heard himself say to Tonya, though he knew she couldn't understand. With her folded in his arms, he let himself enjoy the love she gave him.

He hadn't meant to look toward Melinda, but her gaze drew him as surely as a magnet draws steel. In her eyes, he saw a longing that aroused in him a desire to have her for himself alone and for all time. He'd felt it before but never with such intensity. If only he could let himself go with her. She pleased him as no woman ever had, but he didn't please himself, not even in their torrid lovemaking just before the storm. He winked at her, and she lowered her gaze.

* * *

Sunday night when he parked in front of Melinda's door, he knew she didn't expect him to come in. "This has been a wonderful weekend," she said. "I'm so full. It's as if I'll bubble over any minute."

Immediately anxious for her, he took her hand. "I hope this doesn't mean you're unhappy."

Her eyes widened. "Unhappy? Not one bit. Maybe the opposite. It's . . . I don't know. Maybe I feel as if I finally have a handle on things, though I can't imagine why. But I'm definitely not unhappy."

"I'd better check things out with Tillman. Sit here for a minute. Okay?"

It was not Tillman, but a man who introduced himself as Robinson who stood guard. "Where's Tillman?"

"His wife's having a baby. I'm his replacement." He asked the man for his ID, checked it, and probed, "Who's at the back?"

"Hawkins."

Seemed all right, but he had to be sure. He walked back to the driver's side of his car, leaned against it, and called Hawkins on his cell phone, keeping an eye on the fellow who called himself Robinson.

"Hawkins speaking."

"Hunter. Where's Tillman?"

"At the front door, as far as I know. Why're you asking?"

"This isn't Tillman on the door. Walk around the side of the house with your gun handy, but be cautious." He called the police next and then the company from which he'd engaged the two guards.

"We don't have a Robinson on our roster, Mr. Blake," the receptionist said, "and Tillman hasn't asked for leave. I'll send the police at once."

"I've already called them."

He didn't want to get too far from Melinda, because he didn't know the intruder's goals, and relief spread through him when Hawkins appeared with his gun showing.

"Where's this—"

The moment Robinson heard the second male voice and saw the gun, he dashed from the steps, ran to the side of the property, and jumped over a cluster of shrubbery. Hawkins fired his first shot in the air and the second one missed as Robinson dashed to his left, over the bushes and out of sight.

"I've never killed a man," Hawkins explained to Blake. "I'm sorry, but I aimed for his leg, and I guess I missed." He looked down at his gun. "I've never missed before."

"What's the matter?" Melinda shouted, jumping from his car. He grabbed her. "It's all right. Just stay right here. The guy might fire back."

"What guy? This is my house, and I want to know what's going on."

He held her in spite of her agitation. "That wasn't Tillman on duty, and we don't know where Tillman is. I suspect foul play, but we can't be sure yet."

The sheriff's car drove up and behind it a squad car. When told of the problem, the sheriff turned to the policeman. "I was telling you just this morning that Ellicott City is not a dull town. Lots of things happen here."

"Yeah," the policeman said, "a regular Madison Square Garden." He recorded the particulars. "I'll put a watch on this house," he told Melinda, "but you be careful who you open the door for."

"What about Tillman?" Blake and Melinda asked in unison.

"We'll find him."

"I got a good look at that guy who calls himself Robinson. The man even had proper ID," Blake told the officer.

"How about coming with me, tell our artist what he looks like, and we'll take it from there."

Blake shook his head. "I can't leave here until the agency sends a replacement for Tillman."

After another hour, while he alternately assured Melinda it wouldn't happen again and fought his fear that it would, he remembered the camera. She hooked it up to the television and rolled the tape. Pictures of the man from every angle. She reversed it. Robinson walked up to Tillman and seemed to ask questions. After a minute, Robinson shook hands with the guard and left. The camera swept the gardens and the street. And then Robinson walked back up the front steps, attempted to open first the door and then the windows, none of which would yield entry. He then positioned himself in front of the door. Tillman was nowhere to be seen.

"What do you think?" Blake asked Melinda.

"I'm not a detective, but I believe he either drugged or poisoned Tillman during that handshake."

"But where do you think he went? He didn't just vanish."

She shook her head. "It takes the camera almost five minutes to complete that half circle. Whatever happened took place when the camera was pointed in the opposite direction."

"I'll buy that. As soon as the new guard arrives, I'll take the tape to the police."

Melinda answered the phone. "It's the agency chief. You want to speak with him?"

He took the phone from her. "No, we don't know where Tillman is."

When questioned, the chief said, "Tillman is a widower. So that business about his wife having a baby was a lie. I'm sending Mrs. Rodgers one of our detectives. He won't stand at the door, but will park across the street and sit in his car. He should be there in half an hour. His name's Jonathan Gordon."

He told Melinda what he'd learned, and then it hit him.

Robinson was waiting for Melinda to return alone, hopefully after dark. There was something in that house that someone wanted, and it was valuable. He'd bet Melinda didn't know it was there. How many times had he represented a woman who had a serious problem because she hadn't familiarized herself with her husband's business deals? He hoped his faith in Prescott hadn't been misplaced.

After speaking with Gordon for half an hour, he'd satisfied himself as to the man's professionalism. "I'm going now," he told Melinda, "but I'll have my cell phone with me every minute. If you need me, call that number. If there's a problem call Gordon and then phone me. All right?"

"I'll be fine, Blake. But starting tomorrow morning, I'm going to try and find out what this is all about."

"I agree that you have to, but before that, could we have a talk? I may have some ideas."

"Tomorrow?"

"Call me as soon as you're ready to start your day. And don't worry. If you're uncomfortable about . . . what happened to Tillman today, say so, and I'll stay with you for as long as you want me to."

She stepped closer to him, placed her hands on his shoulders, and looked into his eyes. That familiar warmth headed for its inevitable home in the pit of his belly, but he knew he had to control it, and he did.

"What is it? You want me to stay?"

"You know I do. But it's not the solution. I'm a hot enough topic in this town as it is."

Her mouth was so soft and sweet, glistening in its pouting fullness, and her eyes had that dreamy look that could start his blood on a fast journey to his loins like molten lava rushing down the slopes of a volcano.

He sucked in his breath and ordered his libido under control. "If you can't sleep, come stay with me."

She laughed, and the weight of her predicament lifted from his shoulders. "If I stay with you, I'll sleep?" she asked him. "Don't make jokes."

"I have a guest room."

To his amazement, she laughed aloud. "Yeah. Right. Who'd be sleeping in it?"

He wrapped his arms around her and hugged her. "You walk in your sleep? What on earth was I thinking?"

Her lips grazed his cheek and when she looked at him, a hint of wickedness gleamed in her brown eyes. "The board meets Tuesday, and I can see Martha purse her thin lips and say, " 'When I want to reach you, Melinda, should I call you at Mr. Rodgers's home or Mr. Hunter's home?' "

He laughed, not because it amused him, but because the light banter cheered her up. "I'd better be going. Don't forget to call me if you need me. Idly, his fingers stroked the smooth Italian marble that outlined the fireplace in the Rodgers's living room. He hadn't previously noticed its uniqueness. He studied it for a minute. *A hefty sum of money went into that,* he said to himself. And the house contained three of them on the first floor. He made a note to examine his records and find out when they were purchased.

She walked with him to the door, and he held her briefly for a kiss. Once outside, he called the guard at the back of the house as a check, and spoke with the detective who sat in a dark green car in front of Melinda's house. Then he took the tape from Melinda's surveillance camera to the police station, waited while an officer made a copy, and went home, taking the original tape with him. He'd be remiss as a lawyer if he gave up the only evidence of Robinson that he had.

Melinda walked into Blake's office at exactly ten o'clock Tuesday morning, half an hour before the board's scheduled meeting. "You sounded so serious on the phone," she told him. "What's up?"

He sat on the edge of his desk, and she knew he'd done it so that their talk wouldn't seem formal, though it dealt with business. "I want you to go through Prescott's papers. I know what's here, but if he kept important papers at home, you're the only person who has the right to examine them. I was his lawyer and friend, but someone knows something I don't know. I'm convinced that he withheld information from both of us, and we need to know what it is. I don't know what you'll be looking for, but I'll bet anything that you'll know when you find it.

"But . . . but that's like invading his privacy. I mean—"

"There's something in your house that a person wants badly enough to try breaking in and maybe to harm your guard. Aren't you even curious?"

Her eyebrows shot up. "I hadn't seen it that way. Come over and let's do this together in case I don't know it when I see it."

He stroked his chin as he mused over her suggestion, not sure he wanted to wade through another man's secrets, especially those of his friend.

"You sure that's a good idea? If he'd wanted me to know about it, he would have entrusted me with it."

"On the other hand, whatever it is—and we don't know that there *is* anything—could have taken place before he met you. Right?"

"Possible. Can we get started this week?" He pressed the intercom. "Irene, how's my docket for Thursday?"

"Friday is your only clear day this week, and I have two requests for appointments for that day. Shall I make them?"

"I'll let you know." He flicked off the intercom. "How's Friday?" She agreed, reluctantly, he thought, and wondered whether she anticipated something unpleasant. "I won't be in Friday," he told Irene.

Martha Greene was first to arrive for the board meeting, and as far as Melinda was concerned that signaled the tenor of the deliberations, as the members couldn't agree on anything except the date for the next meeting. Throughout the bickering and jostling for status, Blake remained silent, his long graceful fingers strumming the table as he watched each participant. With luck, she thought, Martha Greene would finally accost Jonathan Riley, the school principal, and they could leave. She couldn't have had a worse disaster even if she'd put her father on the board. After forty minutes, she asked Betty Leeds to close the meeting.

"Don't worry," Betty assured Melinda, "whenever you get this crowd together, they scrap and argue at first, but eventually they get down to business. Martha's a troublemaker, but she understands the importance of this foundation and its work."

"What do you think?" Melinda asked Blake after the others left.

"It's to be expected. They're all prima donnas. The foundation exists, registered and with a tax-exempt status. If it doesn't work with this group, we'll change."

"I thought they were uncooperative because of me. I can feel Martha's hostility."

"Then I'll get rid of her."

She grasped his right wrist. "Oh, no. She doesn't intimidate me, though she tries. When I'm ready, I'll put her in her place."

His left hand grazed her shoulder with such gentleness she could hardly resist stepping into him and knowing again the comfort of his arms and the sweetness of his mouth. She must have telegraphed to him her feelings, for she saw the sudden blaze in his eyes.

"I don't feel like teasing myself," he said. "I always want

you, but when you let me see that you need me—the way you did just then—I know I'm in trouble.''

"You can kiss me, can't you?" she asked him, enjoying knowing that the man she wanted desired her.

He looked at her and slowly a grin curled around his lips. "You witch." With his arms locking her to him, he pressed a quick kiss on her mouth. "If you don't get out of here, I'll have to take the day off."

She held up both hands, palms out. "All right, all right. See you Friday."

"I'm going to see my mother tomorrow, but I'll be back tomorrow night. My father didn't leave a will, and we've had one heck of a time settling my mother's affairs. I hope I can clear things up tomorrow. If you have a problem, call the agency."

"Will do. Good luck down in Six Mile. Here's a kiss." She hadn't meant to let him feel her frustration, and when he stepped back and looked at her as though puzzled, she said, "It's . . . I didn't know I was going to do that. See you Friday." With that, she rushed from the office.

Blake glanced at his watch, a twenty-year-old, five-dollar Timex that he kept to remind himself of leaner days, put his briefcase in his desk and locked it. He trusted his secretary, but he didn't want to give her the burden of keeping her mouth shut about information clients had given him in confidence.

"Be back at one-thirty, Irene."

After dashing to the elevator only to see the door close as he arrived, he sped down the four flights of stairs. Long strides took him to Mill Towne Tavern three blocks away. He'd pounded into Ethan's head the importance of being on time, and he'd almost made himself late for their meeting.

He imagined that he gaped when he saw the boy striding

toward his table dressed in a business suit. He stood and extended his hand, stunned by the change in his protégé.

"Ethan, you're a brand-new man," he said, getting recognition of the change out of the way as quickly as possible.

"Thanks, Mr. Hunter. They're paying me real good for those lectures, so I bought this suit. Would you believe soon as I showed up looking like this, the principal raised me from five eighty-five to eleven-fifty an hour."

"Sure I believe it. You think I don't enjoy wearing jeans, a sweatshirt, and a baseball cap?" He pointed to his white shirt and red and blue paisley tie. "I put this stuff on because I want to be taken seriously."

"Yeah," Ethan said, "but I get tired of this stupid tie strangling me."

"It's working."

"Looks like it. They said the kids talk about what I say in their social science class. One girl cried when I told them what it was like to be in a place where you couldn't eat until somebody fed you and even the toilet wasn't private. Last week, the principal sent me to that high school near the post office. Mostly white kids over there, and they were all upset because a boy in their school just got a twenty-five-year sentence. I did the best I could, but I felt real bad for them. Sick, man. Like walking dead."

He ordered crab cakes, french fries, and a green salad and noticed that Ethan ordered the same. "Do they serve Cokes in here?" the boy asked. Tentatively.

"Sure." He ordered a Coke for Ethan and iced tea for himself. He thought of Johnny and Phil. If only they would turn out as well as Ethan. Later, he shook hands with the boy and promised they'd have lunch again soon.

"Thanks," Ethan said. "I'm glad I had this suit. This is the first time I ate in a place like this." He raised his hand for a high five. "You da man, Mr. Hunter." The boy strode down the street, and for the first time, Blake didn't see Ethan's arrogant swagger. He didn't know when he'd felt so good about someone else's life.

His early flight the next morning brought him to Birmingham at nine-twenty. Once he'd settled in his rental car, he headed back in time. Back to the place that reminded him how far he'd come and what he'd accomplished. As he drove along the two-lane road, his heart bled for the old black women in their wide straw hats chopping autumn corn in the broiling sunshine and humidity. One woman wiped her sunburned neck with a bath towel that she kept wrapped around her waist. He looked the other way, hoping to chase the memory of his own days chopping corn in the scorching heat, and his gaze fell on the men, women, and children who crawled along rows of string beans, harvesting them by the basketful. He hoped they earned more than the thirty-five cents per five-peck basket that he made as a twelve-year-old.

He crossed the brook, the one bit of picturesque scenery he'd enjoyed as a boy, and when he'd learned how to fish and often taken home a sizable catch, his father hadn't minded the time he spent there. Dreaming. As he drove up to his mother's house, no longer an unpainted shack in need of repair, but a glistening white bungalow with green shutters and awnings, he remembered that whenever one of them came home from school or the fields where they'd been working, she always greeted them at the door. He smiled as she stepped out on the porch before he cut the motor. Her arms enveloped him and he understood again the meaning of the word home. Home, the place where one could count on unconditional love. Immediately, he asked himself if he could find that with Melinda.

"It's so good you're here. Come on in," she said. "I'm all ready to go."

He asked how she managed alone. "Emotionally, I mean."

"I get a call from one of you children almost every evening, and the ladies at church ... well, you wouldn't believe how faithful they are. I'm hardly ever alone on the weekends." She waved her hand around to encompass all she saw. "And you can see that I have more than I need."

"Anything you need done here in the house?"

"Thanks, but John did what was needed last weekend. I'm fine."

After a lunch of fried ham, crackling corn bread, string beans stewed with smoked ham hocks, and butter beans with okra, he told her, "You're lucky if I don't stretch out and go to sleep. I haven't had a meal like that since the last time I was home."

"Don't you want some peach pie?"

"Sure I do, but where will I put it?" He looked around. "You can't know how happy I am that you're so comfortable and that Papa could enjoy the last years of his life."

She walked with him to the glass-enclosed, air-conditioned back porch and sat with him in the swing. "What about you, son? John and Callie have someone in their lives. I don't know if it's permanent, but at least they're not alone. Have you found someone special?"

"I think I have," he said, "but it's so complicated." He told her about Melinda and her marriage to Prescott Rodgers. "I want to believe in her integrity. I need to believe it, but whenever I do, something happens to shake my faith."

She took his hand. "Do you love her?"

He nodded. "I don't doubt that, at least."

"Then why can't you ask her questions and accept her answers? Ask her how she came to know him and what their agreement was about their marriage."

"She's told me, and I believe her." He told his mother about the will.

"What would you have done if she'd found someone and told you she was getting married?"

He heard the groans that eased from his throat and the words of truth that came from his lips. "I don't think I would have let her do it. I don't know what I would have done, but I'd have stopped it."

"And she'd have lost the inheritance."

"Thank God it didn't come to that."

She shook his arm as if to make certain he heard her. "Are you going to make her give it up?"

He turned and looked at her. "What choice do I have?"

A long sigh escaped her. "I never dreamed that a stupid person was capable of getting a law degree from Columbia University. I thought that was an Ivy League school."

His head spun around, and he eyed her until she got up and left the porch. "I'm ready to go when you are," she threw over her shoulder, and walked on into the house singing "Precious Memories."

At the office of the county clerk in Birmingham, they settled the material legacy of Woodrow Wilson Hunter's life. Then, Blake drove his mother back to Six Mile and accepted the peach pie that she gave him to take home.

"Maybe in the winter you'll come up to Ellicott City and spend a few weeks with me."

Observing him closely, she said, "All right. I wouldn't promise, but I want to meet that girl."

"Melinda."

"Nice. I hope she's like her name."

He thought for a minute. "She is." He hugged his mother, got in the car, and headed for the Birmingham airport.

On an impulse, Melinda drove to her parents' home after she left Blake's office. She had expected to find her mother alone, but her father answered the door.

"So you came by to lick your wounds, did you?" he said before she could greet him.

"I don't understand," she said, and that was the truth.

"I hear tell your board meeting this morning was a flop. Martha screwed the bunch of you. If I'd been there, I would have shut her up quicker than she could say 'ugly.' Don't stand out there. Come on in."

Her father was tall and lanky, and she had to reach up to kiss his cheek. "Papa, when I get good and tired of her, you'll hear about it. Where's Mama?"

"She's at the senior center arranging a birthday party for one of 'em. She doesn't have enough to do here." He rubbed his chin and looked at his hand as if to examine the damage done by the stubble. "And wouldn't you think that poor ninety-seven-year-old woman is bored with birthday parties by now? Same old tasteless cake and—"

She stared at the merriment dancing in his brown eyes and interrupted him, though she knew he hated that. "Papa, you are meddling with that poor woman. Do you know her?"

He rolled his eyes and looked toward the heavens. "Do I? Ever since I could crawl. I wonder if she's still chewing Sir Walter Raleigh pipe tobacco." He shook his head. "Never knew where she'd spit."

"She lived near your folks?" This was getting interesting. If she'd ever caught him in such a frivolous mood, she didn't remember it.

"Right across the street. She'd sit on that old front porch and beg everybody who passed. 'Gimmie little somethin'. God'll bless you.' Spitting and begging. We used to go out the back way and steal up the other street where she couldn't see us."

In her mind's eye, she could see her grandparents and parents tipping stealthily in and out of their own home, and all of a sudden, giggles poured out of her. Uncontrollable.

"Why is she living at the seniors' home, Papa?" Melinda asked after she gained control.

He put his hands in the back pockets of his slacks. "She outlived all of her kin and most everybody else she knew when she was able to get around. Who's going to help her, other than my wife? Everybody who remembers her is scared of getting spit on."

He headed for the kitchen, opened the refrigerator, and poured two glasses of lemonade. "Here. Have a seat," he said. "Daughter, I don't want you to fool around and waste your fortune. If you don't want it, give it to somebody who needs it. That's your Christian duty." She should have known he would get around to that.

"Papa, would you expect me to marry a man just so I could get money? I'd have to share a bed with him, Papa, and I can't do that."

He cleared his throat. "Well, when you put it like that, it sounds awfully bad. But I keep thinking there's a reason why Prescott tacked that rider onto his will. He wasn't my favorite person, but he wasn't stupid or foolish. Now you think about that."

"I will, Papa. I promise." She kissed his cheek, and for a man who hated to be touched, he smiled and patted her shoulder. She left him, wondering if he'd had a vision of his imminent demise.

If only she didn't have to tackle Prescott's things. She'd never been in his walk-in closet, though she'd looked in it a time or two, and his clothes still hung there. The thought of sifting through all that, plus Lord knows what was in the basement, was sick making. She'd planned to ask Rachel to help her, but since Blake suspected they might find secrets, that wouldn't be clever. She hated to ask her mother, because she had too much to do as it was.

She stopped in Ludie's Good Eatings, around the corner

from the Ellicott City B&O Railroad Station Museum, the oldest railroad station in the United States, to buy some homemade raspberry jam.

"Rachel," she said, "what a nice surprise. I was just going to eat lunch alone. Can you join me?"

Rachel appeared to think it over. "Okay. Maybe we need to air out some things. I called you Friday night, but Ruby said you'd gone away for the weekend. Mind if I ask where you went?"

They took a table in Ludie's outdoor café in the back of the store and ordered lemonade. Melinda didn't want to give up Rachel's friendship, and now was as good a time as any to find out whether the woman planned to continue her pursuit of Blake.

"I spent the weekend on the Chesapeake Bay and got caught in an electric storm while I was out on the water. I'll never forget it."

"You weren't by yourself."

"No, thank goodness."

"I'm glad you're safe. I know I haven't acted like it, but you're still my best friend. Like you said, I just have this terrible habit of getting interested in men who don't show an interest in me. I want you to know that I . . . I took your advice, and I'm getting help for it. I don't think it's pathological because I hardly ever think about Blake these days."

Melinda searched Rachel's face for evidence that she was fabricating the story and saw none. "I'm glad, because I also want us to be friends. We couldn't be, though, if you decided to go for Blake. He's . . . He's very important to me."

"I know that, and I know he's interested in you. I can't imagine what got into me, Melinda."

They ate their club sandwiches and ice cream and prepared to leave. "I hear Martha Greene trashed the board meeting yesterday morning. If I were you, I'd kick her off. She's such a busybody. She'll give you trouble as long as she's on that board.''

Melinda's father claimed that a dog who brings a bone will carry a bone. Rachel was her friend, but in Ellicott City, gossip ruled, and being the first to tell something could put your status on a par with that of the mayor, at least temporarily. She changed the subject.

"I'm considering adding my brother Paul, not as a board member, but as an advisor to the board. He's just what that board needs.''

"That'll upset some of them.''

Melinda's shrug, long and leisurely, indicated that she didn't care. "Let it. They're all convinced that I'm a woman of questionable virtue, so they'll probably say I violated the terms of the will. To them, I'm a scarlet woman. They have no proof, but that's what they think. I'm not going to waste time trying to please them.''

She bade Rachel good-bye, glad that they'd mended their relationship. However, she had never been one to learn a lesson a second time, and she intended to keep a little distance between them.

As she turned into her garage, Gordon, the detective, got out of his car and walked over to her. "Mrs. Rodgers, I thought you'd like to know we've located Tillman.''

Chapter Ten

Around seven-thirty that evening, Blake turned off Route 40 into Ridge Road and headed home. Six blocks from his house, his cell phone rang, and he pulled over to the curb because he didn't talk on the phone while driving if he could avoid it.

"Hunter."

"This is Gordon, Mr. Hunter. I'm going off duty in half an hour, and a guard named Mitchell will replace me. We've located Tillman, and you'll get a full report in a day or two."

A day or two! "I just got back in town, Gordon, and I'll be over there in ten minutes. I don't want to wait 'a day or two' to find out what happened to the man. This is important."

"Okay. I'll wait here for you."

Blake swung the Cougar around, and in less than ten minutes parked in Melinda's driveway. The detective walked around to meet him.

"What happened?"

"We don't really know. Around one o'clock today, Tillman came to himself sitting in a park in Alexandria, Virginia. He had no identification, no money, and he was hungry. He hailed a Virginia park policeman who took him to a police station. He remembers shaking hands with a man who asked him for directions, but nothing after that until he came to himself on that park bench. The police called the agency, verified his story, and the agency sent a guy to bring him back here."

"In other words, our man drugged Tillman when he shook his hand."

"Looks like it. I won't be shaking anybody's hand unless I know 'em," Gordon said. "You can put your life on that."

"Does Mrs. Rodgers know this?"

Gordon nodded. "I told her as soon as we heard from Tillman."

She might be uneasy, maybe even frightened. "Thanks. I'll see how she's doing. Let me know when Mitchell arrives."

He phoned Melinda. "Hi. Gordon told me what happened. I'd like to speak with you. Would you please open the door?"

"I'll be right down."

After telling her what he knew of the case, he added, "Instead of starting on sorting out Prescott's papers Friday, I think we'd better begin tomorrow if you haven't planned anything more pressing. I'll clear my appointments."

Strains of fatigue showed in her sweet face and in the slope of her shoulders, and it pained him to tax her more, but he wasn't satisfied as to her safety, not even with around-the-clock guards. Guards that were expensive Band-Aids on a problem the dimensions and dangers of which they couldn't even guess.

"I realize this may be getting to you, honey, but we have to find out what the guy's after. I'll be with you all the way."

She patted his arm, though with little apparent enthusiasm. "I know you will. All right. We'll start tomorrow. Incidentally,

I'm going to ask my brother, Paul, to serve as permanent advisor to the board. If he's there, they won't behave as they did yesterday.''

"He's straitlaced?"

She laughed, obviously enjoying a private joke. "He likes to make other people toe the line, although if he ever toed it, I wasn't there to see it. He's efficient. You'll like him."

"If he's like you, I will. Kiss me, and don't lay it on thick; I'm tired."

Her eyes sparkled in that devilish way that fascinated him and made him want to explore every facet of her. "I'm not. Why should I bother if I can't do it like I want to?"

"I'm not going to ask you to explain that. Kiss me, woman."

"Hmmm," she said and raised her arms to him at what seemed like a snail's pace. Her fingers skimmed the side of his face, moved slowly to his neck and then to the back of his head, taking her time as if postponing the minute she would reach her goal. He waited, and heat began to sear his loins as he anticipated the second that she would open her mouth to him. Just before she parted her lips, she glanced up at him, and let him see the desire in her eyes, heating him to boiling point. He squeezed her to him, held her head, and plunged into her. When she gripped his hips, locking him to her body, he rose against her. She battled him for his tongue, got it, and sucked it deep into her mouth. He'd promised himself it wouldn't happen again until he'd cleared his mind of doubt about her and could give himself to her totally. But she moved against him, letting him know that she needed him, and he jumped against her belly. Fully aroused.

"Melinda, baby, I don't think—"

"I need you."

She loosened his tie and slipped it from his neck, and tremors raced through him at the thrill of her fingers unbuttoning first his shirt, then unhooking his belt and reaching for his zipper.

Having a woman undress him until she had him naked, an experience he'd last had when he was four years old, sent his libido into high gear and his blood racing through his veins. She unzipped him, and he took the packet from his pocket and let his trousers drop to the floor. He stepped out of them and kicked them aside, never taking his gaze from the heat and excitement in her eyes.

With one hand, she let the strap of her sundress fall to her left elbow, exposing one full and glistening globe, and he didn't try to control the wildness that flared up in him like a raging storm. Then she locked her gaze to his own and lowered the other strap, baring herself fully to his pleasure. He stared at her, mesmerized, as her tongue moved slowly around her lips, dampening them.

"Kiss me. Love me. Drive me out of my mind," she murmured.

Captivated, he unzipped the dress and let it pool at her feet, exposing all but her lover's gate, hidden from his eyes by the skimpiest of red bikinis. Erotic. She was an aphrodisiac wiggling in his arms, and he hardened against her belly.

For a minute, he fought the savage, uncivilized, and unfamiliar hunger gnawing his insides.

She whispered, "Darling, I'm—"

The drunken sheen in her eyes hurled him over the edge, and he swallowed the remainder of her words in his kiss, picked her up, and looked around. Everything seemed to swim before him, to merge, chair into sofa, window into wall, floor into ceiling, as desire ravaged his nervous system. He knelt with her on the carpet in front of the fireplace, but he sensed at once that she wanted command, handed her the condom, and rolled over on his back. She peeled off his bikini underwear, shielded him, and straddled his body, her beautiful breasts inches from his hungry mouth. He suckled her left one and fondled the right breast until she moaned and squirmed above him. Excited at

her brazenness, he let his fingers trail down her body past her
navel to her secret folds and found her damp and ready. Quickly,
he penetrated her heat, and she moved upon him until he was
helpless beneath the onslaught of her merciless motions. He
sucked her breast into his mouth and stroked her back and her
buttocks, and still she rode him. Her quivers, squeezing and
pumping, began, dragging him out of himself, possessing him,
sucking him in like quicksand until he threw his arms wide
and shouted in surrender. Nothing remained of his own as he
gave her the essence of his loins and of himself. She leaned
forward and kissed his lips, as moisture from her eyes dripped
onto his cheeks.

He lay beneath her, stunned and shattered, depleted of energy.
It cost him an effort even to open his eyes, but he had to look
at her, at this woman who had finally brought him to heel, in
whose body he had at last lost the will to resist and had finally
enjoyed the glory of complete fulfillment and total release.

"How do you feel?" he asked her. "You had me in such a
fog that I couldn't make sure I'd . . . that you got what you
needed. Did you get straightened out?"

Her arms went around his shoulders, and she hugged him
and kissed his neck. "You mean release? Yes, I had that.
Thank you. But you gave me something more than that, more
precious." She smiled through the tears that rolled down her
cheeks. "You . . . I don't quite know what happened, but I felt
you were mine. At the end there, you'd never given yourself
to me like that. . . ."

He kissed the tears that rolled down her cheeks. "Why are
you crying?"

"I . . . I'm not crying. I'm . . . I'm just . . . happy."

He closed his eyes, separated them, and held her in his arms.
No doubt about it, he had to get to the bottom of the mysteries
surrounding her because he couldn't see beyond the place she
occupied in his heart.

Minutes later, he said, "I've never felt this way before."

She didn't answer nor did she caress him. When he could no longer stand her silence, he leaned over and looked into her face to gauge her mood. Her eyes were closed, and her breasts rose and fell rhythmically as he observed her in peaceful sleep. This sweet and tender loving woman. He grazed her lips with his own, and she opened her eyes.

"I need to go home. If I'm coming here tomorrow morning, I have to write a brief and draw up a contract before I sleep tonight."

With her hands over her head, she yawned and stretched, long and leisurely. "I could help."

"I don't doubt that you'd want to, but on this night with you in my house, my mind wouldn't be on contracts and legal briefs. I wouldn't sleep a wink and neither would you. So I'll see you in the morning."

For once, he didn't find his work inviting as he dragged himself away from her. "Every time I'm with you," he whispered, "I find something else that endears you to me even more." Covering her with her sundress, he said, "Stay where you are. I'll be here around ten."

He knelt and brushed her mouth with his own, then held her gaze as she stared at him with luminous eyes, her feelings bare. Humbled by what she'd given him and what her eyes promised, he sucked in his breath and left, wondering at his luck.

Later that night, lying in bed, Melinda mused over their lovemaking, trying to figure out what had happened that night that was so different from the other times they'd made love. At the beginning, he'd been slow to cooperate, as if he didn't like their reversed positions. And then he'd caught fire, transmitted it to her and literally abandoned himself to her, moving as she moved until, at the end, he'd given himself over to her.

She hadn't known a person could experience what she felt when his body shook with release and he lay vulnerable and bare in her arms. Happy. She'd never been so happy. Was it the beginning of a new day for them? She turned out the light and slept soundly.

At ten o'clock the next morning, dressed in a red T-shirt, stretch jeans, and sneakers, she opened the door for Blake, who picked up the *Maryland Journal* and handed it to her.

"Good morning, Mrs. Rodgers," he said and walked in past her.

Her eyes widened, and the bottom dropped out of her belly. Had last night been something she dreamed? She spun around to confront him, and the glare in her eyes dissolved into a grin. That six-foot-four-inch, one-hundred-and-ninety-pound man stood there open, vulnerable, and almost scared. One thing was certain, he looked as if he were defenseless, that he needed protection. Her first reaction was, *What a great time to have my way with him.* She couldn't control the mirth that poured out of her in peals of laughter.

"Something's funny?"

She straightened up as best she could. "Uh, yes . . . I mean no. I mean . . . I'm not going to . . . to get out of line. Besides, I can't. Ruby's here."

It was the best she could do, but that didn't erase his frown. "I just want to make sure we spend the day doing what we're supposed to be doing."

"And when did we ever do something we weren't supposed to be doing?"

At that, his vulnerableness evaporated, his face took on a dark and thunderous expression, and his eyes seemed to shoot fire. "You know exactly what I'm talking about."

In other words, don't play with him this morning. "Coffee's ready. Want some toast or a crumpet? Have you had anything to eat?"

The thunderclouds disappeared, and his eyes sparkled with the smile that always made his face beautiful. "I had orange juice. A cup of coffee would make me human."

Her eyebrows went up. "Lord, let me get that coffee." She went into the kitchen and asked Ruby to bring them coffee on the sun porch. "Mr. Hunter will be helping me here in the house today."

"All right. I knows what he likes. I'll bring the coffee. For the rest, give me 'bout ten minutes."

Blake finished the buttermilk biscuits, grits, scrambled eggs, and sausage and sipped his third cup of coffee. "Ruby knows how to feed a man. This was wonderful, like being home with my mother." He took a sheet of paper from his shirt pocket. "Unless you know what's in the basement, I mean what's on the inside of every box and piece of furniture, I suggest we start there."

She put her right elbow on the table and propped up her chin. "I can see that this may take days."

"It may, but if there's an alternative, I don't know what it is."

"Okay, let's get with it. We're in the basement," she called to Ruby.

"Yes, ma'am, Miz Melinda. What time y'all gonna be wantin' lunch?"

"One o'clock will be fine?" She looked at Blake, and he nodded.

"One o'clock," she called to Ruby.

"I haven't spent a lot of time down here," she said, opening a big seaman's trunk. They found rolls of parchment containing diagrams of chemical processes drawn in different colors of ink.

"Wonder why this wasn't locked?" she asked, more herself than Blake.

"That occurred to me too."

An ancient Aetna cedar chest that might have been inherited from Prescott's mother revealed several silver trays, a silver flatware service for twelve, blackened with age and neglect, and linen tablecloths and napkins. She'd attempted to open the chest once while Prescott was alive, but it had been locked. She mentioned it to him, but he didn't open it. She told Blake as much.

"He might have unlocked this chest and the trunk when he realized he was terminally ill. That would make sense," Blake said.

By lunchtime, their search had yielded nothing that might tell them why a man wanted to get in that house.

"What's next?" Blake asked after they'd eaten. "Feel like going through his personal things?"

"I don't feel like it, but we have to do it. Let's start in the den, and if we don't find anything there, we'll check the bedroom."

Finding nothing in the den, they went to his bedroom, which was as Prescott left it when he went to the hospital.

"I don't feel right going through a man's personal things," Blake told her. "I'll just sit in here with you."

She didn't feel like it either, but it had to be done. "I wish I could drop the whole thing."

Around four, Ruby walked into the room with a tray of iced tea and oatmeal cookies. "I don't know what you lookin' for, but the one place he always kept locked from the time I come here was that closet across the hall beside Miz Melinda's room. I ain't never seed it unlocked."

Blake tried the doorknob. "It's locked. Got a screwdriver and pair of pliers?" he asked Ruby.

"In the closet on the back porch. I'll be right back with 'em."

"I'll get them." He opened the closet door and gasped. Rows

of cassettes obviously arranged in an order understandable to their owner. "Come here, Melinda, and look at this."

"Well, I'll be . . ." she said when she could force a sound from her lips.

She remembered Prescott having told her, "That's my old chemical stuff in there. I keep it locked, because that's all behind me now."

"Let's take a couple from the top and play them," she said.

Blake jumped to his feet when he heard his voice. Prescott had taped their conversation about his funeral arrangements. "What the hell! He didn't have to do that. I gave him a signed statement of everything he'd agreed to. I thought the man trusted me."

So Blake didn't know. She stopped the tape, pulled a chair over to where he sat, and took a seat beside him. "You didn't know that Prescott had dyslexia and couldn't read or write? He could barely sign his name, and sometimes he got the letters in the wrong order."

"What? You're telling me that . . . I knew that man well for seven years. He was one of my first clients, and we were close friends. Now you're telling me—"

She placed a hand on his arm. "Did you ever see him write or read anything?"

He thought for a long time, bemusement mirrored on his face. "Only his signature, and I once teased him about that, suggesting that he should have been a doctor. I remember my uneasiness at his response: 'I wish I could have been. It was my childhood dream.' He was so solemn." Blake shook his head.

"Blake," she said, pressing his wrist with her hand, "it's because of that affliction that I knew Prescott." She told him how they met and about the conditions he offered for marriage. "I was so glad to be out from under my father and to have a friend whose company I enjoyed. Yes, the comfort of his home attracted me, because I had spent a couple of hours a day with him for nearly a year before he mentioned marriage, and I knew the place. You must know the terms of our marriage, since you were his attorney.''

"He didn't share that with me. Unable to read and write. That boggles my mind. A brilliant man. Think what he might have done and who he could have become if he'd been literate.''

"I've thought of that many times. I'm the only person in this town who knew, or so I think. He remembered whatever he heard and saw, compensating for his handicap.''

Blake stretched out his legs and locked his hands behind his head, deep in thought. "Whenever I invited him out to lunch or dinner, he gave me an excuse for wanting to eat here at home. And now, I see it was because he couldn't read a menu.''

She got up. "Let's see what else we'll find.'' More cassettes revealed that Prescott recorded all of his business conversations and everything about his work, including his inventions.

"Let's finish this tomorrow. I've had a surfeit of chemical terms, stuff I haven't thought of since my first year in college.''

"What time tomorrow?'' she asked.

"Same time. Okay?'' She nodded, and he laughed. "You're going to behave yourself tonight, baby, because Ruby is here.''

"She's not my mother.''

A grin began around his bottom lip and strayed up to those eyes that she adored. "No? Well, for tonight, at least, she's mine, and I am circumspect around my mother. Come here, and keep the heat down.''

"You're joking. That's like pouring oil on a fire and expecting it to die out. How'm I supposed to keep it down when you're a human generator?''

"Try. You'd be surprised at what you can do with a little self-control.''

"Says you. I had over twenty-nine years of self-control. You let this bird out of the cage, honey, and you needn't expect her to fly back in there willingly.''

He grasped her shoulders and smiled. Sweet. Lord, she adored him. "You like it out here, do you?" he asked her, barely containing the grin.

"If I need self-control, you could use a little ego deflation.'' She reached up and grazed his mouth with her lips. "Don't expect this often. But since I wore you out last night, I'm letting you off."

His laugh, full throated and rippling with mirth, excited and thrilled her. "I don't accept challenges, baby, when they're aimed at bending my will. I'm on to you. Kiss me."

Just as she leaned into him, his fingers gripped her waist, and he set her away from him. Then he brushed her lips, her cheeks, and her eyelids with such tenderness that she felt chastened and, in a symbol of remorse, rested her head on his shoulder.

"I don't just want you," she whispered. "I care for you. See you tomorrow morning."

He gazed into her face until she became giddy from the pounding of her heart and the lurching of her pulse. "And I care for you," he said. "A whole lot."

He released her then, and loped down the stairs. "What's for breakfast in the morning?" he called to Ruby, who responded, "Same thing, Mr. Blake. You know I knows what you likes."

Melinda heard the door close. He cared for her. How could she go through with her plan to leave Ellicott City as soon as the board was functioning smoothly? How could she leave Blake?

He spoke with Mitchell, the guard, for a few minutes, got in his car, and headed home. In the kitchen, he took a pepperoni pizza from the freezer and put it in the microwave. Totally at loose ends, he wandered through the living and dining room until he heard the microwave's beep. With a bottle of Pilsner and the pizza, he sat in front of the TV and tried to eat his dinner. Something was totally out of kilter and he hadn't put his finger on it. While surfing TV channels, he passed Chris Rock, all teeth and smiles, and flicked back, because something the man said pricked his memory. He thought he'd heard the comedian say that lonely women didn't do wicked things because they were too desperate. Rock was already on another subject. Blake flicked off the TV and got another Pilsner.

The telephone interrupted his mental meandering. "Hi, Callie," he said after hearing her voice. "What's up?"

"I just talked with Mama, and I thought she seemed kind of down." They talked for a while, and he promised to visit their mother the following weekend.

"You don't have to. I'm going there for the week. Just give her a call. Maybe she's lonely."

He imagined she was, but she didn't appear to be when he called her, so he satisfied himself that he could stay with Melinda until they finished searching Prescott's effects. Imagine spending a lifetime hiding illiteracy. He nearly jumped from his chair. Rather than cheat Prescott, Melinda had befriended him, and Prescott had adored her. Whenever she was in the room with them, Prescott's gaze had followed his wife's every move with an expression that was nothing short of adoration. How could Blake have been so wrong? But why was she so lackadaisical about that inheritance? It didn't make sense.

He spent an hour and a half in his office before going to Melinda's house. Ruby greeted him. "Your breakfast is ready, and I got some good old hot buttermilk biscuits I made this morning. I loves cooking for mens. Miz Melinda don't eat enough to keep a bird flying. You come on in the sun porch. I'll tell her you here."

After breakfast, he kissed Ruby on each cheek, took Melinda's hand, and the two of them streaked up the stairs. "With luck, we'll get at least a clue out of these cassettes."

After listening to each one, they labeled it. "Let's check out some of these," she said, pointing to the bottom of a row.

"You have no claim to this process." It was Prescott's voice, though much younger than in recent years. "I told you about it, thinking you were a friend, and you have the gall to claim partnership!"

"You read this contract and signed it, making me your legal fifty/fifty partner not only in that film-processing fluid, but in the company we'll set up to produce it," a male voice replied.

"Don't be a fool, Reginald. I don't sign contracts, and that is not my signature."

"Nobody will be able to tell the difference. Nobody on the face of this earth. I worked for you for five years and got a pittance compared to what you stashed away. I'll get my share or else."

"I can afford to forget about that fluid and let it die right where it is, a sketch on my drafting table. I don't need another penny, and before I'll let you cheat me out of my work, I won't develop it. You and I are finished. If you don't want to be sued for blackmail, stay out of my life."

Blake looked at Melinda. "Blackmail? What ... What a mess. This fellow, Reginald, must have discovered that Prescott couldn't read."

They played the last of the tape: "Light green on yellow parchment. The end."

They stood as one. "The trunk," they said simultaneously and headed for the basement.

"Here it is," he said, after unrolling the diagram that was clearly the work of a chemist. Tubes, glass globes, Bunsen burner, and cylinders drawn in intricate architectural fashion, with an assortment of colors that were evidently for identification.

They stared at each other. "This is it," she said. "What else could it be?"

"Let's put it back for now. The next thing is to ask Ruby what she knows about the man named Reginald."

"Why y'all want to know?" Ruby asked.

"We're trying to straighten out all of Prescott's affairs," Melinda said, and he gave her points for discretion.

Ruby sat down. "I told you 'bout him, didn't I? He was the last friend coming here till Mr. Blake here come to dinner that first time. A few years 'fore that, Mr. Reginald practically lived here. I tell you that man done et more of my food than Mr. Rodgers ever et."

"Did he ever come here when my husband wasn't home?" Melinda asked Ruby, and he could see the anxiety in her face.

"All the time, Miz Melinda. He kept a lot of his things up there in that closet of yours."

"Did you like him?" he asked her, hoping to get a clue as to the man's personality.

Ruby lowered her head. "No, sir. He thought he was better'n me."

He thanked her and let his hand graze her shoulder. "Nobody's better than you are, Ruby, and anyone who thinks so is your inferior."

He'd seen Melinda vexed, but not angry, and the fury blazing in her eyes now as she asked Ruby, "What was his last name?" surprised him.

"Goodman or Goodwin, I think. I never remembers for sure, Yes. Reginald Goodwin. But Mr. Rodgers ain't had nothin' to do with him in years."

"What did he look like?" Melissa asked her.

"Real ordinary, except for them thick eyebrows. He wont young, 'cause his hair was salt and pepper, almost silver. But he sure had plenty of it. And he wore them black, horn-rimmed glasses what made him look like a professor."

She'd mentioned those eyebrows when she saw Tillman's camcorder photo of the man who drove by the house in a green Chevrolet. Blake went upstairs and called the police station.

"This is Blake Hunter. Brick, you remember the picture of that man who drove by Melinda Rodgers's house in a green Chevrolet? Yeah. Could you get an artist to change that picture to gray hair and eyebrows and black horn-rimmed glasses? Great. I think we may have him."

After hanging up, he said to Melinda, "I'd lock that cassette up if I were you. Better still, if you have a blank cassette, I'll copy it for you. You may have to give the original to a prosecuting attorney." He copied it and gave them both to her. "Don't forget the board meeting Monday morning."

She stared at him, or was that a glare? "Today is Friday, and you're telling me what will happen on Monday? That's three days from now."

Where was his head? "When it comes to mixing business and pleasure, I'm rough around the edges. Never done it before."

She parked her fists on her hipbones and looked at him from slightly lowered lashes. "What were you mixing with me Wednesday night on the living room floor? Oh, yes. And that kiss last night that knocked my socks off, you do that for all your clients? If I'm getting my signals mixed, please forgive me."

He walked over to her and wrapped his arms around her. "Baby, will you stop acting out and have dinner with me tomorrow night? I was going to call you, but if leaving like this raises your dander, I'll just save myself a phone call. If I get here around seven, will you open the door?" He didn't want to laugh as he watched her deflate, but he couldn't help it.

Her faced softened, and she began to laugh. He stroked her, soft, warm, and sweet in his arms, and when she reached up and kissed him, joy suffused him. "Honey," he said, "we don't have to hit the pinnacle every single time we're together, do we? The thought of you has had me keyed up for so long, I wouldn't mind unwinding, but I'd have to do it slowly. Want to spend a weekend at Cape May? The water's still great.''

With her face relaxed and a smile playing around her lovely brown eyes, he didn't think he'd ever seen her look so mischievous. ''You are one sweet-talking con man.'' She pinched his nose. ''I'll let you know. See you tomorrow at seven.'' He kissed her cheek and left, satisfied that he'd get a warm welcome the next evening.

''Miz Melinda, is that Reginald what's-his-name been up to somethin'? I tell you I never did trust that man, and I told Mr. Rodgers that more'n once.'' She rambled on, not waiting for an answer. ''Mr. Blake ain't staying for dinner? He such a good eater. I loves to cook for him. Well, I guess it's a bunch of veggies and a piece of broiled fish again tonight,'' she grumbled. ''At this rate, I'll lose my skills.''

She didn't want to give Ruby too much information. She trusted her, but Ruby would tell Piper who would tell ... ''Ruby, I hadn't touched Mr. Rodgers's things, and I'm fortunate that Mr. Hunter offered to help me sort them out. After a while, I'll do some entertaining, and you'll have a chance to show off your cooking. Is that better?''

''Shore is.''

Melinda went up to her room and telephoned her brother. ''Paul, I want you to do something for me,'' she said after they had talked for a while. She explained about the will. ''Everybody in this town is convinced that if I'd been a decent woman, I wouldn't have married Prescott. Now I've formed the board, and they're being disrespectful. I can't make you a member of the board, but I want you to be permanent advisor. We hope to meet once a month, and I'll ask Blake Hunter, the executor of Prescott's will, to pay your travel expenses. With you there—''

"You won't have one thing to worry about. I'll see that they shape up."

"Monday morning at ten?"

"Sure. Meet me at the airport at nine."

Monday morning at ten-fifteen, Melinda walked into Blake's conference room, Paul at her side, looked around, and enjoyed a private joke. Martha Greene nodded slowly and pursed her lips as if to say, "Didn't I tell you so?" and Melinda didn't doubt that everyone present except Blake expected her to announce that she'd be marrying the man at her side, her inheritance now ensured.

She walked over to Blake, who had stood when she entered the room. "Mr. Hunter, this is my brother, Professor Paul Jones." After introducing each board member, she grasped Blake's arm, held it, and said softly, "Paul, this is Blake."

She turned around, looked at them, and nearly laughed at the disappointment on their faces. "Ms. Leeds, Paul will be permanent advisor to the board and will attend all of its meetings. Paul, Betty Leeds is board president."

Melinda didn't miss the wry amusement in Betty's face and tone as she opened the meeting. Martha Greene picked up her discussion of rules of procedure where she'd left off at the previous raucous meeting.

"Parliamentary wrangling is out of place here," Paul said. "Let's get down to business." He looked at Betty. "Madam president, go right ahead."

Melinda watched in awe at the orderly interventions and discussion. Even Martha asked permission to speak.

After the meeting, Blake congratulated Paul. "She said you'd do it. Neither she nor I could have put Martha in her place, since the woman is suspicious of us both. I'm glad you're with us."

"I think I'm going to enjoy it, but I need all the advice you care to give me. I'm a professor of civil engineering. This stuff is Greek to me."

She felt good. They liked each other. "Let's get some lunch."

"Great," Paul said. "How about Fisherman's Creek?"

They walked the four blocks to the air-conditioned restaurant, and the sun, hot for early September, made the short hike nearly unbearable.

"I don't believe this," Melinda said.

"You don't believe what?" Blake asked her.

"That's Rachel waiting in line for a table, and she's alone. I'm having lunch with her here tomorrow."

"So it is." He paused, as though in deep thought. "Why don't you ask her to join us?"

She stared at him for a minute, and then asked Paul, "Do you know Rachel Perkins?"

"I don't think so." Melinda pointed Rachel out to him. "No, I don't," he affirmed, "but I wouldn't mind meeting her."

Blake looked at her, grinned, and shrugged. "Go ahead. One man's poison . . ."

When the four of them were seated, Melinda said, "Rachel, you know Blake. This is my brother, Paul."

She couldn't believe her eyes. Paul was attracted to Rachel. "Why did you want her to join us?" she whispered to Blake.

"Because I saw him watching her and figured he'd like to meet her. Wasn't I right?"

"Yes, and she doesn't seem immune."

After lunch, she took Rachel's arm. "I'm so glad we ran into you. Let's be in touch." But Rachel, apparently flabbergasted, just nodded. "See you later," Melinda called to Paul, knowing that he'd either stay with her or with their parents, or go immediately back to Durham, North Carolina, where he lived and taught.

"First time I've known Rachel to be speechless," Melinda said to Blake, as they walked toward her car.

"That'll be interesting to watch. I gather he isn't married."

"No. He's single. Wonder what Papa will say about that?"

"Irene told me your father sent practically everybody in Ellicott City to hell Sunday morning," Blake said. "Did you hear the sermon?"

She shook her head. "Mercifully, I overslept."

"Apparently, somebody stole a woman's pocketbook or snatched it, I don't know which, while the woman was in a booth in the church's ladies' room. From what I heard, he said that if the person doesn't confess and give it back, he'd commend their soul to the devil."

"And he'll do it, too. When may I give this board over to Betty Leeds and go on with my life like the rest of the local citizenry?"

He pulled in his top lip, took a deep breath, and let it out slowly. "Are you telling me you've done all you plan to do in fulfillment of this will?"

"Exactly."

He kicked at the pavement with the toe of his left shoe. "In that case, you have to work with me to decide how to dispose of the estate among charitable organizations, or help me decide on one. And let's keep this under wraps."

"Whatever you say. You're the boss."

"Yeah. Right. I'll call you after I go to the police station to see what the artist did with that photo."

He gazed into her eyes, and she had the impression that he was trying to communicate something to her, something for which he didn't have words, or had them but wasn't ready to use them. *Lord, please don't let me imagine things,* she said as she slowly became enmeshed in his masculine aura. Standing on Columbia Pike Road beneath a broiling sun, the man in him leaped out at her and her breathing accelerated. He must have seen the desire that gripped her, because his eyes held an answering torch. She burned with the need to touch him, to be in his arms.

"Blake, honey, I—"

"It's all right. It just means that we . . . there's more to this than either of us realized. He squeezed her hand and smiled before walking off, but if she'd ever seen a more wooden, forced smile, she didn't recall it.

At home, she made a list of things she needed, and decided to shop for them around six o'clock when the day began to cool. She'd better track Paul down and find out whether he planned to have dinner with her.

She phoned her mother. "Mama, has Paul gotten over there yet?"

"My Paul? He's in town?"

"Yes. He's helping me with the foundation. He'll call you."

She hung up. Wow! She didn't want to call Rachel so she'd play it by ear. If he was hungry, they'd eat out.

When Blake called, his words disturbed her. "If Ruby's there, we'd like her to come to the police station and look at this photo."

"Blake, honey, I'd rather Ruby didn't get involved in this."

"So would I, but that can't be helped. If she doesn't come voluntarily, she'll get a summons. You want me to talk with her?"

"I'll drive her down there."

"Ain't no problem, Miz Melinda. If anybody done something they oughtna, they needs to be punished. Just let me get my umbrella. This sun is too much."

Ruby made a positive identification of Reginald Goodwin, and a judge issued a warrant for his arrest. "But he wasn't the goon who drugged Tillman," the chief of the detective agency said after Tillman examined the photo.

"But he knows who did it," an officer said, "and we'll get both of them."

Melinda took Ruby back to her house and drove to the shopping mall. She stepped out of the office-supply store at dusk, put her packages in the trunk, started around to the driver's side of the car, and screamed. A man lay sprawled supine between her car and the one in front of it. The mall's security arrived, detained her, and called the nearest police station.

"Well, if you didn't hit him," the officer said after she'd pleaded her innocence for twenty minutes, "you'll have an opportunity to prove it."

At the station house, she phoned Blakc. "I'll be there in a few minutes."

"The man was dead when the ambulance arrived," the policeman told Blake when he arrived.

"I was in the mall for nearly two hours," Melinda said. "You can check the time of my purchases from the cash register receipts."

"All right, ma'am. If we can get hold of that judge, you'll be free to go soon as you post bail."

"I'll take care of that," Blake said. "Let me have those receipts. I wouldn't get too upset about this if I were you. The coroner will establish the time of death, and you'll be exonerated. Tonight, you go home with me."

He called the night guard and explained that Melinda wouldn't be home. Then he took her home with him.

The next morning, Blake searched for the coffee filters. He was going to throw out the pot and all the filters. He didn't like that coffee, and he hated to give it to Melinda. He looked up and nearly laughed as she strolled into the kitchen wearing his cotton robe. "Where are you in that thing? For a minute there, I thought my robe walked in here under its own steam. Take a seat. I'll have this blasted coffee ready in a few minutes."

"Not like that, you won't. You have to put the filter in that gadget that's shaped like it, place the two over the pot, put the ground coffee in the filter, and *then* pour boiling water over it.''

He looked from her to the filter. ''You're kidding.''

''Definitely not.''

''Maybe this stuff will finally taste like coffee.'' He lit the oven. ''While those biscuits are warming, I'll cook some bacon and scrambled eggs. Or would you rather have some bran flakes?''

''Hmmm. A man who can cook. I could get used to this.''

''And I've got a few other things I'd like you to get used to.''

She raised soft round eyes to him, and he worked hard at steadying his nerves. She trusted him now, but he wouldn't bet on how she'd feel about him if she knew the role he'd played in drawing up that will. He didn't want to think about it.

Chapter Eleven

"No wonder you didn't bring the paper inside," Melinda said to Blake as they left his house. She pointed to the headline: *Melinda Jones Rodgers arrested for hit-and-run driving and possibly murder.*

"I didn't know about that." He frowned in displeasure. "I hadn't seen it."

Last night when he'd comforted and cherished her, making no demands, she'd thought her world had at last righted itself. And now this. "But you must have expected it. How can they say I hit the man and ran away? When I found him lying there, I stayed and called the police. What are these people trying to do to me?"

His arms eased around her as if to ward off the late October chill, but it failed to temper her rising anger. "Until I married, people avoided me because I was the daughter of Booker Jones, righteous judge of everybody in town. After I married, people shunned me because they decided I'd hoodwinked an old man and married him for his money.''

''Melinda. Sweetheart, don't. Stop it. You're innocent, and I'll prove it.''

She moved from the circle of his arms. ''And those ridiculous stipulations in that will, as if I'd been a lousy wife and had to do penance in order to inherit what I hadn't known existed. Prescott neither acted nor lived like a rich man.''

''Where are you going?'' he asked when she hastened down the steps.

''Home. It's mine at least for the next six months.''

''I'm taking you home.''

She didn't feel the joy that always pervaded her when his arms went around her, and she knew he realized it. They didn't speak during the short drive to her house. Feeling alienated and misrepresented, she didn't try to pretend camaraderie.

Blake stopped in front of her house, put the car in park, and left the motor running. ''You tell me you care for me, but in this crisis, you shut me out. Let me know when you feel you can talk to me. Be seeing you.'' He didn't get out to open the door for her and accompany her up the walkway to the house as he always did.

As she opened the car door, she stopped, turned, and faced him. ''As Prescott's lawyer, why did you let him do this to me? Give the money to the Belly Dancers of the World. Whoever. I don't care. Thanks for bringing me home.'' She didn't wait for his answer.

Tillman stood at the door, and she greeted him as one would an old friend. ''I'm so happy you're safe,'' she said.

''Thank you, ma'am. I sure learned me lesson. From now on, I won't be shaking hands with any man but me brother. I'm lucky I got me life.''

''Anyone snooping around this morning?''

"Not a soul, ma'am."

She put her pocketbook and the newspaper beside the vase of yellow, orange, and white chrysanthemums that adorned the table in the foyer and went to the kitchen to speak with Ruby.

"I shore was glad you left that note on the icebox." Ruby always referred to the refrigerator as the icebox. "I'd a been outa my mind. You didn't see them morning papers, did you? I declare these people is something nasty."

"I saw *The Illustrated*, that muckraking scandal sheet, and that was enough."

"Humph," Ruby said and put her hands on her hips, signifying the onset of a diatribe against somebody or something. "What they says on the inside is worse'n the headlines. I'd like to take a stick and go up against the heads of them people on that paper."

"Thanks." She didn't wait to hear more, but when she reached the foyer, she couldn't resist opening the paper.

Scarlet woman shows her colors

Widowed less than a month, Melinda Rodgers advertised for a husband. If that weren't enough, she made a spectacle of herself on a public dance floor. And now, she's accused of knocking a man dead and failing to stop and call for help. Maybe old Prescott Rodgers knew what he was doing when he made it difficult for her to inherit his fortune.

She left the paper on the table and trudged slowly up the stairs, wondering what she'd done to deserve a public flogging such as that one. She rubbed her forehead to ease the sudden pain. If only she hadn't mistreated Blake that morning. He deserved her trust and caring, but after seeing that headline, she didn't have it to give. Longing to make amends, she welcomed the ring of the phone and rushed to answer it, hoping that it was he.

"Hello." She held her breath as she waited for his voice, but it was Rachel who responded.

"Hey, girl. What's up?"

"Rachel! I ought to be asking *you* that. How are you getting on with Paul?"

"Oh, Melinda. He's ... He's super. I've never met a man like him. Sweet as sugar and absolutely no nonsense."

"That's Paul, all right. Are you ... uh ... in touch with him? Often, I mean?"

The voice softened to a purr. "He calls me all the time, and for once I don't feel as if I have to ... you know ... go after him. It's a great feeling. Look, I called to say I'm sorry about ... about all this mess. If you need me, just pick up the phone."

She thanked her, and they talked for a while, but her mind wasn't on the conversation, and she soon said good-bye. *Do what's right and take your medicine, girl.* She phoned him.

"Hello, Melinda. What can I do for you?"

At such times, she wished caller ID had never been invented. Well, only honesty worked with Blake.

"You ... you can forgive me. I shouldn't have taken my misery out on you."

His silence was deafening, and she had no choice but to wait for the verdict. After what seemed like hours, he said, "No, you shouldn't have taken it out on me, and you shouldn't have walked off with my newspaper either."

" Blake—"

"Just don't shut me out, Melinda. I want to be there for you when you need me. Are you coming to the board meeting tomorrow morning?"

"I'll be there."

"Don't let the stories in these papers drag you down. As soon as this case is settled, we'll get a retraction, or we'll sue for damages in civil court."

Winding the telephone cord around her right wrist absent-mindedly, she heard him and didn't hear him. "All I want right now is to get away from here and shake the Ellicott City dirt off my feet for good."

"You can walk off and leave me"—she heard the snap of his finger—"just like that?"

A strange tiredness seeped into her and she sat down on the bed with a sense of hopelessness. "I may not have a choice," she said and realized that she was offering him an opportunity to give her a reason to stay.

What he said was, "You will have a choice. The question is whether you'll take it."

Her nerves quickened in anticipation. "I'd appreciate a little plain English, Blake. Break it down for me so I'll know exactly what you said."

"I'm in deep. If you leave here, I'll go get you. You belong to me. You understand that? You're mine."

By the time he uttered the last word, she was standing on her feet with her left arm tight around her middle and her mouth agape. When she could collect her wits, she said, "Does that mean you no longer doubt me and mistrust me?"

"It means when I'm arm's length from you, you're too far away. You told me the circumstances of your marriage, and you gave me the proof. You said you wouldn't have deceived Prescott, that you would never have divorced him. I believe you. My gut feeling is that you're honorable, and that's what I'm going to hold on to until you disprove it."

"What a thing for you to tell me on the phone."

"I would have told you this morning, if you'd given me the chance. When your head starts to rule your heart, the way it does sometimes, let yourself remember what you and I are like when we're locked together the way God intended us to be. That ought to tell you that nothing's going to keep us apart for long."

"Are you telling me you've finally sorted things out, that *your* heart is finally ruling *your* head?"

"I doubt that will ever happen, and it doesn't have to. Last night, for the very first time, you slept in my arms. All I wanted was your contentment and safety. You must have realized that I was on fire for you, but you were more important to me than satisfying my need to make love with you. So why should you be surprised to learn that I feel this way about you?"

"Blake, I'm full to the brim. Oh, honey, I need you, but Ellicott City is beginning to suffocate me."

"Then we'll take that trip to Cape May where we'll be alone. Are you willing to try and get rid of everything that stands between us?"

"Yes. I want that more than anything."

"All right. I'll make the reservations. See you in the morning."

She hung up, and for a long time she couldn't move. Had he told her she didn't have to marry in order to receive her inheritance, or was he saying *they* should marry? *Or did he even realize what his words implied?*

Blake knew what he'd said to her, because he hadn't spoken on impulse. Sleep had come in spurts, fitful, the night before when she lay so peacefully and trusting in his arms. He'd ached with desire, but he hadn't let that bother him. What kept him from sleeping was his fear of rolling over on her, of crushing her with his big body, and of not being awake to soothe her if she awakened alarmed and needing him. While he'd cuddled her as if she were a baby, it had struck him forcibly that his reservations about her integrity were excuses not to let himself love her, not to give himself. He'd known all along that if he opened his heart fully to her, he wouldn't want to live without her. Maybe if he reread Irene's dictations of Prescott's own words stipulating the second condition in that will, he'd find an out for her, because she didn't intend to fulfill it. Furthermore, he wasn't about to give her up to another man.

He answered his cell phone. "Hunter."

"Say, Blake, this is Phil. Me and Johnny passed our tests, and we're going to regular eleventh grade classes. We already got parts in the school play, and Johnny's testing for the debating team. It's a gas, man."

He could hardly believe what he heard, that six months could bring such a change. "I'm proud of you both. Soon as I can manage it, we'll spend a Saturday afternoon doing whatever you guys want to do."

"I can tell you right now. Make it Sunday so we can see either the Ravens or the Redskins."

"Right. I'll get the tickets. Heard anything from Lobo?"

"Our counselor said he got in a nasty fight over at the Hagerstown prison where they sent him. We're not in touch with him."

One more life down the drain. "I'll let you know about the football game. Stay in touch."

Irene's notes didn't tell him anything new. Melinda either fulfilled both terms of that will or he had no choice but to give the money to charity. He lifted his shoulders in a shrug. Prescott had tied his hands, and he'd done it deliberately.

He walked into his conference room the next morning to find Martha Greene already there and ready to pounce.

She didn't waste time on preliminaries. "Melinda Rodgers shouldn't be in charge of a foundation that's so important to this community. Who's going to respect anything run by a woman blasted by every paper in town? Imagine! Running away and leaving a man to die. And that's just one of her cute little tricks. As executor of that will, it's your duty to put her off this board.''

"Good morning, Miss Greene," he said and watched her blanch at his reprimand for not having greeted him more politely. He told his temper to take a walk, leaned back in his chair, and looked her in the eye.

"Prescott Rodgers's will stipulates that, without Mrs. Rodgers, there will be no foundation. Anything else?''

Her pursed lips and jutting chin betrayed her hostility, but if she pushed him, even a little bit, he'd give her the obvious alternative.

"Yes, there is," she said between clenched teeth. "I don't see why I should spend my precious time working on this committee for free.''

He showed his teeth in what he supposed passed for a grin. "You knew when you agreed to serve that the will requires board members to volunteer their service. You said you wanted to enhance literacy and education in Ellicott City. Changed your mind?''

"Well, I have to think about it. I'll bet I'm not the only one of us who doesn't like being used like this.''

So she planned to stir up trouble. "I don't know what you've got against Mrs. Rodgers, but she discharged her responsibility when she established the board. It exists in fact and in law. Nothing you do about it will affect her personally. If you don't want to serve . . .'' He let it hang.

"I'd hate for you to miss the reception I'm planning as an occasion to introduce the board members to the community.'' Let her digest that.

Blake stood when Melinda and Paul arrived. He knew his gaze devoured her and that Martha would broadcast what she saw as soon as she left his office, but he was powerless to withhold the evidence of his adoration. He walked toward them.

"Hello, Melinda. Good to see you, Paul." Paul's quizzical glances from Melinda to him told him that he'd bared his feelings. Suddenly, he didn't care. Still, relief spread through him, when the other board members arrived and he could concentrate on business rather than on Melinda. He didn't want to subject her to the gossip that would begin even before the meeting closed.

"What about at least paying expenses for board members?" Martha began. "We ought to be remunerated, but if that's not legal, Mr. Hunter has to take care of what it costs us to attend these meetings."

"If any of you spends more than a dollar for gas getting to and from these meetings," Paul said, "let me know, and I'll gladly reimburse you out of my own pocket. Now, let's get down to business."

At the end of the discussions, Blake stood and thanked them for their work on behalf of the community. "Saturday after Thanksgiving, I'll host a reception for the board, at the Dumbarton Hotel ballroom, to let the citizens of Ellicott City know what you're doing for them. Black tie." He looked at Martha. "This is my treat. The will doesn't allow frivolous use of the money available to the board."

Paul's wide grin gave Blake enormous satisfaction. "If any one of you plans to resign," Paul said, "we need at least a week's notice. Several people are anxious to get on this board."

Martha must have known that everyone looked at her, for she busied herself looking over her papers and left without telling anyone good-bye.

"What do you think?" Paul asked Blake when the three of them left the office.

"She won't resign, because she doesn't want to be left out. This board is the latest status symbol. I hope you'll be here for the reception."

"Sure thing. What about guests?"

Blake couldn't stop the laugh that floated out of him. He'd bet on the woman's identity. "You mean Rachel?"

"Uh . . . why, yes. How'd you know?"

"I got my information the same way you got yours this morning."

"You mean about you and my sister?"

He slipped his arm around her waist. "Who else?"

"Blake, we're walking on Main Street," Melinda said.

He tightened his grip. "I know what street it is."

Paul made a show of looking at his watch. "I'd better hurry. I promised Rachel I'd meet her at one, and I have to stop by to see the folks before I head back to Durham. You two have a good time."

As they walked into a nearby restaurant, Melinda looked at Blake from beneath lowered lashes and said, "At least Paul doesn't have a problem with our being together. Don't you think it'll be cool in Cape May this time of year?"

"We may not be able to swim, but it's warm enough still for walking. Would you rather go somewhere else?"

She stopped and looked into his eyes. "I just want to be with you."

He put his hands in his pockets to keep them off her. "And you say *I* chose a bad time to say what I feel. If I had you alone right now, you wouldn't be standing on your feet."

Her wink, slow and impudent, challenged his control, and when she said, "What would I be standing on?" he laughed for want of a better way to slow down his racing heart.

He ate half of the hamburger he'd ordered and noticed that she barely touched hers. "You take my breath, my appetite, my caution—"

"Good grief," she said, "here comes Papa. I didn't know he ate here. And he's made up his face to reproach me right here in this restaurant. Let's go—"

He interrupted. "Let him try it."

"Well, now, miss, you're playing hookey from school. You ought to be thankful they haven't fired you after that trick you pulled. Leaving a man for dead. I'm ashamed of you."

Never had Blake wanted a piece of a man so badly. His fists ached for a spot beside Booker Jones's head. "How does it feel to be the only righteous person in Ellicott City? You must get lonely for company. Don't you know everybody in this restaurant is staring at you while you make a spectacle of yourself?"

"How dare you?" Booker said between clenched teeth.

"Don't challenge me. Don't even think it. If you weren't Melinda's father, I'd have a few things to say to you and they wouldn't be pretty. Whatever you have to say to her, say it in private."

Taken aback, Booker looked at Blake with alarm. "I'll say what I like; she's my daughter."

"But you don't protect her. I do and I will, even from you. You haven't asked her what happened, so I assume you don't care. I can't wait to see you eat crow." He paid the bill, left a tip, and held out his hand to Melinda. "Are you ready to go?"

"Yes. Good-bye, Papa." She walked around him as if to avoid the appearance of disrespect. "I don't let myself be humiliated when he acts like this," she said as they left the restaurant. "He thrives on an audience, and he did this a lot when I was a teenager."

He noticed that she looked straight ahead, avoiding eye contact with anyone in the restaurant. "I think he needs badly to be accepted," she said with a sigh, "but he doesn't know how to get people to like and accept him."

He looked down at her with a compassion that he knew she read in his eyes. "I'm beginning to understand that you've been through a lot. I thought I had a wretched childhood because

I was treated almost as a workhorse, but I see that yours was no more pleasant than mine, only different.''

"He can be so harsh, Blake, and the next hour or so, he's kind and thoughtful. I love him, but I've never felt free to express it as I'd like."

"Your mother loves him?"

"She sure does, and he loves her, or at least, that's what she says. I need a different kind of love."

He knew that, and he intended to give it to her. "We'll talk later," he said. "Try not to let this upset you."

The smile didn't make it to her eyes. "It won't. I'm used to his public posturing."

She might be used to Booker's taunts and accusations, but why couldn't she tell him it hurt, as it surely must? He wondered if she'd ever open herself to him, if they'd ever trust each other enough to expose their doubts, fears, and pain. He was almost there; if she'd trust him, he'd knock down walls to meet her halfway. He slapped his left hand against his forehead. The private investigator he'd hired hadn't gotten back to him. He wanted a report.

Melinda left school at three-thirty, shopped for groceries and wiled away the time, dreading being alone. Ruby greeted her at the door with the look of one thoroughly harassed.

"What's wrong, Ruby?"

"Nobody knowed where you was. The police been after me to go down to the station, but I told them I wasn't going noplace till you come home."

"What did they want?"

"They got this man down there for me to identify. Suppose I fingers that man and they lets him loose. If it's Goodwin, I wouldn't trust him far as I could throw him. What you think I should do?"

"I'll go with you."

"Seems to me like you wouldn't want to see them cops after what they done to you."

"It's not settled yet. Let's go."

"That ain't Reginald Goodwin," Ruby told the policemen. "I ain't never seen that one before."

"Are you sure?"

"Course I'm sure," she said, bristling. "I'd recognize Reginald Goodwin anywhere, and ifn' I ever heard him talk, there wouldn't possibly be no doubt. You can't miss that nasal twang of his."

Melinda watched the perplexity on the policemen's faces. "Could he be an accessory? If he's innocent, why won't he look me in the face?" she asked them.

"Good question," the detective said. "You're free to go, buddy, but don't move from that address and don't leave town. If you do, you'll be in trouble."

"Yes, sir." The man sauntered out, yanking at his oversize jeans as he went.

"I don't trust that one," the detective said.

"Neither do I," Melinda told him. "He is not the man who rang my bell late one night and who I later caught on my surveillance camera."

"No," Ruby said, "and he sure ain't the one heading up the steps toward Mr. Tillman in that scene the camera took. They's somebody else in this."

The detective walked with them to Melinda's car and thanked them. "But we'll get whoever it is we're looking for. You can be sure of that."

She whirled around and tugged at the detective's sleeve. "Did you ask Tillman if he could identify the man?"

The detective shook his head. "That guy is miles from the

description Tillman gave of the man who slipped him that drug. Don't worry. We'll stay on it.''

"Yes," she said. "I suppose he is.''

When they returned to Melinda's house, Paul was talking with Tillman. "What are you doing with guards around the house?" he asked Melinda.

"Tell you later," she said, opened the door, and walked in with him.

"I thought I'd spend the night with you. I'm hanging around town this weekend.''

Her eyes widened, and she nodded her head as though acknowledging a fact. "I'd have thought you'd stay at Rachel's place.''

"We haven't gotten that far. You know me. I don't rush into anything I might get stuck in.''

"If you ask me, you can get stuck even if you don't rush into it.''

"You talking about yourself and Blake? When did that start?''

She gave him an edited history of the relationship. "I didn't stand a chance from the minute I saw him, but I'm proud that as long as Prescott lived, Blake didn't guess how I felt.''

"My hat's off to both of you. What's holding you back now?''

"I'm still a recent widow, Paul. The local citizenry thinks I'm a gold digger, and now there's the chance I'll be tried for hit-and-run driving.''

"Yeah. Papa was ranting about it this afternoon. I told him he should be ashamed of himself for castigating you, that he should be supporting you. Mama told him the same. Is this holding Blake back?''

"No. He's with me in all of this." She told him about the mystery man who wanted access to Prescott's invention.

"Good Lord. You're getting it from every side. I'm glad you

have Blake; he's a good man. You giving up your inheritance? If you love Blake, you can't marry some Joe just to get that money."

"And I never intended to, but Blake doesn't seem to realize it's possible to marry me."

"He will. If you don't believe it, walk off and see what happens."

"He said something to that effect. How're things with you and Rachel? Wait a minute. Let me answer the phone.

"Yes?"

"Our friend's driving by again. I alerted the police and Mr. Hunter. Just want to let you know," Tillman said.

She thanked him. "Where were we? Oh, yes. Rachel. What about her?"

Paul propped his right foot across his left knee and closed his eyes. "I think a lot of her. A lot of things about her suit me, but there's still much more to be discovered. I'm keeping my fingers crossed."

"I hope it works for you."

"Y'all come an' eat," Ruby called. "I cooked a nice dinner 'cause mens always eats good." After a meal of fried Norfolk spots, braised celery, jalapeño cornbread, grilled eggplant, green salad, and sour cream lime pie, they waited in the living room where Ruby preferred to serve the coffee.

"Play something," Paul said.

"I haven't played the piano since Prescott passed away, I—"

"Come on," he said, "that man was crazy about you. He'd want you to play or do anything that made you happy. Play something rousing like Sinding's 'Rustle of Spring.' "

She sat down, rubbed her hands together, and was soon lost in the music; as she finished one composition, she began another. Finally, her fingers and arms sore from that workout after not having practiced for months, she stopped, lowered her head, and closed her eyes. Startled by the applause, she looked around to see that Blake and Rachel had joined her and Paul.

"I couldn't leave the music," Paul explained, "so I asked Rachel to come over here."

"And I came as soon as Tillman reached me with the news that Goodwin or someone like him is on the prowl again. I never heard you play like that. You were always subdued, but this . . . this was as if the music had been locked inside of you and you suddenly let it fly free. It was . . . it was magical."

A loud noise suddenly rang out.

"Good gracious, what was that?" Rachel asked as she moved closer to Paul.

"Get in the back, all of you," Blake said. "That was a gunshot."

"Melinda, what's going on?" Rachel asked, obviously welcoming the opportunity to clutch Paul's arm.

Blake answered his cell phone. "Thanks, Tillman."

"A guy's been harassing Melinda, driving up and down the street past the house. Tillman just shot the man's tires up, and he's on his way to jail," Blake said. "Nothing to get upset about."

Melinda thanked Blake with her eyes. She hadn't wanted to explain the situation to Rachel, but considering Paul's interest in her friend, she wanted to be as gracious as possible. Who knew? Rachel might become her sister-in-law.

"It ought to be safe to leave," Paul said to Rachel. "You must be starved."

"Not exactly," she said, and Melinda's head snapped around. Who was this Rachel? The one she knew would have screamed at the sound of a gunshot, and would certainly have grumbled and held her belly if she couldn't eat dinner at six-thirty. According to her watch, it was nine o'clock. She glanced at her brother, whose gaze devoured the woman beside him, and hoped he'd found what he'd been looking for.

They left arm in arm, but the room seemed no less crowded. How large a man Blake seemed standing in front of her chair! The open-collared T-shirt, black jeans, and black leather jacket emphasized his heady masculinity and enhanced the aura of danger that always clung to him. She patted the place beside her on the sofa, and he sat there.

"I was here ten minutes after Tillman called me. Thank God I was home. Seems the guy had been casing this house for the past hour and a half. You and Ruby will have to go to the police station again tomorrow morning."

She looked down at her hands when she realized she'd been squeezing and unsqueezing her fists. "I figured we'd have to do that. You think this is the end of it?" It wasn't tension, but anger that she needed guards to ensure her safety from a man her late husband had once trusted.

He draped an arm around her shoulder and warmed her with a quick squeeze. "Who knows? If he identifies the man who drugged Tillman, that might end the danger, but we still don't know how far he'd go to get that invention—provided he *is* the guy we're after—or what we're in for legally."

"The more brazen he gets," she said, "the more determined I am that he won't get his hands on that design. He's not dealing with a woman who'll cringe in a corner and beg for mercy." That wonderful laughter rumbled in his throat and spilled over. How she loved to hear it.

"The thought of you cringing anywhere is mind-blowing." He stopped laughing and turned to her, as serious as she'd ever seen him. "We have the ammunition to send him to jail for a long time, but even if he gets ten years, with that invention, he'd be rich when he got out and young enough to enjoy the proceeds. We have to make certain that every one of his henchmen involved in this is with him behind bars."

He was telling her that he would stand by her through whatever she faced. Her eyes must have communicated the love she nurtured for him in her heart, for his own eyes glistened with tenderness. She gripped his arm, and those eyes she loved darkened into obsidian pools of desire. Knowing what would come next, she pressed her hand against his chest in warning.

"Paul's spending the night with me."

With disbelief mirrored in his eyes, he looked toward the ceiling. "Maybe you believe that, but it's not what I saw when he got up to leave. Want to take bets?"

She shook her head. "No, because I have the advantage. I know him. He's enough like you that he's prepared for every eventuality long before it comes."

"Yeah? Then, I'd better leave right now, sweetheart. What I need would take all night, if not longer. See you in the morning around nine."

She walked with him to the front door. "Maybe—"

A wicked grin crawled over his face in slow motion. "Oh, no. I'm not letting that straitlaced brother of yours challenge me tomorrow morning." He kissed the tip of her nose. "See you in the morning."

She stood at the half-open door, watching Blake talk with Tillman, and used as much restraint as she'd ever mustered when she managed not to call him back.

The next morning, Ruby's jovial manner deserted her as soon as she learned that another trip to the police station awaited her. "When is I gonna get this silver polished and these ovens cleaned?" she grumbled, mostly to herself. But when Blake arrived, put his arm around her, and thanked her for her willingness to help, whatever displeasure she'd felt dissipated like a puff of smoke in the wind.

"You knows I'd do anything I can to hold up the law, Mr. Blake." Her smile was luminous. "We just got time for me to give you a little breakfast."

Melinda stared at the two of them. Who'd have guessed it? Ruby Clark was a man's woman, loved being around them and doing things for them, and Blake knew it. If she gave Goodwin bad notices, he deserved it.

At the station house, Ruby's deference to men was nowhere in evidence. She stared at the man sitting beneath the light in the examining room and laughed. "Well. Well, Mr. Goodwin. You ain't looking down your nose at me now, is you? You ain't gonna catch me sitting under no light with the police grillin' me. I'm good as you is now, ain't I?"

The detective touched Ruby's arm. "You say this is Reginald Goodwin, the man Tillman photographed with his camcorder? This is the same man?"

"Yes, sir. Same man what had the run of Mr. Rodgers's house for years, coming and going as he pleased. Even had his own key. It's him, all right."

"You're sure?" Blake asked her.

"He's dyed his hair, but he can't hide them eyebrows and that mole on his nose. You know, I'd forgotten about that mole. It's him."

"Officer, I want this man arrested for entering my house without permission, unlawfully, and for harassment," Melinda said.

The detective nodded, and looked at Goodwin. "Do you know a man who goes by the name of Robinson?"

Goodwin glared at the officer. "Do you think I'm foolish enough to answer any of your questions without a lawyer?"

Ruby jumped up and clapped her hands. "Shore is him. Shore as you born. It ain't possible I'd forget that twang of his, not even if fifty years had passed."

"We're almost there," the detective told them as they left. "We've posted Mrs. Rodgers's reward for information leading to arrests in this case. My hunch is that someone's being paid to steal something in your house. As long as he's out here, you'd be wise to keep those guards stationed at your doors."

As they walked to his car, Blake's arm around her waist

communicated more than the protectiveness she sensed when-ever he touched her. What she felt in his caress now was far deeper, exceeding even possessiveness. It was as if, in that one gesture, he said, "You and I are together in this and all things." Not knowing how she should respond, whether she read him correctly, she merely accepted the sweetness of the moment.

He drove Ruby back to Melinda's house and, when Melinda would have gotten out of the car, he detained her. "Let's go over to the Patapsco, sit on the banks and talk."

The autumn leaves were at their most brilliant hue that Satur-day morning, dazzling in colors of orange, red, brown, purple, and gold. Evergreen pines stood out among them, asserting their authority in nature. Blake and Melinda had their choice of benches facing the rapidly rushing water and chose one several feet from a huge boulder.

Melinda took in her surroundings and wondered why she didn't go there often. "It's so beautiful here, so peaceful and serene," she said, and couldn't help musing over the sense of rightness she suddenly had about her relationship with Blake. If there was such a thing as fate, she had a hunch she'd met it.

"That's why I wanted us to come here. It's another world." From now on, he intended to avoid making mistakes with Melinda. He took her hand and held it close to his body.

"I ought to have told you this before, but . . . well, I engaged a private investigator to track down whoever hit that man you found lying beside your car. It's obvious to me that whoever did it parked beside you not too long after you left your car. If that coroner knows his job, your cash register receipts will be all we need." He adjusted his trouser leg and draped his right foot across his left knee. "I'm also going to tell him to locate this guy, Robinson. As long as he's loose, we can't relax."

"I know. Whoever he is, he's getting paid to commit a crime.

I don't think Goodwin will reveal the man's identity, because he's hell-bent on getting that invention."

He put an arm around her. "Let's not dwell on that right now. If you don't want to go to Cape May, we can go to the Virgin Islands, the Bahamas, or—"

"I want to go to Cape May. We don't have to swim."

Ray Sinclair, who had been watching the couple from afar, came up to them and said, "Well, well. If it isn't the lovers. Sorry about your ... er ... accident, Melinda. Everybody's talking about it; the poor man had a wife and four kids. You—"

Blake told himself not to lose his temper. "Shut up, Sinclair," he said, getting to his feet and towering over the man. "You heckle Melinda one more time, just one more word, and you're going to see stars. You've got a lot of nerve, brother."

"Don't tell me you'd start a brawl right here in public. Not the high-minded Mr. Blake Hunter."

"That's what you think, huh? Well, let me tell you something: as a teenager in Atlanta, I knew every street man in that city, and they knew me. Nobody bothered me, because the reputation of my fists preceded me wherever I went. Get that?" He slapped his right fist into his left palm. "Don't mess with me, man."

"You don't have to get uptight."

He shoved his hands in his pockets, away from temptation. "Just beat it.

"What I need you to understand," he said to Melinda, as if Ray Sinclair hadn't interrupted him, "is that I want us to have some time together, but only if you want it and wherever you want it, whether that place is here or in the Antarctic. You said you couldn't lie in another man's arms, and I don't want anyone but you. But we don't know whether that's enough."

He could feel her tense. "Haven't we been over this before?"

"I seem to recall that we have, but that was months ago

when . . . when joining our bodies was the most pressing thing we felt. It's more than that now. Haven't you considered whether we can make a life together? I have."

"Yes, it's been on my mind a lot, but your insistence that I find a husband in order to satisfy the terms of that will confused me."

He let out a long breath. "I hope you don't think it didn't bug the hell out of me. I was doing what Prescott wanted, but you've convinced me the price is too high, and I accept that." He rubbed his chin with his free hand. "I don't believe I would have let you do it."

"I couldn't do that to myself a second time. I'd known Prescott for more than a year, and he was a gentleman, but . . . there is no fortune worth what I would have faced."

"It's getting toward lunchtime," he said. "Want to go to the Mill Towne Tavern?"

Her face mirrored her disappointment. "Ruby would never let me forget it. She's prepared lunch, which she hates doing, since I won't consume those high-calorie meals she loves to cook. If I don't show up to eat it, I'll never hear the end of it."

"By the way," he said, and winked to push his point. "Was Paul still asleep when we left your place this morning? I'd have thought he wouldn't miss that fantastic breakfast Ruby cooked." He barely managed to control a laugh when she pursed her lips, frowned, and managed not to look at him.

"You didn't think I'd forget it, did you? From the look in Paul's eyes, Rachel didn't stand a chance. I'll let you know when I'm ready to collect on that bet."

"Oh, you! A gentleman doesn't press his advantage."

He had to laugh; he couldn't help it. "Tut, tut. What gentleman led you to believe that? Surely, you're not so gullible. From now on, I intend to press every advantage you give me."

"Don't be so cocky. I may not give you any."

He pinched her nose. "Then I'll make my own advantages. Woman, can't you see I'm getting desperate?"

She looked up at him, and he wondered at her seriousness. "Do you think Rachel's right for Paul?"

"You can't judge another's needs. If she floats his boat, he'll let us know soon enough."

Falling leaves drifted down around them, and for reasons he didn't examine, he picked up a handful of golden, red, and purple ones from the boulder near where they sat, made a bouquet of them, and handed them to her. If ever eyes bore stars, hers did at that moment. He'd never kissed a woman in full view of anyone who wanted to look, but he had to feel the sweetness of her mouth.

Her lips clung to his. He broke the kiss and stared down into her eyes. "I love you."

She gaped as though in surprise, but he hadn't meant to say it right then, so he didn't elaborate. With her hand in his, he strolled with her back to his car, oblivious to Ellicott City's gossiping citizens.

Chapter Twelve

He meant it; she knew he did. He hadn't said it in the grip of passion and, as usual, he'd been the epitome of sobriety. He'd looked her in the eye and told her in a voice unsteady with emotion that he loved her. Somehow, though, she didn't feel like shouting for joy because in spite of all that had passed between them, he still belonged to himself alone. Yet, they were closer in that moment than when they made love. He communicated to her a caring that she hadn't received from anyone else except, perhaps, her mother. She thanked Ruby for her lunch of shrimp salad on lettuce leaves, sliced tomatoes, whole wheat toast, and tea.

"Don't thank me," Ruby said. "Only reason I concoct that stuff is so I don't have to go out and find another job. I declare, Miz Melinda, real food ain't gonna kill you."

"You're a dear," Melinda said. "You make the best shrimp salad I ever ate, and I've eaten a lot of it."

Ruby folded her hands in front of her and allowed herself a moment of modesty. "You go 'way from here, Miz Melinda. I never made that for anybody but you, but if you likes it . . . Course, I'd rather cook real food, but for a nice person like yourself . . ." She let it hang.

Melinda's laughter filled the room, pouring out of her, and with it the tension she'd felt since Blake's declaration of love that noon.

"Ruby, if you ever want to take acting lessons, I'll be glad to spring for them," she said and hurried up the stairs so she wouldn't hear the woman's comeback.

When she was home on Saturday afternoons during the school term, she usually wrote letters, did lesson plans, checked her clothing, or took care of some personal matters. She didn't want to do any of that, and she didn't feel like reading. On an impulse, she called her mother.

"Have they found that hit-and-run driver yet?" her mother wanted to know. "Anybody with sense would know you're too responsible a person to go off and leave a man for dead. Besides, you're the one who called the police."

Melinda didn't want to go over that again. "The police are still looking. How's Papa?"

"Well, I guess he's worried about all this news. You know how he is."

Did she ever! "I'll see you at church Sunday," she told her mother after they'd talked awhile.

Before the Sunday service was over, however, she wished the thought hadn't occurred to her. Booker Jones was on the warpath. "God sees you even if I don't. You can hide from your parents, your siblings, friends, husbands, or wives, and from the law, but not from the Lord. Your sins will find you out. And if you don't confess and repent, you will surely burn eternally in hell fire and brimstone. The Lord does not like ugly.''

He looked directly at his only daughter and shook his finger. ''I do not except anybody under the sound of my voice.''

Melinda tuned him out along with the amens and yes, Lords that encouraged him. ''If you weren't sitting here,'' she whispered to her mother, ''I might get up and leave. I . . . oh, I don't know.''

''Don't stay on my account,'' Lurlane said. ''If I wasn't married to him, I might go with you.''

''What a spectacle that would be! Half the people in this town seem to think I'm a sinner beyond redemption. I refuse to give them or him the satisfaction of seeing me stalk out of here.''

She stayed until the last amen, but after she got home, she ignored the ringing phone, certain that the caller was her father bent on reemphasizing the thinly veiled accusations he made during his preaching.

''Miz Melinda,'' Ruby called, ''it's Mr. Blake on the line.''

She rushed to the phone. ''Hello, Blake.''

''Hi. I need to see you about something. Mind if I come over in a few minutes?''

Why would she mind? ''Of course not. See you in a few minutes.''

That didn't sound right. She changed into brown slacks and a burnt-orange cowl-neck sweater, twisted her hair into a French knot, and looked around for something to do while she waited for him. It was then that she made the decision that would prove momentous in her life. Every afternoon after school she would work at straightening out the closets, sorting and packing for charity everything that had belonged to Prescott, except his cassettes and the plans he'd stored in that trunk. She heard the doorbell and hastened down the stairs.

She opened the door for him, and shock at his somber expression curled her nerve ends. "Blake! What is it? What's the matter?"

He put an arm tight around her and walked with her into the living room. "Sit down here with me, honey," he said, pointing to the sofa. "The detective called me. The coroner's report placed the man's death at eleven minutes before you bought that blouse, your first purchase that night. We're not in the clear."

Her breath lodged in her throat, and she had to cough before she could breathe. "I was in that store a long time looking for a blouse to wear with my beige suit. The clerk will testify that I tried on at least four before I settled for the one I bought."

"I hope you remember who she was."

"I certainly do. Her left eyelid drooped noticeably. She's worked there a long time."

"All right. Eleven minutes isn't a lot, but it may prove crucial, and especially since the detective I hired can't find anything about the person who might have done it. I'm going to see that clerk this evening. I hope she's on duty today."

"I hope so too, Blake. I don't see how I could be charged with something I didn't do."

"It happens all the time, but the evidence here is so flimsy that I don't believe it'll stand in court." He looked at his watch. "I have an appointment a few minutes from now. I'll be in touch." He brushed her lips with his own, locked her to him for a second, and was gone.

To Blake's chagrin, the clerk didn't want to get involved. "I don't want nothin' to do wif no law. I don't know nothin', didn't see nothin', and didn't hear nothin,' " she said. Nineteen years old, he surmised, a dozen earrings in her ears and enough makeup to last a normal woman for a year. Not a good witness.

"Would you rather I subpoena you?" he asked her.

She observed him from the corners of her eyes. "I still won't know nothin'."

He produced the receipt. "According to this, you're the clerk who handled the sale."

Her shrug was nothing less than callous. "That don't mean I remember it."

He tried another tactic. "You ever been jailed for drug use?"

Her eyebrows shot up and her bottom lip dropped. Then she said, "You're just fishing."

"And you'd better stay clean. I mean clean as a saint."

He had the pleasure of seeing her wither and knew he had her where he wanted her. "I'll be in touch," he promised, though he made it sound like a threat.

His unease about the case mounted steadily. No lawyer wanted to go to court with a single, recalcitrant witness, but he had to work with what he had. And Melinda wasn't going to spend a minute behind bars for that crime. He told his investigator to find out everything about the witness. He didn't know what he'd do with the information, but he believed in being ready for all eventualities.

He got in his car and phoned Lieutenant Cochrane, the police detective, on his cell phone. "This is Hunter. I need to see you as soon as possible."

"I'll be here for another couple of hours. Come on over."

"I'm laying my cards on the table," Blake told the lieutenant at the station a short while later. "I have a witness, but she's scared of law enforcement officers. She may have a record."

"Who is she?"

"She's the clerk who sold Mrs. Rodgers the first purchase she made that evening."

"I see. She's . . . Not now, Ken," he said to the officer trying to get his attention.

"But, Lieutenant, this old lady is either hysterical or she's killed somebody."

Lieutenant Cochrane spun around and Blake followed him, his adrenaline flowing at high speed.

"Where is she?" Cochrane asked.

Blake saw her then, at least eighty-five years old, wringing her hands, and her dim eyes reflecting the pain she felt.

"Are you the officer I have to speak to?" Cochrane nodded. "Well, I did a horrible thing. Lord knows I didn't mean to, but I ran away, because I was scared. I've been so upset I can't sleep and Sunday, Reverend Jones said that if I don't confess and ask forgiveness, I'm lost."

"Come over here, ma'am," Cochrane said. "Have a seat. What did you do?"

"Well, it was night, and I can't see so good at night. When I went to park, I didn't see the man till it was too late. I hit him when he was getting out of his car, and I backed up and drove out of the parking lot. I never did do my shopping."

"What time was this?"

"About seven or a little after. I'm not sure. Will I have to go to jail?"

"I doubt it, but you will certainly clear someone else's name."

"Yes, sir. That's one reason why I couldn't sleep. People said such awful things about her when it was me that did it. I'll have to ask her to forgive me like the reverend said."

Lieutenant Cochrane walked over to where Blake stood making notes. "There's your case. We'll take it from here."

"You're not going to prosecute that poor woman, are you?" Blake asked him.

"The fault is with the law. If she can't see when it's dark, she shouldn't be driving at night, but she isn't forced to take a test for night blindness. Too bad."

"No word on who's in cahoots with Goodwin?"

"Nothing, and the man won't budge, but I haven't given up."

Blake raced to his car and headed for Melinda's house. When she opened the door, he picked her up and twirled around and around with her. "It's settled, sweetheart. It's settled."

"What's settled?"

"An old lady confessed to hitting that man. Poor woman didn't see him."

"What woman? Who?"

He hugged her over and over. "I didn't get her name. It's all over, thank God." But, no it wasn't, he reflected. Three newspaper editors were going to print a retraction and an apology to Melinda on the front page, and he intended to write the accompanying editorial about newspaper slander and muckraking himself. It they didn't print it, he'd sue. But that could wait for another time. The sparkle in her eyes and the joyous glow on her face were too beautiful to spoil, and that's what he'd do if he shifted the focus to a campaign for retribution.

Suddenly, a frown creased her forehead, chasing the glow from her face, darkness displacing sunshine. "I wonder why she decided to confess. She's probably in real trouble now."

"What can anybody do to an old woman? Anyway, we can thank your father for this. Seems he—"

"Thank my father?" Her face, indeed her entire demeanor suggested that he might not be rowing with both oars. "What did he do other than castigate me, accusing me of murdering a man without asking me if I did it? If he preached my funeral, he'd probably blame me for dying."

"Well, recently he preached one of his 'Sinners at the Angry Gates of Hell' sermons about burning in hell if you didn't confess your sins and ask forgiveness. Scared the poor old lady to death."

She slapped her hand over her mouth and stared at him. "Wait a minute. I was in church last Sunday morning, and I heard that. Well, I'll be! I was so mad, I could hardly keep myself from walking out. Looks like some good came of it. I'll have to call and thank him."

"Thank him? Or serve him a plate of crow?"

"Come to think of it, I'd enjoy ... No, I'd better not do that. It would be just the cue he'd need to give me an hour-long sermon about forgiveness. I'll call him."

Blake had thought it over and didn't see how it could be avoided unless she gave her father an out. "You mind if I invite him to the reception I'm giving for the board? It's safe. I'll introduce the board members, but there won't be any speeches. If there were, Martha Greene and your father would make me wish I'd never thought of a reception."

He might yet wish that, but she didn't see how she could countenance her father's exclusion from such an important social event. "Of course, I don't mind. Be sure the invitation includes Mama. I'm going to enjoy dressing her up like a glamour girl and watching his reaction."

The grin began around his lips and got broader and broader until it enveloped his face and he laughed aloud. That wonderful laugh that warmed her all over and nourished her soul. "In that case, will you be my date for the evening? With Booker's gaze glued to his wife, he'll be less likely to focus on me. He thinks my interest in you is mercenary, and he had the temerity to tell me so."

She thought about that for a minute and, in her mind's eye, she saw her father's posturing, using his clerical collar as an excuse to be overbearing. He wanted so badly to be liked, to be accepted. Why couldn't he realize people would like him if he were less strident and not so judgmental?

"I think I'd better go see him and thank him for that sermon and for accidentally getting me cleared of those charges."

He shrugged as if he didn't think much of the idea. "I suppose that's better than fighting with him, but I don't want to hear that he accused you or bullied you. You understand?"

She nodded. "He won't."

She didn't go to church the next Sunday, not as a show of independence, but because she couldn't take the chance until her father knew the charges against her had been dropped. Instead, she timed a visit to her parents' home to coincide with her father's after-lunch rest period, when he listened to music, usually Monteverdi or Bach, classical music with religious themes. She often wondered why he preached "gospel" sermons, but rarely listened to gospel music.

"I'm so happy it's over," Lurlane said, as tears streamed from her eyes after learning that one of their parishioners had confessed to the crime. "Your father's in the study where he usually is this time of day. Don't be too hard on him, child. You know he'll beat himself to death about it for months to come."

"He ought to have a good talk with himself before he points his finger; a little humility would be good for him."

"I know," Lurlane said, as she brushed out her long, stringy hair, "but he's a good man, just misguided sometimes like all the rest of us, you and me included. Remember that."

She wondered what made Lurlane Jones so faithful to a man who had so many visible flaws. Maybe one day, she'd get the courage to ask her. She opened the door of the study, and her gaze fell on her father, his hands clasped across his still slim waist and his eyes closed as though in reverence. It seemed a pity to interrupt his reverie.

"Papa. How are you? It's me, Melinda." She walked over and placed a kiss on his cheek. Risked it, ignoring then as she always had, his feelings about such things, though he accepted it from her.

"Sit down, girl, and enjoy the music. When you listen to Bach, you have to thank God for your ears. If I ever get to Germany, I'm going to that little church in Leipzig and see the organ he used when he composed all this wonderful music.

He's been dead since 1750, and not a day goes by that somebody somewhere doesn't play his music.''

She sat in an overstuffed chair facing him. "Papa—"

"Wait while I put on the Brandenburg Concerto Number Five. It's my favorite, you know."

Her antennae shot up. Her father had the sensors of an animal in the wild, and he suspected she'd come to speak to him about his sermon the previous Sunday when she'd contemplated walking out of church. Well, he wasn't going to hamstring her by portraying himself as a harmless music lover.

"Papa, I think you'll be happy to know that one of your parishioners, a woman of about eighty-five or so, confessed to the police that she struck the man found lying beside my car, and that she ran away because she was scared. Seems she can't see well at night."

He flicked off the CD and sat up straight in the recliner. "What woman are you talking about?"

"I didn't get her name." She described her and related what Blake had told her of the confession.

"Mittie Williams. Can you beat that? Maybe I do some good in this town."

She rolled her eyes toward the ceiling. "I don't think that's been disputed, Papa, but I'd appreciate your telling the congregation about it next Sunday, so they'll all know it wasn't me."

"You're saying I should announce you've been exonerated? You think that's called for?"

"Yes, Papa, I do. You shook your finger at me, accusing me of I don't know what, and what had I done? Nothing. You're always making examples of me. I'm tired of it, and if you keep it up, I'm going to join another church."

"You'd do that to your father?"

How many times had she seen that cloak of innocence without recognizing it for what it was? Not anymore. "Yes, Papa. I don't get anything out of the sermon when I'm mad, and you make me angry. Just tell the folks the Lord answered your prayers, and the police found the person who did it. Closed subject.''

''I never thought you looked at it that way. I've been trying to help you.''

She stared at him in disbelief. He actually believed that. She got up, walked over, and kissed his cheek. ''I'd better go. Sorry to interrupt your music.''

He stood and waved a hand as if to dismiss the idea. ''Oh, that! It's good to spend a few minutes with you. Come back soon.''

Lurlane waited for her in the living room. ''How'd it go? It kinda worried me that he stopped the Brandenburg, much as he loves it.''

She looked at her mother, anxious for her husband and her daughter. ''Fine, Mama. I think he just gets carried away sometime. See you in a day or so.''

Lurlane raised an eyebrow and headed for the study.

''Mama!'' Lurlane turned around with a look of expectancy on her face. ''I'm coming over tomorrow and take you shopping. I'll call you.''

''Won't that be nice. I need a couple of housedresses.''

Housedresses. Not this time, Melinda vowed.

Blake didn't intend to let tension between Booker and himself ruin his party, so he dialed Booker's number.

''This is Blake Hunter. I'm having a reception for Prescott Rodgers Foundation board members the Saturday night after Thanksgiving, and I want you to be there.''

''Any special reason?''

''Yes. I want to introduce the board members to the town's leading citizens, and that automatically includes you and Mrs. Jones.''

Booker cleared his throat. "Well—"

He didn't want to hear the word no, so he interrupted. "I can imagine you've preached many sermons on letting bygones be bygones, and I think that's appropriate in our case. Besides, I want Melinda to be happy, and that means having her family there."

"That so?"

He wanted a little urging, did he? "Yes, sir. Paul's coming."

"You know? Haven't been to a real social event in years. People seem afraid to invite me."

"Well, I'm not. You'll go in my car. We'll be at your house at six-thirty."

"Now, that will be just lovely. Lurlane needs a night out in company." His voice warmed to a melodious baritone. "Yes, she'll love it. Thank you."

"My pleasure." He hung up, satisfied that Booker wouldn't feel the need for public posturing.

Two weeks later, the Saturday night after Thanksgiving, Melinda paced the floor in her bedroom, occasionally glancing at herself in the mirror, not certain that a long red, shimmering silk sheath was the appropriate attire for a widow. But six and a half months after Prescott's death seemed long enough to deck herself out in white, beige, or navy blue. Prescott had forbidden her to wear black, claiming that the color drowned her personality. At last, the doorbell rang. She draped her silver-fox stole around her shoulders and took one last look in the mirror. She wanted to look perfect this night. The stole, her silver shoes and bag, and the diamond and blue-pearl earrings that hung from her earlobes complemented the red dress. *They can whisper about me all they want to, but they can't say I don't look great.*

With that assurance, she left the room and headed for the

stairs. She took a step down, looked at Blake, and stopped. She couldn't close her mouth. He was resplendent in a black tuxedo with a white shirt, red cummerbund, handkerchief, studs, and ruby cuff links.

"Hi," he called to her. "Somehow, I figured you'd wear red."

She let herself breathe and drifted toward him. At the bottom step, he reached for her hand. "You look fantastic," he said. "Honey, you're a dream walking."

"You don't think the red is too much? You know how—"

"You know what they say. Never let 'em see you sweat. Show you don't care. To me, you look great. Perfect."

"Thanks. You look wonderful. Everybody will think we planned what we'd wear."

"Yeah. Next time we'll make sure."

"What's this?" she asked when she saw the limousine.

"Think I'd expect my best girl to sit in the front seat and get her dress wrinkled?" The chauffeur seated them in the stretch limousine, got in, and drove off. "Er . . . we're picking up your parents; then we're going by Rachel's to get her and Paul."

"You planned all this behind my back? I hope Rachel isn't wearing red."

She felt his arm ease around her shoulders. "If she is, so what? Neither she nor any other woman will look as good as you do, no matter what she's wearing."

Happiness suffused her. "I'd put my head on your shoulder if I didn't think I'd muss my hair."

The car stopped. "Be back in a minute," Blake said, and she wondered whether her father had raised a ruckus when he saw her mother dressed for the evening.

"You both look real nice," Booker said when they were on the way to Rachel's house.

Melinda nearly swallowed her teeth when she saw her

father's grip on her mother's hand. "She made me rent a tuxedo. First time I ever got into one of these things. If I had refused, I expect she'd have filed for divorce. Such a commotion! Hunter, don't make the mistake of letting a woman know you're putty in her hands. Sooner or later, she'll take advantage of you."

Blake cut a quick glance at Melinda. "Well, sir, that's one of those things that sneaks in before you know it." He turned up the light, and she stared at her mother who seemed ten years younger and glittered like starlight, her silver-gray ball gown and silver accessories set off with a short, stylish hairdo and flawless makeup.

"Mama, if I'd met you in the street, I don't think I would have recognized you."

Booker's dry "I certainly would have. This is the way she looked when I was trying to get her—the town belle—to marry me" brought a smile from Lurlane.

"I might have looked like this once," Lurlane said, "but that was so long ago that even I'd forgotten it."

"Well," Booker said, "we're going shopping next week and buy you some clothes, and from now on, somebody else is going to do the housework. The Lord didn't intend for us to hide what he gave us."

Melinda managed to squelch the laughter that bubbled up in her throat. Her father was so turned on by his wife that he hadn't noticed the berry-red dress his widowed daughter wore. She'd always thought Paul handsome, and she knew he looked good in a tux, but with Rachel wearing a navy-sequined gown and Paul in a navy blue tux and accessories, they made a dashing pair.

"This looks serious," Blake whispered to Melinda when he got in the car.

"Anybody else coming?" Booker asked.

"No," Blake said, "but a few friends will join us at our table."

"I didn't know you two were seeing each other," Booker said, his mood jovial. "I'm glad somebody's seeing Paul. It's time I had some grandchildren, but my four children don't seem to be thinking along those lines." Still holding Lurlane's hand, he put his free arm around her shoulder. "You think we ought to run a contest to see which one on them has a child first?"

Lurlane leaned away from her husband in order to look into his eyes. "If you embarrass them, they might not let you know when they have them. We're going to have a wonderful time and not get personal."

Booker blessed them with a smile and pointed to his wife. "She told me I had to behave myself tonight."

Melinda stared at her parents. What on earth had come over Booker Jones? She whispered the question to Blake.

"I think that's probably the way he was when they were young and in love," Blake said softly, "before he settled into the small-town preacher's persona. Seeing her young and lovely brings it all back to him. I wouldn't have missed this for the world."

"You may be right. She's a shock to me, so I can imagine how it affects Papa."

"I rather doubt that," he said dryly.

The limousine arrived at the hotel, and as they started in, the first person Melinda saw was Ray Sinclair. "Did you invite him?" she asked Blake.

"Of course not. He's probably hanging around to see who the guests are."

But he couldn't have been more wrong. "I figured you were sore at me," Ray said to Blake, "but can't we just let bygones be bygones? It seems everybody's invited but me."

Blake raised an eyebrow. "Good evening, Sinclair. Sorry about that."

She hoped Ray didn't decide to get revenge for the snub, but she wouldn't put it past him.

Blake introduced his group to Justine and Duncan Banks, who awaited him at his table.

"Who's looking after my godchild?" he asked them.

"Mattie," Duncan said. "Only problem is that Tonya treats Mattie as if she's a big doll that changes hair color several times a day."

By the time Blake accustomed himself to the new Booker Jones, Melinda smiled at him and said, "May I please have a Bloody Mary?"

He nearly spilled his club soda. What they would drink and whether they'd drink it in the reverend's presence hadn't occurred to him. *You're slipping up, man. The woman has bamboozled you,* he told himself.

"But you don't drink."

Her smile was that of an innocent, but he wasn't fooled. "It goes with my dress."

"Listen, honey," he pleaded. "Everything's going great. You don't want to test your father's mettle here in front of everybody, do you? Why do you think I'm drinking club soda?"

She winked at him. "Probably because you're chicken."

Never one to shirk his responsibility, he leaned toward Booker. "Sir, I haven't asked everyone what they want to drink, but I think I ought to ask whether you'd be offended if I ordered drinks for those who want it?"

He wished Melinda would breathe while they waited for Booker's answer. "I'll just have a glass of ginger ale with a little bit of lemon, thank you. I'm not responsible for anybody's soul tonight but my own. My wife will probably want a glass of wine, though. I remember that in our day, she used to love champagne."

"Then I'll have champagne," Duncan said.

"Me too," Justine and Rachel chorused.

He looked at Paul and Melinda, Booker's children. And with the most pleading look he could muster, beseeched Melinda to join with the others.

"All right, all right. Champagne," she said at last.

"And you, Paul?"

"I'm going with the flow, man. Champagne."

He ordered ginger ale with lemon and two bottles of Veuve Cliquot champagne, and released a long, deep breath. Thank heavens Booker hadn't rocked the boat. He found Melinda's hand and squeezed her fingers. She turned to him, her eyes shining with a look that was for him alone, and he thought his heart would burst. The waiter filled their glasses with champagne, and placed the ginger ale in front of Lurlane, but Blake hadn't noticed until Lurlane said to the waiter, "Whatever gave you that idea?"

She pointed to her husband. "He's the teetotaler at this table."

Blake would have skipped the toast in deference to Booker, but Lurlane raised her glass. "Thank you, Blake, for arranging this party. It's . . . it's wonderful."

"And thank you for giving Lurlane this opportunity to shine like the beauty she's always been," Booker said and took a sip of his ginger ale. "I don't know when I last saw Melinda look so beautiful, either. Truth is, I doubt I ever did."

Blake glanced at Paul, who arched both eyebrows when Booker added, "There're four beautiful women at this table. Makes a man proud."

"Right on," Duncan said, and lifted his glass first to his wife and then to the group.

Blake promised himself he'd say a prayer of thanks first chance he got. He excused himself. "It's time I introduced the board members."

He began by saying there would be no speeches, that he only wanted to thank the board members for helping him carry out Prescott Rodgers's wishes by serving on the board of the Prescott Rodgers Foundation. He asked each one to take a bow when introduced, and it didn't escape him that Martha Greene, who wore an expensive white ball gown, bowed to each corner of the room and took three times as long doing it as was necessary. He introduced Paul as the board's advisor, and made a show of thanking Booker for giving the foundation his blessing, though it only occurred to him at the last minute, for Booker had done no such thing. Yet, the man stood and bowed, acknowledging the applause with smiles and a wave of his hand. Oh, the power of human vanity, Blake thought. Because of that one gesture, Booker Jones had become his ally.

The three strolling violinists he'd chosen from a concert bureau in Baltimore strolled from table to table playing whatever the guests requested. At their table, the leader asked Booker's preference.

"You're going to request one of the Brandenburg concerti," Lurlane whispered, in a tone that said maybe he shouldn't.

"Why not?" Booker asked. "Can you give us a little of Number Five?"

As if they had waited all evening for the opportunity, the three musicians smiled with obvious delight and played the first movement to wild applause.

"Doesn't hurt to reach for the sky once in a while," Booker preened. "Good for the soul even if you don't make it."

"It's a good thing you didn't hire a belly dancer," Paul said to Blake. "A man can take just so many shocks in one evening."

Booker cut a glance toward his son. "Since you'll probably still be here tomorrow, I look forward to a visit from you and Miss Perkins. You shouldn't keep such a lovely woman to yourself."

Paul's white teeth glistened against his high brown complexion as he smiled the smile of a happy man. "Not to worry, Papa. We'd planned to do precisely that."

"I bet something's cooking between those two," Melinda whispered to Blake. "He's here every weekend, and he doesn't stay with me."

Duncan lifted his glass. "Here's to the women we love," he said and looked at Paul as if to see whether he'd drink to that toast.

With a grin as wide as Blake had ever seen, Paul raised his glass in Duncan's direction. "Brilliant move, man."

After the waiters served a meal of cold, smoked sable, filet mignon or chicken cordon bleu, roast potatoes, green beans, meslun salad, and vanilla ice cream with raspberry sauce, Blake thanked his guests and asked them to support the foundation's work.

He didn't know when he'd enjoyed a public gathering so much. He'd have to think about this other side of Booker Jones. Maybe all the man wanted was acceptance. Then, too, a woman who looked as Lurlane Jones did could bring out the best in any man. It was something to think about.

After taking his guests home, he settled back in the limousine with Melinda's hand tight in his. "I feel good about this evening. What about you?"

"It's no wonder. You did yourself proud, and I'm still trying to digest it. I think my mother just taught me a lesson. She always said Papa loved her deeply, but I never saw it until tonight. He wanted the occasion to be special for her, because she looked so special, and something tells me she won't be looking dowdy any time soon."

"She's a beautiful woman and, tonight, she gave him back his youth."

The car stopped in front of Melinda's house. "I'd like to continue this evening," he said, "but I dare not risk walking out of your house tomorrow morning in this tuxedo." The thought of leaving her didn't sit well with him, but he didn't want to compromise her. "Can I see you tomorrow night?"

She nodded. "Come on in for a few minutes."

With her sweet and inviting smile, the scent of her perfume teasing his nostrils and the décolletage of her fiery red dress exposing the tops of her lush mounds, he felt the sexual heat begin a slow rise in his blood. And when she squeezed his fingers as they walked up the path to her door, his blood pounded in his ears. He told himself that there was always tomorrow, but that didn't diffuse the desire that had begun its mad race to his loins.

He nodded to the guard, took her key, opened the front door, and closed it. He had himself in check, he'd swear to it, but she looked up at him with her big, soft brown eyes, telling him without words that he was king of the hill, and he lifted her, locked her to him, and plunged his tongue into her mouth. Her soft breasts rose and fell against his chest, and he held her closer until he could feel her hard nipples through the fabric of his shirt. Half insane with desire, his fingers slipped into the top of her dress and she flung her head back as if in ecstasy, her breath short and fast. Crazed with want, he pulled her breast from the confines of her dress and suckled her.

She cried out, "You can't leave me like this."

Shocked at his loss of control, he worked at covering her breast with the revealing dress until she laughed at his fumbling.

"Wait here," she said. "I'll be back in a few minutes."

He thought she'd gone to make herself presentable, but ten minutes later, she was back wearing a red woolen dress.

"My coat's in the closet here," she said. "Ready to go?"

His pulse took off like a runaway train. "You're . . . You bet I am."

* * *

If he'd thought he was leaving her to twist and turn in a rumpled bed alone all night, he didn't know her. From the time she'd seen him standing at the bottom of her steps waiting to take her to the reception, she'd had her own plan for the evening's end. As she put her toothbrush, deodorant, and fresh underwear in her pocketbook and changed her dress, her mind focused on the evening's magic.

To her surprise, her mother had welcomed enthusiastically the idea of spending the day in a Baltimore spa being made over. "That dress you got me needs some glamour," Lurlane had said. "In my day, I didn't take a backseat to any woman anywhere."

She'd learned something wonderful about her parents, too, and she had Blake to thank for it. She suspected her mother could teach classes in the ways to handle a man. Booker Jones had made his children proud.

"I couldn't imagine being away from you this night," she told Blake, as they got into the limousine and headed for his house.

He stretched out his long legs, one of the luxuries the limousine offered. "Nor I, you. Not after that session in your foyer a few minutes ago. I'd have left, but with feet of lead." He opened the bar and poured them each a glass of champagne. "It's getting to the place where I never want to be away from you, not even for a minute. " He locked arms with her as they took the first sip.

When she leaned against his shoulder, he put their glasses in the wine rack, tipped up her chin, and gazed into her eyes. She sucked in her breath at what she saw in him then and parted her lips for his tongue. His kiss was quick and hot.

"I want to be able to walk into my house," he quipped. "When you get going, your heady kissing can cripple a man."

He took the champagne from the limousine's bar and handed her the two glasses. Then he leaned forward and placed a kiss at her throat, sending tremors arrow straight to her feminine core. He opened the door to his house with his free hand, locked it after them, and turned on the light.

"You want to sit down here for a while?" he asked, and she knew he was merely being polite. She didn't need further affirmation that he was a gentleman; she needed what he'd been promising her all evening.

"What for?" she said, wondering at her new brazenness. "We can drink it upstairs."

He hung her coat in a closet, got a tray for the wine and their glasses, and held out his hand to her. "Come."

At the top of the stairs, he asked her, "Am I being presumptuous in assuming that you'll share my room tonight?"

For reasons she didn't understand, laughter pealed out of her. When she managed to control it, she let her finger brush gently over his jaw, feeling the beginnings of stubble and glorying in the masculine feel of it.

"Don't you know how much I love to be with you?" She didn't think she'd ever get used to the joy of knowing that the man she loved and desired loved and wanted her.

The expression in his eyes nearly unglued her, and a wild recklessness overcame her, as it always did when she knew he was going to make love to her. She told herself to let him take the lead. He put the champagne bottle and glasses on a table in the hallway, picked her up, and carried her to his room. A small lamp on his dresser, obviously capable of little more than a night glow, bathed his face in a soft mellow radiance when he turned it on, and she watched, fascinated, as he walked to her in that loose-jointed sexy way of his, a slight smile on his lips. When he reached her, his fingers stroked her right cheek and she looked up into the fierce, blazing storm in his eyes.

Unstrung by the sweet and terrible hunger he stirred in her, she grasped his arm to steady herself. If knowing what to expect hadn't been sufficient, his masculine scent and his powerful male aura possessed her, stripping her of her strength and making her will his will. His arms gripped her to his body and she stared into the dark desire of his mesmerizing eyes.

"You're everything to me," he whispered, his voice hoarse and minus its deep, velvet vibrato. "Do you love me?"

"Yes. Yes, I love you."

His mouth was on her then, hot and demanding, shattering her reserve until she grasped his hips, straining for what she needed to feel. His answer was the rise of his sex against her belly, letting her feel the force of his passion until, of their own volition, her hips shifted against him. But he stilled her and cherished her mouth, her eyes, and her cheeks with his lips. She wanted his hands on her naked skin so badly that she thought she'd scream. In desperation she moved her breast from left to right across his chest, and at last his precious fingers rubbed her tortured nipple.

"Blake. Honey, please."

He unzipped the red dress, and when she stepped out of it, flung it across a chair, though the busy fingers of his left hand never ceased stroking and caressing her.

"Blake!"

"Yes, sweetheart." He lifted her breast from the scant bra, pulled it into his mouth, and started the pulling and sucking that drove her crazy. She heard her moans and was helpless to control them. He picked her up, wrapped her legs around him, and let her feel him, all of him, never taking his lips from her breast. When she tried to force his entry, he lay her on the bed and stood looking down at her while he tore out of his clothes. Then he shielded himself for her protection and joined her.

"I'm going out of my mind," she told him.

"But we've got all night, baby. It's our first night like this. The other time, we didn't make love."

"But—"

"Shhh. Just let me love you. Let me have you." He kissed her shoulders, her breasts, and her belly, skimming his fingers on the insides of her thighs as though oblivious to her frantic movements. Then he hooked her legs over his shoulder and tortured her with his lips and tongue until she screamed, "Oh, Lord. I can't stand it."

He rose above her, and she brought him to her, raised her hips, and welcomed him as he drove home. Immediately the heat he'd built within her burst into a flame, and the powerful clenching began as he rocked her. Enthralled by his passion and enmeshed in the violent, frenzied storm he built around her and in her, she thought she'd die. Her body gave itself up to him, and he soon sucked her into a vortex of passion, refusing to release her until they both shouted aloud their eternal love, and he lay defenseless and vulnerable in her arms.

For a long time, he breathed deeply, his head on her breasts and his weight braced on his forearms. Thinking him asleep, she stroked his back in a soothing fashion, ran her fingers lightly over the tight curls on his head, caressing him as one would a baby. Cherishing him.

"I can't let you go out of my life," he said. "I can't. I just can't."

Was he asleep? Did he know what he was saying? She continued stroking, and words of endearment slipped through her lips.

"My darling. My love," she whispered.

Suddenly, he hardened within her, raised himself up and looked into her face. "There's so much unfinished business between us, but no matter. I won't give you up." He gave her shoulders a gentle shake. "Do you understand what I'm saying to you?"

Tension gathered inside of her, and her heart fluttered madly.

"I don't want you to give me up," she said. "There's no one else for me. There never was."

She felt the tremors that raced through him, and hot needles of desire stabbed relentlessly at her feminine center. He put an arm around her shoulder, his other hand beneath her buttocks, his lips to her breast, and rocked them both to the world that was theirs alone.

Chapter Thirteen

"I would have preferred to spend this afternoon with you," Blake told her, when he called around noon, "but I have to attend Ethan's first public talk on adolescent rebellion and delinquency. This won't be a talk to young people of his own age as he's done in the past, but to an assemblage of their parents at the local YWCA, and he needs support and encouragement. He phoned me a couple of minutes ago and asked me what would happen if he backed out."

"He can't do that. If he does, he may make a habit of it."

"That's what I told him. Look, sweetheart, I hate not to see you today, and especially after what we shared last night. Ethan thinks he isn't up to this, but I know he is, and I have to be there for him."

"It's all right, darling. I'll see you tomorrow morning at the board meeting. However, I don't advise you to catch my eye, because I know I'll give it all away."

"I don't care what they see; I'm through hiding my feelings. Stay sweet."

"You, too. Bye."

She'd been too discombobulated to consider church that morning, and she knew that with her mind on the night before in Blake's arms, she wouldn't have heard a word of her father's sermon. Feeling guilty, she wished she'd gone if only to let him know that she appreciated his graciousness at Blake's party. On an impulse, she got into her car and drove to her father's house.

"I was disappointed not to see you in church this morning, girl," he said. "You're just in time for a bite to eat. Come on in. Your brother's here with his Rachel."

She leaned forward to kiss him on the cheek and nearly froze when he put both arms around her for a brief hug. She could hardly believe it when he said, "You looked good last night, just like your mother when she was your age." Maybe she ought to pinch herself to see if she was asleep. Wasn't he going to lecture her about her sinfulness and the hell she faced for not attending church?

He walked with her to the living room with his hand grazing her shoulder, offering the warmth she'd longed for since she first knew herself. "Wish the other two were here," Booker said when they sat down to dinner, their midday meal. "I don't know when we last had all our children here with us. Why don't we plan a family reunion?"

She caught Paul's gaze and saw his concern. Was their father sick and preparing for his imminent demise? What had caused this . . . this reaching out, this considerateness? She looked at their mother, but Lurlane didn't seem concerned. Instead, she wore the serene expression of a happy woman.

"What a wonderful idea!" Lurlane said. "We could plan it

for Paul's birthday." She looked at Rachel. "We're a small family. My only sister never married, and I didn't have any brothers. Booker has a brother, Rafe, but he's in Alaska getting rich and can't leave his gold long enough to do more than eat and take a short nap. I expect he sleeps with one eye open. We can't count on him, nor his only child, a daughter, who married a Frenchman and lives somewhere in Provence, France."

"Where's his wife?" Rachel asked, sitting forward, her interest piqued.

"Miriam?" Booker asked with a short snort. "She got tired of that gold years ago. Said she couldn't eat it, drink it, wear it, nor sleep with it."

Rachel turned to Paul. "Where do you stand on gold?"

Paul shrugged eloquently. "Me? Greenbacks suit me fine. If Uncle Rafe had a warm, loving woman, he wouldn't spend so much time thinking about gold."

A secretive smile floated over Rachel's face, broadcasting her self-satisfaction and contentment that Paul wouldn't be chasing money at her expense. Lurlane looked from Rachel to Paul, then glanced at her husband, who was also watching them. Booker Jones took his wife's hand, leaned back, and closed his eyes, the picture of contentment. She wished she knew how to interpret her father's unusual behavior.

She nearly sprang from her chair when Booker stood, looked around the table, and asked them, "Anybody want coffee? A meal like this one deserves a good cup of coffee."

"Zip it up, Mindy," Paul said, reminding her of their childhood, when he'd tell her to shut her mouth. With eyes wide and her mouth gaping, it wasn't the first time she'd wished for her brother's poker face.

"Mama, what's come over him?" she whispered, as her father headed toward the kitchen to get coffee for everyone.

A smile drifted over Lurlane's face. "Thanks for the evening gown and accessories and the day at the beauty spa."

"You mean—"

"I mean he just discovered that he can be a loving man and still serve God. He also noticed that nobody got high and misbehaved last night, in spite of all the alcohol consumed at that party, and most of all, the people applauded him. I don't know when he's been so happy. He needs to get out among people more."

She stared at Lurlane. "You sure that's all there is to this? Mama, this is a different man."

"I know, and isn't it wonderful? I think it started when you told him you weren't going to our church anymore, that his sermons made you mad and resentful. He talked about that for the rest of the week, and I think it forced him to so some self-searching."

"But, Mama," Paul said, "I told him practically the same thing when he launched into that diatribe against Melinda with no proof whatever. And look what happened. The charges have been dropped."

"That's another thing. He preached about that this morning, and he meant for Melinda to hear what, for him, was an apology, but she wasn't there."

"Good Lord, I should hope not," Paul said, a wicked gleam dancing in his eyes.

"Last night put a cap on it," Lurlane told them. "He was so happy that Blake introduced him the way he did. Your father isn't used to having people applaud him. When he talked about it after we got home, I thought he would cry."

"I don't suppose you'd share the real reason for this with your children," Paul said, "but you can tell Rachel."

"Sure," Lurlane said dryly, "and she won't breathe it to a soul, not even in her prayers."

"Well, here we are," Booker said, returning with the tray of coffee, milk, and sugar.

It didn't escape Melinda that Rachel rushed to his aid when he looked around for a place to put the tray.

"Let me help you with that, Reverend Jones," she said, and placed the tray on the sideboard.

Anybody could see that Booker Jones wasn't accustomed to serving anything, Melinda thought, but after thirty years of watching her mother work herself to a frazzle with no help from her husband, only the Lord knew how glad she was to see him try.

"Can I drop you and Rachel somewhere?" Melinda asked Paul as they left their parents' home.

"We're going to Rachel's place. Since I have to be at the board meeting tomorrow morning, I won't go back to Durham till tomorrow evening." She noticed that he held Rachel's hand, and she wanted to ask him so many questions, but it wasn't the right time.

"Do you think Papa's all right? I never saw such a change in a man."

"Know what I think?" Rachel said. "Something's happened between him and your mother. I sensed a kind of renewal. They've been married for thirty-five years, and today he held her hand and looked at her as if he'd just fallen in love."

"Yeah," Paul said, "and they must have had a talk, too, because I noticed she didn't jump up and tell him she'd get the coffee. She sat there like a queen and let him do it."

"We'd better have a family reunion," Melinda said. "If John and Peter walk in on this alone, they'll think our parents have gone into mental decline."

"I never dreamed your father could be so . . . so charming. I was always scared to death of him, " Rachel said, "but he's actually . . . uh . . . He's nice."

Paul opened the back door of Melinda's Mercury Sable and held it for Rachel. "I'll say this much; I don't know what got into him, but whatever it is, it works for me."

He walked around to the driver's side of the car where Melinda wiped away fragments of dry leaves caught beneath the windshield wipers. "I'm staying with Rachel tonight. We'll talk after the board meeting." He opened the door for her and got in the back with Rachel. "It isn't often a man has such a sharp chick for a chauffeur. How about driving along the Patapsco?"

She ignored his quip and was about to tell him she wasn't going that way when she remembered it had been there that Blake told her he loved her. She parked near the big boulder and the bench where she'd sat with Blake. Maybe the spot would work a miracle for Paul and Rachel.

"Want to get out and breathe the fresh air?" she asked them.

"No," Paul said, "but you can."

She turned around and gave him a level look. "I should stand out there in the cold while you make out in this warm car? Don't let it enter your mind."

He shrugged and wrapped his arm around the woman beside him. "Just testing the water, sis. No need to get out of joint."

With the days growing shorter, night fell early, so she took them home. As long as her nemesis remained at large, she wouldn't travel alone at night. If the police didn't find Goodwin's accomplices soon, she'd board up the house and leave, because her tolerance for guards at her front and back door was diminishing hourly.

Blake hadn't expected the board members to behave differently that morning, but they did. Even the mayor, who obtained Blake's permission to sit in on the meeting, refrained from asking him whether Melinda had given up the idea of marrying in order to get her inheritance. And a good thing. He had hardly a modicum of tolerance for His Honor, and even less for the idea that some other man would touch any part of Melinda.

Martha Greene rose at the start of the meeting. "Thank you so much, Mr. Hunter, for that wonderful reception you gave for the board members. I'm sure I speak for all of us when I say it was the biggest thing ever to happen here in Ellicott City and an honor to the board and the Prescott Rodgers Foundation."

He smiled, showing the measure of graciousness that the comment required, but he wished the hell she'd sit down. As much trouble as she'd caused him, her tightly shut mouth was all the peace offering he needed.

"Thank you, Mrs. Greene," he said. "We'll start as soon as Mrs. Rodgers arrives."

She walked in with her coat on her arm and her skin glowing from the chill of the brisk wind. He didn't care what any of them said, did, or thought as he walked to meet her and took her coat.

"Consider yourself kissed," he whispered. "I mean from head to toe."

The panic mirrored on her face didn't elicit remorse; rather, the joy inside of him brought a sparkle to his eyes along with the memory of her as his lover.

"We were waiting for you, Mrs. Rodgers," he said. "Where's Dr. Jones?"

"Paul's parking the car. We couldn't find a parking space, and it's cold, so he let me out in front of the building."

None of the board members mentioned Booker Jones's attire and behavior at the reception, and if any of them noticed that Melinda had been Blake's date, none broached the subject. But the devil would have his day; after the meeting, the mayor took him aside.

"It looks as if she isn't doing a thing about getting married, so I'm putting you on notice. This city deserves the largest share of that money, and I'm prepared to go to court to get it."

"Frank, you've known me how many years? Seven? You ever know me to dodge a confrontation? Man, I thrive on the kind of challenge you just threw at me. I'm going by the terms of that will. To the letter. Prescott left instructions as to what I should do if Melinda didn't fulfill the terms of the will. Giving you the money is nowhere in that document. Besides, what did this town ever do for Prescott Rodgers but reject him?"

Frank's face screwed itself into an angry snarl. "I'll see you in hell."

"Hardly. I don't expect to be there."

Frank Washington had sounded desperate, which meant he needed money for more than the city's operation. As Blake headed for Melinda's car, he dialed his private investigator on his cell phone.

"See what you can find out about the financial dealings of Mayor Frank Washington. Soon."

When he reached his car, he asked Melinda, "You going to school now?"

"I took the day off for the board meeting and so I can drive Paul to the airport. That's where we're going now."

He walked around to the passenger's side and shook hands with Paul. "Looks as if things are coming together for you, man. Rachel's a fine woman."

"I think so, too, Blake, and I notice there've been some changes between you and Melinda. I wish you the best. She holds out for what she believes in, so you have to ... well, just hang in there."

"Tell me about it. I had five rough years to look but not to touch or even reveal what I felt. I'm not in this now for fun."

"I didn't think so, man."

"From this conversation, anybody would think I'm not here," Melinda said.

"Then pretend you're not," Paul said.

"I'll call you this evening," Melinda told Blake, ignited the engine, and headed for Baltimore.

He went back to his office, ruminating about the Jones family, Prescott Rodgers, and the man who'd tried to blackmail Prescott into giving away a fortune in an invention. And he thought about his feelings for Melinda and how long he'd have to wait until she was his forever.

The last thing he expected was a call from Booker Jones. "Blake, if I may call you that," Booker began, "I'm worried about those guards at Melinda's house. Haven't the police found out *anything?*"

Blake sat down, draped his left foot over his right knee, and collected his thoughts. "We have the man who's behind it, and we suspect he's the one who got into Melinda's house while she was in Italy. However, we're certain he has an accomplice or two, and until we find them we don't want to go to court."

"I expect you're on top of it. I . . . uh . . . want to thank you for inviting me and my wife to that reception. It's . . . Well, you couldn't imagine the good it's done. I hope you're willing to let go of the past."

Who *was* this guy? "Of course, sir, and I thank you and Mrs. Jones for coming."

Now what? He heard Booker clear his throat and wondered whether the man's preceding conversation had been a prelude to less palatable words.

"Blake, I'm still worried that Melinda won't someday regret passing up her inheritance. She told me she couldn't live in a loveless marriage, and I don't blame her. Besides, after what I saw between the two of you Saturday night, she'd be stupid to do it. I . . . uh . . . hope you can find a way to see that she gets what's rightfully hers. You will, won't you?"

It appeared that the man's conversion hadn't changed his character completely. Blake ran his hands back and forth over his hair. "Booker, I swore in a signed affidavit that I'd carry out the terms of that will to the letter. I've racked my brain, and so far, I haven't found a legal escape.''

Booker's sigh sounded as if fear had pushed it out of him. "Look after her as best you can. She can be stubborn; always was like that. I looked at her Saturday night." For a long minute, he didn't continue. Then he said, as if in reverence, "She was never that beautiful before; looked exactly like her mother did at that age. Well . . . it's good talking with you. Lurlane sends regards. God bless."

Blake stared at the phone long after the man hung up. He'd give anything to know what had caused the change in Booker Jones. He knocked his left fist into the palm of his right hand. Booker was right; those guards were merely a bandage on a serious wound. They had to catch the man who drugged Tillman before he harmed Melinda.

Melinda parked in her garage, locked it, and started to the front door. When a dampness brushed her face, she looked up at the gray November sky and the tiny flakes that heralded the coming of winter. No one could expect men to stand beside her door and freeze in the snow and blustery wind.

"You'll have to come inside, Mr. Tillman. I can't allow you and Mr. Hawkins to stand out here in this weather."

He touched his hat with his finger. "Thanks, ma'am, but it's not too bad today. Later, we may have to sit in the car, but we'll manage. I'm not one to back away from doing me job."

She went into the kitchen, and because Ruby wasn't there, she made a pot of coffee and took a mugful to each of the guards. "If you get cold," she told them, "come inside."

She put on a shirt and an old pair of pants and got to work on the closet, telling herself she'd finish sorting, storing, and dispensing with Prescott's effects before Christmas. She listened to the tapes while packing his clothes for delivery to local charity thrift shops. Suddenly she stopped, ran to the radio and reversed the tape, certain she hadn't heard it properly.

Blake's voice came to her clear and strong: "You ought to make it a condition. People don't appreciate what they get for free, but if you make them earn it, they're more likely to cherish it. Besides, it will be your legacy to the community."

"Spell it out," Prescott said. "What would she have to do?"

"I'm talking about a foundation that would support literacy. Give her a year in which to set it up, put together a board of directors, and get a working plan to promote literacy in Ellicott City."

"And if she doesn't?" Prescott asked, his voice communicating a wariness. "Then what?"

"She wouldn't inherit, but my feeling is that she could do it easily. She's smart."

"Yeah. I know she is. All right. I accept that. Make certain that the foundation supports both literacy and reading disabilities, and the help should be available to everybody who needs it. Got that?"

"Right. Consider it done."

"Now," Prescott said, "I have another condition that's very dear to me, but we'll talk about that one another time."

Melinda sat down without looking for the chair and landed on the floor. *"How could he?"* So she didn't deserve what she hadn't earned! How could he claim to have loved her from the minute he first saw her, yet say she should earn her inheritance and then force her to do it. When she thought of what she'd gone through trying to set up that board . . . Well, he was in for a surprise. She could do without that inheritance *and* him.

I can't stand duplicity, she said to herself. *I don't care how much the sun sets in him. It could rise in him for that matter. He can't tell me he loves me and cook up that kind of torture for me.* She got up and slammed the lid on the box of clothing. *The hell with Blake Edmund Hunter!*

From the window of Prescott's bedroom, she stood with her faced pressed to the glass, watching the snow fall thicker and thicker as her tears streamed silently from her chin to her blouse. She wanted to be rid of Blake and everything that reminded her of him and of the hours in his arms when he'd loved her to distraction. How could he do such a thing?

Increasingly outraged, she put on a heavy sweater and went to the front door. "Mr. Tillman, you and Hawkins are discharged as of now. There's no longer any need for your service. I appreciate your help and protection, but you may both leave now."

He stared at her with eyes wide and mouth open. "But, ma'am, they haven't caught the guy who—"

"Those are my last words on the subject, Mr. Tillman. Thank you."

She closed the door, locked it, and went back up the stairs. She couldn't decide whether to call Blake and give him a piece of her mind or wait till he kept their appointment and confront him.

Chapter Fourteen

"What do you mean, you dismissed Tillman and Hawkins?" he screamed into the phone, unable to believe she'd said it. "Have you gone out of your mind? That guy could be watching everything that happens in your house, every person who goes in there and comes out. Those guards are going right back there. This day!"

"Now you listen to me," she yelled right back. "It's my house until May the eleventh, and until then I'll do as I please with it. They're out. Gone. Caput. Period."

"Melinda, sweetheart, what's come over you? Why are you doing this?"

"*Why?* Because you're no longer running my life. All this talk about loving me from the minute you first saw me, and you could make my husband agree that I should establish that foundation in order to earn the right to inherit what was right-

fully and legally mine, or else. Earn it? How did you know I
hadn't already earned it? You didn't. You didn't know we had
a marriage of convenience. I don't ever want to see you again.''
She hung up.

The weight in his chest pulled him down into the nearest
chair. Half an hour earlier, he'd been thinking of ways to make
a future with her a reality. Now the issue was as dead as the
gold standard. Why hadn't he told her? After they'd discovered
Prescott's way of taking notes, he should have known she'd
eventually come across a cassette that contained his prophetic
remarks. He pulled himself up, walked from one end of his
den to the other, looked out the window at the season's first
blizzard, and hoped the weather would discourage anyone who
wanted to break into her house. He considered calling her father,
but discarded the idea.

Finally, he phoned Lieutenant Cochrane and reported what
she'd done.

''I'll send a squad car past there every so often for as long
as the weather will permit. It's already too thick and too deep
for all but especially equipped cars.''

''I hear you. I'd go over there, but it's almost impossible
walking or riding. Thanks for whatever you can do.''

He'd never felt so helpless. She'd cut him out of her life
without giving him a chance to defend himself or to explain
that when he and Prescott discussed that will, she was Prescott's
wife, and in those days he didn't let himself harbor romantic
notions about her. He kicked his prized Turkish carpet with
the toe of his left shoe. If that was the way she wanted it, she
could have her wish, and it wouldn't kill him. He headed for
the refrigerator to get a bottle of beer, opened the door, and
suddenly their shattered relationship took its toll, shortening
his breath, and he let the refrigerator take his weight. Like hell
it wouldn't kill him.

He told himself to get it together, opened the beer, got a bag of chips, and sat down to watch the Giants-Redskins Monday-night football game. Who'd be calling him on his cell phone at eight o'clock on the evening?

"Hunter."

"Got some news for you, sir." His antennae went up. His private investigator never identified himself.

"What is it?"

"The mayor's been dipping into city coffers. Seems he likes to go to out to Pimlico and play the horses. The man's credit rating is nil, he's overcharged on five credit cards, and, like I said, he's helping himself to the city till."

"Thanks, man. Keep up the good work." At least he didn't have to worry that the mayor would bring suit over Prescott's will. He made a note to get a copy of the man's credit rating.

"And another thing," the investigator continued, "Goodwin was just seen talking to a man who'll do anything for money, but that's all I could get."

"Goodwin's out on bail?"

"Evidently, for the last two days, at least."

"Do you know that man's name?"

"My informant wouldn't give it, which means the guy plays rough. I'm trying to find out more."

"When was Goodwin seen talking with that man?"

"Day before yesterday, around four-thirty in the afternoon at Pim's Bar. That's it. Be in touch." He hung up.

Blake waited about ten minutes and rang the number from which his investigator called. As he'd expected, his informant had used a pay phone. The man was being very careful. He phoned Lieutenant Cochrane at the police station and relayed the information.

"Thanks. I'll have a patrol car spot Mrs. Rodgers's house."

But that didn't satisfy him. She was in that house alone. Vulnerable. He caught himself just before he threw the telephone receiver against the wall. Why had she picked a day like this one to do such a foolish thing?

He flipped on the television and was treated to the sight of cars stalled and, in accident after accident, cars crumpled like accordions. He didn't care if Melinda said she didn't want to see him again. He put on the hip boots he wore when trout fishing, dressed in layers of sweaters, an overcoat, heavy scarf, woolen cap, gloves. and goggles, got the walking cane he used when hiking, locked his door, and set out for Melinda's house. He had to make it; her life might depend on it.

What a job! Melinda filled two pillowcases with boots, shoes, and house slippers, tied them, and placed them in the hallway. She didn't like going through the pockets of Prescott's pants and jackets, but she had to do it, and in no time, she found thirty-two dollars in coins and bills. She thought of the drawers in his bedroom furniture, threw up her hands, and decided to call it a night.

Somewhere downstairs, the sound of crashing glass and of a heavy object slamming against a piece of furniture sent a chill through her and goose pimples popped up all over her body. For a minute, fear rooted her to the spot, but she recovered, grabbed a brass bookend, and rushed to the top of the stairs. She thought she screamed, but she didn't hear a sound, as a hand reached through the broken glass panel beside the door and strained toward the key chain. She dashed down the stairs and slammed the bookend against the intruding hand with such force that the would-be intruder screamed in anguish. With her adrenalin pumping at top speed, she forgot her fear, picked up the hall phone, and punched in the precoded number for the police station.

Minutes later, she heard a knock on her door but, rather than answer it, she turned out all of the downstairs lights and stood at the bottom of the stairs, shivering from the blast of cold air that swept through the broken glass pane.

She answered the phone. "It's the security agency at your door, ma'am, Tillman, Hawkins, and Gordon. Can you open up?"

She'd forgotten that her house was wired to the agency's office. With the chain on, she cracked the door, saw Tillman, and opened it.

"You don't know how glad I am to see you," she told them. "Did you catch him?"

"We didn't," Hawkins said. "Policemen were putting him in a police car as we drove up. Fortunately, we have this John Deere snow shovel hooked to the front of the truck. An ordinary car can't move in this stuff. The snow is so deep the man couldn't run."

"Did you recognize him?" she asked Tillman.

"Yes, ma'am, I sure did."

"Now who could that be?" she asked when the doorbell rang again.

"I'll get it," Lieutenant Gordon, the agency's detective, said, drew his gun, and opened the door.

"*Blake!*"

"Mr. Hunter. Come on in," Gordon said. "You just missed the commotion."

"Hardly," Blake said, his voice and demeanor the epitome of gloom. "That guy spun around right into my arms. Fortunately the police patrol appeared, because he carried a thirty-eight revolver with a silencer." He pulled off his cap and gloves. "As cold as I am, it was all I could do to hold on to him until the policemen could cross the street and handcuff him."

"We don't think it's safe for her to be here alone tonight," Gordon said. "The guy who's behind this is out there free to finish the job himself."

Blake looked at her then, his sadness as obvious as a flashing neon sign. "It's up to Mrs. Rodgers."

If she hadn't seen in his eyes the bleakness of the wintry weather that surrounded them, she might have turned her back, but no matter what he'd done, she loved him. He'd braved the most fierce storm she had ever witnessed, because he feared for her well-being, and how right he'd been.

"You'd better get warm," she said. "I'll run some hot water, so you can get your body temperature back to normal."

"Sure you want to do that?" he asked.

The three men looked from her to Blake, obviously aware that more was going on than what they saw and heard. "We'd better patch up this pane," Gordon said. "You got any cardboard boxes, heavy paper, and tape?"

She thought for a minute. "I think there's some plywood in the basement. Prescott had planned to build a storage closet down there, but didn't get around to it. I'll show you."

She glanced at Blake and saw him shiver. "First I'd better help Mr. Hunter get warm. Come on up to the guest room." She said it pointedly, and for a minute she thought he'd leave.

Instead, he thanked the three men and, as if reluctant to do so, walked slowly behind her up the stairs. At the top, she asked him, "How long did it take you to walk here from your house?"

"Three hours."

"I'll help you out of those clothes," she said, reaching for the buttons on his coat.

"I'll manage. If you'll just put some hot water in that tub, I'll—" He staggered toward the bathroom, and she ran to him, but he held on to the door, sending her the message that he didn't want her help. Unstrung by the obvious incapacity of the man who was, to her, the personification of strength, she sped down the steps and asked Tillman to go up and see if Blake needed help.

"Maybe you could show me that plywood, ma'am," Gordon said. "Stay here, Hawkins. We can't leave that window unattended."

While Gordon and Hawkins boarded up the broken window, she made coffee and ham sandwiches. With Blake in mind, she opened four cans of chicken stock and combined it with pieces of chicken breast, chopped green pepper, and noodles. It wouldn't win a prize in a gourmet magazine, but if you were half frozen, you wouldn't sneeze at it. She put some of Ruby's brownies and chocolate chip cookies on a tray and put that on the table with the sandwiches. By the time Tillman came downstairs, she'd set the breakfast-room table for five.

She didn't want to appear overly anxious about Blake, but she couldn't help it. "How is he?"

"I'd say not so good. He insisted on a shower, which was dangerous, because he could hardly stand up straight. Hypothermia is a serious thing, and you don't get over it by fighting it."

"And that's what he's doing?"

"Yeah."

"Where . . . I mean, what is he doing now?"

"He's lying across the bed, but he said he'd be down in a minute. If you could take him something hot . . ."

"I will. The three of you go in there and eat something. I'll be back in a few minutes."

She put a bowl of soup and the remainder of the meal on a tray along with a napkin and serving utensils and took it upstairs to him. He took his time answering her knock, so she opened the door and walked in without his invitation.

She pulled a chair to the side of the bed, put the tray on it, and sat down beside him. The chill she felt wasn't from the weather, but the frosty reception he gave her. He sat up, with effort, she noticed, and looked at her. "You said you never wanted to see me again. What are you doing up here?"

Taken aback by his blatant hostility, she bristled. "My reason is the same as the one you had for walking here in this blizzard and subzero weather. Now don't give me a hard time. If you don't eat this, you're going to be awfully sick."

He grasped the coffee mug in his long, slim fingers, took several quick swallows and looked around him as if seeing the room for the first time. "You must have decorated this room. Lilac and rose. Soft and feminine like you. And almost like your bedroom."

She supposed her alarm at his reference to her bedroom must have been reflected on her face, for he said it with what was just short of a sneer, "Oh, yes. Your bedroom. I remember everything about it, not the least of which was the way you writhed under my body."

"That's not worthy of you, Blake."

He held the cup to his lips with both hands and drained it. "Then you'll forgive me, Mrs. Rodgers, if I'm not myself tonight."

Refusing to be baited, she put the tray on the bed. "This isn't the best soup I ever made, but it's filling, and you need to eat. If I bring you a pair of Prescott's pajamas, will you stay here tonight?"

"I don't sleep in pajamas. Anyway, where would I sleep?" he asked, eating the soup.

Where did he think? Though it pained her to see him lethargic and weak, his baiting annoyed her and she swung around, a glare on her face.

"Sleep any doggoned place you please."

He finished the soup, pushed the tray away from him, and eased back onto the pillow. "And if it pleases me to sleep with you?"

"Weak as you are, it wouldn't make an iota of difference," she shot back. "I have to go down and give those men something to eat. Be back after a while."

"I'll stay tonight," Tillman said, "and Hawkins will be here tomorrow morning. How's Mr. Hunter?"

"About forty percent of his normal vigor. I hope he'll remain here tonight."

"He needs rest, a lot of it," Hawkins said. "I'll be here when you get up in the morning, ma'am."

She told them good night, went upstairs to deal with Blake, and found him beneath the covers fast asleep.

Aware that Ruby wouldn't be able to come to work, she got up at seven, dressed, and went down to the kitchen to cook breakfast for herself and Blake. She phoned Hawkins, who was responsible for the front door that morning, and asked if he'd come in for breakfast.

"I already ate, ma'am, but I sure would like a cup of coffee."

They talked for a few minutes; then he stunned her with the information that Blake had left.

"What? You mean he walked home?"

"No, ma'am. I came in the truck and Tillman drove it back to the agency. On the way, he dropped Mr. Hunter off at his house. Worked out fine."

"Why ... uh ... that's wonderful. I hope he manages to rest today."

"Seemed a hundred percent when he left here."

"I'll have the coffee for you in two minutes," she said, and came close to adding that she'd like to have Blake Hunter's scalp. How could he leave without saying good-bye? She had a mind to ... Why should he say good-bye? Hadn't she told him she never wanted to see him again? She put the coffee in a thermos, went to the door, and waited until Hawkins, who sat in the agency's car, walked across the street to the house.

"Thanks, ma'am. I know you'll be glad when your problems are over, but after this job, my next assignment will seem like punishment."

"Punishment comes in a lot of forms, Hawkins, but it's least bearable when the source is close to you."

"Tell me about it. It's my middle name."

She didn't ask him to elaborate, she had her own problems to deal with, and considering how hard she'd prayed for sleep the night before and still hadn't had one wink of it at seven that morning, she was in for a rough time. Breaking off from Blake was a matter of words, but getting him out of her soul would take a lot more.

Her pulse kicked into a mad race when the phone rang, and she had to fight for calm before answering it. "Hey, girl. Imagine no school today and probably none tomorrow," Rachel said, her spirits obviously high.

"Too bad Paul went back to Durham yesterday." She didn't feel like bantering. The letdown at hearing her friend's voice and not Blake's stunned her.

"You in the dumps? What's going on with you and Blake?"

If you got a headache, did that mean you had problems with your man? She asked Rachel as much.

"Honey, a headache wouldn't make you sound like that. You've had the wind sucked out of you. What's the matter?"

She took a deep breath and summoned her patience. "Rachel, I don't think you want to know. When I get it all straightened out, I'll broadcast it to all my friends."

"Whoa there. Sorry I butted in."

"Somebody tried to break in on me last night and almost made it. That, and I don't know how many other problems, aren't likely to make me want to dance."

"I guess not. I'm sorry. I told you to let me know if you needed me, but you never have. I'd offer to come stay with you, but I figured Blake was keeping you company."

Blake. Always Blake. "When's Paul coming back?"

"Soon as the airport opens, I guess."

"Are you two making plans?"

"It's getting to that point. I hope I have your blessing, Melinda. If Paul and I got married, you'd be my sister."

Best news she'd had all day, because she suspected Rachel wasn't in a position to tell all of it. "Paul's my favorite sibling. If you make him happy, how could I not be happy myself? I'm glad you two found each other."

"I love him, Melinda. For the first time in my life, I'm in love. I don't know what the problem is between you and Blake, but you love each other. Anybody can see it. If he needs forgiveness, forgive him. That man's worth loving."

"My grandfather used to say, 'Talk's easy done, but it takes money to buy land.' A small thing to some is a behemoth to others."

"Be stubborn and see if he comes crawling. Not in a million years."

Blake swore he'd never again serve as executor of anybody's will. He'd done it a dozen times, but this one was more than he'd bargained for. After telephoning first Ethan and then Phil and Johnny and satisfying himself that they were all right, he phoned his mother, because he knew she'd worry if she saw that snow in the television newscasts.

"You promised to come visit me. I know you said you'd come this winter, but you don't have to wait till then."

"I promise I'll be up there the first part of the year. I've joined a sewing club, and we're making sweaters, mittens, scarves, and caps for homeless children. These will be the only Christmas gift some of them will have."

"If you're enjoying it, great. You need anything?"

She told him she didn't. "You don't seem to have your usual energy. Is anything wrong? What about that girl?"

He should have known she'd ask about Melinda. "I wish I

knew the answer to that. I had great hopes but, well . . . that's life.''

Her loud gasp was as much evidence as he needed that she had hoped for a different outcome of his relationship with Melinda. ''You can't patch it up?''

''I don't know.'' He gave her the essence of the problem. ''I think she's devastated and hurt. I'm sorry, but that doesn't solve anything.''

''But you're not giving up. That's not a bit like you. Besides, being mad with you doesn't mean she's stopped loving you.''

He had to laugh when he remembered Melinda sitting on the side of the bed holding a spoonful of that awful, strange-tasting soup to his mouth. ''I know she loves me, and I probably should have told her of my part in the wording of that will. I didn't get a chance to explain before she gave me a taste of her vituperative tongue, and—''

''Oh, for goodness' sake. We've all said things when we were angry that we later wanted to take back. You can be rigid when you believe you're right, and this time, I'm not sure you are.''

Neither was he. He told her good-bye and hung up. He had to get to his office and prepare for his encounter with the mayor. A desperate man made a worthy opponent, but he was forearmed, and right now he'd welcome a good fight with just about anybody. He put in a call to the sanitation department to check the condition of the streets and learned that if he shoveled his driveway, he could drive to within a block of his office. He brought out the snowplow he hadn't used in four years and went to work. Two hours later, he walked into his office.

He tried to work, but a restlessness pervaded him and he found himself pacing from his desk to the window and back. Eventually, anger replaced his discontent, and in a fit of temper, he telephoned her. But like a dream at daybreak, the anger vanished when he heard her voice, and the only things that mattered were his need of her and whether she loved him.

"Melinda, this is Blake."

"I know. Your breakfast is still on the table where I'd already put it when I learned that you'd been home for nearly an hour."

"If you're mad at me, why would you cook breakfast for me?"

"Because you risked your life for me last night, and I was raised to be grateful for kindness."

"No kidding." He didn't mean to sound sarcastic, but *grateful for kindness* indeed. "I expect you were taught forgiveness, too."

"That's something you have to ask for. Even the Lord demands that."

"Can I see you?"

"I . . . uh . . . I don't think so. You don't know what a torture this whole thing is for me. There've been times when I've actually disliked Prescott, believed he wasn't the man I'd thought. If I was so precious to him, how could he have done this to me? I don't want his money. Blake, I wish you well, but I . . . I still hurt. Bye."

He had to dig into himself, force himself to work, using all his power of concentration, and yet she dashed across the page on which he wrote, laughing, mocking. When at last he finished the draft, he thought of calling her again and telling her he'd done it in spite of her. The idea brought a laugh from him and, with it, the reminder that before he'd opened himself up to her, he'd rarely laughed. She'd given him laughter and so much more.

On the way to his car, he passed the drug store, the only establishment open for business, thanks to Ellicott City's first blizzard in twenty years. His glance caught something in the window and on an impulse he went in and bought it. He had it wrapped in lavender paper and tied with a rose-colored bow, stopped by her house, and asked Tillman to give it to her. If that didn't move her, he'd find something that would.

"Mr. Hunter asked me to give you this, ma'am," Tillman said, handing her a small lavender-colored shopping bag.

"Thanks. " She said it almost absentmindedly, as if neither that nor anything else interested her.

Blake had never given her a gift, and her curiosity sent her barreling up the stairs to her room, where she sat down, calmed herself, and tried to steady her fingers enough to open it. Her gaze focused on the little box wrapped daintily in her favorite colors, and her heart constricted. If only . . . She loosened the bow, eased the ribbon off the paper, opened the box, and stared at the tiger-striped kitten half the size of her hand. He'd chosen a happy little cat that had the slightest suggestion of arrogance, its head tilted upward and its tail up high and curved forward as if it didn't give a hoot. She opened the envelope and read *Her name is Lindy, because she reminded me of you. Love, B.*

"I will not cry. I don't care what he does, I will not cry," she said aloud as moisture dampened her cheeks. She put the kitten on her night table and went back to the drudgery of sorting out the remainder of Prescott's effects. She couldn't call him, because she'd break down if she did, and she didn't want to give in to him. She wanted to forget about Blake, Prescott, and that will and get on with her life. But it was not to be; both had found nesting places in her mind and refused to move.

The following day, with the streets still clogged with what had once been snow but was now ice, school remained closed, and she continued the task of going through her late husband's things. The most difficult job still faced her, for she hadn't touched his bedroom. She heard a loud pop like the sound of a firecracker and rushed to the back window just as a man jumped from the fence into the street. She called Tillman and told him what had happened and, because she knew he'd report it to Blake, she phoned him.

"Thanks for the kitten," she said. "I'm trying to figure out what it is about that little cat that reminds you of me."

"Shouldn't be too difficult. That cat says if you like it, fine; if you don't, tough. And like you, she's so graceful."

"Anyway, I think she's cute. There's something I . . . maybe ought to tell you about." She described the incident. "It happened just a minute ago."

His silence rang in her ears. After a minute, he said, "Thanks for telling me. I expect Tillman's trying to phone me right now. It seems as if Goodwin's getting reckless, and that's what we've been waiting for. He's discovered that there's no guard at the back and he'll try it again, so I'm calling the agency and ordering a guard for that post."

She didn't protest, because she realized dismissing the guards hadn't been a wise move; indeed it could have cost Blake his life. She pulled air through her teeth. Blake. Always Blake. It could have caused *her own* demise.

"Do what you think best," she heard herself say and added, "I'm not used to the taste of crow, but if I have to eat it . . ." She let the thought speak for itself.

"I wouldn't ask for your humility," he said, "not now, not ever, no matter what transpires between us. All I ask is your understanding and a chance to—"

"Please, Blake, I'm not ready to deal with that yet. I'm . . . I'm . . . I put so much of myself into it that I need to breathe a different air for a while."

"Are you telling me you don't . . . that you're no longer interested? If you are, make it plain."

She was irritated by her own inconsistency, her inability to get her heart in sync with her head; anger threatened to sharpen her tongue and she had to exert great effort to control it.

"You want to know where you stand, and I don't fault you for that, but I . . . I need time."

"You're saying you haven't given up on us entirely?"

She told herself he had a right to probe, but that she was entitled to stand her ground. "Blake, you're a smart man. You know how I feel about you, so stop pushing me. Put yourself in my place, and see if you wouldn't feel betrayed."

"All right. Let me know when you have a change of heart. But don't wait too long. I'm going to call Lieutenant Cochrane at the police station and see what they're doing about Goodwin."

"Maybe that wasn't Goodwin."

"I've thought of that. Could be another of his henchmen. Mind if I drop by there tomorrow evening?"

"I may be in school."

"School's closed for the remainder of this week. Well?"

"I'll be here." She could have kicked herself, but she admitted to herself that she wanted to see him.

"Around six. See you then."

She put away her lesson plans at around five that evening, showered, dressed, and still had half an hour to burn before Blake arrived. After pacing the floor for a few minutes, she sat down at the piano and began to play Liszt's Hungarian rhapsodies. Tension seeped out of her muscles, and the stress she hadn't recognized eased from her mind. She closed her eyes and let the music wash away her cares. A kaleidoscope of brilliant colors, ever changing, dancing and flying, exploded in her head as she mastered the keyboard, unaware of all but the music, out of herself. Lost now, somewhere in time, her fingers produced Liszt's magical Rhapsody Number Four in D Minor. When at last she played the final note and an eerie hush was all she heard, she glanced at her watch. Twenty minutes past six. How could it be? Blake was never late.

The doorbell rang and she went to open the door. "Hi," she

said, her animosity gone, a casualty of the music she'd just played.

"Hi," he said. Banal greetings that served as poor substitutes for dashing into each other's arms.

"I didn't want to disturb your wonderful playing, so I waited out here until you finished the piece. You are certainly accomplished."

She walked with him to the living room and offered him a seat. "I should play more often. Music does wonders for me."

He handed her a small package wrapped in rose-colored paper and tied with a lavender velvet bow. "You shouldn't do this, Blake. You're seducing me."

He looked her in the eye and didn't smile. "That's my intention; it's what this male-female thing is all about. But in the meantime, I hope I'm pleasing you."

Before she could answer, his cell phone rang. "Hunter. No, he's dangerous. I'll alert the police out back."

"What is it? What's going on?" She was doggoned if she'd be treated as if she were a helpless child to be kept out of harm's way.

"After your call yesterday afternoon, we set a trap for the guy. He thinks nobody's guarding the place, but in addition to the agency's guards, you have six cops hiding out. When you stopped playing, I had exactly one minute to get inside this house. We'd put the word out that the day guards would leave and that the night guard at the front door was supposed to be there at six, but was in school and always got there between six-fifteen and six-thirty."

"I could have walked right into it. Thanks for not telling me."

"With a detective at each door, there wasn't a chance."

"What was the noise I heard yesterday afternoon, that popping sound out back just before that man jumped over the fence?"

"The guy tried to blow off the back door, but that crude, handmade stick of dynamite he used didn't detonate."

A peculiar fatigue settled in him and around him; he was tired of the fencing, one-upmanship, and discontent, but he had to wait until she came to terms with his having had that clause inserted. He stared at her, wanting to ask how she could be so soft and sweet, how she could give herself up to him so completely, and now be so unyielding.

"I suppose he's in custody now," he said, "but we'd better stay put for a while in case there are any shots."

"Then, maybe I'd better go upstairs out of the range of gunfire. Gee," she said, swung around, and reached for the package, as if suddenly remembering it. "My Lord, look at this! A mahogany and mother-of pearl miniature baby grand." She shook her head in wonder. "Blake, this is . . . I can't believe . . . this is fantastic."

His grin took her aback momentarily, because he hadn't smiled much recently. "Does that mean you like it?"

She raced to him, threw her arms around his neck, and hugged him, and he grasped her to him in a fierce caress. Nervous and self-conscious about her impetuousness, her "Thanks" was barely audible and she moved away from him.

The doorbell rang. "I'll get it," Blake said.

"All clear, Mr. Hunter. He left here in the squad car protesting that Goodwin set him up. Won't he be surprised to see Goodwin when he gets downtown? I don't think they'll be greeting us at Christmas."

"You bet. Thanks, Lieutenant. I'll be down to the agency tomorrow to take care of the bill." He turned to her. "Open the piano, why don't you?"

She lifted the lid and found that the piano was a music box that played the tune, "If I Loved You." At the music's end, she looked up into eyes that shone with love, and her heart seemed to stampede in her chest.

"It's precious, Blake. I've never had one before, and you knew I'd love it."

"I hoped. You're safe now. I'll be in touch."

Gazing at his departing back, she wondered whether he'd come because as executor of the estate, he thought it his duty, or because he wanted to protect her. Then she looked at the music box that she still held in her hand, put it to her lips, kissed it, and wandered in the direction of the kitchen. She had to eat, but the thought of food nearly sickened her.

Chapter Fifteen

Blake usually completed his Christmas shopping before the first of December, but with Christmas only days away, he hadn't managed to buy more than a few gifts. He told himself that he'd been too busy preparing a brief for the trial of Goodwin and his two cohorts, but he'd never been successful at fooling himself. Everything in his life was dragging along like a car with two flat tires. He found a brown leather jacket for his brother, a matching Burberry raincoat, umbrella, and rain hat for Callie, his sister, and a red velour robe and slippers for his mother. He went to the smoking section to look for pipes and remembered. It would be their first Christmas without his father.

With the gifts in shopping bags, he browsed through the store. Nothing he saw looked like her. During the past three weeks, he'd sent her scented candles, a tiny pink satin pillow on which were embroidered the words *What about tonight?*, and a silver chain on which hung a silver key inserted into a silver heart. She'd responded with *Thank you* on scented, personalized notepaper. He didn't care if she didn't call, because those notes told him she didn't trust herself to talk with him. He walked through the book and record department and stopped. At last, he'd found what he wanted.

At home, he took the packages to his den, just as his phone began to ring. He picked it up and heard the mayor's voice.

"Blake, this is your mayor. The whole town knows that Melinda Rodgers isn't trying to find a husband. According to Ray Sinclair, she's on record as saying she's not going to marry anybody, and I'd think he'd be the best candidate, so he should know."

He took a deep breath and decided to let Frank Washington hang himself. "You're suggesting I should start parceling out this man's effects before the deadline for Melinda's compliance with the will. You're a lawyer and an elected official and you're suggesting I break a legal, registered will?"

The mayor's breathing accelerated as if he'd been frightened. "No, you know I'm not saying that, Blake. But she's not going to find a decent man to marry her, not in this town, so you might as well plan now to give that money to the city."

He'd been sitting on the edge of his desk, and he bounded up and nearly snatched the phone wire from its socket. "What the hell do you mean by that statement? Where do you get off with assassinating her character?"

"Now, now, Blake. There're things you don't know. I wouldn't want this to get back to Mrs. Washington, but I know more about Melinda Rodgers than you'd think. I've been having an affair with her for years, and I wouldn't be surprised if I wasn't the only one."

"You're lying, Frank, and I'm the one man who can prove it. Now, let me tell you what you've *really* been doing for years." He repeated what his private investigator had discovered and which he himself had documented. "You either eat that lie or I'll give the facts, documented and with a signed affidavit, to the daily paper tomorrow morning. What'll it be?"

"You can't prove—"

"Give me your fax machine number, and I'll send you copies."

"Don't expose me, please, Blake. I never touched her, not once. I—"

"I know you haven't, but you'd malign her. Don't expect mercy from me." He hung up. That took care of the mayor.

He couldn't leave Ellicott City without giving her the gifts he'd bought for her and knowing that she wouldn't be alone on Christmas Eve. He packed his bags, put them in the trunk of his car, and drove to 391 College Avenue. Darkness had already set in at five-thirty in the afternoon, and his spirits lifted when he saw the wreaths glowing from her door and windows. At least she'd gotten the Christmas spirit. She answered the door at once, and he was gratified to see that she'd taken the precaution first to look through the peephole.

"Hi."

He gazed at her, a sight for his sore eyes, lovely in a red jumpsuit.

"Hi," he said. "I couldn't leave town without seeing you and wishing you a Merry Christmas. Did you dress a tree?"

"Uh-huh. Want to see it?"

He followed her into the living room, and when she flicked a light switch, the six-foot balsam fir—beautifully decorated with red, green, and silver bells, fairies, angels, munchkins, and the like—glowed beside the lighted fireplace. A warm, cozy environment where a man could love a woman to distraction. He opened the shopping bag and placed two packages under the tree.

Her mouth worked the way it did when she was struggling

for composure, but he figured it best to pretend he didn't notice.
"Thanks for the presents. Would you ... er ... like some
eggnog or some mulled wine?"

"I can't have more than a sip, because I'm driving to the
Baltimore airport. Mulled wine will be fine."

She brought a glass for him and one for herself and sat in
a beige overstuffed chair facing him. "Cheers. Will you be
with your folks in Alabama for Christmas?"

She already knew the answer to that. He nodded. "It's our
first Christmas without our father, and we'll all be there to give
our mother moral support, though I'm not so sure she needs
it. She's a strong woman." He sipped the wine and looked at
his watch. "I'd better get moving. You'll be with your family,
I suppose."

"Yes. We're having a family reunion. I ... uh, hope you
have a wonderful Christmas."

She walked over to the tree and picked up a package wrapped
in a golden brown iridescent paper and tied with a brown ribbon.
He looked at the package, then at her. She'd said his eyes were
that color. Was she telling him something?

"Thanks for remembering me," was as much as he could
manage. The scene, barren of warmth, lacking all he'd envi-
sioned for the holidays, cut him to the quick.

She walked with him to the door, and he didn't think he'd
ever seen her so subdued, nor would he have expected it. "Have
a good time." She looked down at her feet and said, "Drive
carefully, and get back safely."

She wouldn't look at him, and he'd learned early to seize
the moment. If he hadn't he wouldn't be where he was.

"Do you care whether I get back here in one piece?"

She didn't look at him, so he tipped up her chin with his
fingers, forcing her to let him see her eyes. The pain in them
nearly rocked him on his heels.

"Melinda. Oh, Melinda! Sweetheart, don't ... Don't do this

to us." He opened his arms, and the feel of her soft, sweet body tight in his embrace sent shocks reverberating throughout his system.

Her arms went to his shoulders, and she gripped him with more force than he would have imagined she could muster. He hungered for her mouth, but when he attempted to kiss her, she lowered her head.

"I'm ... I'm ... Go on home," she said, "and when you come back, maybe we can talk."

"I'll be back on the thirtieth, can we spend New Year's Eve together?"

"I. . .yes, I want that."

He couldn't leave as things were. "Can't you ... kiss me?"

He watched her struggle with her inner conflict, but he'd waited a month, and he'd wait as long as he had to. She was his, and he meant to let her know it.

"Kiss me," he whispered. Slowly she raised parted lips to his, and he plunged into her. Shudders plowed through him and tremors shook him as he wrapped her to his body. She battled him for his tongue, and he'd have given her the world if he'd owned it. Her breath came short and fast as she feasted on his tongue. He thought she'd devour him, and he didn't care. Then, as if she'd come to herself and realized what she was doing, she braced her hands against his chest. He released her.

"It won't go away for me either, sweetheart," he said. "I'll barely make my flight, and Callie's meeting it. Be here for me when I get back."

She nodded but didn't answer, and he realized she'd surprised herself when she went into his arms. Nothing had changed, and when he got back, he'd bring that home to her forcibly.

* * *

He sat at the Christmas dinner table with his family, thinking of the warmth and love that surrounded him, and he was almost happy. He and Melinda should have been together, but their course wasn't yet smooth. At least he knew she still loved him; he'd take it from there.

"I was hoping you'd bring Melinda with you," his mother said. "You must have gotten it straightened out, because you've hardly stopped laughing since you've been here." John and Callie stopped eating and focused their attention on him.

"It's better, and it'll get better still."

"How the mighty have fallen," John said, raising his glass. "Here's to Melinda." As his mother and sister joined in the toast, he thought: *Just wait till next year.*

Melinda sat with her parents and her brothers, John and Peter, waiting for Paul and Rachel to arrive for Christmas dinner. "Melinda, you have to find a way to keep your money. If you don't want it, divide it among those who need it, but it would be a crime to let it go to the city and state," Booker said.

"I know, Papa. Blake said he's trying to find a way, and I believe him."

"Of course," Lurlane said, "but you have to help him."

She stared at her mother. "What can *I* do?"

Lurlane rolled her eyes. "This is twice recently you've given me reason to wonder about your intelligence."

She was saved the trouble of answering, for Paul arrived with Rachel, who greeted them with her left hand stretched out in front of her. Melinda ran to her friend and hugged her.

"We're engaged," Paul announced. He greeted his parents, hugged his brothers, and kissed Melinda. "Get your act together, Mindy. Guys like Blake don't show up in this town every day."

Lurlane poured a glass of eggnog for Booker, and then laced the remainder with rum. She knew that none of her children would mention the added kick. But Booker decided he'd like a second glassful.

"Just spit it out, Papa," Melinda said when he tasted it and made a face. "That way, it can't make you high."

Booker glared at her. "Young lady, I want you to know that a teaspoon of liquor isn't likely to make me unsteady. I have stronger willpower."

His four children stared at him, each wondering at his calm acceptance of rum in the eggnog and his failure to spoil their day by sending their souls to hell.

Lurlane raised her glass. "Merry Christmas, all of you." She turned to her husband. "Thank you, my dear, for being the man I married." To Rachel, she said, "Welcome to our family, my daughter."

With the aroma of roasting turkey, buttermilk biscuits, and sweet potato pie filling the house, Lurlane took her husband's hand and started toward the dining room. "Dinner's ready."

"I'd like a word with you, girl," Booker said to Melinda after dinner, and she followed him into his study. Normally, he'd have said whatever he thought in the presence of the others, and she couldn't help being grateful that if he was going to say something that would embarrass her, he'd at least do it in private.

Apprehension settled over her as she followed him, fearing he'd cap a wonderful day with a lecture. "What's happened between you and Blake?" he asked, surprising her. "How come he's where he is and you're here? I know what was going on just a month ago, so this doesn't make sense."

She sat down, weary from fighting herself and lonely for Blake, and told him she'd broken off the relationship and why.

He paced in front of her, his thumbs in his vest pocket, as when he was about to preach. "I can't believe what I'm hearing.

If there was nothing between you, it was his sacred duty to protect his client's interest, not yours. So what if he didn't tell you; was he obligated to tell you how that will was written? Even if he wronged you, what did I teach you since you were born? What? Tell me."

"You said if we don't forgive, we're lost, and that the person who bears the grudge has a bigger burden than the one against whom the grudge is held."

"You're the one holding the resentment. So am I right? Aren't you miserable?"

"Yes, sir."

His arm grazed her shoulder in a gesture of affection that, six weeks earlier, would have startled her. "Don't ruin your life for spite. Don't be too small a person to forgive. Blake's a good man, and he loves you. Get it straightened out. You hear me?"

"I want to, but I can't figure out how."

He half-closed one eye and raised his eyebrow above the other one. "I don't believe you. You have to know you can get that man to do anything you want him to do. If you have a problem with it, talk to your mother."

She kissed his cheek. "Thanks, Santa Claus."

She didn't want to seem too anxious, but every time she heard a car pass her house, she bounded toward the door, slowed down, walked back into the living room, and sat down. She figured that, in the last half hour, she'd lost fifteen pounds jumping up at the slightest sound and sitting back down. Finally, the doorbell rang. She inspected her appearance in the hall mirror, checked her right wrist to make sure her Fendi perfume was working, and made herself walk slowly to the door. After looking through the peephole, she yanked it open.

"Hi," she said, as casually as she could. "Come on in."

But Blake apparently didn't have games in mind. He stepped in, kicked the door closed, took her in his arms, and brushed his lips across hers.

"Hi," he said. "Thanks for the beautiful cuff links. Did Federal Express bring you a flat envelope today?"

"I don't know. Ruby can't get over the habit of putting the mail on Prescott's desk, and I haven't been in the den today."

"Would you mind checking?" As she started for the stairs, she glanced at him over her shoulder. Hmmm. He was not a worried man. If anything, he was as self-assured as Paul's old peacock. She ran up the steps as fast as her long, slim black skirt would allow and, a minute later, returned with the envelope.

He took the cassette from his own envelope. "I have a feeling we each got one and that they're identical," he said, "but we can play them both."

"Why do you think what's on here is important?"

His eyes sparkled with the glint that always gave her a warm feeling. "There's a note on mine that says 'copy two,' and the return address says 'Estate of Prescott Rodgers, care of Attorney J. L. Whittaker.' I'm executor of the estate, so this is something he deliberately withheld from me."

He put the cassette on. "Sit over here with me. If we don't want to hear it, we can at least comfort each other."

She snuggled up to him, shamelessly, maybe, but she'd missed him so much. "Blake, I'm . . . I'm so sorry I messed things up. I mean, I was mad, but I didn't have to act like I did. And all these little presents you sent me, and the book of poems. I've almost worn out that CD of Brook Benton love songs. I'd never heard of him. He's wonderful. Here's something I got for you," she said, handing him a box.

He opened it, and then his wonderful laughter filled the room. "I'll be doggoned. A necktie with your telephone number on it. Now that's clever!" .

"I bought it in case you decided not to accept my request for forgiveness."

"Don't tell me. You've been talking with your father."

She figured her expression was deprecating at best. "Play the cassette."

He hit the button, and the cassette rolled a full minute before they heard his voice.

"Dear Blake and Melinda,

"I instructed Whittaker to deliver duplicate copies of this tape to the two of you on December the thirty-first of this year. By now, it's clear to both of you that Melinda won't marry a man just to get an inheritance. I inserted that clause because it would force the two of you to accept the fact that you love each other. I knew it from the start, and I loved both of you the more for your strength and virtue, your refusal to dishonor me. You belong together, have from the moment you met. I didn't care a hoot about that foundation, Blake, but I accepted the idea, because it would make it necessary for you and Melinda to spend a lot of time in each other's company. I'm certain that, by now, my scheme has worked because your attraction to each other is so strong. Melinda, my dear, the inheritance is yours. Blake is yours as well. Love him with all your heart. Prescott."

She didn't try to stop the tears, much as she hated to cry, and soon wrenching sobs poured out of her. "I th . . . thought all kinds of me . . . mean things about him for inserting that clause, and he only wanted to help us get together."

"Shhh. It's over now. Please. Honey, stop it. Don't sob like that. I can't stand it. I—"

He hooked an arm under her knees and the other around her shoulders and pulled her into his lap. "Honey, please stop it."

The feel of his lips caressing her eyelids, her ears, neck, and face filled her with another kind of emotion, the drive to explode in passion. Her fingers traced his jaw, his forehead, his cheeks, and his bottom lip.

"Kiss me, Blake. Kiss me as if you mean it."

Immediately that fiery storm she knew so well raged in his eyes, but he gazed at her for the longest time while his eyes seemed to grow stormier and wilder by the second.

"I once told you that if you made love with me, there'd be no turning back," he said, "and if you take me up those stairs with you, you're making a commitment. Is that clear?"

She slid off his lap, stood, and reached for his hand. In a second, he was on his feet and had her locked in his arms with the hard tips of her breasts rubbing against his chest. He brushed his hand across one turgid nipple.

"Yeah! You missed me."

His lips came down on hers in a powerful statement of possession, and she welcomed his velvet tongue into her mouth. Lord, she needed him so badly. Standing on tiptoe, she fastened her hands to his buttocks and pulled him to her.

"Slow down, hon," he said, "I'm short of control tonight."

"I don't want your control. I want to know who you are, and if you're uncorked, I don't care."

He stared at her. "You don't know what you're saying."

He had a wild, feral look now, a little scary, but she wanted him like that, without the polish and the suave lawyer's persona. She wanted down-to-earth, gut-bucket man. As if he read her mind, he picked her up and dashed up the stairs. At the top, he reached for the zipper on her blouse and had if off her by the time he got her into her room. She unzipped her skirt and stepped out of it.

"Good Lord," he whispered, as his gaze swept over her body, bare but for the tiny red bikini panties. He picked her up, dumped her onto the bed, knelt beside it, and slowly, methodically pulled the panties down her legs, kissing every spot they touched. He stood then and took his time getting out of his clothes, never taking his gaze from her.

"I'm going to help myself to you this night," he said, almost to himself. After putting his clothes and her skirt and blouse across a chair, he walked back to the bed and stared down at her. She could see him swallow the liquid that accumulated in his mouth. When she crossed her knees, his familiarity with her body told him desire had begun its strumming in the seat of her passion, and he jumped to full readiness. She opened her arms to him and a loud, hoarse groan escaped him.

She wanted wildness, and he let her have it, plunging his tongue into her mouth and showing her what was to come. He nipped her lip and her ears, and bathed them with the tip of his tongue. His fingers skimmed her arms, neck, and shoulders, teasing her though he had to know she wanted his mouth on her breast. Frantic for it, she put her hand on his head and led him there, and he went at her as if he'd been starved for the taste of her. He suckled vigorously, and stroked the other one until she cried out loud.

"Honey, I need you inside of me." She felt his hand skim her belly and held her breath for that second when he'd touch her and she'd start aching for more. He stroked slowly, driving her nearly mad, until she began to undulate wildly. Frustrated, she slapped his buttocks, and his fingers began their dance, turning her into the earthy, primitive female she knew only when she was in his arms. She swung her hips up to him, but he wouldn't be rushed. She thought she'd die if he didn't get inside of her.

Out of her mind with desire, hot arrows of need pounding her feminine center, she reached for him, but he moved away and continued his onslaught. Sucking vigorously and stroking the diamond between her legs. Love's liquid dampened his fingers, and when he rose above her, she sheathed him with the condom he'd placed on the night table.

"Look at me, baby. You belong to me now. No other man exists."

"Yes. Yes, I'm yours. I—"

He plunged into her hot and furious the way he'd taught her to like it, and within minutes he had her out of control, not certain where she was or how she got there. He stroked with the fury of a fast-moving train, claiming, possessing. He seemed to crawl as he moved up higher, shocking her senses with a feeling she hadn't known before, triggering the awful deathlike fullness. She wanted to die of the half pain, half pleasure, and then he locked her to him with steellike arms. "We're together this time. Give yourself up to me. Let me have you."

He stroked powerfully, until that sweet and awful explosion plowed through her.

"Blake. Blake. I love you, I always loved you," she gasped, shattered by the loving.

He screamed her name, "Melinda. Melinda, my love, my life," and came apart in her arms.

He lay that way for a long while, and she had time to wonder how she'd been so foolish. After about twenty minutes, he raised his head from her breast and looked at her.

"You knocked the stuffing out of me just now."

"It's what you deserved. You did something to me you hadn't done before."

"You weren't committed to me before. I was breaking ground for the future. I want to marry you, Melinda. I had hoped we could announce it this Christmas, but—"

"Would have been nice, too. Paul and Rachel announced their engagement at my parents' house Christmas Day."

He braced himself on his forearms and stared down at her. "Did you just agree to marry me?"

"I sure did. I'm honored, even if you didn't get on your knees to ask me."

"Considering where I am right now, that would be impossible."

"Oh, Blake, I'm so happy."

His smile, so brilliant and sweet, confirmed his words. "I love you now, and I will forever."

"Wait a minute." She remembered the will and its bequeathal of millions. "What will we do with all that money?"

"Whatever you like," he said, nibbling at her breast. "With all these poor people in Ellicott City, spending it won't be a problem. Happy New Year, sweetheart."

"Happy New Year, darling."

Dear Reader:

Greetings! This is my first romance novel and my first letter to you in this, the third millennium. I hope it began as well for you as for me, and that SCARLET WOMAN enriched your life in some way, if only to give you a couple hours respite from the problems of daily living. And I hope, too, that Melinda and Blake will have a place among your favorite romance couples. Love and romance are to be treasured. Having that special person in our lives, there for us through every crisis, and sharing with us our joys, dreams, and successes, are blessings beyond measure. It is soul sustenance of the rarest kind. This is the pinnacle of living, and I find inexplicable pleasure in leading the strong and supportive yet gentle and vulnerable hero and the capable, loving heroine to this fountain of ecstasy. During the months that I spend with these people, they are real, live beings who exist in the world that I create for them. That so many of you embrace these characters is a source of immense satisfaction to me. Thank you also for making SECRET DESIRE such a stunning success. I appreciate your support.

Don't forget to write. I answer every letter and E-mail promptly. E-mail: GwynneF@aol.com; Web page: http://www.gwynneforster.com. Letters may be addressed to me at P.O. Box 45, New York, NY 10044. Please include a self-addressed, stamped, legal size envelope if you would like a reply.

I wish each of you many blessings.

Fond regards,
Gwynne Forster

ABOUT THE AUTHOR

Gwynne Forster is a best-selling and award-winning author of eleven romance novels and four novellas. *Romantic Times* nominated her first interracial romance, AGAINST THE WIND—which Genesis Press published in November 1999—for its award of Best Ethnic Romance of 1999, and nominated Gwynne for a Lifetime Achievement Award. The Romance In Color internet site gave AGAINST THE WIND its Award of Excellence and named Gwynne 1999 Author of the Year. FOOLS RUSH IN, which BET Books published in November 1999, received the *Affaire de Coeur* magazine award for Best Romance with an African-American Hero and Heroine. Her books won that award in 1997 and 1998 also. Her January 1999 book, BEYOND DESIRE, is a Doubleday Book Club, Literary Guild and Black Expressions club selection.

Gwynne holds a bachelor's and master's degree in sociology and a master's degree in economics/demography. As a demographer, she is widely published. She is formerly chief of (nonmedical) research in fertility and family planning in the Population Division of the United Nations in New York and served for four years as chairperson of the International Programme Committee of the International Planned Parenthood Federation (London, England). These positions took her to sixty-three countries. Gwynne sings in her church choir, loves to entertain, and is a gourmet cook and avid gardener. She lives with her husband in New York City.

BOOK YOUR PLACE ON OUR WEBSITE AND MAKE THE ARABESQUE ROMANCE CONNECTION!

We've created a customized website just for our very special Arabesque readers, where you can get the inside scoop on everything that's going on with Arabesque romance novels.

When you come online, you'll have the exciting opportunity to:

- View covers of upcoming books

- Learn about our future publishing schedule (listed by publication month and author)

- Find out when your favorite authors will be visiting a city near you

- Search for and order backlist books

- Check out author bios and background information

- Send e-mail to your favorite authors

- Join us in weekly chats with authors, readers and other guests

- Get writing guidelines

- AND MUCH MORE!

Visit our website at
http://www.arabesquebooks.com

More Sizzling Romance by
Gwynne Forster